GODSLAYERS

ZOE HANA MIKUTA

FEIWEL AND FRIENDS
NEW YORK

Content warning: This book contains suicide and graphic violence.

A FEIWEL AND FRIENDS BOOK
An imprint of Macmillan Publishing Group, LLC
120 Broadway, New York, NY 10271 • fiercereads.com

Our books may be purchased in bulk for promotional, educational, or
business use. Please contact your local bookseller or the Macmillan
Corporate and Premium Sales Department at (800) 221-7945 ext. 5442 or
by email at MacmillanSpecialMarkets@macmillan.com.

Library of Congress Cataloging-in-Publication Data is available.

First edition, 2022
Book design by Mike Burroughs and Mallory Grigg
Feiwel and Friends logo designed by Filomena Tuosto

Printed in the United States of America

ISBN 978-1-250-26952-2 (hardcover)
10 9 8 7 6 5 4 3 2 1

To the runaways.
Keep going. We'll find it eventually.

PROLOGUE

The twenty-nine remaining Gearbreakers lie asleep. They are guarded by Starbreach, on watch that night, and so they are entirely safe in her brilliant, cruel hands. One of those hands holds a knife, and the other, after she pushes through the door, James Voxter's hair.

Jenny waits until he wakes up, until he meets her eyes, to cut off his head and make the count twenty-eight.

She'd figured it out over the past few weeks, after Eris and Sona didn't come back, after the Gods came to call in Winterward. After they lost. You can tell a lot about a person from when they want to run. Voxter wanted to evacuate as soon as Eris and Sona had departed in her darling, shitty Archangel, hours before the Paladins came in, because he knew they would. He *knew*.

The Winterward ice had splintered beneath her feet—she can still feel the sound it had made in her marrow, like the breaking of a bone, the breaking of the world. Never seen a tear that big, couldn't see where it started or ended, could've ringed the entire earth from where she was standing, and then swimming.

Jenny drags the two pieces of Voxter, creator and traitor of the Gearbreakers, through the halls of the safe house, calling for her crew to wake up, that it's time to leave. Some of the others stir awake, see the body, see the blood. Some reach for weapons, but the shock leaves them still— What is there to stop? It's already done. They were already scared of her, already hated her—for the Archangel, for plugging a Pilot into it. Only her known loyalty to the Gearbreakers maintained their trust, and this is why they put her on guard for the night. Expecting her to watch the surrounding Iolite mountainscape for Windups, instead of killing one of their own.

Well. *Oops*, as traitorous wirefuckers tend to say.

Voxter wasn't one of their own. Hadn't been for a while now, Jenny suspected. This is why she drags what's left of him out of the safe house and into the snow.

Her crew trails behind, shouting her name. It's sunrise by the time they manage to shove their fearless leader into a coat. Jenny shrugs off their hands and does the button under her chin, kneeling in the permafrost to cut Voxter's body apart. Her crew watches silently, and she likes it, that trust set sure and taut as a wire trap—or she would like it, if she could focus on their quiet and not the wet pulling of her knife.

This is what they do for one another—horrible, perhaps even petty, things. They would do anything at all. This is the reason that they do not simply lie down in the cold and wait for it all to go dark. It is already so dark.

They find Windups doing patrols in the Iolite Peaks and take them down, leaving pieces of Voxter behind inside each dead mecha. They are so efficient with all of it. So professional. Jenny remembers, distantly, how fun it all used to seem.

She can't go back to face the rest of the Gearbreakers. She failed them. Jenny Shindanai is brilliant and deadly and wants to break things and doesn't want to lose anyone else. She is a fearless leader and a feared rebel and barely more than a kid, only twenty-four years old, and people had counted on her.

And look where that had gotten them. Torched and crushed and flung into pieces.

But Starbreach can fix this. She can kill more Gods. There are abandoned Godolia Windup hangars hidden around the Iolite Peaks, old caches from the Springtide War—smaller than the monolith under Godolia, but they'll do. Who knows how many mechas Sona managed to take down on Heavensday? Godolia might be tapping into these holds even now, cracking open the hangars like eggs to find the weaker, older Gods they might have left behind.

Jenny leads her crew to the eastward Peaks, guided by an electrical resistivity tomography imager of her mother's design. The device was originally for mapping out caverns in resource villages if Windups were ever called to collapse their mining tunnels. People could flee into these openings Godolia didn't know to crush flat—and then, hopefully, the Gearbreakers would be able to dig them out. But it was hard to get a signal out from that far underground. A good try, anyway.

But it's all guesswork. Really, Jenny expects to find nothing at all.

She definitely does not expect to find, at the base of the hollow mountain, a working elevator.

They go down. They go down because they cannot turn away and maybe because they are fools and they want a fight, or an end—anything but the slow decay of the grief-stricken Gearbreakers they left behind.

The elevator doors creak open to a vast, dark space.

Jenny's hands rise to skim over the shadows, fingertips searching to catch on a loose seam and pull it free, to unravel the world. It was already coming undone, anyway. She sighs, and it bubbles out of her as a laugh.

Fingers curl under Jenny's jaw, and Zamaya Haan meets her eyes steadily. The gear tattoos on her cheeks tick as she says, words silk and venom, "Get a Godsdamn grip on yourself."

Zamaya's fingernails bite into her jaw, and Jen stands still, lets their imprints set right as she digs through her pack. Flare sticks slip from her grip and clatter against the stone floor. She gets a hold on one, and her crew crane their necks to watch. Seung had made a bet with Gwen whether or not Jen would burn her eyebrows off—again.

Working the cap of the flare stick against her teeth, Jenny breathes, "Oh, darling. Your eyes aren't accustomed like mine; you weren't born so voidlike, brushed up against a cosmic power so unfathomable it nearly disintegrated you; no, I was ash and then I was not, and turned out so damn pretty, too. Watch yourself, now. I see them. I see them."

She hasn't spoken in weeks—trekking through the cold, scattering Voxter. Her own head feels scattered, too; thoughts reel from her, a lack of sleep and loads of hurt working tirelessly to uproot coherence as soon as it sprouts. She thinks she's rambling. It doesn't matter. It doesn't matter.

The flare gasps to life, and Jenny tosses it high and far into the darkness.

Light skips across shadow and stone, then curves of steel and iron.

Humanoid faces and limbs scrape the cavern heights with terrible, extraordinary unnaturalness. There should not be forms so arrogant as to crowd the collision of tectonic plates.

An army of Windups, row after hellish row, spiraling out of the flare's reach.

"Well." Jenny scans the dumbfounded expressions of her crew. "Well, well. These should not be here. That makes all of us."

Flashlights click on, needles of light branching from the crew, up across the mechas looming closest, red eyes dull in their sockets. A chill works its way from Jenny's toes up to the crown of her pretty head. This is interesting. This feels quite right.

"I've never seen models like these . . . ," whispers Seung.

The mechas have teeth. Nonfunctional, Jen guesses, paired with a lack of lips, two shallow divots marking the impression of a nose, and a shadowed, sunken stare. And then there are the bones. The tilled valley of ribs, hip bones a small hill of steel on each side, hands spilling five long lines of metal talons—like a dehydrated body, skin sucking close to frame. Each digit—long, much too long, nearly gracing the knees—is dotted with a row of small, black holes.

Gwen runs a nervous hand through her strawberry-blond curls. "Jenny, what the—"

"Doesn't matter," says Jenny. "They won't be anything soon enough."

All her life, Jenny had been pissing Godolia off, and they had struck back hard. First the Hollows, burned to the ground, then Winterward, sent straight through the ice after Heavensday. A new, crueler king on the throne, the Gearbreakers fragmented, and her sister—she doesn't know.

At least she wishes she didn't know.

But it didn't take a genius to figure out what had happened to Eris.

Jenny can't just go around breaking apart one God after another anymore. It's different now. She has to tear the whole damn heaven from the sky.

But she doesn't know how she will.

Ah, she's being dramatic. She'll figure it out . . . if they get through this next bit.

"Aw, you can come out! It'd be rude not to introduce yourselves," Jenny calls into the darkness.

"Rot," Gwen rasps, loosening the pistols at her sides. Each hand finds arrow, trigger, or blade.

Where there's Windups . . .

Up in the shadows ahead, dots of red flick into view.

"No? I can go first," Jenny says to their silence. "Jenny Shindanai, aka Starbreach, corrosives expert—well, *everything* expert—captain of the deadliest Gearbreaker crew in the Badlands. And you are?"

"The Gearbreakers are dead," responds a grating voice.

Faces peel from the shadows, gazes spiked with biting red, guns cradled almost lovingly in hands. But Jen isn't worried—why should she be worried? They've always been outnumbered. This is an edge she's used to, the black void of all her mortal fears she likes to bow herself over, just to spit into. Any amount of terror she feels just signifies she isn't dead, not yet, so she welcomes it.

Besides, maybe she can be a little bit proud of the grandness of dying here.

Jenny Shindanai flicks her wrists at her sides, the veins in her gloves breathing awake in a web of molten gold.

"The Gearbreakers"—Starbreach smiles, because she told herself she would, at the end of it all—"dabble in necromancy."

CHAPTER ONE

BELLSONA

I have an odd dream. Senseless—Godolia, like a mouth in the desert. It breathes in.

In comes the world. Out come its Gods.

I think, in the midst of that divine hunger, I become someone else.

He is there when I wake from it. The Zenith. Just a boy. The only one left.

I was close. I was very, very close.

He stands at the foot of my bed. I crawl toward him, dropping my brow to the frame.

"Now," Enyo says. I feel his eyes, dark as Phantom skin. His voice is gentle. "Do you feel like yourself again?"

"Yes, my Zenith," I whisper, closing my eyes against the feel of sheer, splintering relief. "I am feeling quite like myself again."

I was so lost. She . . . made me lost.

And Enyo.

I have done the worst to him, to my nation. And still he saved me, plucked me from the depths of the Gearbreakers' corruption, instead of slaughtering me like I slaughtered them.

Lost, but found. And home again.

In Godolia. This holy place.

This merciful place.

CHAPTER TWO

ERIS

I guess I do believe in deities, after all.

There's supposed to be millions of them, so when I pray, it's really more of a blanket statement than pinning it to just one. One doesn't seem like enough.

My head bowed over my knees, the metal shell of the transport shudders around me. As I sit shoved between two guards amid about a dozen others—which seems excessive, seeing as my wrists and ankles are bound, and a clamp is fastened over my mouth because as of late I've been what some would consider "bite-y"—I work on sending a careful, concise message up to the heavens. They must be crowded and loud, and I want to get this right.

You're assholes, I pray, but maybe that isn't the right word for what I'm doing. Is there another word for when humans speak to Gods? Did we bother to make one? *You're assholes, every single one of you.*

The train slows, and the transport doors glide open, spilling light. It stings my eyes; must be months since I've been outside.

I go limp when they try to shove me to my feet.

Because it's been months. And the only reason they'd have to move me is to kill me.

I am going to come for every last one of you.

They lift me easily. I let my head loll back, the sun warming my bruises. It feels like spring. It feels like they harvested me from my grave just so they could kill me again for kicks.

I will rip your divinity out by its roots.

The transport rumbles away, and my eyes follow it to a massive spire rising a few dozen feet to the left, its black throat craning for the sky. A cannon. I realize, faintly, that we're on the wall ringing the city. Light glints off the bleached stretch of the Badlands, webbed with the metal of train tracks. I can just see the point where the smog of Godolia fades to blue sky.

It all feels out of place—me muttering profanities into the broad shoulder flattening my cheek, the raised platform set at the wall's edge, this ugly, ugly place and its billion people pressed in like a rotted spot in the sand. Random things dumped into the blank part of a map.

Save me and I won't do shit for any of you, I pray as they lug me up onto the platform, promptly tossing me onto my hands and knees. The plastic surface is slick with humidity, but I still drop my brow to it and close my eyes. I need a little rest. I need there not to be so much buildup.

You dealt me a rotten world, and the very least *you can do is not let it kill me like this.*

Footsteps shake the platform, but no one hauls me upright. I don't really want to get my brains blown out with my face already touching the ground, so I roll onto my back, but the light still sears, and I have to put my hands to my face, shackles awkward but blissfully cool against my cheeks. The breeze picks up in just about the nicest way possible. There's not even an unreasonable amount of sand scraping my hair.

A few weeks ago, someone politely informed me my entire family was dead. That hours after Heavensday, Paladins were sent to crack the Winterward ice. That everyone I have ever loved probably froze before they could drown.

Well.

Everyone except for one, but she's dead, too.

And that is entirely on me.

I'm coming for you either way. It's your decision whether it's now or in a few years, when you'll have time to get ready for me, or apologize, or just die, *or bring them all back, just . . . just bring them all back—*

"Get her to her feet."

They pull me up. I go limp again, chin bumping my collarbone. They don't find it as funny as I do, and someone steps forward and grasps my jaw. I wince, their nails slipping beneath skin. I expect to open my eyes to a gun between my brows—which makes me really not want to open my eyes, to just let this darkness bleed easily into the next, barely a transition, hardly a difference—*Oh Gods*—I don't want this I don't want this—*Save me please* please *I'm scared to die*—

Then I open my eyes anyway, because I refuse to go out both begging and blind, not after *everything* . . . and the panic hesitates.

It's her, the blue of the sky behind her, and the world doesn't seem so empty anymore.

She's cut her hair.

Those perfect, chestnut curls scrape her chin, dark lashes drawn low so she can look at me properly. Backlit by the sun, her glare is vicious, and she's alive, and she's alive, and she's *alive*.

There's no way in hells I'm letting them kill me now.

"Should I take off her mask?" Sona asks someone I don't care about, but who seems to respond in the affirmative, because she unhooks the bind from around my mouth.

I try to kiss her, and she hits me across the face.

"Uh-huh, completely deserved that," I rasp out of cracked lips, which split even farther when I grin. My vision is still tilting when I look back at her, cheekbone stinging. "So, we're getting out of here?"

I haven't spoken in weeks, and my words peel out drily, incomprehensible.

They must be incomprehensible, because Sona fixes me with a strange look. She doesn't answer.

Also, instead of unshackling me, she moves behind me and hooks her arm around mine, one hand tangling in my hair and forcing my chin skyward.

My heartbeat spills up my throat. This isn't right. *She* isn't right.

Her lips brush my ear, and mine part, and I think to myself *please please please*—why would I pray to the Gods when *she's* right here—and Sona says, "You will show respect for your Zenith."

I start laughing.

It comes out splintered and gasping, and I can't stop it. Even when she punches me again, even when I hit the platform and the shock snaps my teeth, even as she leans over to shake me, curls floating off her chin. Because of course it would be her of all people, one of the unlucky few strong enough to survive corruption. Thoughts ripped out and dropped back in with new roots.

We just need to start running, I think, dazed, as Sona lifts me onto my knees and forces my head back again. *We just need to get home.*

Someone else leans over me—a tall boy with dark hair pulled into a small knot, and sharp black eyes, a sullenness to his mouth that in a flash of hurt reminds me of Xander. Low freaking blow.

And then it goes lower, because there's an insignia on his jacket that really shouldn't be there, really shouldn't be anywhere now. Because it means we missed one. We failed.

"I'm sorry," I rasp, and keep saying it. Apologies bubble up my throat, my rambling soon smudged by laughter again when I realize she thinks I'm begging for my life, and that these words aren't for her. Because I've doomed her here. I thought I was leaving her to a Zenithless world, to Godolia in a state of chaos. I was going to die, and maybe she was going to hate me for it, but it didn't matter because she would be *alive*. She would fight and get out, and it was going to be okay because she had people to go home to.

Does she even remember them?

Does she even know how loved she is?

The Zenith starts speaking. I don't care what he has to say, so I pitch forward and try to bite off his ear.

He pulls back, and my teeth snap against open air. Sona snarls, her grip winding tighter in my hair.

"How *dare* you—" she spits.

"Gwaenchanha. Bellsona, it's fine," the Zenith assures her, raising his hand. And he really does look fine, as unfazed and clean-cut as the tracks against the pale sand. He's just a kid, now in charge of a big, messy world. At the very least there should be some Godsdamn black circles around his eyes, and a suit that doesn't fit him so perfectly. He smiles brightly at Sona, which makes me want to not only go for his ear again, but also gnaw on it. "Everything's intact, see? I'd heard Miss Shindanai was getting a tad bite-y."

"Why—" My voice breaks. It startles me. The Zenith's eyes stay steady on mine, watching. The corruption couldn't have stuck the first time. She's too freaking stubborn for it. She's going to come back, and I might already be gone. "Why didn't you kill her?"

"Do you really not know?" the Zenith asks—he seems like he's actually asking. His gaze drifts to Sona, and there's something in his eyes I don't understand. Something careful. "She's worth saving."

The cool edge of a blade slips beneath my jaw, Sona's hands are perfectly steady, lining it up right.

"Wait," the Zenith says, and she does.

Heat builds fast behind my eyes and trickles out slow, the fight leaving me with the simple realization that she's going to be the one to pull me from this world, just like she's done countless times before in little, euphoric bursts—her head on my shoulder in the soft light of the hallway; her fingers tracing mine under the wide, star-cluttered sky; the warmth of her lips inside the dead mecha, tugging me away into something quieter, despite everything else—

The Zenith comes closer. And then he kneels down in front of me, dark, focused eyes on mine. Past the heartbeat in my ears, everything is suddenly still as he observes me. Finding a worthless Badlands girl. A heretic. Full of anger and hatred and hurt that means *nothing* to him.

"Worth saving . . . ," I whisper, throat moving against the blade. "Just to kill me?"

"No, no. Not just you." The Zenith smiles. It could be considered gentle. He leans in, lips nearly gracing my ear. He breathes—I close my eyes as the tears break. That startles me, too. The fear, its suddenness. I've killed Godolia's Gods before, but I haven't met one, haven't had one speak to me, soft and promising. "Bellsona is going to end the Gearbreakers."

He pulls back. I stay perfectly still, watching his shoes through the hair in front of my eyes.

"So," I say. "Starbreach is alive."

The Zenith chuckles. "Are either of us really surprised?"

He moves his hand. Sona forces me around, knee in the middle of my back, grip in my hair pitching me up and forward. And suddenly there's not ground under my chest, but a two-hundred-foot drop down a cold, black wall, into a Badlands full of deities.

A dry, panicked gasp cracks out of my throat.

"Sona—" I rasp. "Sona, *please.*"

Windups. There must be dozens of them, mismatched and red-eyed with their chins tilted back, craning for a view. That's what really scares me shitless, I think—the disarray of it, a mob instead of an army tailored into orderly lines.

We were good Gearbreakers. Glitch left the Windup army a fraction of its formal glory. But we didn't get all of them. The ones out on rotations, the ones stationed in the Iolite Peaks. We knew there would be a few leftovers. A fraction.

But it seems all of them wanted to come watch me die, and they had the right idea. Let the last thing I see be that all we did and all we gave up was for *nothing.* Despite our efforts, the world is still crawling with Gods.

And Sona's hand is the only thing keeping me on it. Tears pool out of my eyes and into open air, my mouth wet with spittle as she readjusts the blade at the side of my neck with perfectly steady hands. I'm going to die. *I'mgoingtodieI'mgoingtodieI'mgoingtodie—*

"All right, dear," says the Zenith. "Proceed."

It startles me, when the blade draws blood; I wasn't ready for it. I was waiting for her to look down, but she doesn't, and I realize that this is really happening, that she's going to kill me without even meeting my eyes. And when she wakes up from this—*she* will *wake up from this*—it's going to destroy her—

"Sona," I gasp, sob rattling in my chest, sounding like a little kid. "You said you're here as long as I want you to be, remember? I want you here. Don't do this. *Please don't do this.*"

The blade hesitates. Blood runs in a warm, steady line down one side of my neck, soaking my shirt collar.

"You *know me*," I choke. "We belong to each other. Remember?"

Sona blinks twice, and then, for a split second, her eyes drop to mine.

Then, hurriedly, her gaze lifts back to the Zenith. He stares at her steadily, and I can tell he saw it, too.

It happens too quickly.

His hand lifts, and Sona jolts me to my feet, shoves the knife into my shackled hands, and pushes me away. And she's screaming *go, go, go*, and I'm screaming *come with me you have to come with me*, and the air comes alive with gunfire.

I'm back on the platform. Sona hits it a second later, warmth spotting my cheekbone before I roll for cover.

"Put down your guns, you might hit her! Bellsona! These are not your roots!" the Zenith growls. She flinches, but dives for me when I twist the knife in my hands and lunge for him. Entangled, we skitter toward the wall's edge, my feet kicking out over the open drop.

"Go!" she screams, pulling away from me.

"Come with me." It barely matters that there's nowhere to run to. "I love you, *please come with me.*"

Faintly, I realize the bullets have stopped flying. Crouched above me, Sona presses a hand to her ribs, to the blood slicking her side. The Zenith is standing a dozen feet away, mouth closed despite the ease of a kill order.

"I don't know you," Sona rasps, wry smile on her lips, and she's so desperate and so confused; I can feel it in the way her hand grips my arm, that this is familiar to her, but she says it again anyway. *"I don't know you."*

Her skin knows mine. But they messed up her head, and she doesn't know how it got to be that way.

"We'll fix it," I beg wetly, tears smudging the image of her head bent over mine, warbling the tight line of her mouth. "Please, love, I promise—"

And then I'm airborne.

She pushed me. She *killed*—

No. Greedy things, Gods—their hands rise, searching for me, and I hit a palm. Metal fingers curl to block out the sky, but I'm already gone, sliding down a wrist and then an arm. Metal bodies rise around me, heads and necks and collarbones. I hit a shoulder running, fingers reaching for me from a dozen hands, and this is it, one of my hells, Windups and nothing else . . .

I'm down the line of the shoulder, reach the side of the Argus's head, and there's only one place left to go.

Down.

Down.

Down.

Back-to-back with the Windup, below all of them.

I hit the ground. Sooner than I was expecting. Alive-r than I was expecting.

No. Fuck. There's another freaking palm under my feet, I—

The hand is closing. It's the worst way to go, a Gearbreaker way to go, being crushed—

We're moving, and the force of the motion brings me to my knees. The world above is mechas, spines and chests and grins, edges outlined by sky, heads turning . . . The Windup's other hand closes over my head and goes still.

It's just the dark and me, breathing hard. Waiting. *Nothing. Nothing. Nothing.* My pulse throbs in my teeth. *Alive alive alive.*

"Did you just—" It comes out as a whisper. "Cup me in?"

What the hells is happening? Did the rest of them really not see?

I slam my foot against the fingers that have replaced the sky. The scream comes first from the pain and then from everything else, and I double over in the darkness. "You f— you have to let me out!"

My hands scramble against the pockmarked metal of the mecha's fingers—a Berserker. But there's something else here, between the valves. Lips parting, my touch moves, following the scratches. Finding words.

No—finding my name.

Eris Don't Panic.

I trace it again. *Don't Panic.*

Oh, I think distantly, my head going blank with dry delirium, like static eating a screen. *I get it. I'm dead.*

Sona's still up there. With the Zenith. He said he was going to kill Jenny. The look in his eyes was just like one I've found in hers again and again—the careful observation, the next step already lined up neatly in their heads.

Didn't I always wonder what it would be like, if Jenny had been born on their side?

He saw Sona's corruption waver, and he's going to try it all over again. Until he gets it right.

Until it sticks.

CHAPTER THREE

BELLSONA

"Good," I say. **"Good. I feel fine."**

Fray watches me, her features stone. I adjust my legs on the low-lying couch, socked feet curling over the edge of the cushion. The material wrinkles under my weight, and a startled, naked feeling gasps to the surface: Tether barking at me to straighten my spine, the hair on the back of my neck like needles, whole parts of me going numb with fear as his hand lifts from his side . . . I almost reach for my shoes, almost drop my eyes to the ugly tongue of carpet between us.

The moment rolls through me. Tether is dead, and I never much liked looking to the floor.

Besides, I am far from a student now. Maybe Pilots should be more formal, but Enyo acts like a child, so I treat him as such. He does not mind, and I think it has made me comfortable. Perhaps I figure if no one has killed me yet, I can put my socks on the couch cushions. Perhaps I am pushing, testing for a line. Perhaps I am giving them a reason. Or perhaps I am just rude naturally, mean when I am bored, and the questions Fray asks are veiled and dull, so every time she frowns, I take a sugar cube from the tea tray between us and set it on the table. After months, she still cannot seem to figure out what the hells it correlates to. It's just so Godsdamn funny.

"Do you have any anxieties about today's incident, Bell-sona?" Fray asks, tablet balanced on her crossed knees, held steady by a thin hand tipped with pretty manicured fingernails.

"For my clarification, the 'incident' is the small massacre that took place a few stories up, correct?"

"That is correct."

Then, because Enyo would prefer I try to play nice, I say, "I feel . . . unnerved."

This morning was like any other. Enyo and I were eating breakfast together in the Zenith wing, his feet knocking against mine beneath the table, a familiar habit by now. I do not complain because it means that he, too, has grown comfortable with me, because we have the same thoughts sometimes and it feels good not only to feel known, but twinned. I do not complain because I killed his entire family and yet this morning he sat there, smiling; he had just made me laugh, and the sound was not fully free from my throat before I remembered how I burned them all alive, and still he was smiling at me because I found his stupid joke funny. This is what I was thinking of when the glasses on the table started to shake.

The tremor was violent, and brief. I had already pulled him to the ground, where spilled coffee darkened the rug fibers.

Four stories down, we found a frozen laboratory. A plume of ice stretched floor to ceiling, a table, the remnants of a microscope, and one arm blooming from its side—frozen and stuck, moth wings to honey. Around the room other bodies were slicked to the walls, tossed back by the blast.

I turned in a slow circle, taking it in. Not a single soul had been spared. When I was saved, the doctors had to peel the Gearbreakers' corruption from my memory moment by moment. It had left the moments darkened, but I remember that much of her. How she was cruel, how she smiled when she fought.

How she tore my head to bits, and when she was finished, dropped me from the sky.

"Can you articulate why you are unnerved?" Fray asks me now.

"I am not fond of frozen corpses."

"Or of death?"

"Is anyone?"

"Not usually, but you are a little odd," Fray says with a soft smile that reaches her eyes, but the bitterness hovers no matter how warm her expression is. I am not here to heal. I am here to see if the healing stuck.

Or if it's coming loose.

If *I* am coming loose.

"They should not have been attempting to reverse engineer the Frostbringer's gloves," I murmur. They should have known Starbreach would not let anyone take too close of a look inside one of her creations.

The doctor waits, I think, for me to continue. I only tug up my sock, then lean forward and pull a sugar cube from the dish. Fray tenses up, the slick, blond bun pulling at her temples, but I just drop it into my untouched tea, biting back a laugh.

Enyo loves it. He says her notes all contain a little box in the corner where she keeps a tally of the sugar. In our last session she frowned ten times, almost imperceptibly, so ten sugar cubes dotted the wood in a tailored row. Later that night there were ten particularly angry tally marks for Enyo and me to chuckle over.

Like always, after our laughter had died down, I had asked

him about the rest of it. The other words Fray scrawled as I talked or fidgeted or sat quietly, the notes she handed him afterward. It's never the first question I ask him, but always the last. Best to ease him into it, before he realizes I am prying, that I am nervous and a bit desperate and a bit angry. It all clots like cobwebs at the back of my throat, and I start when I am still laughing so he cannot hear the grate to my voice.

I think she thinks me vain because I fixed my hair in the reflection of my socket Mods. *You are vain, Bellsona. And your hair looks lovely.* I know. I am sure it is not the worst thing she thought of me. *You're absolutely right. In fact, she wrote right here that "Bellsona Steelcrest is a bitch."* Is that an official diagnosis? *Yes. She also wrote she does not think you're sleeping well.* I told her I am. *Did you lie?* Is she more concerned about the lying or my insomnia? Does she say it is going to amount to me killing you in your sleep? *Not specifically. Are you going to kill me in my sleep?* Not specifically. What about brief suffocation? *I don't like that, either.* No, did she say anything about suffocation? *Ah. Bellsona—*

Did she say you should lock your door tonight?

Come on.

You can tell me.

"What is the last you remember of your time with the Gearbreakers?" Fray asks, sensing I am finished with the other topic.

I smooth my palm in a slow line, collarbone to shoulder. And then, quietly, I say, "Falling."

Weightlessness. Sky slipping against my spine, and far off, my feet drifting up from the glass. A breath I did not need snapping against the back of my throat.

It's the same thing I say every time. The same truth. Fray does not need me to elaborate again, unless I give her reason to.

The first half hour of our sessions is always white noise. Fray asks me how I am feeling, or sleeping, or dreaming. I am uninterested in the exchange, and I give uninteresting answers. She dislikes them, and I put sugar on the table.

But then come the questions that matter, and I pay attention.

"What is the first you remember?"

"Their hideout," I say. "After the Frostbringer took me."

"What about it?"

"The crowd. Moving between the trees."

"Can you recall any faces?"

"No. I believe some were welcoming. Most were angry."

"Anything else?"

"The forest foliage."

It would get boring, spitting out the same answers to the same questions every few days, but the little omissions sink like rot into my words—those keep me focused.

I am scared of hurting Enyo. I have hurt him enough. The only reason he survived me is because he got lucky. Or perhaps that is the worst word for it.

But I am also scared of him. Of what he could do, of what he *should* do, if the Gearbreakers still own a part of me.

So I give foliage, but not the sky tucked up above it, blue, and not red, for a reason I do not know.

"What is the last you remember of the Frostbringer?"

"She was in the Archangel with me. To make sure I carried out the mission." *And I did.* "I do not remember if we talked."

"Do you remember any of your conversations with her?"

"Not much. Archangel semantics. The test run."

Pale light against paler wallpaper, carpet beneath my bare heels . . .

Something in my tone makes Fray wait, and I drag my eyes to her left, to the window yawning behind her. Her office faces east, the Badlands desert a thin, broken thread between horizon and the teeth of cityscape. A handful of months ago, one could see the dark, brilliant pillar of the Academy, the vein tethering the earth to the heavens. Now, where the skyscraper once rose there is a grove of golden trees, one leaf for every life lost, one shimmering trunk for every dead Zenith.

"Bellsona?" Fray finally presses.

We never found her body. The Pilots were greedy, reaching for her—I could understand it. Enyo tells me I suffered a corruption relapse, after seeing her. The details are all blurry. I think I remember her crying.

"I think . . ." A spike of selfish self-preservation snags my words; I curl my fingers into the couch fabric and rip them free. "I think we talked about my parents, once."

Fray angles her pen to her tablet, her expression blank. "Did you just recently recall this?"

No. "After the incident this morning. I just . . . I do not understand it."

"Understand what, Bellsona?" Fray asks softly.

"Why she would ask. Why I would tell her." Shame catches at the back of my throat as I watch digital ink bleed from beneath the strokes of Fray's fingers. "Why it would not fracture the corruption, even just a little, telling her about the building collapse, about how the Academy took me in when I had no one else. Was I really so far gone?"

24

Her silence pulls my attention away from the window, my eyes hitching on hers.

"Bellsona, it is important for you to know that they were cruel to you."

"I know that," I say with a bit of poison.

The kindness in her gaze makes me ache. "They were cruel to you, and fear is a natural response. Allow yourself the possibility that you acted in the way your fear permitted you to."

I stare at her. "No."

She raises a perfectly tailored brow. "No?"

"No." A smile cracks across my lips. "No, I was not so terrified of her that I rolled over whenever she asked and told her about my dead parents and killed a skyscraper's worth of Godolia children. No. No, I fought her, all right? I—I had to have fought her; I could not have simply . . . just . . ."

"Bellsona."

I stop. There is spittle on the corners of my lips; I quickly drag my sleeve against my mouth, and air flickers against the backs of my fingers.

I am breathing.

Fray's pen has paused.

"Bellsona," she says again, and cold splinters inside my chest. I should have kept my Godsdamn mouth shut. I knew there was something wrong with me, and I knew the script that kept it quiet, that kept me alive.

Fray's blouse ripples around her waist as she leans slightly forward, two small lines settled between her brows. "Bellsona. It's okay to be scared."

My mouth opens.

And, quietly, something slips out of place.

"I—"

Tell me, Enyo.

"I—I am not scared of her."

Am I getting better?

"I am just so . . . *angry*." I am on my feet, immediately tripping on my discarded boots; I right myself and tangle my fingers into the plaited laces, send them both crashing into the door; Fray jumps at the shock of the impact. A dry laugh hews my words. "Deities, is it not enough? When will it be enough for her? She just wants *death*, and it is unimaginative and indulgent. So, no, Fray, she does not get my fear or anything so soft; she gets a meaningless end, and after all she has done to Godolia, to Enyo, to *me* . . . I get to provide her that."

Fray looks up at me, tablet dark on her knee. The pen does not move in her hand. The cold portions of me go still as stone.

Then she smiles again, but the expression is not warm or kind, and it feels real.

"Well," Fray says. "I think we will end there for today."

CHAPTER FOUR

ERIS

The knife hesitates at my temple. It hovers and tilts, indecisive, steel throwing a thin line of dull light against the wall. I'm a bit unsure about the angle. In the three-inch mirror balanced against the bed frame, my teeth find my bottom lip. Both my hands—one holding the hair and one holding the knife—are losing circulation, static eating at my fingertips.

You're overthinking this, I tell myself, and the blade moves.

Black strands dust my sweatpants. I sit back for a second, observing, then move to my knees to get a better look in the mirror. The single bulb makes for shit light to do this in. Not that I should be complaining. Shoved a few hundred feet belowground, it's a new kind of dark when the lights are off. And they should be off, at this hour. But, you know, it's funny. For some reason I haven't been sleeping that well.

I go a little farther, then pause to thumb through the cut. When I lean back to start again, two other faces have wedged themselves in the mirror, crowding the small square. I put the knife on the ground and turn.

"June?" I ask.

"Yeah," Theo says, ruffling his bedhead. Nova's in one of her quiet phases again, but she nods, bouncing anxiously on her toes.

I follow them a short distance down the passage, bare feet

spared from the stone floor by a path of mismatched rugs the Hydra Pilots used to line our *accommodations*. They all sleep in the hangar and left us with the short network of natural tunnels, which sounds crude, but there's little smoothed platforms to support the beds, heat lamps to keep the chill away, and sounds carry, so I can keep tabs on the kids. My crew occupies a passage just off the main tunnel, a jagged crescent with two dead ends—Nova and Theo shoved up on one side, June and Arsen on the other, and me set in the middle curve, where I can lean over the edge of my bed to see a good distance up the tunnel, plus a sliver of the passage that Jenny's crew sleeps in.

The lights clipped to the ends of June's and Arsen's bed frames are bent up toward the short, uneven ceiling, teethlike shadows reaching down the walls. Two sets of pillows and blankets are gathered between the beds—Theo and Nova are sleeping on this side this week. June and Arsen will migrate in a couple of days so the other two will have a chance to sleep in their own beds. I used to sleep in their pileup—or, at least, lie there and wait for someone to come tell us the sun came up—but that was only for the first week. It made me anxious, not being able to keep watch. Where my bed is now, the breeze can reach, the one that will tell me if the mechas start to move.

I kneel before the low wood frame of the bed on the left. Theo told me when Juniper's night terrors began—all those months ago when I wasn't here, when they all thought I was dead (again)—Arsen couldn't stop crying. Now he just sits on the mattress beside her, looking far, far too tired for his age when she wakes up choking on her bad thoughts.

"Hey, June," I murmur, hand on her hand, thumbing her knuckles. It's always panic first, when she jolts awake. And then it's quieter, the grief so deep that she can't make a sound over it.

Her dark brown eyes brim beneath low lids, teeth on her bottom lip. Thinking about Xander, thinking about Sona, and all the others—there are *so many* others.

We all think about them; June with her nightmares, Nova with her quiet spells, Theo and Arsen flinching at things they didn't before. Me . . . what? Ha. No, I'm good. I'm *all* good. It's just I want to punch something, and the impulse never really passes. Just like how the strange, physical feeling that my heart is seasick hasn't really stopped since I first saw my crew again. The four of them looked so small from the mecha hand as it lowered me to the ground, bundled together on the hangar floor, and when Sheils set me down in that borrowed Berserker, they didn't look any bigger.

The Hydra hangar—the one that Jenny stumbled into months ago—is tapped into the broadcast system Godolia hooked up in their Ore Cities, about twenty miles southeast. That's how they heard about my execution, that Godolia was inviting any and all Pilots to attend in their Windups. To watch their Valkyrie, saved from the Gearbreakers' savage corruption by the grace of the Zenith, cut the Frostbringer's throat.

My crew just wanted eyes on the situation; the not knowing if it was really done would have been worse. It had been June's idea to scratch that note into the Berserker's palm, but it was really just to pretend, to do anything besides nothing. They didn't actually expect Sheils to catch me. I don't even think Sheils expected me to jump, let alone for us to get out alive, walking straight back into the desert alongside the rest of the Windups picking up their rounds after their bit of fun was over.

The crew seemed strange—stranger than the cavern full of mechas, stranger than their being alive at all after what I'd been told happened at Winterward. Like all the fight had been peeled from them, like it had been a superficial sticker all along and not the red in their cheeks.

My heart had rolled over in my rib cage and snagged, and it hasn't felt like unsticking since.

Nova takes a seat beside me and tugs her blankets over our legs. Theo carefully flops onto the bed behind Arsen to trace slow circles between June's shoulder blades. It's still quiet for a while after her tears have slowed, knees pulled up to her chin and eyes trained to the floor. Nova and Theo, ankles pressed together, tilt their feet back and forth in a steady metronome. One of my hands is in Nova's hair—the blond now fed by the dark brown of her roots, since she can't bleach it weekly, brutally, like she did in the Hollows—the other supporting my cheek. Back at the Hollows, late at night we'd do the same nothing as this, steeping comfortably in each other's silence while the hearth logs crumbled, but it feels different now. Like it's not a choice anymore, just a lacking of things and people, just a peace that isn't going to stick around.

After a while, June looks at me and says, "What's with your hair?"

"I wanted an undercut thing. Just on one side." I thumb through the choppy path again. "For my birthday."

June smiles and taps the bed frame beneath her. "Well, come here. I couldn't get you anything this year, anyway. Knife, Novs?"

Hours later, when the sun's probably up, Jenny finds Nova

and me asleep on Arsen's bed, the other three curled up on June's with Theo snug in the middle. My sister knocks her hand against my shoulder and looms over me while I blink awake, her dark sheet of hair brushing my newly shorn scalp.

"Hey, so . . ." She scratches the back of her neck with what I would call a sheepish look, if it were anyone but Jenny. "Listen. Just so you know . . . I might've killed Sona."

The rest of the morning is kind of blurry.

By the time my vision stops shaking, I've run Jenny into the hangar. I bat away my crew members' hands and take another swing. Jen dodges, but judging by the flush of her lip and the ache in my knuckles, I got her at least once. We've gathered an audience around us; an unwound mecha looms above us, rubbernecking Hydra Pilots grouped around its feet.

For some reason, it's the toes of the Hydra Windups that really get me. Why the fuck would you give mechas toes? I would've still gotten the skeleton picture without those thin, maggot-colored metal nubs. My crew thought I was delirious when I demanded an answer for this particularly horrific creative choice; it was my very first question after Jenny had finished explaining that Sona wasn't the first to defect, that the Hydra Pilots ended up here, in the Mutts—their name for this forgotten, hidden hangar—after they saw what their mechas were built to do. The first and only wave of Hydras debuted forty years ago, Jen had said, and the Zeniths did a superb job covering the embarrassment up when they all ran off. Blueprints blotted from history, the Academy told to give a blank stare to anyone who asked around.

The defected Hydras did their bit, of course, killing the Pilots in their class who didn't want to leave alongside them—which, as it turns out, was most of them. The morality of it is kind of cool. Kind of useless, since they did have to pick off the ones who stayed, but cool. Then they'd detonated another Springtide-era hangar in the Iolite Peaks to leave some of their mechas behind in the rubble, so Godolia would think it was dead and done with, when really they'd migrated east. Decades later, I hadn't heard about the existence of the Hydras until I'd been brought back to the Mutts hangar.

When Jenny was done, I'd looked at her and asked hotly, *Who the hells authorized the* toes?

Jenny takes my wrist and pivots out of my way, barely a tug to send me stumbling over my own momentum. She's snatched Zamaya by the time I turn back, ducking behind her.

The demolitionist, unimpressed with the role of human shield, turns and bites Jenny's earlobe. My sister startles, then blushes, grinning shamelessly. Zamaya ignores her, slipping from her hold. I lunge at Jenny again, but Z catches my elbow and yanks me back, her arm pinned across my collarbone.

"Hear her out," she says softly, and it's not a request. I go still. My sister is afraid of exactly one person in this world, and that still holds weight despite the temporary suspension of my fear of Jenny. Especially since that one person is currently pressing her dimpled, tattooed cheek to mine.

Jenny fiddles with the swelling on her lip. "Thank you, babe."

Zamaya fixes her with a dead stare that makes her spine go straight. "We're having words after this, too."

"Ah. Okay. Eris, you're free to continue to chase me, drag this out and such. Z, if you could just let her g—oh, no? Get on with it quickly, you say? Yes, dear." Jenny takes a breath and slides her eyes over to mine. "Okay . . . so after you escaped the Academy the first time, I put a tracker in your gloves." She glances quickly back at Z, receiving a nod to continue. "It flickered out today."

"So?" I grit out, choosing to ignore the fact that I have no idea when she took my gloves.

"So, I last had it marked in Godolia, probably wherever they built their new Academy. And they tried messing with it." Jenny raises her chin. "I put in a fail-safe. The tracker's out, so that means they opened the gloves up too far. So . . . they detonated."

My throat is raw; I must've been screaming at some point. "You could've killed her."

"You said the Zenith had her standing at his side. You said it looked like they were friends," Jenny rasps, and a dark expression touches her features. This is what Jenny's always done: hit just so she could be the one to hit first. So I know what she's going to say before she says it—because this world is cruel, and she's going to keep a hells of a lot of people alive because she's cruel, too: "I hope I killed her."

Even though he's a Zenith, we guess that Enyo is lacking support in Godolia, support that was supposed to be unquestionably guaranteed to him about thirty years from now. But the fact of the matter is, people don't like taking orders from kids. He inherited the aftermath of the Archangel disgrace—most likely striking the model from any chance of production, judging by the lack of wings in the skies—a devastated Pilot army, and a fragment of their once almighty Windup arsenal. Underlings were thrown into promotions they weren't prepared for, probably pissing off any more-senior officials who managed to survive Heavensday. Even with the miracle of the corrupted Valkyrie Pilot, a Zenith repairing a soul ripped apart by the Gearbreakers, I can't imagine every single person in their army being happy about the decision to let Sona live. Not after how close we got to killing them all.

Cupped in the Berserker's hands, I'd thought about how she had cut her hair.

The decision to keep her alive, to keep her at his side, becomes less questionable if Enyo handed her the scissors and she didn't immediately push them into his temple, or if he called someone else to do it and she just sat still while it happened. It becomes something worse when he calls her *dear* and she doesn't snap his neck for it.

The words boil out of me. "Take it back."

"I won't."

Zamaya unhooks from around me. I stay frozen in place. "Take. It. Back."

Please.

Instead of answering me, Jenny turns to our watching crews and the hovering Pilots, one of whom leans casually against the side of the mecha's feet, the red glow of her eye a startling complement to her silver-shot black curls. She has on dark boots that reach over her knees, black pants, the edge of one suspender strap peeking out of her dark green Hydra jacket. Fingerless gloves that show the tattoos decorating her knuckles clasp easily behind her head as she watches the spectacle with morbid—but utterly shameless—interest.

Every time I see Captain Soo Yun Sheils my first thought is, *Gods, if I ever manage to be that old, please let me look as cool as her.*

"Listen up!" Jenny snaps, and the murmuring and exchanging

of bets dies down. "Now, some of you already know this, but late last night, some of Sheils's scouts returned from Ira Sol. We knew they were constructing something in that cleared northern stretch, but we didn't know what it was up till now. At this point, it's clear that it's another Academy."

The breath trickles from me. The Pilots react just the same as my crew—with quick, narrowed glances, sharp words muttered low.

One of them, Nyla, pushes to the front of the crowd. She's a defected Berserker Pilot—it was her Windup Sheils had used to get to me. "Another Academy? In the Badlands?"

"They wouldn't do that," I breathe. "The Zenith can barely keep control of Godolia as it is."

"You know the Ore Cities aren't like the other resource villages," Jenny replies. "Badlands people with Windup fanaticism. But the Mechvespers aren't our problem. Another Academy dropped a desert away is an odd choice." She releases a sigh, and then shrugs. "Unless this Academy isn't intended for Godolia kids."

She turns on me as the outrage around us crests, as dread soaks me through, leaning over to put her hand on my sleeve. I can see that tired, harrowed look in her eyes, a rare thickness in her voice when she says, "I can't take it back. You'd better hope she's dead, too." Jen cares about Sona, too, I know she does. Some part of her is hurting for it. Just not the part she gives power. Her grip tightens. "Because if not, it's about to get worse."

Worse for all of us. But all I can think is, *We're already there.*

Badlands kids shipped off to get their heads slowly stuffed with mecha fanaticism, raised to be Gods of a nation that makes mine fodder of their families. A new Academy, a new army that fragments their problem population, that twists them against their own.

More Pilots. More Windups. And fewer Gearbreakers than ever.

My head feels fuzzy, the skin around my fingers too tight. I force my feet to move, brushing past Jen, brushing past the crew. "Then it's about to get worse. She's alive."

She's alive. I have to think so, because I think mourning her will kill me. I know by now that grief starts at the throat, like the beginning of a bad cold. I'm too tired to fend off the rot of it. Tired of kids dying. Tired of this world making kids murder other kids.

"Get your coats," I say hoarsely to my crew. "We're going out."

I need a nap and a fight, in that order, but I know I wouldn't get any sleep right now.

Sheils has moved next to Jenny as we head toward the exit. "You have a plan B, Miss Starbreach?" she asks, fingers in her front pants pockets. "If your fail-safe did not obliterate those poor children?"

"A plan B, C, and all the way through Z, halmeoninim," Jen responds, the Pilot smirking at the honorific like she always does. "But you don't know if A shot through yet."

I button up my jacket and tuck a loose strand of Nova's hair into her cap, very aware of Sheils's slow glance over her shoulder toward me.

"It is too easy," the captain muses to Jenny.

Like our home burning to the ground was too easy. Like bodies upon bodies of Gearbreakers is too easy, and yet we still can't find much to bury.

"You would know all about easy," I say under my breath as I pass, knowing the captain can hear me just fine, "hiding down here for decades."

"Have you already forgotten who brought you here?" Sheils meets my eyes with a chilled focus. "We have done our part, Shindanai. Your Gearbreakers would not have been able to fight against the Hydras."

"Are you sure?" I ask. "A Windup is only as good as its Pilot. And all I've seen you do is wait around to die. So." I shoulder my bag. The Mutts hangar is stark-quiet. I look to the rest of my crew and find half-slack jaws, Sheils's glare burning into the back of my head. "Okay. Are we good to go?"

CHAPTER FIVE

BELLSONA

The elevator breaches the fog. It stretches so plush and still across the cityscape, it looks as if I could take a step and it would not let me drop, but swallow me up to my throat and hold me there, toes scraping open air above the streetlights.

I had told Enyo this once, expecting him to laugh at me. He only fixed me with a serious look and said he imagined the same exact thing, except that he was always headfirst with his eyes watering from the pollution, and to never tell the good doctor I was thinking of jumping out of windows.

What if I was pushed? I had asked lightly, to which he had responded, *Then you are paranoid instead of suicidal, and I still have to deal with it accordingly.*

We were in his study, lying on our stomachs across his desk, the single lamp like a drop of sun in the night air filtering in from his windows. He was scribbling on a notepad, new, better haircut, so the light traced the pale shell of his ear.

What about you? I had asked him. *Were you pushed, or did you jump?*

I remember the way his pen stopped midletter, ink swelling in a heavy bead.

He looked at me, and it had startled me. It was not just that he did not look like himself in that flash of anger, but that he looked like he expected anger in return. Like I was going to hit him, and when I did, he would hit me, too, and he would not stop.

Then he blinked, and whatever was there smoothed over. He had smiled as he answered, *I was pushed, dear.*

The elevator doors open. I blink at the familiar, cold stretch of the hall into the sparring rooms level—almost identical to that of the old Academy—instead of the floor-to-ceiling elegance in the Valkyrie apartments. My fingers twitch at my sides. Did I hit the wrong floor?

I never come down here, even though I am allowed to go wherever I please. Usually I train in the sparring room up the hall from my room, where it is just me and I do not have the chance to run into other Pilots.

The sound of swords clashing, metal ringing against metal in quick succession. The notes thrum through me. Is someone laughing? It is so bright. *Oh, you are* good. I am good? Someone is charging me, their weapon flashing—no. It is dropped at her side, defenseless. Red curls. Red beading from her neck, slow, then quicker—good—did it so I could be good—am I good—

My hand braces against the wall as I gasp. I have moved out of the elevator without even realizing it. Swallowing, I step back and punch the Valkyrie level button, leaning against the glass as the doors shut.

Here. Squeezing my eyes closed. I am here.

I am *this.*

The desperation of it cracks through me. My hands over my face now and I *shudder.*

I hate her so much. The Frostbringer did this to me, split me. I am still finding my pieces, but I think . . . I think she took some for herself.

I do not complain to Enyo how sometimes I wake up in the dead of night frenzied, pulled from a dream where I was not quite myself. I do not complain, because he could have killed me for what I did, yet he saved me instead. I am alive only because he thinks he fixed me.

I do not think I am fixed.

The same words. Someone else. Cold air. Bile stinging my throat. Sand grains cutting into my ankles, her hand in mine—*why*—starlight making the sky glow like a healing bruise. *It's okay to be scared.*

I think I am missing pieces, and Godolia needs their Gods to be whole.

CHAPTER SIX

ERIS

I wrap my scarf tighter around my chin and breathe out slow, then reach out. My thumb traces the slope of the bluff that makes up one end of the mountain pass. We're looking north, but the Windup will be heading south, the path of its past rounds marked by the pale dots of exposed tree hearts, trunks bowing in unclean breaks on both sides of the narrow ridge. I trace down, where the rapids hiss below the bluff, about thirty feet out. "It'll hit the river."

Theo, crouched on the branch beside mine, adjusts the rifle strap around his shoulder. "We far enough back, Eris?"

"A Phantom is a hundred and sixty feet tall. The pass is two hundred feet out, give or take, and it's not going to get a chance to brace itself." I crane my neck slightly, a leaf brushing my forehead; I bat it away. "That pass is too slim for it to go straight-on. It has to step over. Right foot first's going to give us more of a push, but left'll be fine, too. I think . . ." I point down from our perch, where the edge of the water runs below us, faintly visible through the foliage with the way the light of the half moon hits its surface. "The head will hit there, see? Just off the riverbank. We'll probably have about fifteen seconds before it gets back on its feet. Take an arm up if it gives it to us. Or a head. We might need to move out of the way for that." I consider the angle again. "You know what, never mind, we're perfect. What, Nova?"

She shifts, small frame balanced on the branch to my upper left, green eyes jumping to the foliage above. "I didn't say anything."

I glance at Arsen, silent on my right, to find his glance skittering from mine, and then back at June, spine against the tree trunk with her legs dangling over the sides of our branch. She has the detonator cradled like a baby in one arm, other hand picking at the holes in her cargo pants, gazed dropped attentively.

"Well? If any of you have a problem, just say it," I bark, to continued, careful silence. Theo coughs innocuously. I sigh. "Loves, after everything, honesty's not going to kill me. Am I being crazy?"

"Yes," they all say.

"Yeah? Rot. I don't care," I snap anyway, instead of asking the next reasonable question (*Why do you think I'm being crazy?*), which they would answer incorrectly (*Eris, this is a terrible way of coping*). Because I am, in fact, *not* coping. Because I'm not even thinking about it—I've *chosen* to be crazy instead. See? It's a loop that solves itself. They might not understand, not like I do, which I can't fault them for.

Because I might be acting a little unhinged, but I'm still a damn fantastic Gearbreaker—crew captain for some damn good reasons, and still alive for just one: to kill some metal Gods. And that's enough.

I pull my goggles down into place and say, "Can you guys just chill out a little and help me blow up this deity?"

"You're being an ass, Eris," Nova says flatly, and throws a twig at me.

"What? Because I'm being completely insensitive and oblivious to anyone's devastation but my own? Because we're hanging out in a tree solely so I can ignore my problems and all of yours, too? I know you little shits better than anyone, and you're on a low, and I can do something about it, so I will." I pull the twig from my hair. "I don't have the proof to be devastated, by the way, so I'm not. That'd just be wasted energy. But this . . . this is productive."

I look around at them again. Their glances don't scatter this time. Nova's mouth has a little twist to it. She's prepared another twig in her hand but doesn't let it drop.

"What?" I ask, warmth crawling into my cheeks.

Theo gawks. "This is you trying to cheer us up?"

I roll my eyes. "Deities, do you have to sound so shocked? I know I'm prickly, but of course I care about—oh, *shit!* Hold that thought. The bastard is here. We primed, June?"

"Uh—yes!" she squeaks, her slight start wobbling the branch. "When—"

"I don't see it," Arsen says.

"You don't have to." My eyes flick from the gnatlike flock of birds rising from behind the peak to the mouth of the narrow pass. Then ten silent, held-breath seconds later . . . against the black, a massive hand wraps itself around the rock.

"Hold, Juniper," I murmur.

From behind the bluff, the Phantom's face pulls into view. Red eyes blare from sunken sockets, mouth a thin but effective sliver in the metal, a starved grimace. An instinctive unease stings my chest. You can't hear the damn thing chasing you, and then imagine you glance up to follow skinny legs to emaciated torso to pinched neck . . . and find that sick mug balanced a near two hundred feet above you, staring with that twisted grin. You're frozen (and soon after, dead) if you aren't prepared for it.

The Phoenixes have their grandeur, the Valkyries their strange, terrifying elegance. But models like the Phantoms, like the Hydras . . . I think that's where the Godolia architects really got it right. Deities captured in their physical forms. The Gods as sickly, happy creatures. Revolting things. After all the poison they let wither the world, after *everything*, they don't get to be beautiful. They can grin all they like, but they have to rot alongside us.

"Eris," Arsen warns as the edge of its hip moves into view, nearly indistinguishable against the dark, forested mountainscape.

"I see it," I say, one side of my lip pulled between my teeth. The Phantom's gait is off; it's listing its weight against the bluff more than it should have to. Its forearm knocks against a tree trunk, fragmenting it instantly, and presses fast against the mountainside, pulling itself forward. The moonlight shines in a dull sheen against the metal of its thigh—right side—as it lifts to step over the pass. "You have got to be kidding me."

There's a hole blown in its outer ankle.

A dark laugh sounds behind me.

"June, *wait*," I hiss.

"Oh, I'm waiting, Cap," she says, and I can hear the feral grin in her words.

"Maybe we shouldn't—" Arsen starts.

"They threw us out," Juniper snaps. "They sure as hells aren't stealing our takedown, too."

Something bright and fanged flares to life behind my ribs. After Winterward, what was left of the Gearbreakers fled to our Iolite refuges—cabins hidden a few miles past the foot-hills. My crew knows how to hold their own, but when Jenny split, it was them against everyone else blaming the collapse on their acceptance of Sona. Jenny, anticipating this, gave the kids a trail to follow when she left. But that doesn't mean I don't have a score to settle with the Gearbreakers who thought they could drop my kids without consequence.

The Phantom makes the pass, weight listing onto its right foot. *Could you please remove your hand from the mountainside . . .*

Its left knee moves, rises. The Phantom's arm lifts, finger-tips braced against the rock. That'll do it.

"Now."

We'd spent all day planting explosives. It was a nice time, too—good weather for a hike, ice-blue skies overhead. I could've gone for a little more bickering, but we got the job done.

Or I thought we did.

"June, *now*."

I spin back to see her frantically pressing the detonator. "I'm trying!"

"It's moving," Theo calls.

"She's out of range, Eris!" Arsen snaps.

"Toss it!" June does, and I catch it and slam my finger to the black button.

Nothing.

The mecha's other foot makes the pass. My feet scrape beneath me, the fabric of my pants tearing at the knee as I lurch up the branch. Press. Nothing. I get to my feet, my crew shouting, and move before I can wobble. Press. Nothing. Press. Nothing. The branch gets thin too quickly, my steps going heel to toe, and ahead, the mecha begins to move from the passage.

I snap my arm out, detonator balanced on the ends of my fingers, and press. "Wirefu—"

A blast ruptures the mountainside and hits the Phantom on the back of its shoulder. A shock wave rips up the valley, throwing me head over knees from the tree.

The fall happens quickly. I hit branches but don't feel where until after I hit the earth—miraculously meeting dirt instead of a rock, catching on tree roots before I go rolling too far. I sit up immediately—a mistake that makes the world go briefly fuzzy—and numbly take in the angry scrapes on both arms, bruises blooming underneath.

I look up, dazed, through the foliage at the black of the sky, and note faintly that the stars have blinked out.

"Eris!" someone screams above me, which jolts the realization of what's actually coming down.

I scramble backward on hands and heels and make it about ten feet before the Phantom head hits the ground with a violent, consuming protest of earth and wood giving way to metal. The impact lifts me for about a second and a half, and I land *hard*, with a slack-jawed expression and a choked laugh halfway out of my throat.

I tap the toes of my boots against the curve of the Phantom's skull. I don't even have to extend my foot all the way.

Well. That was a little close.

My crew quickly hops from what's left of the tree onto the back of the Phantom's head, just as it begins to lift.

"How are you alive?" Theo hoots, a grin on his face— grins light all their faces, which makes a nice, glittering feeling glow beside my relief at not being crushed flat.

"I told you we were perfect!" I call, pulling the mallet from my belt. Red light begins to trickle over my shoes. "Meet me inside."

The Phantom's head rises. Crown, brow, socket rim—the night is all black edges and crimson sheen, and I go for the source of the red as soon as it picks up from the earth. I take off at a sprint, leap, hinge my heels and a hand against the right socket, and—aware that now there's a hand reaching for me—smash the mallet against the glass. Its searing glow brings tears prickling to my eyes; I squint and swing again, cracking the exterior layer, my teeth gritting as the ground shrinks behind me. The crew better have made it onto the shoulders.

I swing the mallet a third time, finger slipping against the small trigger at its handle. Jenny's exact words were, *Yeah, so. It'll release enough acoustic energy to shatter the glass, but probably not your skull.*

What's the mallet bit for, then? I'd asked.

Oh, well, I don't know if it's going to work.

I have the faint thought that she said it just to mess with me. It works.

Shr—tink.

Mecha fingers close around me, looking to pop my rib cage like a blister.

I dive into the fragmented opening of the eye, yelping as something cold and solid closes around my ankle. I land hard and twist off my stomach, panicked hands tracking down my leg, knee to shin to ankle to toes—all intact. But my sock is halfway off my foot, boot nowhere in sight.

"Asshole," I mutter, getting to my feet.

I turn toward the Pilot, who is off the glass mat, nose

crooked and bloody. She looks me dead in the eyes and says, "Shit," but the word shouldn't be for me.

The Pilot touches her neck, at one end of the reddening line drawn across it.

The Gearbreaker behind the Pilot holds on to the collar of her jacket so she can't buckle; she can only claw at her neck and jerk mutely against him as the mecha shudders and dies around us.

He drops her once it's over; at the same time Juniper hauls herself into the head, followed closely by the rest of the crew. They go still at the sight of him. The Gearbreaker tosses them a wave, and I step closer. He turns back to look down at me with that telltale smirk, with that little dimple pushed into the left cheek.

"Hey, Eris," Milo says. "Oh! Happy birthday."

I slug him across the face.

"You threw my kids out?!" I snarl, and cradle my bruising hand to my chest. "Agh—*wither*—"

There is a vastly uncomfortable, wet warmth seeping into my sock. I look down and find the Pilot's head bent close to my feet, parted lips almost gracing my ankle. Revulsion, paired with a dark, funny kind of hopelessness, twists through me.

"Deities." I shake out my hand and step over the body.

Milo straightens with a groan that sounds like a growl, gingerly skimming his thumb across his swelling cheekbone, and then slower, traces the gears inked from his jaw down beneath his shirt collar. I recognize the gesture, his chin lifting, the freaking arrogance of it. Used to be hot. I think I used to be more fun. "Where are you going?"

"I need a nap." I take inventory of the kids, touching Theo lightly on the shoulder. The look on his face is carefully blank, but he holds his hand slightly behind him, so Nova's pinkie can link around his. "Let's go."

Milo stalks up to me and leans casually against the hull of the Phantom's head. "Where to?"

"Eat dirt," Arsen offers, grasping June's hand to help her down into the neck.

"I just want to make sure you all found a place to live," he says softly.

"Like hells you do." I bat back his attempt to ruffle Nova's hair. June pauses partway on the ladder, head poking out from the neck to observe.

Milo runs a hand through his hair, overgrown now, so it curls slightly. Dark circles rim his blue eyes, stubble prickling on his chin, even though I know he doesn't like the way it feels. He looks rough, which should not give me such an arguably immature bite of satisfaction, but it does, so I let it happen.

"Look," Milo says, "I didn't want exile for you guys. I haven't been able to sleep much since."

"What a tragedy," says Nova, monotone.

"We sleep in the woods, and sleep great," June says from below. They all know it's not the best idea to tell him we're living with a bunch of rogue Pilots, alongside a small handful of other defected Godolia guards, surgeons, and Academy students, inside an abandoned pre–Springtide War automecha hangar. "And eat dirt. I mean, really, eat *dirt*, Milo, you freaking—"

"It's been a couple of months. The rest of them have cooled off a bit, and our numbers are low. You know that. You're obviously fighting on the right side." He raps his knuckles against the skull. "I can convince them to let you come back."

I bark out a laugh. "You can stop. We don't know where Jenny is."

The easy, pitying mask falls away. Then Milo's just angry again, so, so *angry*, and it makes me ache. It makes him look like he's been alive for so long. I know it's a strange thing to think, but that's what comes up. He looks like he's seen the entire world and found every corner serrated.

But then he speaks, and he just sounds tired.

"We're split," Milo says, gesturing faintly to all of us. "It's fine, and I mean that. Glitch did good." He laughs. *Laughs*, and it's drained, more surprised than dark. "I've had time to think about it. We all did what we could. Your end goal was the same as mine—ending all of this. That's still it for me, Eris, and I think it's the same for you. I might have not liked the way you wanted to fight, and I still don't, like you don't like the way we wanted to fight, and it's fine. It's fine that we ended up here."

He breathes out slow. He doesn't mean *fine* as in *good*. He means *fine* in the tired way, like a collapse, like *at least we're not dead, too*.

"But what Jenny did to Voxter." Milo laughs again, and this one is cracked and stinging. "That will never be something that's *right*."

His voice is a hard and cold thing ricocheting in the space of the mecha head. I wince without moving, and meet his eyes. "Have you ever known Jenny to be wrong?"

The kids told me how they woke up to Jenny dragging Voxter, two pieces in her hands, across the cabin floor. How everyone's shock quieted the air. How she was crying, and still managed to look each of them in the eye to scare away any thought of moving from their cots.

I know this: Jenny would never kill another Gearbreaker. If she didn't consider Voxter one anymore, I trust her on it. But she knew not everyone would and that's why she left, and that must've hurt. Leaving, when so many of us were already gone.

"Well," I say, attempting to scrape the blood from my sock onto the floor, "this has been loads of fun. We're going. Go rot somewhere."

Milo shrugs, excruciatingly unbothered. "Should I expect to see you in Ira Sol next week?"

"What for?"

"The Badlands Academy opening. There's going to be a masquerade ball, hosted by the Zenith himself." He spreads his fingers wide and says, fake awe hushing his words, "The beginning of a new era."

"Ha," June says after a beat of silence, voice small. "That's scary."

It's a gesture weeping with Godolia generosity, a gesture that's going to infatuate a whole generation of Badlands kids until they're falling over themselves to enroll. But Godolia will only cull their most devout; they'll take the children already sick with awe and worship and offer them a gift they'll do anything to be worthy of.

Enyo isn't using fear. He's using grandeur, and religion.

June's right. It's the scariest thing I can think of.

"But I'm assuming you've heard the other broadcasts," Milo continues. "A lone Zenith surviving Heavensday, what a miracle! And even more, he's *merciful*." His mouth curls into a thin grin. "Saving the lost Valkyrie Pilot from the Gearbreakers' corruption. Bringing her home."

Wire*fucker*. "What is *wrong* with you?"

"Me?" Milo says. "Are you going after the Zenith? Because you'll have to kill her, too."

My heartbeat's in my ears. *Bellsona is going to end the Gearbreakers.*

Theo spits in Milo's face.

He probably does it for himself but also in part for me, because the crew takes care of me, and they knew one of them had to do something before the rabid thing in my chest got wound too tight and split. Before I brought the mallet to Milo's temple like it would fix anything. Like it would make him less right.

"Well," Arsen says mildly.

"Well," Milo echoes, and carefully wipes the wetness from his chin. "Just for you to remember, Eris. It's going to be the only time that the Zenith is out of Godolia. So if you're going to make a move, you should be ready to see it through."

He gives one last look to Theo, and then June's hugging the side of the ladder to let him pass. And then he's gone.

I can feel their eyes lift to me, all of them careful. Mine are on the floor. Thinking it over.

Bringing her home.

But Sona's not going to be in Godolia. She's going to be right at Enyo's side, just where he likes to keep her. And he's about to be in the Badlands.

In Ira Sol. Only a hike away.

CHAPTER SEVEN

ERIS

"Talk," Sheils says.

She and Jenny are both looking at me, my sister with her usual amusement, which I have learned to stomach, and Captain Sheils with her cool stare—half-dark, half–glowing red—fixed on me like a steady headshot. For some reason I get to my feet too quickly, smacking my wrist against the table edge, and my mouth purses to keep from yelling. Theo snickers, and the look I shoot him only makes the rest of the crew join in.

Around the table sits a strange mixture of Godolia defectors and Gearbreakers—a combination that continuously startled me when I first got here, but it's hard to summon that jolt of fight or flight when Captain Sheils is looking at me through the steam from her teacup, and Nyla is standing behind Nova, braiding Nova's partially bleached hair. On either side of them sit pale and sullen-eyed Hyun-Woo, the Mutts' nurse, and Dr. Park, a short woman with dark brown skin and a shaved head—both deserters from the Godolia Academy's hospital staff. Flew right out on a stolen medical helicopter. Very metal. At the opposite end of the table, Nolan whispers something to a Hydra Pilot named Astrid—Jen's crew has really been enjoying the new gambling crowd. They're probably gambling right now, on what I'm about to say next. Whether it's brilliant or suicidal.

"The Zenith might've been killed yesterday morning, I don't know. We don't know," I say, off to a wildly confident start. "If not, he's throwing a ball in Ira Sol for the opening of the Badlands Academy. Um. Yeah. So, if he's alive, as in, not blown up—so, alive . . . yeah, *if* he's alive, this means he'll be at this ball."

"Alive?" Seung asks drily, and passes what looks like papered toffee to Gwen.

"Godsdamn it. Yes. Alive. So—Godsdamn it."

I don't have any problem with the Pilots here looking at me—except maybe Sheils, but that's only because I want to impress her, like a child—it's the mechas behind them that bug me. A series of large, staggering platforms are built against the front wall of the hangar, housing sleeping quarters, a small armory, the infirmary, and this meeting room, which doubles as the dining room-slash-kitchen. This level happens to be exactly at the eye level of the Hydra Windups. Sheils doesn't waste generator power on lighting up the hangar, but the light of the platform reaches far enough that I can see the first couple of faces, sunken sockets staring in from the black.

I circle the table and find it not much better, with their stares now fixed on my spine. I take a deep breath and try to ignore that Nolan seems to have just lost whatever his wager was—he hands Astrid a spool of thread.

"If he's *alive*," I start again, "he'll be in Ira Sol within a week. He's going to have heavy guard, but he's also going to be outside Godolia, in the Badlands, on our turf. The ball is the only place we can be sure he'll be in public. We might never get another shot at this."

"A shot at what?" Sheils asks, fingertip tracing the rim of

her cup. The knuckle has a dark tattoo of what June tells me is a belladonna leaf. Which is *so kick-ass.*

"At killing him."

It's ugly, for some reason, saying it so simply. I've killed before. Hells, I've killed a lot. Gets easier, in a sticky way—easier until you start thinking about it. That's the mistake, when you realize there's killers on both sides of this. That's when you've messed up.

Sona thought about it a lot, and it hurt her. I worry about it. That I might have disgusted her by being so numb to all the violence.

Or maybe not numb, but used to it to an extent that I'm forgetful, that I find it uncomplicated sometimes.

Because it is uncomplicated, how this unravels. The Zenith dies. Godolia has an internal power struggle that skews the chain of command in the Windup army. Mechas stop getting sent out to slaughter Badlands people for missed quotas, or to keep the others in line, or for kicks. Within the city, factions are created. Pilots choose sides. People keep dying, but I can sleep at night. Fitfully, maybe, a little nightmare ridden, but with the people I love still breathing in the next room over.

It's simple. It's us or them.

Except. They have one of us.

"There's a Pilot the Zenith keeps at his side." I close my eyes. "She's a Gearbreaker under Godolia corruption. We don't know exactly what the Zenith put in her head, but right now her loyalties are to him. But—"

"The Pilot," Sheils interrupts. "Bellsona Steelcrest."

"Sona," my entire crew corrects, which makes my heart tick in my throat.

Sheils takes a slow sip of her tea, waiting—the look on my face gave her enough of an answer of what Sona means to me.

"She's still in there." I'm not mumbling my words anymore. "I saw it. I saw *her*. And a lot of you don't believe me, that she's still in there, but you know what? Neither does the Zenith."

Sheils is silent for a moment, then leans back in her seat. "Keep talking."

"We get her. We undo the corruption. And then . . . we send her back." The knot in my chest, the one that doesn't ever really go away, now snaps taut. "She tells Enyo that we kidnapped her, that she escaped. That—that she left bodies in her wake. He thinks her corruption is ironclad. Her returning to him will prove it."

The corner of Sheils's mouth tucks into a cold smirk, because she knows my next words. Suddenly I want to stop talking, but I force them out. "And when she gets a chance, she kills him."

The room is silent. Behind Sheils, the light over the stove top flickers lazily. She takes her time looking over my face, taking another slow swallow of her tea.

"Undo the corruption," Sheils repeats finally. "You do not know how the Zenith has had her memories altered. And Sona Steelcrest is not going to believe you when you try to set them straight."

"But she might believe it from another Valkyrie."

There's doubt in the pitying way her small smile twitches, and her two-toned eyes brush briefly over the tattoos rising from my shirt collar. "Ah. That is why you are coming to me with this. You want my prisoner."

The flatness of her voice makes me break, a nervous,

idiotic grin pulling at my lips. "I mean, I've heard you say on multiple occasions that she's nothing but a pain in your ass."

"You and her have that in common."

No. She's going to say no, and I need that Valkyrie to make Sona wake up . . .

"Is this because of what I said this morning?" I ask. Out of the corner of my eye I see June giving me a wary look, Arsen matching her with a small shake of his head. "About you hiding down here? What? Did I hit a nerve or something? Did I say something that was *wrong*, and now you're seriously going to fuck me over because—"

"You are fucking yourself over, with this absurd plan," Sheils says, the words steel. "I took all of you in. I do not regret it—*that* is what I am doing down here, by the way, Shindanai. Just because you Gearbreakers put a gun in the hands of every orphan who walks through your gates does not mean I should be expected to do the same."

Her words wash me cold, head to toe.

Jenny blows her hair out of her eyes and muses quietly to herself, "Hmm. Yeah. Got us there."

There's a nasty scar curling under Jen's jaw that I haven't asked her about, but it was probably from the Winterward assault. The Phoenix attack on the Hollows was a slaughter, but we were all soldiers there. Winterward had civilians. The Paladins sent entire buildings full of Badlands people under the ice, and met the same fate when they were taken down, with Gearbreakers still trapped inside. Jenny had managed to get out of the Windup she felled, half-frozen, and tried to dive back in to rescue others. Seung and Gwen had dragged her back from the water, kicking and screaming.

Now Jen looks at Sheils, black eyes, black circles drawn

around them, black hair pooling around her shoulders in a messy shroud. There's not a trace of a smile on her face.

"You walked away when you saw what your mechas were built to do," Jenny says to Sheils, voice quiet and sharp. Around the table, the Hydras collectively stiffen. "They may not make Hydras anymore, but they still make Windups. They still make kids into killers. Badlands people may not be dying by being dissolved into puddles, but they're still dying, in what I promise you is a lot of other super fun ways. Now it's going to be their children doing the killing, and *us* who are going to have to kill *them*. I don't want to do that."

Jenny picks up a lock of her hair and starts twisting the strands. "That Zenith . . ." Her other hand ghosts over the scar at her neck. "I adore you viciously, halmeoninim. But that Zenith crossed me. And whatever you say, we're taking that prisoner."

A look passes between them. Sheils and Jen have some strange, electric connection that I can't really place. If I think too much about it, then their relationship resembles the one Jenny and our mom had. A little intense, a lot of tough love. It was partly an angsty teenager thing, but probably mostly attributed to the fact that they were both so smart and *so freaking stubborn* for it.

Sheils finally shrugs. "Fine, Miss Starbreach, take her off my hands. Whoever wants to go with you, I can't stop them."

Someone at the table murmurs, and we glance over to see Nurse Hyun-Woo speaking low to Dr. Park, whose thin brows are knitted in a troubled expression. Hyun-Woo shuts his mouth and sits back with pale cheeks pinking. His eyes slide, I think, to Jenny before skittering back to the doc. Just like that, in that brief, abrupt silence, there's a shift in the air. I realize I don't understand what's just happened.

"Jenny," Dr. Park says, in what seems like a careful voice for some reason. "I would not recommend you leaving so soon after—"

"You're not going to get anywhere with her," Zamaya says, her words a little hurried. I look at Jenny to see what the hells is going on, but my sister's face is expressionless. Maybe she's bored now that Sheils isn't fighting her.

"And Eris?" the captain calls. I snap my head back toward her. "Wherever you bring Sona Steelcrest back to, it won't be here. Am I understood?"

I nod, blatantly eager, but I don't care. Sheils puts her mug in the sink and makes for the stairs, the skeletal two-headed snake on the back of her Hydra jacket baring its fangs.

The Hydra Pilots get up and follow her out, then Hyun-Woo and Dr. Park leave, until it's my and Jen's crews left, plus Nyla, who finishes Nova's braid and places it gently over one shoulder. June hands her a hair elastic to tie it off.

Nova runs a hand over her head. "Hot."

"Yeah," Nyla and Theo say.

"Nyla," I say, "are you absolutely sure you want in on this?"

She's one of the few younger Pilots here—not a Hydra, but defected from the Windup ranks about two months after her surgery. I guess not everyone had bought that Sona had been corrupted by us—I guess not all Pilots are so different from her, needing somewhere to run to—because Nyla, out on Iolite Peaks patrol for the first time, paused her Berserker halfway through her rounds, unwound, killed her guards, and waited. Waited for the Gearbreakers to come and make sure all was still.

She got lucky; after weeks of her camping out in her Windup, my crew started following Jenny's trail to the Mutts, came across Nyla's grounded mecha, and found her waiting inside. Luckier still that they had known Sona—they didn't kill her at the first sight of the Mod in her left socket.

Now, she's been hanging around the crew a decent amount, even lent me her mirror to cut my hair.

"I want to help." Nyla pulls back a loose strand of hair behind Nova's ear. "Just, please . . . do not leave me alone with that Valkyrie you are taking from Sheils. She scares me."

"And what's in it for you?" Nova asks, brash grin sparking. June flicks her knee under the table.

Nyla's ruddy cheeks go a little brighter, but she manages the recovery. "I do not want other kids to have to run. They should not have to run."

Nova hangs her head back so Nyla can see how pleased she is. Arsen murmurs something to Theo, who shakes his head with a smirk and smacks him in the shoulder. It's nice that they can act like this now. Because the crew told me about their first meeting. How they'd passed the rotting bodies of the guards as they made their way up. How Nyla sat cross-legged in the Berserker's head, blood dried black on her clothes, hands already up, with her eyes hungry on their gears. *Is it true? Are you taking Pilots?* Her bottom lip trembling. *If I'm wrong, can you make it quick?*

"Touching." Jenny yawns, rolling her chin on the heel of her hand. "Now, Eris. Do you know the specifics of this ball? Are the invitations paper, biometric?"

"I know there's a resource village nearby. Nivim. It's the closest town outside the Ore Cities."

"I know it," Jen says. "Mechvesper village."

"Exactly. And the Academy is only going to recruit Badlands kids who've already been raised to worship them."

"So . . . what? We're just gonna find whoever got invited and mug them?"

"Yeah. I mean, and, like . . . impersonate them."

"Twin hells."

"Look, I know it's rocky, and I know we don't have a lot of details, but we also don't have a lot of time." I pause to take a breath, or maybe because I've run out of useful things to say, and that's when the memory rushes up. My fingernails curl into my palms, nails bitten down to the quick, unpainted.

Both of us on the floor, common room carpet fibers clinging to our hair. Sona's long legs arcing up onto the couch, feet across Juniper's lap so she could get her toes painted, so hers could match mine. She tilted her head toward me, but I was reading and didn't notice until her breath slid against my cheek, until I started and she asked, *How long does this last?* I didn't realize, at first, that she was talking about the nail polish. I don't remember what I answered. I had lost where I had left off in my book.

"We won't know," I breathe. "We won't know what we're getting into, or hells, even how we're getting into it until we get there. But we'll figure it out, and we'll figure it out fast, because we have to. Because we *can't* . . . we can't just keep sitting here."

We haven't, really—today's Phantom takedown certainly wasn't the first one since we came to the Mutts—but we all know things aren't like they used to be. This war isn't slow anymore. We can't keep picking them off Windup by Windup, and we don't have a lot of people left. Rebuilding our numbers gives Godolia time to rebuild theirs, and then we're right back where we started.

We're not doing that. Not when we got so close to ending it.

Not when we've lost so much because of it.

"So," Jenny says. She still has her chin to the ceiling, feet kicked up onto the arm of Zamaya's chair. Casual, but her eyes are drawn low, and her next words are to her crew. "Are we in?"

Seung puts his palms to his face and rubs vigorously. "You ever have a moment when you can so perfectly realize that the rest of your life hinges on your next decision? And that you're gonna make the one that's going to kill you, for no discernible reason?"

"No. That might be the dumbest thing I've ever heard," says Gwen, then she looks tiredly at Jenny. "But also yes."

"We're the same crew, only a few years younger, aren't we?" Arsen murmurs.

I roll my eyes. "Because I'm such a tyrant."

"No, Cap," June says. "It's all of us or none of us, see? Over a cliff. Underfoot." She runs her fingers over Nova's braid. "It's no fun alone."

CHAPTER EIGHT

BELLSONA

"The good doctor has cleared you for Ira Sol," Enyo tells me later that night. We are in his bedroom, and he is at his desk deciding little fates for the nation, perfectly relaxed, with a cup of the coffee I told him to refrain from held to his lips.

"What do you think of this one?" I ask, standing in the doorway of his closet, pressing one of his suit jackets to my collarbone.

"We will have something for you made. You do not need to borrow from me."

"Wasteful. And I like this."

"Did you hear what I said?"

"About Ira Sol? Yes." I turn and rehang the jacket, selecting another one. I think it is gray. "This one?"

"Aren't you going to ask me about your appointment? Subtly, of course." He nods to the secretary poised beside his desk. "Move four Phoenixes from the second southeast rotations to the south guard. Replace them with the Phantoms from last week's shipment, the fourteenth-A batch."

"The Phantom Pilots are split about the Iolite rotations," I remind him.

"Devoid guard," Enyo says, looking at the secretary's map. "Here, here, and here . . . and here."

Devoid guard—posting an unpiloted mecha to scare off

unwanted activity—is a new tactic, and one that only works for Phantoms, who are expected to stand completely still until something crosses them. Phantoms are visible under a clear night sky if one knows to look out for them. Assuming some sense of self-preservation, this will result in a wide berth, herding passersby into territory protected by a Piloted Windup.

Truly, the Gearbreakers were misguided in targeting the mechas, or even the Zeniths. The former can be reproduced, and the latter can be reaped young and still hold authority, as seen by the entitled youth sipping caffeine and giving military orders, trying to pull together enough protection from barely a sixth of their former army, and even fewer Pilots. Those cannot be made so quickly.

"So?" Enyo says.

"So," I repeat, holding the suit jacket up.

"I am unsure about the blue."

"Blue?"

"Bellsona."

I choose one of his button-downs from the drawer and stand in the doorway to try it on, collar halfway down my face when I speak. "I threw my shoes."

"So I read."

"She is still all right with me going to Ira Sol?"

"Granted you do not kill me before we leave for the opening ceremony." Enyo sets down his coffee and glances at the secretary. "Maybe we should call it a night. Yes. Good night."

The blushing secretary bobs a nod and exits, and Enyo leans forward to drop his brow to the desk's edge. I stand in front of the mirror on his door and pull on the gray-slash-blue-slash-red suit jacket. The sleeves are too long, ending halfway up my palms.

"You are the only one in the world who does not take me so seriously, Bellsona."

"That is because you are a dramatic brat, but everyone else is too afraid to treat you as such," I say, straightening the collar.

"Is it the way I look?"

I run my thumb under my bottom lip, the corner of my left eye. Light filling up the nail. "How do *I* look?"

He does not lift his head. "You are not my type."

"I know."

He glances up. "You look pretty."

"I know. And it is the way you look, yes." I bunch up the sleeves around my wrists, frown to myself in the mirror, and discard the jacket. "Do you want me to help with that?"

He perks up immediately, but I blame the coffee. "Could you?"

I go over to his desk and start rummaging through the drawers, batting him back when he gets in the way. "Call for ice. And a lighter. And earrings."

He pales in my peripheral vision. "Um."

I find the sewing kit and pop open the plastic casing, holding the small row of needles up to the lamp on his desk. "Do not be concerned."

"I can just have someone—"

"My umma did this for me when I was six."

"You do not wear earrings," he says, words strung with a nervous laugh.

I pull out one of the needles by its eye, easing myself onto the arm of his chair. "I sat on our dining table. Took hardly a second on each side."

Enyo stays perfectly still, the needle hovering four inches from his jaw. "Did you flinch?"

"No." A beat. "But I cried afterward."

"I do not like crying."

"Then do not. Call for the supplies."

He does. They come on a little silver platter—a glass bowl of ice, a variety of lovely earrings pressed into a velvet cushion, just for show; we select what we want, and the attendants bring new ones still in their sterile plastic bags. They also provide gloves, which I put on, but I reject the needles they offer.

I strike the lighter and thread the sewing needle through its flame. "Some part of this has to be questionable."

He sits on the desk, holding ice chips to his ears, drops of water darkening his sleeves. "You are trying to kill me."

"The issue is not other people taking you too seriously, Enyo dear, it is that you take *yourself* too seriously. When your ears fall off because of this botched job, you can relax a little. Are you ready?"

"Do I have a choice?"

I smirk, and brace a hip on the table beside him—bracing, because truly, I do not know what I am doing—and grasp his earlobe between two fingers. My other hand rises, and he waits quietly as I study the angle. The wood-fed fireplace at the back of the office burns low and slow, drowsy heat pooling around us. The usual fanfare of choked traffic in the city streets breathes against the window glass; we are far up enough that the blaring horns sound lazy.

The desk was originally facing his doorway. We spent half an afternoon rotating it so it faced out the window instead, Enyo refusing to call for assistance—besides me— embarrassed, for some reason, of his want to look onto the city. We were both pouring sweat by the end and drank iced tea sitting on his floor in front of the desk, our backs to its wooden legs, knees pulled up so our toes rose against the window.

"Did you do it?" Enyo asks hopefully. I can see the corner of his toothy, nervous grin.

"No."

I knock against his jaw lightly to bring his ear farther under the light, the needle hovering above the skin, and I want to grasp his chin and splinter his skull against the tabletop.

What?

I start—I physically start—and the urge is nonexistent, blinked out with no Godsdamn trace. It was there in my head and in my fingertips for the fragment of an instant and then gone, no provocation, no warning, nothing no no no I was doing *better*—

"Enyo," I murmur.

He is already stiff on the edge of the desk, so perceptive of me like he is of everyone; the difference is, with me, he puts his hand on my sleeve because he knows I need him to. "Bellsona?"

"I just thought about cracking your head open," I whisper, voice even but almost inaudible. The warmth gathering in my left eye breaks first, and my right follows a beat after, tears crawling silently toward my chin. "Just for an *instant*. It was me, or . . . no, *no*, I was no one else but someone who wanted—oh Gods. Oh, *fuck*."

I sink into his chair, needle still pinched in one hand, his still holding my sleeve. Shame burns in my cheeks, so heavy it feels like grief, but I force my eyes up to his regardless, because he deserves that much from me—at the very least, after *everything*, I can meet his eyes, even though I am sure the look on his face is going to dissolve me.

But Enyo is not looking at me as if I am a stranger, and it breaks me just as much. Dark hair tousled in untidy waves, soft lamplight clawing one side of his face, black eyes drawn low on mine. He looks so young and so worried for his age, so worried for *me*. I still cannot understand it. Cannot understand how I could berate him and orphan him and threaten him, and still he pulls me out of my chair by my sleeve so he can put his arms around my shoulders.

"Is she gone?" he murmurs softly.

I watch the flames lick in the hearth over the line of his shoulder. "Yes," I say, the word pressed into his shirt fabric.

"Why did you tell me?"

I lift one shoulder. "Too much for me to handle alone."

"Am I helping, or making it worse?"

A fractured laugh spills from me. "Deities, am I?"

"What do you mean?"

Part of the fire sighs into itself, firefly cinders dying fast. I close my eyes. "What happens to me now?"

Enyo goes quiet. I can feel his heartbeat, which means he can feel mine, its frantic, rabid jolts. I grip the moment, the feel of his shirt to my chin, the warmth, the hoarse drawl in his voice. Whatever comes next for me, I can bear it, with this instant tucked away.

"Are your hands shaking?" he asks.

"You know they do not."

"Are you going to finish?"

I lean back. "What?"

Enyo taps my hand, the one still holding the needle. I look at him, disbelieving, and he says, "Go ahead."

And I do, before I can lose my nerve, before someone else comes crashing in and takes my hands, the thoughts in my head. The needle goes in, then the earring, then the left side, repeat. I sit back and Enyo blinks, then hops off the desk and past me to stand in front of the mirror. I follow to stand behind him.

"How do I look?" Enyo asks.

I watch him poke one of the earrings and, of course, wince, and cannot help but smirk. "You are not my type."

"I know," he says. He grins, dimples burrowing deeper. "I did not even cry."

"The night is not over."

Enyo disappears into his closet for a few seconds and emerges with another suit jacket. He pushes me closer to the mirror and offers it ardently. "Try this one."

I do. My eyes are slightly swollen, the glow of my Mod thrown in tiny, threadlike wisps of light across my wetted lashes. I free the hair trapped in the suit collar. "Better?"

Behind me, Enyo nods.

"Better," he says, and I can tell he believes it, by that smile, that gentle stare through feathery lashes. He has the eyes of an old man—not in their appearance, but in the way they rest on mine, like he is weighing me against the knowing that comes from a long life, though he has not lived much longer than me.

I tilt my chin, curls slipping off my shoulder. "Do you truly think this is going to work? Drawing out the Gearbreakers to Ira Sol?"

Drawing the Frostbringer out, if she is alive.

Hells. He could just stay here, have his subordinates throw the opening on his behalf—he *should* stay here.

But no. He would prefer to be bait for his own trap, which doubles as the start of a new era.

His era.

Godolia and the Badlands, hand in hand.

And the age of Gearbreakers dead and done with.

And me, the trap's teeth. Maybe this, too, is a kind of mercy. That Enyo is going to allow me to rip them apart like they did to me.

"Yes." Enyo's dark gaze trains on mine in our shared reflection, and then he puts his chin on my shoulder, closing his eyes. "Everything they want will be in Ira Sol. I think it is all going to work out just fine."

CHAPTER NINE

ERIS

"This is nice," says Juniper, looking down the valley to where Nivim sprawls, cheery structures dotting green hills, everything shot through with streaks of flowers. "I'd live here."

"It's a Mechvesper village," Arsen responds. "You're more spiritual than religious."

"Absolutely. But I like the wildflowers. And *oh*, look at that *river!*" She lifts a hand, tracing a brown, scarred fingertip against the blue line cutting the landscape. "I'd totally live here. The underground life is not for me."

She and Arsen are sitting on a log at the edge of the small clearing we've set up our camp in. It was about a half-day trip from the Mutts to Nivim, the closest Mechvesper village—Badlands people who worship the Windups as deities incarnate, Godolia as the physical plane's heaven, and the Zeniths as . . . I don't know, some sort of super-Gods? It all kind of escapes me. Silvertwin was the same—Sona might've been the same, if she hadn't watched the deities slaughter her entire village. If she'd grown up with her family, one that would duck their heads over their meals every night and thank Godolia for allowing the Gods to walk among them.

Would it have been better that way? For her to believe in something so powerful like that, something twisted and dark but with her mother and father still breathing at her side—caring for her, loving her, seeding faith in the place where rage and hurt are so viciously rooted now?

Yeah. It would have been better.

But I couldn't have loved her like that.

What a sick joke.

Nearby, Nova bends over to pluck a flower, then straightens and offers it to Nyla. Novs grins and points at Theo, stretched out on his back in the clearing. Nyla smacks the flower out of her hand and skitters away, black curls floating off her shoulders.

I roughly pat my hands against my cheeks, scattering my spiraling thoughts. I am so tired of the spiraling.

I walk to where Arsen and Juniper are sitting, dropping my forehead to where their shoulders are touching. Their hands, the ones that hold their tattoos, immediately find my wrists.

"You good, Eris?" Arsen asks.

"Let's live here," I say into their shirts. "Somewhere like here, when we're done with all of it, yeah? We'll all have our own houses. I can sit on my porch and throw shit at you guys on yours whenever I'm in a bad mood. You'll need to be away from the river so whatever chemical stuff you're messing with can't seep in accidentally, but then, June, you can grow all the poison plants you like in your garden. And we'll need to have at least two bedrooms apiece to rotate Nova around, whenever she burns down her house. We might need a wall in case Jenny tries to siege, but otherwise we'll be good."

I can feel them glance at each other over the crown of my head.

"I love it. Deities . . . yeah, I really love it," Juniper says, voice quiet but strained. She wipes her eyes, quickly, sleeve brushing my temple. "You are literally making me so sad, Eris."

Luckily, I don't need to think of a response, because just then we see Jenny circling back from scouting Nivim, sunlight reflecting in twin sparks off the welding goggles loose around her neck. Zamaya and Seung trail her—we left Gwen and Nolan at an old Gearbreaker safe house about five miles back, a few miles outside the Ira Sol walls, to watch over Sheils's prisoner. I thought taking her from the Mutts would be a messy ordeal, but she actually seemed to enjoy the walk, even with her hands bound. She waited all the way until we got to the cabin before she tried to kill one of us, which was nice of her.

The expression on Jenny's face makes me straighten, palms bracing on June's and Arsen's shoulders. "Something's wrong."

Jenny doesn't say anything to me as she stalks past. We follow her into the clearing, where Theo scrambles to his feet, dusting dead pine needles from his shirt. Overhead, the sky is bright. A perfectly nice day.

A warm breeze flits through, and it lifts Jenny's hair from her shoulders in a black sheet. "There's heartbreak grass in the valley, Juniper."

All heads turn toward our chemist. She would consistently dye her hair green when we were in the Hollows, and now the dark brown of her roots has dropped to her ears. A smile tugs her lips, more reflexive than pleased. "Oh? Oh."

Silence. Jenny's stare is fixed on Juniper, which makes her tawny cheeks flush, and I flap a hand. "Hello? What is it?"

Juniper glances at me. "Jenny wants a paralytic."

"You found who has the invitations?" I say, relief swelling in my chest.

"Wasn't hard," says Seung. He turns and points to a bright dot on the villagescape below. "See that? Their entire house is decked out in flowers—to celebrate, probably. Which is absolutely adorable."

His tone and expression actually say *absolutely fucked up*.

"So how many are there?" I ask.

"Two," Zamaya says when Jenny doesn't say anything. I realize, with a start, that she's chewing on her thumbnail. Not a good sign. "But there's a slight complication . . ."

The complication: Godolia tech-fucking-gaudiness. Of course they wouldn't make the invitations something as superficial as a piece of paper. No, of course the Godolia techs would make them implants, would bury them nice and safe in the skin of the Mechvespers' forearms. Which means . . . We would have to dig.

Nova laughs outright when Z's done explaining, no cheer in her voice. "Oh. Okay. Is that all?"

"Wait, wait, wait." I shake my head, one hand running through my hair. "Okay. Okay, so—"

I stop short. I don't know what to say, and I don't know what to do next.

"Eris—" Zamaya starts.

"We still need to get to Ira Sol." I'm pacing, I realize, boots kicking up pine needles. I clap my hands against my cheeks again, a little sting to push my thoughts together. "We can take the tunnels that Sheils's scouts use, right? Slip in with the crowd when the ball starts. Maybe we need a distraction? They're probably going to check the invitations at the entrance, so I doubt they'll be looking once we're inside. So—"

"Eris," Jenny says, her voice hard. "We're taking the invitations before sunrise tomorrow."

The undergrowth settles around my feet. I turn toward

her, where she meets my sight with black eyes, the ones that match mine.

"Gods, Jenny," I rasp. "You can't be serious."

"We overheard that the Nivim family is expected to meet at the Gillian Conflux early in the morning," she says. "There's a ferry waiting to take them and the other Badlands Academy recruits up to Ira Sol. We have to take the invitations before they get to the water."

"Oh, you 'overheard'?" I snap. "Or did you leave some Mechvesper bleeding out in a bush somewhere?"

Her eyes narrow dangerously. "I wouldn't do that."

"But you'd do *this*?"

"We don't have a choice, Eris!"

Her expression flares viciously, scowl flickering to a nasty grin, clearly daring me to continue. When I was younger, it would've sent me scrambling away. "First the gloves, and now this? They're *our people*, Jenny! I know it's been rough—deities, I know it's been hells, but you're forgetting—"

"Rot," Jenny breathes. She's still standing halfway across the clearing from me, but the disdain in her tone singes me anyway. "I don't forget."

There's always been a sharpness to the way my sister stands. Dark gray canvas jacket with the sleeves neatly tucked up, long hair pulled back into a high tail, shoulders straight, pretty features that always, *always* look at you head-on. But now . . .

Now, her jacket has splits around its sides, just above the pockets, and the sleeves are unrolled so they hide her wrists. Her hair hangs unbrushed and matted around her shoulders, which would make her look bigger if you couldn't see how hollow her stomach is, judging by the way her shirt drops limply off her ribs. Her eyes still meet mine, slashed with the same crow's feet she's had all my life, but these too seem empty.

Where her sharpness was made of clean, effortless lines, now her edges are serrated.

"You're being reckless," I hear myself say.

She laughs, hands twitching at her sides. "That is *rich*, coming from you, you little bastard."

Around the clearing, our crews watch in careful silence.

"Fine, Eris," Jenny continues. "What's the backup plan, then? And for the love of the good Gods, make sure to keep the moral high ground! Wouldn't want you to plummet from grace, your empathetic angelic majesty!"

She bows low, her black hair tickling the thistles.

I just stare at her as she picks her head up again. I really could cry, but I don't, because more and more I'm finding it doesn't help—all it really does is just make me so *tired*. And I don't have another plan, and Jenny knows it. That's why I'm guessing she could cry, too, if she had the capacity right now. She doesn't want to do this any more than I do.

I turn toward my crew. Nova is holding another flower, stem choked in her little fist. Juniper's mouth is pressed into a sick, hard smile that doesn't fit her right, and Arsen is viciously rubbing his eyes so he doesn't have to look at me. Even Nyla looks sullen, little heart-shaped face hidden by her curls as she looks at the ground.

Theo breathes out slow, then says with a dry laugh, "Don't say it, Eris."

"I'm serious," I say. My hand reaches out and closes around his wrist. His green eyes snap to mine. "If you want out of this, say so now. Any single one of you . . . and we're out. No questions asked."

I let them exchange glances with one another. Part of me viciously hopes one of them will say, *No. No way in the twin hells, Eris. This isn't who we are. This isn't who we're going to be.*

"All right, Eris," Arsen says quietly. "We're in."

Jenny doesn't look nearly as smug as I'd like her to. I'd rather she be celebrating than the way she sniffs and straightens, throwing a stiff nod before ambling off, muttering something about collecting flowers. Our crews slowly trickle out of the clearing to follow, but my feet slow.

"Zamaya."

The demolitionist stops at the tree line, glancing at me over her shoulder so I can see the gear tattoo set right into where her dimple would sink if she were smiling, which she's not. "Darling."

Something about the look on my face must be particularly concerning, because she turns to me fully, brows furrowed.

I'm suddenly reminded of our old common room—not the one that belonged to my crew, but the one that belonged to Jenny's, with the herbs drying on the windows and the small, bright lights that dropped from the corners. A blackboard on wheels drifted haphazardly to where it was needed, or kicked to, padded with symbols and graphics I never understood, white chalk powdering everything most of the time. There was an ugly olive-colored couch shoved up against the walls, where Jenny would sit on Z's lap and make out and I would shriek about the public display of affection. When I would fall asleep on the rug, Nolan or Seung or Luca would carry me back to my room, and then chuck me onto my bed from the doorway. Gwen lined my windowsill with bullet casings filled with soil and wildflower seeds; Zamaya hid bundles of wax paper for me around the apartment, some containing toffee, some holding tiny caltrops that split my fingertips if I went for them too eagerly.

I swallow hard. "Is Jenny okay?"

Zamaya takes a moment to tuck her violet hair around her ears, and then says calmly, "It's not any of your business, is it?"

I would snap at that, if it weren't basically what I was expecting. "But you are worried about her."

"Jen's been worrying me since the day we met."

"Z."

Now there's a smile, and the tattoo sinks, but there isn't any mirth that reaches her eyes. She runs her fingers down her cheek, each knuckle inked with a gear, and lets out a steady, careful breath. "She's just . . . she feels cornered. She's used to making her own way out, you know, she always has a way to fix it. But after Winterward, after the Hollows . . . deities . . . you know what, Eris? No. No, she's not okay." Her voice cracks a little; her boot makes a scuffing line in the pine needles to mask it. Her chin tilts away from me, and for a moment she stands there, letting the sunlight catch on the deep copper of her skin. "Jenny is really sad, Eris. She's just really fucking sad."

Zamaya presses the heels of her hands to her eyes. I still don't know what to say when she draws them away, but when she speaks this time, her voice is no longer soft; her words have barbs, and she looks at me with a curl to her mouth to make sure every one of them burrows.

"But she's also really fucking smart, okay? Don't you *ever* forget that. Jenny might be reckless and arrogant and a hot-head, but she is the furthest thing from stupid, and she's doing what she can. So you damn well better be thankful for it. She's trying to save everyone even though she has to deal with herself at the same time."

I work my breath around the clot in my throat, but my words sound thick anyway. "What can I do?"

The wind picks up, leaves chattering above our heads. At her sides, Zamaya's fingers briefly tense into the edge of her sleeves. Then she forces herself to relax, palms going limp before lifting in a gesture equal parts helpless and hopeless. Something snags in my chest; it's like her hands are under my ribs, twisting sinew as she traces by.

"Just stay alive." She turns away from me. "Good Gods, if you can manage it . . . just stay alive."

CHAPTER TEN

BELLSONA

The mountainside hitches like a chipped tooth where the Zenith's train was blasted off the tracks. I lean over, my immense shadow washing across the valley, silent and dark. Pick through tangled threads of ripped tracks, smoldering train cars like plastic toys next to my fingertips. One has a hole at its belly, large enough for me to tuck my thumb into. I raise it to my eye level, and somewhere to my left, Enyo hums, so full of interest I could throttle him.

"I could throttle you right now," I say.

"And how is that different from every other moment, Bellsona?" Enyo asks, unbothered. "Charges on the tracks?"

"Mountainside, most likely." I let the train car fall from my hand, the hundred-foot drop shattering whatever pieces were spared from the detonation. I believe we are both thinking the same question—how many Gearbreakers are left?

Wound into my Valkyrie, I cannot see Enyo, cannot see the twitch in his jaw, the hands I know go still at his sides when his anger rises. Never fists, just fingers untucked from palms, a calm and careful mask. I imagine his head tilted down to the glass, black hair untucking from around his ears as he bitterly watches the smoke curl from the metal carnage far below.

Bitterness does not become a Zenith. Maybe it is considered a childish tick, something to outgrow. Coldness is more suited to their divinity. The removal of themselves from their purpose. The removal of their human soul to spare the humanity of others. Zeniths are not meant to be good. They are meant to protect their people.

But Enyo is not cold. I know this. Because I am still alive, and he smiles at me despite what I have done, and he weeps for his dead. He sleeps with his curtains open and says he likes the city lights. I will never tell him I know he is afraid of the dark.

"Would you like me to look for them?"

To pluck the Gearbreakers from their hiding places. To toss them easily back to the earth. I would not be asking if Enyo had been on the train; I would be crawling on steel hands and knees, combing the pines for thin, breakable limbs. I would already be reaping.

"Not particularly. Overwhelmed by what might have been my violent death, I think I would like to get to Ira Sol and have a cup of tea."

Inside my head, my smaller form bites the inside of her cheek. He knew the dangers of leaving Godolia just as he knows the dangers of putting himself in public, especially beside Badlands people—thus the decision to send an unmanned decoy instead, imbued with the Zenith's Aether Tree insignia, and then to accompany me in my Valkyrie rather than in a helicopter. We know there are still Gearbreakers alive—not many, after Winterward, but we do not know *how* many, and this is the problem.

"I am turning around."

"Ani. Please do not, Bellsona," he says politely, but with the bitterness tilted toward me now. "I will beg you."

"Beg, then." I turn back north. When my feet leave the

valley floor, they leave craters. A small group of deer scatter into the woods a few hundred feet away.

Enyo steps onto the glass mat under my stance; I know because when I take my next step, it moves, and he lands with a sharp breath. Irritation flashing, I straighten my spine and rip out the connecting cords from my forearms. When I blink, a red, spring-clear sky and hills dappled with thistles become Enyo's toothy grin beneath me, the mecha humming into silence around us.

"What if the Gearbreakers come?" he asks, framed by the dulling glow of the mat.

"You do realize," I say through gritted teeth, "that twice in the past three days someone has tried to kill you."

"The gloves were an accident. I think."

"Are you trying to make it easier for them? Do you *want* to die?"

"Only the normal amount."

"Fine. I will kill you when we get back to the safety of Godolia."

He goes to thumb one of his newly pierced ears, and I kick his ankle. He puts his hands under his head instead.

"This divide ... ," he says. His tone is light, but a chill drops down my spine. "This distance between Godolia and the Badlands ... It chokes them, and it will suffocate us. The ones who do not worship us despise us, and we are to blame for it. Don't look at me like that. The Badlands have hardly been given a chance. But I can make them more. I can make them good. I can make them Gods." Tone dreamy, and I am cold. "Because we cannot have this hatred, Bellsona. We cannot be so infected with it. I can make them feel holy, and loved. I can keep it from getting worse."

Enyo's dark eyes are drawn low. There is something fever-ish tumbling within his prayerlike words. "No more Badlands people have to loathe us. No more of my people have to die.

"What is it like?" he asks suddenly, gaze drifting to the top of the space, where the connecting cords dangle down, like strange plants. For a brief, cold moment, I think he means killing. "Winding. I have done simulations, of course. But I mean initially. The jump to the greater form. Is it a jump? A drop?"

The sudden topic change jars me, and I roll my eyes. "The first time, the trial run . . . it was a jolt. Like I was thrown out of my body. Amplified."

"And now?"

I ghost my palm over one of the hanging cords. My arm panels are still open, and the silver in them scatters the midday light. "It is nothing now. Just me. Waking up in the morning, that is what Lucindo said. My former Valkyrie captain."

He is the one, Enyo has told me, who fought me in the sky on Heavensday. He failed, too, because I am a fantastic Pilot, and because parts of me were blotted out—save for the skill, the malice, the heartlessness that I cannot remember whether it was mine to begin with or if the Frostbringer forced it to root. Save for what they needed.

I remember Lucindo. The color of his eyes, when I still wanted color. His grin with the dimples, tossed across the Valkyrie dinner table while they all toasted me. All of them dead now. Lucindo, I bested. The rest I fed to the flames.

All of them? Is that right? I can barely remember their names. Enyo says something else, dreamily, but I do not catch it. There is something else here. Something I . . . misplaced. Next to me, at the dinner table . . . a boy. No, a girl, and then a boy. Her hand on my cheek. Pinching. I cannot remember her face. The boy beside her, leaning so he could look at me.

Enyo sits up and says something else, the words muffled. The light from the Valkyrie's eyes drown the pale skin of his hand as he flits it upward. I feel worlds away from where my feet are.

Where is Rose, Sona? A hand in my hair. And I think I thought he was already dead, dead like the rest of them, but that isn't right, because this was after, because he—Jole. Jole's hand in my hair, tangling, lifting, bringing my head to the tabletop. Fluorescent lights smearing right and left. Who is Rose? He is screaming at me. *Answer me, Sona.*

Enyo stops talking, because I am looking at him. He gets to his feet silently, and waits as I search his face with a franticness I cannot mask.

"Jole," I say, the name spilling from me. "Jole, he was a Valkyrie, and he lived—where is he?"

Enyo does not answer me. Instead, he says, "You remember Jole?"

And that scares me. That tells me I've slipped up. I step forward and grasp his shoulders tightly. He lets me jostle him. I could get killed for touching him like this, but I cannot see how it could possibly matter.

"I do not remember killing Lucindo," I gasp. My thoughts are reeling; I can barely focus on Enyo in front of me. "Where are they? Am I really the only Valkyrie left?"

He shakes his head. "Bellsona—"

"Please."

Enyo puts his hands to the back of my arms, I think because I am trembling.

"Please," I say again, quieter, my voice breaking. "Please, my Zenith, I feel like I am going crazy."

"I don't like that," he rasps, voice hard, his eyes flitting away like he is ashamed. "I don't like you calling me that."

I stay clutched to him, frenetic, unspooling, and it's when a sob escapes me that he looks back. Immediately disgusted with myself, I try to step away, but he keeps me in place.

"You are the last Valkyrie," he murmurs, and I still. "Jole lived. Lucindo lived. They survived Heavensday, just like I did."

We survived you.

"What happened?" I whisper. "Where are they?"

I see him swallow hard, and his fingers curl slightly into my arms. "They were angry, that I let you live. One night . . . they were going to do it themselves. They were caught."

I focus on the little fibers making up his shirt. "You had them killed."

"They went against my orders. They undermined—"

"It was for me." There is a line marring the cloth, a wrinkle that needs to be ironed out. "They were going to hurt me, and you killed them for it."

The silent air is warm with sunlight. Outside the Valkyrie's eyes, the sky sinks between the mountains.

Enyo nods.

I shove him back. He could have me killed, too, for that. I shove him again. A laugh twists from him, full and unbelieving.

"Hwana?" he asks, laughing again. He thinks I am joking, that I am playing with him. "You are mad?"

"Why would you *do* that?" The words come out half sob, half shriek. Eyes widening, Enyo stops laughing, and I start, and it chokes me. "They *lived*. There were two entire lives that survived what I did. Two bodies' worth of blood that I could have kept off my hands. And you—you could have *saved* them from me."

"They were going to—"

"You should have let them!"

His hand is instantly around my wrist, voice suddenly a growl. "Do *not*."

"You should have. You know you should have." His hold is soft, even now, barely there, and I hate him for it. "I should be dead. I should be rotting. I *am* rotting, and it is the only thing that is keeping me sane."

In the body of a God, we stand close, loathing each other viciously, but not in a way that will stick.

I want him to kill me, I realize, recoiling from the self-pity, the pathetic darkness of it. I do not want to die, but even more than that, I do not want to go unpunished.

I just want it to stop.

And I would rather feel nothing than feel good.

"They were going to kill you." Enyo's fingers slip from my wrist, and then he flicks me between my brows. I blink, and he smiles. It reaches his eyes, but the look in them is drained and still, like he is too tired to even want to cry. "You're my best friend, and they were going to kill you. I—"

My hand slips over his mouth. "Stop it," I say viciously. Quietly. Am I afraid someone is listening? He is not supposed to have friends. He is not supposed to have anyone. Just like I should not have anyone. That should be it, silencing him, a flare in his expression, maybe, and I would find relief in it. Atonement. "You sound like a child."

"We are children," Enyo says under my touch. "You have done horrible things. And I . . . I will."

The guilt that breathes in Enyo shares an edge with the guilt that breathes in me. I am living, despite all the death I have inflicted, scattered by the fistful, thrown as easily as a late-day shadow over the streets. He is living, despite the same. His guilt comes from being the only one who is.

And he hated me, at first. He must have. Sometimes, late at night, I wonder if he hurt me when I was delirious and corrupted and wanted to hurt him, too.

But it is not in his nature, past initial instinct, past blind grief. I think it could make anyone want to do terrible things. I think I could do terrible things, in mourning, in anger, all on my own.

"I met you at the end of the world." His words work into my skin. "Can we not want to be alone, here?"

I do not want to be alone.

He is different from the Zeniths before him. I have made him different—I should have made him crueler.

But when I draw my hand away, his fingers move and catch mine.

"Can we both be terrible here, Bellsona?" Enyo asks me. "Together?"

CHAPTER ELEVEN

ERIS

I reach out and wrap my fingers around the cool glass of the syringes, pulling them from Juniper's shaking hands. My other palm finds her knuckles. Her dark brown eyes flick up to me, cavernous under the predawn sky, and haunted.

I get to my feet. We're a little way down the road from Nivim, where the invited Mechvespers should be heading to make the Ira Sol ferry. The sky is a black slash above us, starless behind a sheet of clouds. The air feels charged. Thunder's been rumbling low for the past half hour, threads of pale orange lightning clawing at the northern peaks.

Jenny is stretched out on her back in the grass at the side of the road. She glances up at me, then arches her spine, hands extending above her head as she yawns.

I hold out one of the syringes to her; Jenny sits up and takes it. Gaze distant, up toward the sky, she says, "This whole place used to be an ocean, you know." She absentmindedly pats the grass at her side. "Sea floor, all of this. Nearly completely unexplored. It was probably an easier feat when it dried up, after all the bombs and eco meltdowns and the like. But then again, there weren't that many people left to go discovering after all of it. They probably had other things to worry about."

I glance around us. The green seems black right now, but

I know there's a lot of it, the mountainscape spanning all the way east to where the actual ocean is.

"Has it just been war ever since then?" For some reason, the words come out hoarse.

"Who the hells knows." Jenny grabs the syringe and stands, dusting off her black cargo pants. "At least the trees grew in nicely."

Footsteps crunch down the road. We look to see Seung and Zamaya, our scouts, stalking up the dirt path. It's raining by the time they get to us, first a couple of drops, and then a downpour. All of us fold into the grass, the water already pooling on the soil, and I touch my gaze to each of my crew members through the onslaught. I find mouths pressed into tight lines, shoulders braced in anticipation. Nyla has a strip of cloth over her eye to cloak the glow of her Mod, which of course reminds me of Sona.

I can't hear Seung's words over the pounding of the rain, but I follow Jenny's glance down the road. Lights have appeared over the curve of the path, soon flanked by two figures moving quickly toward us.

In the back of my head, some part of me recognizes I'm holding the syringe too tightly. Some other part of me realizes I'm not breathing all that well, that I am really about to do something terrible. The weight of my sodden clothes is suffocating and the rain is so fucking loud I don't even catch that Jenny, Seung, and Zamaya have moved forward until Arsen is shaking my shoulder, shouting, "Eris! Eris?"

My boots kick against the slick ground, and then I'm on the road and then on *them*. Their flashlights clatter out of their hands, slices of light skittering to the side of the path. Seung and Zamaya holding one, a woman, who's screaming. Jenny hovers over her, light glinting off the syringe as she raises it, and then the needle pushes into her neck. The rain sounds like static, and Jenny throws me a snarl alongside a lightning strike that tears the sky, followed by thunder that I can feel between my ribs—no, not thunder, but a fist.

I stumble with a gasp, turning—the other Mechvesper is on me, another flash of lightning dousing her features; she's scared absolutely shitless, but she raises her hand again anyway. She must be the woman's daughter, must only be a year or two younger than I am. She could've run. She could've gotten away, but she turned back, just like I would've. Her next punch goes for my stomach.

But she's not a fighter. Not yet.

I dodge and shove her away, and she's caught by my crew members' hands. She screams, flailing so wildly that they have to force her to the ground. Through the rain I hear Nova's sharp, helpless sob, quickly stifled as her hand clamps the Mechvesper child's arm to the waterlogged earth. Vaguely, I'm aware that her mother is limp on the ground, Jenny at her left hand with a knife, searching, and then *digging*.

Badlands Academy recruiters came around a few weeks ago, apparently, to set the invitation implants. What an honor it must have felt like. To be chosen. To be given this little piece of metal as a gift, with a promise that it wouldn't be the last.

I lean over the Mechvesper. She's crying, shrieking, but with the rain drowning everything out, it only shows in the way her body convulses. And then I'm pushing the syringe into the side of her neck, and emptying it, and she's still.

And the rain just keeps on coming.

"Jen?" Zamaya hisses, and I look, half-dazed, to see my

sister has paused. Her knife lies discarded at her side, a hole opened up in the woman's palm, where between a pair of tweezers held in Jenny's practiced hand a piece of metal glints, small and round like a pill.

And Jenny isn't moving.

"Jenny?" I echo, empty syringe heavy in my fingertips.

"There's no purpose to them," she murmurs, and I see it: the trail of wire stemming off the end of the invite, feeding into the opening of the palm. "Except . . . just to have it root." Her touch drifts to the woman's wrist, and she adds, voice distant, "In the radial vein . . . Hand me the shears, Nolan."

"Wait—" I can't take my eyes away from the woman's palm, spilling bloody, hair-thin threads. "How do you know what they're even for?"

"Because I've seen them before." Nolan hands Jenny shears from his pack. She takes them, closes and opens them once, then lowers them to the implant. There's a wild look in her eyes. "Because they're not wires."

That's when I see. They're not part of the invitation. They're separate, rooted deeper inside the woman's arm and entwined around the implant like vines.

Jenny cuts, and the threads *move.*

The shorter ends go slack around the implant, like string, and fall to the ground. The other ends seem to snake away, retreating back into the woman's palm. Every vein in her wrist bulges outward, the skin above them sucking inward, blue-black lines against her form, and then—

The entire length of her inner forearm splits apart.

Her limb jerks once, violently. My hands snap over my mouth. She twitches again, like an aftershock, and then she's still. Her wrist is a raw, erupted bed, flesh and bones and veins smeared pastelike on the road. Blood in the rainwater. Her eyes are half-open, so, so glassy . . .

Juniper screams, stumbling past me to press her hands against the bleed. It's useless. I'm useless, frozen on the road. "No, we didn't say—we didn't *want*—"

"We weren't getting the implant otherwise." Jenny's voice is quiet and empty, like she's not even here. "I could have shocked them, maybe. It would have fried her, too, made the Worms ease up in her veins and pull out nice and easy. But they wouldn't've let go of the implant." Her hand tightens around the invitation. "And I wasn't about to put those Godsdamn things in *us*."

"Worms," Nyla breathes beside me. She pushes the cloth away from her eye to stare, a red glow falling over the scene. "I did not know Godolia still used them."

Jen's shoulders shake, a silent, mirthless laugh. "They just sat there. While the techs threaded them into their veins. Worms first, then invitations. They just *sat* there. Gods." She smears the back of her hand against her mouth. "What a fucking joke."

Jenny takes a step toward me, toward the girl at my feet. Everything kind of snaps back into place—the roar of the rainfall, the taste of blood in the back of my throat, teeth on the lining of my cheek. Juniper's head is now on the woman's shoulder.

"No." The word scrapes against my tongue. "Jenny, we can't—"

"Do you want to see her again?"

I laugh. I think it sounds like a sob. "You're such a bitch. Just put that one in me. I'll go alone, and I'll get her myself."

"They've marked two bodies from Nivim. There has to be two." The shears glint in her hand. "Do you want to call it off?"

Yes. I want to call it off. I want to stop.

And if this were just about Sona, I would. But this only proves it even more, that the Zenith has to die. The Badlands Academy is going to take kids and never let them leave.

Just because you Gearbreakers put a gun in the hands of every orphan who walks through your gates does not mean I should be expected to do the same.

We're already well past the gates. We're already worse than we might have been.

I drag my hand across my lips, then stand and glance around at the crew. Arsen's the unfortunate one who catches my eyes. He takes a half step back; I don't think he even realizes it.

The syringe drops from my grip, and I hold out my palm for the shears.

"Find it," I say to my sister. "I'll cut."

The sky is still split with the downpour, but I can hardly hear the onslaught. There's water in my shoes, and a dead Badlands girl behind me. Even when the crews leave Jenny and me at the riverside, Mechvesper bodies strung between them to be carried back to the safe house, I can't get the jagged edge of her shrieks out of my head.

I trace the base of my neck with my fingertips until Jenny snaps at me; I'm making my skin red. I'm making a mess. She takes my hand and draws a quick, small cut on my palm with her knife, slipping the implant inside before I even think to flinch. Then she does the same to herself, expression unmoving. In the west, the sun is coming up, the storm clouds fraying with dawn light.

When she's done, Jenny sets her gaze to the edge of the river, and cries in complete silence.

I look away, even though her hands don't rise to cover her face, even though she's never been embarrassed about a single thing in her life.

I think she's ashamed. I think the stones in my chest match the ones filling hers, and I think, more and more, we're kept up at night by the same monsters.

So here it is.

Sona might be sickened by the person I am by the time I get to her. But she'll be home, and I don't care about anything past that. I can't. I pushed her in front of the wolves, and the wolves tore her apart.

I did a bad thing to save her, and it damned her, so I'm going to do worse to get her back.

That's it. I just don't care.

CHAPTER TWELVE

BELLSONA

"Twin hells. You are going to spend half of your life unconscious if you keep this up."

I rip open the bedroom curtains without ceremony, mid-morning light blaring against the furrows of bedding and the Zenith tangled within them. One black eye cracks open, clearly agitated. All his pillows have found their way to the floor at some point or other in the night.

I pluck one up, so when the slurred "That's what I am aiming for, dear," emerges from the bedsheets, I can bring it down beside his head.

"This is not my job, you know," I say after Enyo jumps and scrambles upright. His reflexive, nervous smile pairs oddly with his fine, pretty features. "The attendants here are afraid to drag the Zenith out of bed, even though I told them that the ones back home wake you up with ice water every morning."

He pauses, rubbing his eyes to blink at me through his long fingers. "They do not."

I lift one shoulder and turn toward the window. "It was worth a shot."

The cityscape of Ira Sol carves across the Iolite Peaks in the shape of a dagger, skyscrapers rising in the narrow valley between two mountain ridges, massive slabs of basalt that reach like teeth out of the pine trees.

My eyes trace the bridges linking several skyscrapers in the distance, all joining into one path that reaches across the city in a bold, diagonal line—to the north are the mines, and southward, the mecha hangars. Those make up about half of Ira Sol, though they cannot be seen, the underbelly of the city veined by enormous train tunnels that shuttle the needed materials from the mines.

We stand—well, *I* stand; Enyo still rolls around the bed complaining behind me—in the newly constructed Badlands Academy, set in the thin tip of the dagger, hemmed by forest on one side and the Gillian River on the other, past the pale wall that borders the riverside of the city. A sprawling garden marks the Academy campus, a smattering of stone fountains dotting a meticulous lawn and the garden bleeding from the left edge, slashed by the stretch of road leading to the city. Already, sleek hovercrafts are gliding up to the entrances, the figures of the Badlands invitees like pinpricks from this distance. But I can imagine their chins tilting back as they ascend the steps, the slow, prayer-slick unhinging of their jaws.

"You seem nervous," I say without turning.

"Probably because of the anxiety," Enyo says, voice now floating from the walk-in closet.

This floor is what will one day house the Valkyries, once the Academy sifts out those who are worthy. Sprawling, lush bedrooms, a glittering kitchen and dining room, a library more museum than books—I have not told Enyo how it all makes my skin crawl, remembering the Valkyries and the way their jackets were thrown haphazardly over the leather couches in the living room, feet kicked atop sitting-tables and bodies stretched out on the rug as we listened to one another recounting the runs of the day.

How quickly it must have all burned. One moment suspended against the sky, the next, smearing it in black plumes.

Something rolls in my stomach, and I force myself to move before it comes into focus, stalking over to the closet.

"I am not decent," says Enyo calmly.

"What am I doing tonight?" I demand, batting the door open farther. A thought jolts through me. "I am not being . . . introduced or anything, am I?"

"This is Bellsona Steelcrest." Enyo straightens formally, shirt unbuttoned, one hand gracefully rising in my direction. "Captain of the Valkyrie Windup Unit and occasional voyeur."

Even despising the attempted humor in his words, I cannot help but notice their effortless equanimity. He could be reading from a cookbook and make it sound like a declaration of state.

"Enyo," I say, voice thin. Immediately he glances at me, silent laughter drained. I am vaguely aware I am clinging to the doorjamb.

I am a God to the Godolia people, but only on occasion—when those cords are fastened to my arms—and on one of those occasions I tried to blow them all off the map. Now I am the Valkyrie who was saved by the grace of the child Zenith, evidence of the start of a merciful reign. But from what Enyo told me yesterday about Lucindo and Jole, not everyone cares that my loyalties are steadfast once again.

"It is a masquerade ball, Bellsona. You can hide all you like," he says, buttoning his collar. "I am so tired of the queries about you. You are the captain of the Valkyries—"

A dry laugh tumbles from me. "Because I am the only one *left*—"

Enyo only shrugs. "Anyone is free to take it up with me. I would prefer they address the issue directly rather than attempt to kill you while you sleep and I have to deal with it accordingly."

His tone is light. But when I whirl on him I find those black eyes, those Zenith's eyes, steadily trained on me. Dead serious, even with that little smile on his lips from my reaction. It scares me. He scares me, sometimes.

I am glad for it. He is done for if anyone finds out how kind he can be, too.

Enyo does not care for the gossip. He does not care about the public eye; his image is irrelevant as long as his actions are pushing the nation forward. This is the tenet that every Zenith follows: The individual is immaterial beside their role on earth. But crisis makes humans forgetful, and Enyo, at his age, seems a safe target to place uncertainties that no one dared attach to his predecessors. I do not hear how he has dealt with those. I only know how he is still standing before me, and that means he handles it.

"I heard," I say quietly, "that an alarm went off on the wall last night."

He is silent.

"Have you found them?" I ask. "The Gearbreakers."

Now he meets my eyes. Black, black irises—and a flash of something, a weight in my palm, a dark room—and then it dissipates when Enyo murmurs, "The Leviathans did."

I take a half step back, a brief moment to untangle relief from disbelief from clawing fear. Teeth slowly tracing the inside of my cheek.

"There were nineteen of them," he says gently. "Judging by the equipment the guards found on them, they were planning on blowing the wall and flooding the gardens, then using the water to carry a charge."

"And kill their own people?"

"It might have been a distraction. Maybe they had something messier planned." He eases himself beside me on the bed. "It seemed a desperate operation. They were desperate, Bellsona."

"It's done, then," I say feverishly. "She is—"

"She was not with them. Neither was Starbreach." Enyo breathes out slowly. "The Frostbringer is leading her own renegade sect. Separate from them."

The taste of blood webs across my tongue.

I want her to be alone. I want her to be *ruined*.

But there were others. I cannot remember their faces as much as their presence, how they hovered around her, how they feared her, how they adored her. Loved her, I think. Attention that vicious is also careful, inevitably, and that carefulness—that seems like love.

If they survived the Hollows, if they survived Winterward, they would be at her side. The figures I cannot put names to. The ones I do not loathe as much as I do her, but quite close enough.

Enyo makes to leave the closet, and my arm extends across his path. His gaze steadies on the sleeve of my Valkyrie jacket.

"How do you know that?" I murmur. "You are not telling me something."

"She will be there tonight," he says softly, even though he is perfectly allowed not to tell me anything at all.

"She would have to get an invitation." I know what that would involve, with the Worms.

"So she would."

"You are not—"

"Yes, dear. I am not telling you something." His eyes flick to mine. "Don't say it again."

My arm drops, and he moves past me.

"I am sorry," I say, but not for my insistence. For the deaths. Enyo wanted each implant tangled in the invitees, in the Worms, to protect them. He thought the Gearbreakers would not dare touch their own Badlands people. It is not what we were expecting. It is not what we planned for.

"Deities." I run my hand over my mouth, my horror slow and cold. I start to pace the room, fingers ripping through my hair. "Deities, Enyo. She could already be inside. She—"

"Oh," Enyo says. "Yes. She already is."

Strands I did not feel break away thread my fingers. I reach the window and briefly consider smashing my fist through the glass; instead, my palm flattens softly against the image of the cityscape, forehead dropping to the cool surface. I hear Enyo approach but pause at a safe distance behind me.

"Bellsona?"

"What floor?"

"Not yet."

Another laugh falls from me, full of barbs. "You marked her walking in here, and you did nothing?"

"Her, and Starbreach."

"*Deities*, I am going to *murder you*."

"I, actually, am going to be surrounded by guards." He

leans against the window, gaze thoughtful as he looks up above us, where the glass meets the ceiling.

This is ridiculous. But I turn my head fully to tell him this and my next thought dries on my tongue when I see the dark, dark fury touching his features.

"The Gearbreakers killed them," Enyo says simply. He closes his eyes briefly, then draws them low. "To get to here. I do not want them dead before they see the main event."

I did not know anything about a main event. But Enyo wanting the Frostbringer and Starbreach alive to witness it makes me think it involves the renegades that were caught last night.

"And afterward," Enyo says, "I will pluck Jenny Shindanai from the crowd, and she will remember that, in spite of all her gifts, the extent of her ego, she was never going to win. That she is fated to die, just as the rest of her kind. But for now"—he smiles—"let them think they are safe."

"And the Frostbringer?"

"She has others. The last of the Gearbreakers, outside Ira Sol."

"You want me to follow her back to their safe house." My mind catches against those fractured memories, the closeness of her renegades. "She will not leave Starbreach. She will not leave you alive."

Enyo's hand brushes mine. "She is not only here for me."

The rage rises with startling force. Who knows the person I might have been if not for the Frostbringer? I could have been so much lighter. I could have been able to sleep through the night.

"Bellsona." He looks down at me, a head taller than I am, the intensity in his stare sharpened; it cuts through me like a static shock. I try to look to the left, but his palms are against my cheeks, lifting my chin, gently leveling my eyes to his. "They believe you are theirs."

"She has no part of me," I rasp. *Not anymore.*

Enyo smiles, a soft one that makes my throat twist. "I know it, dear."

His head tucks beside mine, lips moving just above my ear. Sometimes, I forget what it means to be this close to him. How extraordinary it is. This brat. This divinity. This little, mortal God, breathing against my cheek, the crook of his arm tender around my shoulder. My heartbeat trips over the awe in my chest.

"I want to give you a chance to kill your own demons," says Enyo quietly. "You can free yourself, Bellsona. Tonight. You can be at peace."

I give a tight shake of my head. "You are wrong. She does not want me back. She will shoot me on sight."

"The Frostbringer thinks a lot of herself. Act like their corruption still holds you, and she will bring you back to the rest of them eagerly." His hand closes around my arm, and he draws a steady breath. "You know what to do from there."

A chance to kill my own demons. To kill *her*. A chance, a test—no, this is an affirmation. He is releasing me to them, because he knows what I will do; he knows who I am, beyond what I have done. What I have done to *him*. He has untangled the monster from the girl standing before him, and, deities, does he even know what that means? That he *can*, even when I cannot do it for myself?

A weight in my palm, a dark room. Why her hand is around mine, why the edges of her words are murmured soft for me, why I am sure I wake up at some point with her body tucked to mine—it all just melts away.

This moment, Enyo's eyes holding mine with such care . . . this is what is real. This is what I can fight for, kill for, die for.

"I know what to do."

There is a pause that feels weighted—Enyo is not one to hesitate like this—but it is brief. Then, with words that run a beat quicker, smoothing over the lull like it never happened, he says, "You should know this. Her name is Eris Shindanai."

Something delicate snags between my ribs, and I pause.

My name is Eris.

I would tell him right away, if his elegant hands had not trembled a little as he spoke. Afraid of my reaction, which is calm, because I've made it so, because I know he needs me to be.

If I were not so sure it does not matter—if I were not so sure that it means nothing, that truly, it cannot mean *anything*—I would tell him that I already knew that.

CHAPTER THIRTEEN

ERIS

"Something's wrong," Jenny says, and tilts her head to one side, drawing her jawline closer to the mirror. Her gloved hand—not her magma gloves, but black and made of silk, shimmering up the length of her arm—traces her bare, white neck. "Yeah. I need some jewels, obviously. D'you have anything like that?"

The attendant looks briefly weary before snapping back into passiveness. She ducks her head and disappears from the room once more, leaving behind the space absolutely bestrewn with Jenny's rejected attire—tossed suits flopping paper doll–like on the satin couch, dresses with material that flows liquid across the rug where she has discarded them. It's probably all very expensive, though I literally have no concept of money since we never used anything like it in the Hollows. Unless you're counting the toffee that funded the rampant gambling system.

"You're not acting like an awestruck Mechvesper," I say once I hear the attendant's footsteps fade. "You're going to blow it for us."

We arrived at the Ira Sol water gate early this morning. Jenny's plan was to say we fell on the rain-slick path and that's why our palms were freshly split. But on the ferry, surrounded by Academy invitees and their families, flushed-faced and most picking incessantly at the chips in their hands, we were given Spiders as soon as we boarded to seal up the wounds. Before, though, we had to shuffle up the Gillian Conflux's rickety pier alongside the other Badlands guests, up the ferry ramp to where guards grasped wrists and peeled open palms to check the chips with a thin, penlike device. I'd held my breath, and maybe even Jenny did, too—not a weapon between us, her knife discarded in the river since we knew we'd be searched— but the device's light flickered from red to blue, and we were waved onboard.

As the river carried us east toward Ira Sol and the two bordering Ore Cities—Ira Terra to the south and Ira Luna to the north—I folded myself against the railing and watched the hull of the boat cut through the water. Jenny stayed silent beside me, but I could feel the moment she tensed, and I glanced up to see a Paladin treading a lazy path at the edge of the canyon rising up around us.

All heads turned, every mouth moving, yet the deck fell completely silent as we all watched the deity until it disappeared from view. It still looked massive, even from five hundred feet above our heads, footsteps drawing ripples through the water. Halfway up the ferry, a Badlands boy emptied his stomach over the side and came up with glistening lips, still moving in soundless prayer.

The Ore Cities are a different caliber than the rest of the Badlands. Their population lives in cities, but the mountains and forests curving between the three municipalities are teeming with Windups; the ones that were out on rotation on Heavensday make up a good chunk of their remaining ranks, spread more thinly throughout the whole of the Badlands now, but still commonplace in the Cities' vicinities.

It works in a dual sense. It's easy to keep faith in the

faithful when they see their Gods on a regular basis. It's also easy to catch the ones who run. No one has ever heard of a Badlands refugee hailing from the Ore Cities, the three of them ringed by water and canyon walls in a sicklelike shape, making it a perfect natural hunting ground.

But it was easy enough getting in. Way, way too easy.

Something's wrong.

After the water gate we were herded into hovercars that took us up to the Badlands Academy, then split off into rooms on the tenth floor—what would be the instructors' wings, we were enthusiastically informed—where the attendant stood waiting to prepare us for tonight's masquerade.

Jenny took full advantage. Now, she merely flaps a hand in my general direction, thumb tracing the edge of her mouth, lips done over in dark red lipstick. She flashes a grin at her reflection before continuing. "Confidence, kid. It sells no matter what the other party is smoking."

I roll my eyes, which the attendant has outlined in black, and in all honesty, it's kind of kick-ass. Last time I was around mirrors for an extended period of time, it was back in the Academy cell, and I sure as hells didn't look as good then as I do now. "And what is the other party smoking?"

"Deity di— Ah! Wonderful!" The attendant has returned with a handful of creamy silks, peeling them back to reveal a thin gold chain weighed by a black gemstone shaped into a slim cylinder. Jenny eagerly gathers the sheet of her hair over one shoulder, allowing the necklace to be clasped at the nape of her neck. She traces the line of the chain down to where the gemstone marks her sternum—usually patterned by takedown tattoos, but the first thing she did was boot the attendant out to cake our collarbones in makeup—then smooths her palms down her ribs, covered by the sleek, deep red dress she finally decided on, the color of old blood.

The attendant smiles tiredly at me. "Miss Stillwater, is there anything else I can provide for you?"

I return the smile even as I go cold. "I'm good. Thank you."

It's only after it's done that I realize my voice is shaking.

"My daughter and I need some space now, thanks," Jenny says abruptly, dropping her attention from the mirror to level it harshly on the attendant, who—learning from the previous booting, or just realizing she should take any excuse to leave us—exits without another word.

"Jenny—"

She whirls on me. "*I'm* going to blow it for us?"

Sitting on an armchair with too many puffy parts, I cradle my overalls in my lap so I can thumb at the buckles. She gives a short shake of her head, and then I'm yanked to my feet as she reels me over to the mirror. Her fingers close around my chin, tilting my face side to side as she scrutinizes me over my shoulder. I squirm, and she goes, "Hold still."

"Why?"

"You're such a baby." She tucks my hair behind my left ear, where silver rings have been set along the cartilage. "Look. Now, tell yourself you're stunning so you don't vomit when you first see her."

I bark a dry laugh. "Is *that* seriously what you think I'm worried about?"

Her black eyes lock on mine in our reflection. It startles me, how much we actually look like sisters. How much I look like her. Her face is narrower, and her chin is a bit sharper. But the cheekbones and the set of our brow lines are the same, as are our eyes, even though hers are usually tugged by a grin and mine by a scowl. It's more the look in them, though—like she's daring someone to hit her. I didn't realize, before, that it's how I would describe the look in mine.

"No," Jenny says, "but you're worried about a lot, and it's the one thing you can do something about." I open my mouth, but she tugs my chin again so my eyes are back on my reflection. "So we're manifesting. Say 'I'm glorious.' Say 'Tonight I look damn good and I'm going to get my girl back.'"

My cheeks immediately pink, but even though Jen's smile grows wider at it, I don't get the feeling that she's making fun of me. She only gives a short nod of her head, urging me forward.

This feels ridiculous. Jenny's said it before—the world's ending all the time now, and here I am standing in a black dress with a high buttoned collar and fluffy skirt that ends just above my knees, with black *lace tights* with *flowers* patterned all over, feet slipped into tee-strapped shoes. We're going to a party, and the end goal is to kill a kid, and all I can think of is seeing Sona again. Of how I hope she likes my dress, and how I know she will, because I do.

So, it's all ridiculous. The hope, despite everything else. The jolt of excitement, like a giddy kid, at the thought of her coming home. It's ridiculous anyway, so I open my mouth, and I say, "I'm stunning. I'm fucking ethereal, and Sona's coming home."

I don't think I've ever seen Jenny grin this broadly. She releases me and floats over to the table where our masks are laid out—simple and gray for the family members, covering brow to nose, and something a little more for the Badlands recruits. Black masks, eyes outlined in silver, cheekbones cut into peaks, and thin, rootlike veins of metal that drip from the bottom edge. The barest resemblance to a mecha. I have to suppress my shudder as Jenny helps to latch it around my head.

"The safe house is west," she murmurs low once she's finished. "Tell me the route Sheils's scouts use."

"I know it. And you know it, and . . . you'll be with us," I say, a bubble of panic rising in my chest. "Right?"

"That's not a guarantee," Jenny returns offhandedly.

My voice hardens. "Yes, it is."

"We're not on our home playing field, little bastard," she says, copying my tone but somehow sounding a lot scarier. "Tell me the route."

I tell her. Since the docks inside the city's walls are usually used for smaller shipments, like people and foodstuffs from the surrounding Cities, there's another port on the far side of the Gillian where the mecha pieces are shipped out via a transport that runs under the river, fed straight from the mountain Windup hangars. It's lined by service tunnels, including some older ones that are prone to flooding and have been subsequently abandoned, which Sheils's scouts now use to slip in and out of the city to steal medical supplies and other provisions.

"We'll exit the tunnel on the far side of the river, and follow the northeast trail back to the safe house, about three miles. Two knocks if it's me and Sona and she's okay, four if it's me and she's not." And then, because she's already letting me talk and maybe I won't get a chance to say this when it's quiet, I finish with, "And, Jenny, please be careful, okay? I need you to be careful."

I say it even though I know she hates it, because I realize

I've seen this state of her before. She was ragged back then, too, when my parents didn't come back and she did, when she went straight to her bedroom and Zamaya sat me down in the common room on that ugly green couch and told me what had happened. When she wouldn't eat, when she bit off all her nails and shaved her head and stood outside my door all night long, her presence betrayed by the shadow of her feet in the hall light, never once coming in. I hated her for it, for a while, because I'd lost them, too.

For me, with time the grieving inevitably ebbed, but it hooks in Jenny in a different way, like it did for our mom. Maybe if, growing up, Gearbreakers hadn't embedded the idea that softness is weakness, it would've been easier for her. For both of them. She could've come through the door. I could've been there for her, too.

And even though she looks good now—and she knows it, too—she still won't meet her own eyes in the mirror.

"Don't tell me what to do," Jenny says, and starts to laugh.

I grab her wrist, endure the flare in her expression, and snap, "We're not on our home playing field, remember? I need you to make it, too, because with you at least I've still got one person left, okay?"

"Have some self-preservation and let go of me," she says coolly.

"Say you'll be careful."

"Oh, I'll be *so* careful."

"Swear it."

"Ha!"

"Unnie, *please.*"

And my voice cracks, embarrassment rushing to the surface until I realize it startled her, just for a moment, before she collects herself and twists out of my grip. Jenny places her gloved hands on her narrow, silk-covered hips.

"I bind myself to nothing," Jenny says, leaning over me so I'm forced to lift my chin, which is probably the point. "But I'm going to be here for the final act. I have to see how it all turns out, don't I? I deserve that much. And I'm not going to wait around for someone to give it to me. I'm not going to stand for the world killing me before I give it to myself. I'm going to do whatever the hells I want, including surviving the worst of it."

CHAPTER FOURTEEN

BELLSONA

"Take a breath," I say, to which Enyo immediately responds, "You first."

So I do, and it has been a while since I have—the stretch of my stomach is strange, the slow expansion between my ribs brushing skin against the cool fabric of my shirt. I look at Enyo to make sure he follows the next one, and the next. After the third breath he seems less like he is about to bolt, and I stop, ribs settling. My heartbeat echoes, alone in my chest once more, and it sometimes hits me, how this body was not always like this.

It contains more than it did, but there is a lightness here. It is not the same body that grew up with me, that witnessed my parents go quietly under the onslaught of cracked concrete and the metal of our apartment building.

But now . . . This body is a gift.

I watch Enyo's fingers worry at his black tie, which is perfect, and then lift to the silk square folded into his breast pocket, which is also perfect.

"Are you ready?" I ask the moment his motions hesitate for lack of unworried clothing.

I am sure what he says will be, "Does it matter?" and already I am thinking how I cannot respond to that. I know the answer. I just do not know if it would help him to be reminded of it.

But instead, after a beat of almost imperceptible struggle,

his long fingers relax, and his dark eyes list to the banquet hall door. Instead of the reply I was expecting, his feet move, and he says nothing at all.

The hall, like the rest of the Badlands Academy, exists as a monument to sharp, sleek elegance—grand, but far from gaudy, black marble floor glittering beneath crystal lights dripping like a forest of daggers a hundred feet above our heads. The left wall is entirely wrought iron windows looking out over the garden's cherry blossom grove, and past that, the stretch of the Ira Sol wall, the thin sheen of the river unraveling the moon's reflection into threads of white. An orchestra plays from a grotto in the opposite wall, fresh flowers spilling from alcoves every dozen feet. Curved and clothed tables of food send steam up into the high, pale rafters—small mountains of glassy noodles with mushrooms and sesame seeds rising from platters; carafes of champagne and chilled barley tea; golden, fried mandu dotting trays in precise increments, peaks pinched like the edge of my sleeve between my fingers, tighter, tighter; there are *so many Pilots here*—

I force my hands still, focusing on the weight of my mask. It covers my brow down to the end of my nose, black and shimmering with detailed constellations when I turn my head, similar to those stitched on my Valkyrie jacket. Enyo's is black as well, simple save for the cut of it, slashing his face at an angle, left jaw to right brow. For some reason I think of his smile, reflexive and anxious, how cruel it would seem in this current state.

He is not smiling now. Five guards flank him on each side, the crowd pulling apart around the small armory, and me trailing just at his left, watching the outline of his profile as we make our way to the raised dais set against the windows.

The masquerade might give the Gearbreakers a false sense of security, but the idea also fortifies the concept of a Zenith as well. He is at once mortal, walking among us, and more. He is the only one who could take off his mask and still seem as something otherworldly.

A few moments before we walked through the door, I thought the masks were to help him, too. To keep a part of his face hidden when all eyes would roam every other piece. To obscure the blush that likes to stain his cheeks.

But then Enyo reaches the dais, and he turns to face the room, and the movement cuts through me in a cold, thin line.

Even past the metal plating his face, Enyo simply turns and drops the room into a complete and perfect silence.

His arm rises slowly and gracefully, a linchpin, and then he brings his hand to his heart and threads his gaze across the room, like a bullet's path through a hundred slack, veiled faces.

From behind my mask I flick my eyes over the crowd, finding not one head unturned. Some lips move in silent prayer. Others stand completely still but attentions hovering, fixed—and perhaps this is all that worship is. Worship is merely attention; it can be hatred and fear as much as it can be love.

The guards linger at the edges of the dais in a circle, the large guns at their hips gleaming wickedly under the lights. I stand with my hands folded, spine against an iron stile along the window, and accidentally meet a nearby Pilot's eyes. They're wearing a black mask with the eyes outlined in what I know is truly red—part of the Phantom Windup unit. Their lip *curls*, and suddenly the sky is full of smoke, plated wings sprawling like heavenscape, but my feet are light and so is the feeling in my chest—and then I remember to snarl. The Phantom snaps away, attention retreating back to the Zenith, who has opened his mouth.

"The next hour will begin a new era," Enyo says, words heavy silk. "But it would be wasteful to disregard the current one. It is essential that we see the totality of it. The rise and the fall, but not completely, not irreparably. The Gods at our sides, but not without consequence. We have witnessed immense turmoil, and we have witnessed immense strength—from Godolia and Badlands alike—and here tonight, we renew our partnership. It is extraordinary, and it is profound, in a way only survival is."

Survival.

And just like that—I see her.

She is slight in a crowd of masked faces, dressed in all black, marrow wrapped in slit bone. Mouth relaxed under the metal roots clawing for her jawline, one strap of her mask marking a path through a sheared portion of her hair. After a beat, I realize I do not know how I could possibly have recognized her like this.

I also realize that there is nothing in my chest. No breath. No heartbeat.

Corruption, I think, panicking, my palm flattening to my side only to find my heart thudding again. To find that it has not revived alone.

My palm lifts with the expansion of my ribs, and the moment I recognize this, recognize that I do not know *why*, the Frostbringer's eyes lock with mine.

ERIS

Oh shit.

BELLSONA

"We live in a time after the end of the world, and it is a time of deities again. It is my wish and my purpose in this mortal life that it will be a time of prosperity and of peace as well. It is with great admiration and gratitude that I welcome the first Pilot class of the Badlands Windup Academy."

The Zenith drops his chin in humble acceptance of the applause that sweeps the room. The orchestra picks up and the crowd shifts, and the Frostbringer vanishes among the bodies.

I immediately glance up at Enyo to find his gaze already upon me.

He has eyes all over, marking the Frostbringer, marking Starbreach. This morning I thought him overconfident. But there is no need for haste. He has the entire night in the palm of his hand.

I bow low at the waist, hand over my heart.

He would loathe it, under any other circumstances. But I do not know when I will see him again, and I cannot touch him here, cannot say goodbye with my fingers tensing around his sleeve alongside my words—*Do not even think of doing anything stupid while I'm gone*—and when I straighten from the bow, I find that he has not recoiled.

Instead, Enyo looks at me like he is trying to pin the moment to memory, black eyes leveling me, both our expressions cleaved by metal masks. He takes in my suit and my heels and the curls already spilling out from the knot at the back of my head, with that great, careful attention I never know what to do with.

"You were wonderful," I whisper, then turn and melt into the crowd just as his lips part to say something.

The Badlands invitees are quick to part, glances hastily dislodged from my left iris as their bodies sweep from my path. I am hyperaware of the sound of my heels across the marble floor even under the din of the hall—a *click click click* that pairs with the cadence of my teeth biting and softening against the side of my cheek.

Where are you?

A glass shatters somewhere nearby, followed by a peal of high, nervous laughter. The music crests before sighing, until the air is thick with rich legato. The people move more slowly now, disparate with the rabbitlike seize of uncertainty in my chest.

Cold curling suddenly down my spine, I turn back to glance at Enyo, only to find a spire of glittering silk blocking my view—a girl standing closer than anyone else has dared to, and then coming *closer*, gloved hand closing around my waist. And then we are moving.

"Hmm," she says when I open my mouth. I stand almost six feet tall in these shoes, and I still have to tilt my head back to meet her dark, painted eyes, to find her grin splitting ear to ear as she speaks. "You look downright offended, Glitch. I wasn't expecting that. What, no 'Hi, Jen, Unnie, lovely'? You did call me pretty once—if we're only counting what was said out loud."

Her other hand is around mine, held to a graceful height, so we do not draw looks as we shift around the other pairs of dancers, even though her fingers constrict to crush mine as subtly as possible. Strangely, it is the calmest I have felt since we arrived in Ira Sol. The threat being where I can see it, where it can dip its head to unspool that bold, glossy voice into my ear.

"Oh," Starbreach says quietly, just the bare corner of her eye visible in my peripheral vision, iris drawn to its dagger edge, and when I recognize a dark, almost lazy amusement settled there, fear splinters in my throat. "Do you not know me at all?"

The silk of her voice threading through my hair, a wolf crouched over a hare's burrow, it does not matter that she is only human.

"Well. Perhaps it's not my business. You were never the reason I came here anyway."

I drop my eyes to the skin on her bare collarbone. The optics of the Zenith's pet Valkyrie biting off a Gearbreaker's shoulder during the Academy opening ceremony would be kind of optimal, but Starbreach's nails slip into the skin on the back of my hands, blood seeping quietly down to my white sleeve. She laughs and says, "Careful, now. Oh, there's Eris. Ha! She looks *pissed*."

She shifts out of my grip. My hand moves down to catch her wrist, because she clearly just threatened the life of the Zenith, but it snaps away to flatten against my sternum, and then I am stumbling and she is gone, faded into the crowd like an immaterial force. The moment I realize it, the moment I catch myself, a hand closes around my sleeve.

I look down. Her mouth, painted over in black, opens,

spills out only silence before her teeth close over her bottom lip. Her grip tightens around my sleeve viciously, eyes blown wide behind the slots of her mask—

What is happening, this is not right it isn't—what is happening what the hells is happening why can I not move—

It is the hatred. It is the *fear*, made physical in a black dress, five fingers curled to tether me, threaded through me, flat and soft to line my rib bones in her bed, and there is a voice that bursts up. I do not know from what corner of my head it emits, and I do not care: *These are not your roots.*

Enyo. I turn to search for him over the crowd, terror striking at the thought that Starbreach could already be at his side. But the Frostbringer's grip shifts, and suddenly her cheek is pressed to my chest.

Why—

It is just for a moment, and then she steps back. Her hand drops from my sleeve.

"Do you know who I am," she says, in a voice so harsh it does not sound like a question.

I force myself to still. Then, carefully, carefully, I take her hand.

"Dance with me," I say quietly. "Won't you, Eris?"

"Thank Gods." Her voice catches; she closes her eyes for a moment, lets out a slow breath. "Hells yes, Glitch, let's do it."

We do not speak as we begin to move, her with her head just beneath my chin. Me with one palm at the middle of her back, the other fastened to hers, turning it all over in my head so the story lays out in a way I can follow properly.

Enyo speculated that the Frostbringer came to Godolia in the first place with the intention of stealing a Pilot, that she allowed herself to be captured on purpose so that the Gear-breakers could carry out their Heavensday plan. It's unknown whether my corruption somehow started in the Academy or at their base. If the latter is true, it is a mystery how she removed me from the city limits. It is the blank part of my memory that makes me writhe the most, that it was some weakness of mine—one that I cannot even *name*—that marked the start of it all.

"You're bleeding," the Frostbringer says, but her fingers do not pull from mine, even though the blood has reached her own cuticles.

"Starbreach has a dark sense of humor."

"You two have that in common."

"How so?"

"You're kind of trying to kill me, right?"

I physically feel my heartbeat hitch, but in my glance down I see that she is grinning. There is a giddiness to it that reminds me how young she is, and it strikes me then, how small she stands, the lightness of her hand as it rests on my shoulder. "Just—I mean, you look really good."

I raise a brow. "I know."

"Ha. Yeah, of course you do."

It won't matter, whatever fragility all this death grew from. I am going to be the one to fix this, to *end this*, and the end is so very close.

So close that when the song dies down, she can pick up her chin and brush her lips to the underside of my jaw, just as the floor-to-ceiling windows at our left begin to split apart to siphon the crowd into the gardens.

I go stiff. Just for an instant, before I force my limbs to relax.

She does not notice, head tilted toward the massive glass doors fanning out into the hall, letting in a sweet night breeze from the cherry blossom grove. *This does not make any sense.* This is not how it is meant to be. There is not meant to be *affection*.

Because then the story becomes different. Drops into a new context. All those smudged memories of closeness, moments strained from the viewpoint of a fogged window, the ghost of her skin against mine unrooting me from sleep—

A nearness flourished as a threat.

That is what this is. Of course. An unraveling of her power, just because she thinks it is safe to do so. She is having fun with it, with the same cat-and-mouse malice Starbreach held me under, and the rage that rises is so sudden and so dark, and so very needed.

She is not safe. She is too close to me to be safe.

When her grip on me loosens, I bring my hand to her delicate chin, tilting it back so her eyes are on mine. My other arm circles her waist and then she is flush against me, my fingertip lightly tracing the line of her jaw, thumb pausing just on the edge of her lower lip.

"What are you doing," Eris rasps in a hoarse voice, black mouth working under my touch. Still not a question. We are unmoving as the crowd parts around us in their migration to the grove.

Leveling the playing field. "I missed you, Frostbringer."

"You're making fun of me."

"Good thing you adore my sense of humor."

"Absolutely rot." Her eyes roll before cutting to the left, and she pushes away from me. But I can tell she is pleased, by the way she straightens herself afterward, and the way her hand is still in mine. "Let's get out of here, okay?"

"Can we please?"

She laughs. She has done it before, around me. A monstrous thing, just from the fact that it is so bright, so encompassing, that she can laugh so genuinely at the imploring expression on my face when she split open my head and thought I would never notice, thought she would never pay for it.

"Yeah," she says, and I thought she was known to scowl more. "Let's go home, Gl—"

Eris stops short. Her hand drops from mine, and I find myself colder for it.

"No."

And then she is running.

"Fr—Eris!"

I follow after, pushing my way through the stream of people funneling out of the hall and into the grove, pathway melting from marble to cobblestone once we make the glass doors. The night air is cool against my skin, cloud-striated heavenscape soon blocked out by cherry blossom trees, their limbs coiled with string lights to replace the stars. That is when I lose sight of her, a little after I realize this is more forest than grove and a little before the first body, hung by her tattooed ankles at the mouth of the thicket.

"... evidence that the Gods wish for us an era of peace ..." Enyo's voice, a lulling tone from the hall, morphs into distinguishable words once I reach the massive stone pavilion at the center of the grove. Another dais rises at its middle, already ringed by the Zenith's guard, Enyo pacing it in a slow circle as he speaks, so that his eyes can touch on each of the Gearbreaker bodies that sway gently amid the cherry blossoms.

". . . they have delivered to us the message that the destruction of their earthly echoes and the murder of their vessels are not unanswered evils. This display is crude in the manner that all violence must beg, but it is not one committed in senselessness, such as the kind witnessed on Heavensday. Godolia does not pretend that its strength does not lie in a show of that strength, for bloody and unnecessary actions called for bloody and necessary reactions."

I find her under the trees, just off the path. Eris stands with her heels half-sunk into the grass, under the body of a Gearbreaker boy hung from his wrists. The stubble around his mouth and the gear tattoos down his neck are streaked with dried, thick blood from the bullet hole drilled into his temple.

I cannot see her expression, but I hear it in her voice when I come closer. She did not ever need the cryo gloves to earn her alias, just the tundra she can breathe into her words. "Did you know?"

"No," I say. *The main event.* "I did not know."

Gently, Eris touches the cuff of the Gearbreaker's pant leg.

"Theo . . . ," she murmurs, fingers falling away, tears down her cheeks stained black by her makeup. "Poor kid. Gods, Glitch, how am I supposed to tell them?"

People need to feel protected, because fear brings out the worst in them. Zeniths are meant to draw that shield into place, no matter what harsh form it takes. No matter what they need to do to protect their people. For all the power they have, their station is not a wanted one. Everyone praises them for what they do, but they worship them because of what it means.

All Zeniths go to hells.

Enyo should have had decades to learn to cope with that responsibility, and four other people to bear it with. To bear their fate with—that the sins they must commit for the sake of their people trace out their damnation in the next world.

Still turned from me, Eris's hair unhooks from behind her ear and falls to veil her face. I reach out and tuck it back to find her eyes dropped to the earth.

"We will tell them about Theo together, Eris," I say softly. "Okay? I am going to be right here with you."

My fingers are still hovering at the shell of her ear, and when her eyes lift, they trace a slow line from my wrist to my elbow and then up to my gaze, spilling red light across her masked features.

"Bellsona," the Frostbringer says quietly. "Give me your hand."

I do. Her fingers immediately tighten around mine, and for a moment her mouth thins to a tight black line, and I think she is about to start crying harder. Then she blinks, muscle clenching in her jaw as she takes in a breath. An impossible stillness in her fingers where a moment before they trembled like they were trying to crack apart, and we are moving for the pavilion.

"Damn it," she says, pushing the words through gritted teeth as we pass under another body, this one hung by the ankles from the branch that curls the farthest over the pavilion. Three bullet holes in a tight formation bloom over his lower ribs. His hands hang loose over his head, tiny gear tattoos running like rivers along the veins of his wrists, down into his canvas jacket sleeves. Some are worse off, caught by the Leviathan instead of the guards' guns, mutilated forms dangling in the trees. "Jenny's going to lose it—"

The air cracks apart with a gunshot.

Eris looks at me, and I realize, with a strange, perfectly calm clarity, that she loves me.

She cannot look at me as the gunfire starts with so, so much fear for me and think I won't know what it means. You cannot love someone and think they won't feel it.

I do not know how it could have happened. I know, a beat later, that it does not matter. Eris made a mistake: She fell for someone she was going to use. Maybe she recognized it, too, with a lucidity that was insignificant, in the long run—it would be safe, because the thoughts she put in my head would stick. Maybe we could have even been happy.

And it makes all of this so much easier, that she does not want to tear me apart, that she wants me *close*—I could laugh so hard it would fissure me. *She deserves to end like this.*

It all threads through me in an instant, and then I am present again, in a sea of panicked bodies.

Heartbeat thundering, I scan the masked faces for Enyo as Eris pulls me toward the pavilion and upstream of the stampede making for the safety of the Academy doors. I do not realize she is speaking to herself—"What did you do, Jen, what the hells did you *do*?"—until she stops short and I crash into her, sending us both into the stones and underneath the charge of hysterical feet.

What—

All of a sudden I am choking on earth. It's down my throat, teeth scraping the particles.

Bellsona.

The sky is coming apart—no, it's coming *through*, splitting the ground, arching above like a broken seam.

Bellsona!

Something. Someone else. My parents. I'm—screaming—what—

"Sona," Eris gasps, wrenching me to my feet. "We need to go."

"Wait—" Where is Enyo? Only the guards had guns—I am sure I would have noticed one on Starbreach. She did something, and they must have fired, which means she got close. How close? Damn it. There were supposed to be eyes on her the entire time. A surge of nausea, the panic physical now, the need to empty my stomach onto the cobblestones. He can't be—

My eyes catch on a black mask in the crowd. Or it catches on me. He is on the ground, one hand wrapped around the upper sleeve of his suit, something wet ribboning between his long fingers. Bared teeth below the line of his mask, shoulders arched around himself with heaved breath. A strange, pulsing thought that his back is about to burst into massive, terrible wings. But his eyes are on me.

That is what matters—his eyes on mine, and the sharp, snarling mouth that forms into a single word: *Go.*

We escape by delving deeper into the forest of bodies, each hung in a way that most prominently displays their tattoos. The manner in which they are scattered, in the shadows and off the lighted path, tells me that this was not all for show—they were offerings. Oblations. Eris keeps one hand in mine and the other clamped to her mouth. Just when I think she cannot take any more we break out of the grove into a courtyard of irises and ivy-draped statues, and then we are running for the water gate.

It unsettles her, I can tell, how our pathway is clear. How the wall does not light up with spotlights or with gunfire as we rush under its watch. Her eyes cut to the gate's dark height and then behind us, where the Academy seems to grow with each step forward instead of shrinking back, lit up floor to penthouse with flashing alarms. She trips over her own feet at one point, but comes up still attached to me by the fingertips, her heels kicked away in the grass. I follow her example.

We make it to the line of maintenance houses huddled beside the water gate, darting into a narrow sliver of alleyway just before the larger strip of docks. Pausing at the first bend, Eris strips off her mask and sends it clattering to the damp asphalt under our feet, and then—it seems without even thinking about it—reaches up to take away mine. By some miracle I do not startle when her fingers skim my cheek, a slide of metal and momentary blindness as she pulls the mask free.

For a moment, I am sure she is about to say something. Her mask has left imprints like cracks in porcelain across her cheekbones.

"Jen will be all right," I say softly, and do not believe it. The reason we are here so easily, the reason we will escape so easily, is because Enyo has allowed it. But he knows I only require one Gearbreaker to lead me back to the rest. Starbreach is not needed anymore.

Her eyes shut briefly, a breath animating her shoulders, and then open and lift above my head. I follow her line of sight.

Above a leaking gutter, a massive shoulder slopes toward the heavens.

A Leviathan Windup, a guard of the Ira Sol water gate. Designed for underwater assignments during the Spring-tide War, they had the smallest production run of all the units—this is one of only ten remaining. Two are stationed at the other Ore City water gates and two to patrol the major Gillian River system webbing the Iolite Peaks, and the rest are far east, at the ocean border.

The Leviathan head tilts into view, cutting the sky with red light. Its design is humanoid like all other Windups, save for the flat, slitted nose and the wide curl of the mouth. And the etching to mimic scales. And the trio of retractable fins splitting out of its shoulders, lined with valves for its torpedoes.

"Ugly wirefucker," Eris hisses as the Leviathan moves away, wading strides marked by the roar of churning water on the other side of the gate.

She crouches over what looks like a sewer drain, and I help her drag its round opening up and out. We both lean over it, the light of my eye eaten away by the darkness only a few feet down, ladder rungs feeding into black.

"This feels vaguely familiar, doesn't it?" Eris whispers, and I can feel her stare on my cheek.

"It was a long time ago."

"Yeah," she says after a moment. "Yeah, it was."

The tunnel is unlit and half-drowned, water up to my hips and up to Eris's ribs. The only thing that guides our path is a metal cord we have to feel for blindly, that we grip as we wade in silence. Somehow I ended up going first, and I realize it was a mistake. I do not like her at my back. At least I do not have a fear of the dark.

"We made it," she says when the cord meets wall an unknown amount of time later, and we find another ladder leading up to the surface. She sounds more bitter than surprised.

"You sound elated."

"Oh, really, Glitch? I meant to sound *pissed*."

We emerge on the opposite side of the river, a little north of where we went belowground. Eris takes a rock and chucks it high and far into the forest rising above us, and then stands there, slight shoulders heaving, a very clear recognition that this did nothing to cut her mood. "Gods damn it," she snarls, voice broiling but shoved into a whisper, "Jen's such a fucking id—I wish she *was* just a fucking idiot."

Her words are thrown across the water, to where the Academy's alarms have ceased. Its penthouse floor is illuminated, a bright nick in the night sky.

I find Eris's hand in the dark. Wait for her to move without speaking, and then a rocky, winding path is biting into my bare feet; if it pains her, I cannot see it. Her face is turned away from mine.

Separated from the river by a handful of miles and a forest of indiscriminate sprawl, we reach the little cabin when it's still dark. The curtains are drawn over the windows but each bleeds a thin box of light at its edges. It has a small porch with hooks on its ceiling that, maybe, a long time ago held a swing. At some point something must have cut Eris on the path—bloody footprints trail her as she crosses the porch. I stand beside the last one as she drops my hand and gives four knocks on the door. *Thud thud thud thud.*

The number strikes me as strange. Or maybe it's not the number, but the feel of the air afterward; whoever is inside moves silently, but I can tell they are there by the slight wavering of the curtain at our left. A sudden chill draws down my spine.

"Eris," I say quietly.

She just shakes her head, and the frail light from the curtains grazes the roughened skin of her cheek—coarse with the salt of her tears. There in excess and then dried, and I did not notice in the dark, with her hand pulling mine.

The handle turns, and my options flash through me in the same instant. Fight, and they might kill me instantly. Wait and pretend, and I could give myself another chance to end this.

Where did I slip up?

"Eris," I say again, but this time I reach for her. She wrenches away, and then the door is open fully. Someone shoves me away from her, and I'm cast onto the porch. When I cry out it is not from that, not from my skin tearing on the splinters. It is from how many of them there are. How easily those faded images from my memory snap into tangible faces hovering inches from mine.

I cannot help it. It bubbles up in me, this bad thought—I have more fear of the Gearbreakers than I do hatred of them.

She puts her hand on the back of my shoulder fearfully—I can tell by the lightness of it—when she sees I have not moved.

"I'm fine," I murmur, mostly to myself. And faintly I realize that my feet are bleeding, too.

CHAPTER SEVENTEEN

ERIS

"Okay," I say, scratching at the thing still buried in my palm. Pacing. Tearing my cuticles off in little pink strips. "Okayokayokay . . ."

This cabin is about the cutest fucking thing in the world. I'm wearing circles into the floorboards, looping around the dusty couch to the low glow of the fireplace and then back again, my crew huddled in the middle watching me tailspin. My sister's crew decided to hike back down the path to wait by the service tunnel, so they would be there if—no, when—Jenny managed to get out.

"You got it here?" Seung had asked as they shouldered their bags, cutting a glance toward Zamaya where she stood in the open doorway, her face tilted toward the darkened sky. Zamaya had been silent since she saw that Jen hadn't come back with me, her things already packed by the time we locked Sona in—all her things, which was telling enough that she wasn't coming back without Jenny in tow. I couldn't help but be grateful for it, alongside being scared shitless.

"We got it," said Arsen, because I couldn't speak past the lump in my throat.

Gwen had touched my arm, very softly. "If it goes bad," she said—and I thought to myself, *it's already bad*—"we'll meet back at the Mutts, okay?"

Then Nolan told me to get my shit together, and Zamaya

glanced at me once over her shoulder, and they were gone. I'd started talking. Nothing in particular, nonsense really, judging by the look on my crew's faces. I still have my dress on, some twigs stuck in the skirt, tights ripped up to wrap my torn feet in lacy bands.

The ball. Her eyes finding mine like a magnetic, inevitable thing. Her hand on the small of my back. It all seems like years ago. *I was so young then*, I think to myself, or maybe out loud. Dramatically, either way, but I don't find it as funny as I thought I would.

Nyla comes back from the kitchen and hands me a cool rag. I take it and stare at it, unsure. She says, "Your makeup is, uh, smudgy."

It still doesn't click for me. Arsen takes the rag from my hand and drags it under my left eye. My mouth, which I didn't realize was still moving, shuts. I sit down on the couch, dizzy. He moves to my other eye.

"Okay," Juniper says once he's finished, hand gentle on my knee. "Try that again, Eris."

"I just thought I'd know right away," I mutter, my voice hoarse. "If it wasn't her. Like she'd be a whole different person. But she's not."

I thought corruption scrubbed you away; I thought they emptied you and filled you up again with something manufactured. It should give me hope that I don't have to remind her who she is in her entirety, that she's a little arrogant and a little twisted, that she smiles with her eyes first. But it's worse like this. It wouldn't hurt as much if she were someone I couldn't recognize.

"Milo's dead," I say, and immediately I know there was a better way to do this. "The rest of Junha's and Holland's crews.

Nadia and Benny and Dex. They had them in the t-trees. I'm sorry." I drag the back of my hand across my eyes, shocked to find them dry. My voice breaks all the same. "I'm so sorry."

I have a lot to apologize for, but it's not this. Jenny wouldn't apologize. She would be sad, and maybe she'd even show it, but she wouldn't say *I'm sorry*.

Theo stands. I don't know if he wants to leave the room, but he's just standing there, shaking like pine needles. Nova has one of her small fingers in his belt loop, tears on her cheeks.

I learned something new about Sona today: She's a good liar. I mean, up until that point she whispered, *We'll tell them about Theo together* with such gentleness, with Milo's ankles hanging limply next to my temple, I thought it'd be okay. I thought I'd bring her back to the safe house and she wouldn't try to kill all of us.

Because of course that's what she's here for, why she's biding her time. The Zenith had the same idea as us.

It means we're just as cruel as he is.

And that makes me afraid for us.

"Was it quick?" Theo asks quietly, after a while.

"It looked like it." Though I'll never know for sure.

"I—" His hair has grown out, strands framing his face and the rest gathered into a tail at the back of his head; he reaches back and tugs at it, the tattoos on his wrists peeking out from under his sleeve. "I need to go."

"Don't go alone."

"I won't."

"Don't go too far," I say thickly, knowing I sound like a nagging parent.

"I won't, Eris."

He leaves with Nova and Nyla trailing behind. I bring my

arm around Juniper's narrow shoulders. She's taller than me, but still tucks her head into the crook of my neck. She isn't crying, but her breaths come in fits and starts. Arsen, sitting on the ground between our legs, puts his cheek on my knee, curls pressing into the fabric of my skirt.

"Why do I feel like it's just getting worse and worse?" I murmur.

"Because it is," Arsen says, eyes closed.

"Oh," June says in a hard voice. "Is that all?"

"We're still the lucky ones." He doesn't hesitate, but the words aren't light. Gods. I want so badly for them to feel their age, just once, and not a second older.

At our backs there are two doors. A Valkyrie placed behind each one, hands bound behind her back. Both, I think, want to kill everyone in this room.

Lucky. He's right. That's the funny thing.

"Eris," Juniper says as I get off the couch. "What do we do if this doesn't work?"

What do we do with Sona, she means.

"You know," I say softly. "I really don't know."

I think it was always unspoken that Jenny would be the one to do it, if it got to that point. It would maybe ruin us, because I might grow to hate her for it, but we might be half-way there as it is.

It doesn't matter, though, because Jenny isn't here, and I haven't thought about if I could do it or not. If, even after all this time, I could push the barrel of a gun into Sona's temple and feel it kick in my hand.

She's sitting with her back against the post of the wire bed frame, eyes closed when I open the door and send the light in. Her head is leaned back and to the left, the line of jaw and cheek catching the last of the starlight drifting in through the threadbare curtains.

I think this isn't going to go well.

Because she opens her eyes when she hears my footfalls and says, without looking at me, "Can you take off my tie?"

I crouch down in front of her, fingers moving against her shirt collar.

"Do you want your jacket off, too?" I should've asked before I locked her hands in the bed frame. I'll have to literally cut her out of it.

She seems to know this, too, and says, "No. It's cold." A beat. "The top button, though, if you could undo it."

"Yeah." My fingers reach up again, and when the button's free, she turns her head. I didn't bring a weapon, with June and Arsen standing right outside the door, but I still feel like I'm about to cut myself on something.

Red light slides over my face. Sona tilts her chin so her lips brush my knuckles.

I go still. "Don't."

"He tried." The words ghost over my skin, the heat of her breath singeing against my knuckles. "He tried to take you out of my head. You just kept coming back."

I push to my feet, knocking her chin, but she only rights herself with just about the saddest look on her face. It's cruel; we're being cruel to each other. Even when I speak I'm desperately relieved to find my voice cold. I hope it matches the look on my face. "Is this really how you're going to do this?"

"I know it is hard to—"

"No, you don't! You don't know—you're—you're *lying* and you—you have no idea what that means for us. Fuck, I can't even ask myself how we got here because *you're not here.*"

I forgot to breathe. I suck in air raggedly, and she leans toward me, manacles clanking hollowly against the bed frame. She's crying. She's just so *good* at this.

"But Gods." I say it anyway, the heels of my hands pressing into my eyes. Blackness, then fireworks. "How did we get here, Sona? How the hells did we get here?"

"Eris," she says, quieter now. Careful, voice so broken that it cuts. "I am right in front of you, *please*, just look at me—"

My hands are in her shirtfront, twisting, but this doesn't feel like a tether, doesn't feel like anything but a whole-body hurt, skin and muscle and bone parting where I can't reach it.

"Then why didn't you *run*, Sona?" I'm screaming it, and the words don't even sound like mine; they tear out of me as contorted, severed things. "If you knew who you were, if you knew what we *mean* to each other, why did you stay?"

She's sobbing with her entire body, tears leaking down her face, and suddenly she doubles over into me, head bowing into my lap so I can feel the way she shakes, can see the hands I bound behind her back with her wrists rubbed raw, screaming red.

"I did not know where you were!" she pleads into me. My cries could split open the walls. Her cries could bring the whole room crashing down on all of us. "Please, Eris, I did not know where you were! I would have come for you, you know I would have come for you, please Eris you know me I love you I love you I love you—"

I can't get enough breath. "Oh my Gods." I say it over and over again. Sunk onto my knees now, her head cradled in my lap, lips moving against the fabric with *love love love*—"Oh my Gods, please *please stop*."

I'm cold to my fingertips. It's like I have to break them out of ice to force her away, and she catches back on her heels, head rolling so her curls drop down the base of her neck, wet with her tears. She tilts her head up, shoulders completely still. Relaxed. Cheeks ruddy and those large, slender eyes blinking past the salt, tongue moving thoughtfully over her bottom lip as she swallows. I just shake my head. I can't stop crying.

"Damn," Sona says, voice thick with tears but no longer shaking. She shifts to dry her cheek on her shoulder. Her eyes are swollen, but fixed on me with level, apathetic study. Like I'm not even a person. Like I'm a negative she's holding up to the light, turning slowly. Red light, washing over me. "I really did believe that would work."

CHAPTER EIGHTEEN

ERIS

I need air. I go outside to get it, and when I come back, June is closing the door to Sona's room.

"She was bending the bed frame," Arsen says. "We put her on the radiator instead."

He's cradling one hand in the other. I know that's the reason for the look on Juniper's face, why her grip's still on the door like she wants to push back inside.

I cross the room and take Arsen's hand. Turn it over.

"Ha," I say, voice hollow. "No freaking way."

Teeth marks, freshly tilled.

Sona bit him.

She's not here at all, is she?

Maybe it's better that way. Because now Arsen's skin is open in little flushed lines.

And you do not touch my kids.

I turn. The door to my right holds Sona. I go to the one on the left, the one that holds Sheils's Valkyrie. The one her Hydras picked up, half-frozen, on one of the trails months ago. Who wouldn't speak and could barely move, who they thought was another Godolia defector . . . until she thawed back in the Mutts and tried to plug into a Windup. She probably would've rampaged the entire hangar if she hadn't lost most of the fingers of her left hand to frostbite, if she hadn't lost her grip on the ladder and been found writhing in a tangle of artificial nerves, and then broke the nose and wrist of the first Pilot who tried to get her free.

I still don't get why Sheils didn't just kill her after that. I never asked her. I had a feeling that if I ever did, she'd just hand me a knife and say, *Be my absolute guest, Shindanai.* Maybe she wouldn't even look up from her tea.

I unlock the door. She's lying down, shackled hands buried under the small of her back. We haven't attached her to anything since there are no windows in this room, but she hasn't been much of a fighter anyway. Sheils mentioned that was the case as of late, once she realized no one was coming for her.

"Get up."

She doesn't move. I cross the room and grab a fistful of her shirt, lifting her shoulders, neck, and head off the ground. Her chin drops back, hair a golden stream unwinding onto the dirty floor, but her eyes are open now, throwing light to the back wall and then scraping up the ceiling as they roll to meet me. Red and green.

"Victoria," I breathe, and she smiles, a sickly, faraway grin. "You're going to do something for me."

CHAPTER NINETEEN

ERIS

It seemed like it would be an easy trade. Victoria tells Sona she left of her own accord, and the details of that leaving, and then we let her go. But it turns out that Victoria has some fight left in her after all—she just had to be put in a room with Sona.

"Gods damn it," I hiss, Theo at my left to help wrench Victoria back.

She's completely off the ground, head screwed back, shrieking, her feet kicking savagely for Sona's jaw. We end up having to pin her on the floor, end up halfway alongside her. Now her feet kick for the ceiling. Sona, in the corner of the room by the radiator, is unmoving. She doesn't even look startled, chin tilted back slightly so she can look under the curtains.

I force my eyes away and growl, my voice almost animalistic, unrecognizable to me, "Listen, you wirefucker—"

"I am not helping you!" Victoria spits, and then throws her head back to laugh. She has the most perfect set of teeth I've ever seen in a head. "Why the fuck would I help you?"

"A decent point," June observes from the doorway.

Victoria erupts into another peal of laughter. I shoot June a withering look, and then grip Victoria's golden head with one hand and use it to yank her upright.

"Listen," I snap in a whisper, lips so close they scrape

against the shell of her ear. I have the strange feeling that Sona is paying attention to me now, though her head is still turned away. "She doesn't know who the hells you are. Godolia didn't come for you. None of your Valkyries came for you. And then the Academy scrubbed you from Sona's head. You were a loose end. Making you nothing was barely a footnote on a list of more important things."

"Rather cruel, Frostbringer." Sona's voice floats across the room. I don't have to glance over to see she's smiling now.

She thinks I'm faking this. We don't exactly know where the corruption techs put Victoria in Sona's head, if they put her somewhere else in her memory or if there was an attempt to blot her out completely, like we predicted was done with us. The corruption process has messy, bloody roots that can be traced back to before the Springtide War. Religion had already been intertwined with tech since the fortieth century (-ish; humanity has been around for a while now, and there's a lot of history that I'm not exactly committed to learning, though it does seem like religion overlaps consistently with bloodshed), but the development of technological psychedelics marked a turning point, or maybe a downward spiral.

What I do know is the design is similar to the simulation setups they use for Academy students—a helmet and a thin light threaded between your ears, and the way you perceived reality could be shuffled between different lenses at the programmer's discretion. The first programmers of the psychedelic were devout themselves, pious pioneers, and created the tech in pursuit of communication with their higher powers.

There was, of course, the occasional case of those realities sticking, even after the helmet came off. It caused what had been named "neurofeedback shamanism" to go underground, then be outlawed briefly, then decriminalized, before ultimately fading into obscurity under what was the constant onslaught of tech-religious revolutions.

Until eventually, it was unearthed by the radical devout for the same reason it had been cast aside, and altered to target the empathetic component of reality rather than the perception of it in its entirety. It was easy to proselytize when you could pinch the convert's worldview into a shape that perfectly clicked into your creed, cast to a mold.

It probably had some longer, scientifically accurate name at this point. The general population just called it *corruption*, both for what it did to your head and how much any possible good had been choked out of it.

Whew. Actually, I do know my history. Good shit.

"Sona thinks she'd die for Godolia. What an *insult*, right?" I hiss. "She's not herself. Godolia's let her live just to make her think she's the most pious of them all."

"Ha! Oh, how *sad*." Victoria's smile is thin and wide. "How unfortunate."

I thought stripping Victoria's pride would get us there; it would definitely get under her skin if I weren't some Badlands kid she'd love to scrape from under her heel like chewing gum. She couldn't care less about me. Maybe she even doesn't care about Godolia anymore. Sitting in a cell will shift priorities for you, I can tell you that much. All the good you were going to do for the world is very distant when your world gets so small.

But I can only describe the look on Victoria's face as *hate*, and it's not for me.

"It doesn't hurt her now. It's going to." The words sting my throat on the way up. Victoria's eyes flick over to mine, something instantly hungry in them. *Eat it up, you sadistic wirefucker.* "When she sees what they did, it's . . . it's going to hurt her."

Godolia's brand of corruption has a newer gleam than what was used pre–Springtide War; they're able to blot out memories, too—very helpful when you're picking apart loyalties. But the design of a corruption varies programmer to programmer. The Zenith probably requested Sona's empathetic attachments be rearranged a certain way, but there's no way of knowing how.

I remember how the Mods surgery had weighed on her. She once said she felt like a garden, when I asked one night, her words moving in the dark, but it wasn't a good thing. Actually, it made me go cold, and I didn't sleep all that well after. And this is something worse—she'd kept her head after her surgery, but she'd fought for it. And after all of it, the Zenith still tilled her thoughts as easily as earth.

It's going to wreck her. She'd want herself, her actual self, I know she would. But if this works, it's going to be bad for a while.

"Let go of me," Victoria says silkily, smile a little idle now, but just as vain. I've just told her how desperate I am, and she's basking in it.

I release her, even though my anger cuts above the surface again—even though I thought I was too sad to be angry. Apparently I can still feel like wringing Victoria's neck even while simultaneously wanting to sleep until the sun collapses. Theo follows my example, and she drops to her knees.

"Ah," Victoria sighs, stretching her neck. Under her cuffs, her intact hand cradles protectively around the other one, so you can barely notice it's missing three fingers. I know from

Shiels that the gesture is an act, to seem like she's wary. But Victoria and I both know she's just as dangerous as she was with a complete set. Her two-toned eyes slip to me over her shoulder. "You know, I had a lot of time to think about what I'd do to the both of you."

"Calm down," Theo says drily. I'm not sure if he's talking to Victoria or me.

"Pulling out the wires in her veins, inch by inch, like ripping a plant out by the roots." Victoria shivers. "Oh—starving her and then feeding you to her in pieces."

I smile at her. Then I kick her between the shoulder blades and lean over when her cheek hits the wood, my foot growing heavy on her spine. "You should watch yourself," I whisper.

"You need me," Victoria reminds me, allowing herself to be ground down. She doesn't need to use her lungs to speak, and so her voice comes out clear and even. "But the cold room was my favorite place to imagine you two. I'd put you both somewhere locked up nice and tight and let the temperature drop down. I thought it would be like falling asleep . . . But you are both fighters—you are both so strong. Then one of you nods off. Sometimes it's you, sometimes it's Bellsona . . . but how it ends is always the same, as these sweeter things tend to go. One of you cradling the other, *shrieking*—"

I crush my rage down into a dark, hard ball and step off her and back, back, back, so I don't put her head through the floor.

"Ha," I say, dragging my sleeve across my mouth. "Ha, okay, okay. I guess you'd better do your job, then. I don't think she's in a state to cry over my corpse, right, Glitch?"

Sona blows a chestnut curl lazily off her cheek and shoots me a radiant, barbed smirk. "Only tears of joy, love."

"Enough out of you," I say, tone spiked with a half-broken laugh. Even when I'm about to cry and she's fallen apart without even realizing it, our banter reigns supreme. She laughs a little, and I think to myself, as the sound fissures me, *We really do have to end up being okay. This really has to all turn out okay.*

CHAPTER TWENTY

BELLSONA

They keep the Pilot back, like a wild dog, when she gets too worked up and tries to move for me again. I sit with my spine between two radiator bars and wait for her to finish talking, or to get close enough. Whichever comes first. She is not in the best shape. I could snap her like a stem from a cherry pit.

I broke the Frostbringer out of her cell, the Valkyrie tells me. Let her go, let her into my Windup. Wound, and then was thrown down into the ice, soon after, minus a hand. Victoria went looking for me, through the socket of my mecha's skull. She was going to rip my physical body from the cords and let me drip out her clenched fingers.

The dramatics of it all. I do not remember her being so crass.

Half the time I watch Eris's face. She meets my eyes every time, chewing the side of her mouth. Waiting for the look on my face to change. I run my tongue over my lips, slowly, just to see if I can make her blush, but her cheeks are still ruddy from her sobbing and it's difficult to tell.

"You had better look at me when I am talking to you," Victoria sneers, voice liquid poison. "Bellsona, you had better look at me like you are *begging* me—"

"You think I do not remember you at all, but I do," I say. "You bothered me, and I punched you, embarrassed you in front of your entourage. And then you skittered away, a scared, blushing thing."

I am bored, and worried absolutely sick to my stomach for Enyo. He will soon be worried about me, too, now that a soft, rainy dawn has crept into the gap between the curtains and the wall. That is what I tell myself. That he is okay enough to worry himself over me.

Victoria's striking, fine features are acidic. "They had trouble with me, didn't they, sweetheart. With when exactly I was in your head. Standing in an inconvenient place in the narrative they wanted for you. The details on how you could manage to walk out, Gearbreaker ice bitch in tow, when you were stuffed to bursting with Godolia loyalties. Ah, but that's one of the hazy parts, I bet."

My face is clear. I am still bored, still so steadfast. My heartbeat is not slowly rising in my ears.

"The reason it is difficult to remember is because I was difficult to explain. Better get the ink, blot her right out of her pretty mind! But really, Bellsona, every Badlands kid already has a head that's only half-screwed in."

Victoria's voice is high and fraying now; ironically, she is slipping in a way that keeps me focused. This is what the Gearbreakers do. Pull you apart, thread by thread.

"You are insulting our hosts," I say.

"Oh please, do tell me if I am incorrect!" Victoria croons. "Tell me, how did a dirty renegade coax you into allowing her to crawl through the veins of a *God*—"

"Stop."

"—*tell me*, or tell me if it's all just black, black, *black*—"

And it is—it is dark and smeared and blank all at once, and the only consistent thing *ever* is Eris. Eris hovering, Eris changing the weight of the air in the room. I cannot understand it, how this closeness was what stuck in my head, how I could wander blindly through these memories and still draw her outline in the pitch black. A scar is healed but still curls in the shape of the cut. Her nearness is that mark left behind, and she does not fade. I knew her name. I knew it always, and it does not make sense, it doesn't make *sense*—

I smash my temple to the metal edge of the radiator. Wait for the room to come back into focus, then again. Does not hurt, cannot hurt, just smears my vision, smudges nausea up my throat, again—

"Sona!" Eris screams, but I must have distracted her, because suddenly Victoria is free from the Gearbreakers' hold and against me, knee pinning my stomach to the radiator.

And she hovers. Hair ragged around her eyes, just teeth and split, feverish lips stretched ear to ear.

"Wait," Eris snaps to the boy at her side, the others teeming in the doorway. Her hand is up, warning them back. Black, narrowed eyes meet mine over the curve of Victoria's pale shoulder. "Just . . . wait."

Victoria tilts her head to the side, hair slipping off her cheekbone so her Mod's light can glance off mine. She leans closer.

"You do not remember all of me," Victoria rasps, lips ghosting mine. A pause, and then she is kissing me like she is trying to devour me—vicious, terrible, the complete, perfect rage of it. She rips away with the same clean jolt of snapping a bone. She is no longer smiling. "What about that, sweetheart? Remember that? Maybe I cannot even blame you. It's been a while since I was a God."

"You are a mad creature," I say through gritted teeth, the

slick feel of her bloody hand on my cheek, the warmth of her mouth still flickering across mine, and the taste—her hand on my cheek?

Victoria's hands are bound.

The memory—somewhere else, dark . . . someone else. No. We were running. We . . . she leaned in first . . .

I glance at Eris. Maybe it's a reflexive thing, like flinching. It's a mistake.

"Get her out," the Frostbringer growls, and Victoria is brought up and away. No longer snarling, Victoria just gives me another grin followed by a dry, barking laugh, cut short as the door slams shut.

I am silent as Eris crosses the room. Carefully, she kneels down in front of me.

"What is it?" Eris asks quietly. "Did you—"

"You were cruel to me," I say, meaning it to sound cold, and horrified to hear my words grief stricken. Heat builds up in my throat. "Did you ever feel guilty for it, Eris? Did it ever make you hesitate, your love for me? Did you ever hesitate to use me like you did?"

Eris waits a moment. The curtains are threadbare, filling slowly with light clotted in the fabric; she reaches past me to tug them open a few inches, dawn spilling in. "Yes," she says. "But not enough. We hit the street in Godolia and—Gods, Sona—I thought you were dead. I really thought you were dead, and all of it—it wasn't worth it. It was all fucking shot.

"Then you were up. I should have let us die. I was trying to get you out, but it wasn't on your terms, and it wasn't—I was cruel to you. You're right. I was so *cruel*, and I'm so sorry. Gods, I—" Eris turns, hands falling on my cheeks.

She is looking for something in my expression, and she

150

does not find it—but she knows what to look for because I used to give it to her.

She lets go.

Her lips break apart as her next exhale comes in a shudder, tears brimming but she does not let them free. "You don't even know what I'm saying. I've done a lot to you, okay? And you were always wonderful to me. You're wonderful, and I was going to make it up to you." She lifts a limp shoulder. "Maybe this is better, though. I've just gotten worse and worse, but I'm going to keep trying. Even if it can't be for you anymore."

She kisses me once, quick, between my brows. The air separating her skin from mine is a static front. There is something here. Maybe she was a home to me, once. But there is someone else waiting for me.

I love Enyo, the brat, with his ancient eyes and nervous smile, and I love him *now*. That feels real to me in a way that I have to trust.

Eris's hands tighten, but gently, so I can feel that there is something beneath the skin of her left palm. Then she pulls away. I follow her hand as it drops to her lap, see the outline under her skin, like a little pill. Ripped from a child's corpse.

I turn my head to check the time using the sun, but Eris snags my chin. Her touch is no longer gentle. She forces my gaze to hers, which is simmering.

"What was that?" Her voice is a growl. A complete shift. She misses nothing.

"It is not worth it now, is it?" I whisper. "What you had to do to get that invitation."

A flash of hurt crosses her features, and I cling to it. "Actually, I was invited by the Zenith himself. Did you put in a good word for me?"

"You are lying, Frostbringer." I smile, just as we feel the first footfall.

You are not telling me something. I do not need to know how he knows exactly where we are.

Shouting immediately sparks from the other room, and Eris's touch skitters from me. She scrambles to her feet with a shout to her crew members when the next footfall quakes the ground. Eris is thrown sideways and then onto the floorboards, rises with a sound half groan and half snarl, as someone behind the far wall starts to scream.

Then the wall crumples under the weight of a metal heel, alongside half the ceiling.

The last thing I see is Eris throwing her hands over her head, as the rest of the ceiling yawns, and then comes down.

CHAPTER TWENTY-ONE

ERIS

The world is dark, but it's still here. I'm still on it, I mean, which is weird because I should be crushed flat by now. But oh my Gods. I so do not feel good.

Somewhere past the broken wood and the wrecked roof there is shouting and the chest-seizing blast of explosives. There are mechas, two at least, footfalls lifting me in odd pulses, my decently junked body going light in fits and starts.

There's something collapsed on my leg, but I drag myself out from beneath it with just a little tearing of skin and clothes, knee and leg bones unshattered. I'm flat and can't lift my head more than a few inches. I know this because I try too quickly and whack my crown, which does not help my thudding headache.

Sona's next to me, still, her head near my ribs. My hand moves for her in the dark, but this isn't a good idea. She's not here, and I'm not leaving with her.

Damn. That's actually kind of horrible.

But I do check her pulse. It's there, but she's out cold. The radiator's snapped to pieces under her back. Her shackles are probably broken. Should I check? I don't have time. That must be why I'm already moving away.

I crawl. There's a slice of light licking across the floor, bottom of the left wall, probably at the base of the house. Forward and low, carefully, even though I want to be scrambling, even though there could be another Windup foot eased down onto my body at any moment—I could bring the rest of the ceiling down if I panic and knock against something.

I realize the hole is too small only after I reach it. I can see the debris-covered grass and the lower end of the forest, and the earth smells damp from yesterday's rain, but I can't fit my shoulders through.

Panic trickles into my chest—I'm really stuck here. I stick my arm out of the hole. I'm screaming now. Screaming what? Nothing in particular. Another Windup footstep lifts me clean off the ground, and I smack my jaw on the floor when I land.

"Get back!" someone is shouting. "Back away if you can!"

I can't, not really, but I shrink away as much as possible. Then there's kicking and the wood wall splintering inward—then there's light, and hands. I'm dragged out and onto the grass, coughing into the wet soil when I try to suck in fresh air; it's like I haven't breathed this entire time.

"You're good, you're good, can you stand?" Nolan doesn't give me much of a choice, lifting me to my feet.

"Did you get Jenny?" I gasp once I have enough air. "Is she—"

He shakes his head, blond hair soaked against his temples. "We saw the mechas coming up this way. Turned around right away, but the bastards are quick."

Then a Windup drops a shadow on us, and then its hand.

Something shrieks over our heads, followed by another teeth-grating explosion. The Argus emerging from the forest stumbles backward, smoke and fire curling off its left shoulder—but that was a Paladin heel that came down on us, I could tell by that swollen foot, so *where*—

The next arrow hits right between the Argus's eyes when it tries to right itself, and it goes down with a crash that sends Nolan and me both to the ground.

I roll onto my belly and then to my feet, stomach dropping when I realize I can see Zamaya standing with another arrow nocked at the mouth of the path, straight over the plane of the decimated cabin. And there's the Paladin, driven back to the forest but standing sixty feet almost directly above her, reaching its thick, bus-sized fingers for her violet hair.

Z fires at the palm, but it's already too close—the blast sends her back, too, body slamming into the grass and then folding around the trunk of a tree.

"Go!" I yell to Nolan, and he's sprinting for her. There's a hole smoking at the Paladin's ankle, Seung or Gwen probably already inside.

I round what's left of the building, but I don't even know where to start. The Paladin only got to Victoria's room before Nolan's crew showed up, but the old cabin just couldn't take it. I don't know why that's the thought that bubbles up as I tear through the debris for breathing bodies, that I can't blame the house for crumpling after only partial assault. I can really only blame myself.

A crumble of brick marks what was the fireplace, silky smoke rising from the remnants of the embers. Someone is coughing under the teeth of the broken roof, and I rip aside wood and brick until Nova's blond head comes into view, cradled against Juniper, who's conscious, dark brown eyes watery from the grime.

"Arsen?" she chokes weakly.

"Don't know," is all I say, and then, "Come on, come on—"

We haul Nova's small body from the wreckage. She stirs

slightly with a groan, and I can't help the sob of relief that comes up my throat.

"Theo?" she murmurs. "Arsen? Nyla?"

"Wow. It's nice to see you, too," I say truthfully.

"Away from the . . . forest . . . thing," Nova slurs. "Arsen set up stuff . . ."

Then she tries to stand on her own and her knees buckle, leaving blood where her head knocks against my arm.

"Oh, it's okay, I got you, love." My words come frantically as I balance her in my arms, and to June I snap, "I got her. Find the others."

The Argus has risen, on its hands and knees and only half an eye still blaring red, but its shadow still clears the wreckage. Someone from Jen's crew has disabled the Paladin from the inside—the mecha's on its stomach, legs dangling down the valley, arms felling trees as it drags itself through the undergrowth. Root systems snap from the earth in massive, tearing sighs. The Argus moves in a similar state.

They're crawling for the cabin. I hate it when they crawl, the shift from elegant to feral; either still blots out the sky.

I see that Zamaya's up as I make my way off the cabin wreckage. Don't even know where I'm going, don't know what to do, Windups on all sides. I'm still wearing the freaking dress. I lay Nova down on the grass and glance back to June, who's pulling Arsen from the debris by his shoulders, his curls dusted gray. His eyes are open, skittering around the surrounding mechascape before he bats her away with an un-Arsen-like wildness, hands digging in his pockets even after she drops him on the rubble like dead weight.

Then I get it. I bring my hands around my mouth. "Get back from the tree line! *Get back!*" I bring one palm up; judging by the feel of my two feet still on the ground, Arsen sees it, and waits. Zamaya and Nolan have seen me, scurrying back from the tree line. I meet Z's eyes. She knows what's about to happen, knows Gwen and Seung are still in the mecha and Theo and Nyla are still missing—and knows we don't have another choice.

"Wait!" The Argus is a dozen feet from the clearing; I turn to see that the Paladin's head is shadowing the path leading up to the collapsed porch. "Wait! All right, *now*, Ar—"

It starts on my right, so I'm thrown to my left, shoulder hitting grass and then back hitting something tougher, and then I'm crawling blindly, hearing knocked clean out of my head by the roar of splitting ground as the tree line and its mechas vanish behind plumes of earth and flame. The force of each bomb hits me like a full-body gut punch—it's like Arsen was trying to carve out an island for us.

I find Nova's hand first and follow it to the rest of her, slipping a palm under her head to tuck her beneath me. I can see, barely, that she's conscious, green eyes flicking fearfully, tiny fingers clutching onto my skirt as the ground seems to shatter around us. Her lips move, but I can't hear what she's saying, blood glistening brightly on her temple.

I uncurl from her when the earth stops moving, but I have to untangle that feeling from the shaking in the core of my chest. Zamaya and Nolan are close, now, and Nolan takes Nova while Z clenches a firm hand around my shoulder and drags me to my feet.

"Listen to me, Eris!" she shouts, but her voice barely cuts through the ringing in my ears. "There's going to be more. We need to move."

"My crew's missing—"

"Tough shit, Shindanai," Nolan says, and I recoil from the both of them, even though he doesn't say it lightly, says it like he's begging me. Zamaya lets me go easily. She can see that I've made up my mind.

"Get my other kids," I snarl, and then watch Zamaya and Nolan pick their way toward the wreckage, where Arsen is helping June to her feet. They both glance up when Zamaya shouts at them. They miss what she's saying a few times; I know when they do get it, though, because June shouts, "Fuck off!" before turning to continue rummaging through the ruins.

Nova shrieks in Nolan's arms as he and Zamaya make for the forest. He eventually lets her go, too, and she lies still in the grass for a few moments before getting to her knees.

"I miss my freaking truck," she says as she starts to help us look.

I keep an eye on the mechas as we sift. The Argus and the Paladin are down for the count, face-planted in the erupted earth. The Paladin got close enough that the crown of its head is settled on the steps of the porch, two stories of bronzed skull reflecting the sunlight as we search. The room we shoved Victoria back into was completely flattened by that first step. I can't help it, the side of my mouth between my teeth as the thought rises with venom—*It's a really fun way to go, isn't it. Dead bitch.*

We find Theo and Nyla after peeling away a part of the roof angled over the back end of the couch. No sob of relief this time—I'm too shaken for it—but I kiss them both fiercely on the brow once we haul them into open air. After one step and a subsequent collapse, it's clear that Nyla has a broken leg; Theo and Arsen take her arms.

That's when I see the Berserker past the curve of the

Paladin's temple, appearing around the knife edge of the mountain ridge, maybe fifty feet past the heels.

"Move," I hiss as we press against the mecha's skull. We hug close to the Paladin, using the corpse as a cover, making for the forest.

But they're not just coming from the west. Another Berserker steps out around the slope rising above the east side of the cabin, across a forested valley it can cross in five paces. In the Badlands desert they're bigger than everything else, though here the Peaks dwarf them easily—but does it matter? Does it matter that they're not the biggest thing around when we're still ants to them, when they have a chestful of cannons that are opened to the dawn light—

Godsdamn it.

Arsen's bombs left gaps in the earth by the Paladin's neck; we slide into the divots and land mud-slicked as the first round of blasts sails into the clearing. Metal screeches, and through the smoke and ruptured earth, I see the hole opened up in the Paladin's iron shoulder, smoldering, fringed with torn, three-foot-thick peels of skin. *Damn, Arsen . . .*

Wordlessly, the crew scrambles up and out of the divot and into the forest. I'm the last up, bare feet finding a foothold in the mangled earth, and I pull my head aboveground just to see them, thankfully, already running, Nyla still between Theo and Arsen. They're moving quick—Nyla landed on her bad leg, but she's alert without the pain to claw at her.

I make it to my stomach, and then a hand wraps around my ankle and rips me back into the ditch.

I land on my back in an inch of mud, and then Sona's on me, curls wild around her ears, a gash on her cheek that flecks blood onto mine.

"I have to get one of you, at least," she says hoarsely, and then her hands are pressing around my neck.

There's mud in my ears and sucking at the small of my back as my feet kick under her. *Not like this. No freaking way.* I'm screaming and she's silent and then I'm silent, too, and it's happening so fast so fast the black coming in and I bring my fist to her stomach once twice but it's not enough I'm too weak for it and I do it again—

And she releases me. There's no way I threw her off. It doesn't make sense, but I gulp for air and choke on it and just *move*, up and out and into the forest. Snatch up one of the fragments Arsen's work left behind, drag it through my palm to scrape out the chip. I trip over my own feet once and leave the chip behind in the dirt.

I think, at first, that I'm crying, and that's why the world looks blurred. But it's just the forest streaking past. I should have looked back. The last image I have of her in my head is her watching me die. Her killing me. It shocks me so much that I don't think I could cry even if I wanted to.

CHAPTER TWENTY-TWO

BELLSONA

She scrambles away and then she is gone. She's hit me before in the ribs, once, twice, three times, and I think something broke.

I think I let it happen.

Wait—

I think

This isn't   I'm not   all right

my   hand against my side feeling

                    for what

Am I here? But that does not make sense not completely

YOU LOOK LIKE YOU'RE ALL HERE TO ME *because why*

does it come up where else would I be

RIGHT WHERE YOU'RE SUPPOSED TO BE.

Doesn't it feel like it, Sona?

No. No. No.

I

I am not meant to be like this.

CHAPTER TWENTY-THREE

SONA

"Eris," I breathe.

But she is already gone.

If she had just waited for a *second*—but I scared her.

Better, I think to myself, as my brow touches the earth, fingers digging into the back of my head, even as I am screaming. *Better I am here after she ran than after I snapped her neck.*

Gulping down air and mud all at once. Trying to line everything up. The ground sucking at my legs shakes with the approaching Berserkers, their gunfire—it's better that it is. It matches, the splintering of pines and the frayed ends of my thoughts, the ricochet of bullets and the chatter of panic.

I should run.

But that comes to me too late, that I could do that. That I could just leave Enyo behind and not look back.

A Berserker leans over the trench and leaves me uncrushed, because Enyo told it to. Instead I clamber up onto its extended hand, watch the ground shrink as the other Berserker fills the forest with lead and flame, splitting tree trunks into meaty, white hearts.

I could just not look back.

If I did not have to kill Enyo, I could just go *home*.

The thought arrives without rage, settled in a strange

calm. I realize I may be in shock, that I have disassociated from it entirely.

It hardly matters, I think. What Enyo did to me, how he cares for me—it's a little thing.

We are on a playing board larger than what we might mean to each other.

Right?

The Berserker deposits me on the far side of the river, a ferry shuttling me across the water and then a hovercar waiting for me on the docks. My temple is pressed against the window as it glides up to the Badlands Academy shimmering at the city's apex. I watch the line of water warble thinly above the reach of the wall. No Leviathan. It must be north, maybe, combing the waters for Gearbreakers.

I close my eyes, let it all go dark.

There are guards waiting for me at the Academy steps, one attendant pressed between them to give me a winning smile as the driver opens the door. I brush past and walk straight up to the attendant, feet bare and shredded, muddy pants and a shirt half-open and untucked. To his credit he does not move, just freezing his grin as I stop a foot away.

"Bring me to the Zenith."

"Of course, Captain Steelcrest," the attendant says smoothly, and I could laugh in his face, like I laughed in Enyo's when he told me this was my title. I am only captain of the Valkyries because there are no other Valkyries left. Rose, first. I got the rest eventually. I laughed then because it was ridiculous and dark and I hated myself. I could have laughed or I could have lain on the floor and just drowned in all of it.

Again. I think it viciously. *Say it again.*

I *hated* myself.

I do not laugh now.

I am guided—guards trailing behind, clearly watchful—to the elevators, bringing us up to the penthouse. A tangle of branches and leaves marks the edge of the cherry blossom grove. A lump hitches in my throat. The dead Gearbreakers are still there, probably will be until there is nothing left for the crows to pick at. *Milo* . . . He may not have liked me, but he was still doing good for the world. Still saving people, and he deserved more than this.

"Right through here, Captain Steelcrest," the attendant says after we make our way down the hall. I pass through the double doors and into the dining room, then freeze when I realize the room is completely empty.

I do not turn as I hear the innocent click of the lock. Dread seals me in place, makes the whole room look fake, like it's made of plastic—the gleam of the silverware in front of empty chairs, the dish of glassy japchae noodles turning dull in the air, the coiling tail of steam rising silent from a vat of barley tea. I cross the room and pour myself a glass with perfectly steady hands, watch as I overfill the cup and spill it all over my fingers anyway, skin flushing as it scalds.

I should run. I could run—I could take whoever stands guard in the hallway; breaking apart the lock would be the harder part. But I need to see Enyo.

Why? I think to myself harshly, and my response is just as vicious: *Because I am going to kill him. Because I* have *to kill him.*

I am locked in all day long. Pacing. Watching the sun carve a line and then disappear completely from the sky. When the moon has made fair progress, a helicopter appears in the distance, the sound of its rotors beating against the window as it coasts close to the Academy and then disappears from sight. I think it's on the roof.

Deities. Stay *calm.*

About five minutes later, the doors open, closing again once a single person glides into the room. She promptly takes a seat, eyes drawing low across the untouched food and the cold tea stain on the table linen.

"Dr. Fray," I say without a smile, because she knows me as arrogant, maybe as a little angry, too. Rough edges all around. It's a good thing, I tell myself. I do not have to fabricate as many lies, just enough to get me to Enyo. "Is our Zenith concerned about me?"

And I thought he trusted me. The thought diffuses drily.

And then another startles me—I am a little bit hurt by this. Hurt by what? That he thought he needed defense from me? He does.

Dr. Fray smiles warmly. There might be pity in it that she wants me to see. "Zenith Enyo knows the weight of what he asked of you." A pause. "Even if it was unsuccessful."

It's a fact—one that I am grateful for—but my lip curls despite that, even though her tone hovers without judgment. Eris and I can laugh about it later.

You couldn't kill me if you tried, love.

I sit across the table from her, collecting myself as much as I can in my current state. Latch a button or two and tuck my hair behind my ears. Roll my muddy sleeves neatly up my arms. She watches this movement with particular attention. She has to, as much as I have to keep my expression steady, bored, as my left forearm panel comes into view.

No gears. Just smooth, dirty skin. Not one ounce of evidence that he—

Enyo—

Cut

Them

Out

Of

Me.

"Can we start?" I say evenly—still, so still, even though I am panicking now. Where did I learn to sit so perfectly still when the thoughts that are *eating* me feel bigger than me? I'm so scared and sad that I feel little. I want to crawl under the table and curl in on myself in the soft carpet so badly it aches. But my voice is steady. My chin is on the edge of my hand, and I look at Fray like she is bothering me, like I do not want to stand up and run away. "It has been a long day."

"Sure," Fray says, easing back in her chair. Her tablet balances on the crook of her arm, pen held delicately in her manicured fingers. I realize it, then. That it was her, all this time.

My corruption tech, checking in on her programming.

"How about we start with when you left the Zenith's side," she says.

This I can do. I do not need to lie about much. The dancing, the grove, the tunnel. The cabin and my capture and

Victoria. The roof coming down, and then my hands around the Frostbringer's throat. How I did not expect her to act as she did, to be how she is. Did not expect her to cry. To love me.

The latter I tell Fray with a vicious triumph. My tone says I think it's funny, and pitiful, and disappointing. But what I am really saying is, *Listen carefully. Pay close attention. This is why you are going to lose.*

Eris Shindanai loves me. Fuck everything else. Through everything that this world threw at us—how it wrecked us and cost us and how much distance it dropped between us— she did not give up on me. On Heavensday she fought for me, and she fought with everything. I would have done the same.

Eris did not give me a choice. She did not give me a choice, but there was not another one besides dying together, and I only want that later. Much, much later. Because I need to know her for most of my life.

I scared her and she ran and it's going to be okay. She is a riot with skin and I love her I love her *I love her* and we really do have to end up being okay—

I finish talking. Fray's pen, a half minute later, stops moving. She lets the tablet screen go dark, and sets it on the table between us with a small thud. Her hand rises to draw back a thin length of blond hair that has escaped her bun, and I realize that has not happened before. Always put together— her, and everything else about her city. Because what a delicate thing, all these lives held together by the same threads of belief.

Enyo was never afraid of a coup, even with the blatant skepticism aimed at him because of his age. I see now it would have been a wasted fear. Zeniths, captains, Pilots—a simple, carefully tended hierarchy. Godolia balanced on these slender foundations, like a hairline fracture.

Everyone can see how fragile it all is. Maybe they can see how Enyo alone is too small for the weight of it. But it does not matter, it cannot matter, because they are all scared senseless of the chaos that would come with a shift. They should be. Panic is the easiest human act.

Fray lifts her eyes from the tabletop, meeting mine. And she pauses for a moment, hand still hovering at her ear, before dropping it down into her lap.

Something's wrong.

"Bellsona," Fray says. Her warmth is gone, replaced by a hardness, but I do not think it is directed at me. It's more like she is trying to hold herself together—

She does not have to say it.

This is what you wanted. The thought is desperate and useless to the small, black hole that opens up in my chest. *This is what you* wanted.

Please don't say it.

But she does, quietly. Like it could actually be true, if not for everything that comes after it. If not for how anarchic the world is about to get.

"The Zenith is dead."

CHAPTER TWENTY-FOUR

ERIS

I catch up to the rest of them eventually, aching spots in the shape of Sona's fingers blooming around my throat; I can tell by the looks on their faces that I'm already bruising. I also can tell by the blood on Theo's shirtfront that he's been shot.

I kneel in the undergrowth that they've lowered him in, steadying my hand before smoothing it over his freckled forehead. His wrist lifts, and his fingers seem so little as they search for mine.

"What happened to you?" Theo asks thinly, with the audacity to be concerned.

Rot, I want to say, but I just shake my head—I know I can't speak yet anyway, what with Sona having crushed my vocal cords—and scowl at him, now that I see he's not going to die. He got a round in his shoulder, already bandaged but the bullet's probably still lodged inside, and what looks like a graze or two tearing his upper arm. Also Nova's bleeding from her head. Also Arsen and June have cuts all up their arms and legs, battle wounds synced up, how they unexplainably usually do. But it hasn't been this bad in a while. Nyla's leg is still broken, go figure; she's on her stomach in the undergrowth, breath brushing spring moss and Theo's cheek.

I nod. *Okay.* I mouth it and they see it. *Okay. We're good.*

We go slowly, rotating who Nyla leans up against and who half carries Theo and who takes care of Nova when she pauses to empty her already-empty stomach on the side of the trail. But we make it back—that's what matters, that we make it back—long after sundown because we just can't stop, the harsh rise of the Mutts lacerating a clear, starry sky.

Sheils stationed some Hydras out by where the entrance yawns under the cover of forest—once a natural cave but scraped open when the hangar was made during the Springtide War, smooth and cold stone striated and split to a mouth about sixty feet wide—but it's not a friendly gesture. They could probably feel the tremor of the ambush even in the caverns. Anyone else but us coming out of the woods they probably would've shot. Though the Berserkers partially beat them to it. It's a good thing I can't speak or maybe I'd mention this. Or I wouldn't. It's not really that funny.

For a moment we stare at one another, unmoving. Pilots in the mouth of the cave and Gearbreakers in the tree line. Plus Nyla, who kind of teeters in the middle, who then limps forward after a few silent seconds and goes, "Don't be dicks. Please."

The Hydras lead us down into the Mutts, which means filing into the old grated elevator set in the wall of the entrance, followed by a few minutes enveloped by the groan of metal and the clicking of our teeth as the box shakes, and darkness, save for the yellow light in the corner.

But I'm relieved for all of it, and when that hits me, I drop my cheek against June's arm and close my eyes. She's too tall for me to reach her shoulder when I'm barefoot.

"How the hells did you beat us here?" June spits.

Seung glances up from the infirmary bed, black hair peeking out in tufts from the bandage wrapped around his head. Gwen, sitting at his feet, looks fine, but her smile is only just there—just so, so tired. Nolan and Zamaya flank the bed, battered and filthy and both looking furious with me. With one hand still steadying Theo, I could honestly not care less.

As Nurse Hyun-Woo and Dr. Park lead Nova, Theo, and Nyla to beds, Zamaya and Nolan cross the room. I go completely still as they both take turns hugging me—Nolan lingering, Zamaya quick and practically shoving me away—and for a moment it's just my face in the softness of their shirts, like I could ever be someone who's completely safe.

Then I look at Zamaya, standing on my shredded feet in *this fucking dress* and say, "We need to get Jenny."

It's impossible. It's delirium. But because Jenny is to Zamaya what Sona is to me, and because Jenny might actually still be here, she nods. Nods like Jen's in the next room over.

That's when I start crying.

I sit down with my back against the leg of Nova's bed and sob with my whole body. I cry while Arsen forces me to drink water. I cry while Hyun-Woo kneels down to bandage my feet. I cry harder than I did when Xander died, like when my parents died—I'm sorry, X and Appa and Mom, I wish I could say this doesn't feel worse, I wish this *didn't* feel worse, like I'm in pieces, or halved, missing an edge like an open wound—and I wrap my arms around myself and just shake when I run out of tears.

She's gone. Out of her head.

The love of my fucking life, and she's gone.

I wake up on my side in what must be the middle of the

night—I can't possibly know what time it is down here. The infirmary's fluorescent lights have clicked off, just the glow of the kitchen a floor below crawling up over the railing. I get to my feet slowly to find Arsen and Theo curled up on one bed, Novs and June in another, touching my eyes on each chest to make sure they rise.

Nolan sits in a chair next to Seung's bed, slouched halfway over the mattress in his sleep, cheek on Gwen's arm as she sleeps with her head to the baseboard. No Zamaya. Seung is snoring the way he always did, like an ancient halabeoji, when I was in the bedroom next to his and I would plot to smother him in his sleep. But I like it now.

Nyla is in the bed beside his. She's awake. I ease myself onto the mattress, feet on the frame, so my back is partially toward her as I look out over the hangar, at the Hydras standing there. The tubes—the veins—that run up their arms and into openings dotting the palms of their hands, are all still filled with liquid poison. Each finger connected by a tube to a twenty-gallon tank of fluid, tucked up in the lower biceps. Jenny said that Sheils was wary of dumping the stuff, or even handling it to begin with, though it was probably more of an unprompted psych analyzation on Jen's part than the captain actually telling her she was afraid.

So the Hydras don't move, and nobody touches them. One of the worst parts of Godolia history locked up underground so no one has to know, which wasn't Sheils's intention, I know, but that's what it is.

"I did not know her," Nyla finally says, and I look at her, startled. The distant kitchen glow edges her ever-flushed cheeks, softening the crow's feet as it works its way across her skin. "Steelcrest, I mean. I know you have been wanting to ask. She was in my year and I probably heard about her more than I saw her, but I did not know her. I do not think anyone really did."

I scrub at the salt lines dried on my face. I don't want to talk about Sona, so I ask, "Did you know you might run when you first enrolled?"

Nyla shakes her head. "Hells no. I enlisted because the Academy was the only place I could be something. Something . . . incredible." She looks past me, out into the hangar. One hand wanders up to touch her left cheek, right under the Mod eye. "That's the deal with a lot of the students, you know. You go to the Academy because the city can just swallow you up. I mean that in the worst way." Her voice is hard. "As much as the Badlands are monitored, there are parts of Godolia that are just plain lawless. But the Academy takes in everyone. That is why kids are convinced it is good. They will feed you. They will feed your family. They will make you a God."

"That does sound pretty good," I say truthfully.

I've never looked at it like that. I'm stunned, then ashamed, that I haven't. Godolia is massive. Not all of it could be flourishing like they evangelize that it is. Not when they were pumping out the number of mechas that they were pre-Heavensday. Pouring everything into their military even while parts of their country starved.

"Yeah." Nyla chuckles softly. I expect it to be bitter, because that's how I would sound, but it's not. "It was not the surgery that freaked me out. I like it, actually." Her fingers absent-mindedly trace the panel set into her arm, peppered with cuts from the cabin collapse. "Then I passed the trial period, my test runs. Then some Badlands people hopped a train going east hoping to get out of their resource village, maybe make it to the ocean. It just didn't hit me until afterward. After I was done, you know, it just—"

I reach out and lay a hand over hers. She leaves it there and uses the other to rub her tearing eyes.

"It's okay," I say, and this time I'm lying. She's okay, but this world isn't.

She lifts her eyes to mine. Red and brown, and the look in them reminds me of the look in Sona's, but it's not just hers. It's all of theirs, the kids sleeping in damaged bodies a few feet away, and it's mine, too. A tiredness. A resolution that right now feels all right, but move carefully or you'll scare it off.

"No," Nyla says finally. "It's not."

A beat of silence.

"But," she adds, "I think it's going to be. Okay, eventually. We just have to trust."

"Trust what?" I ask.

She smiles at me. It's a little shy. "Each other."

CHAPTER TWENTY-FIVE

SONA

I do not know how long I have been here, watching my fingers grip the edge of the table, every knuckle white. I have never been so still. *I am cracked,* I realize. *If I move I will break apart.*

Finally, I say, "No."

No, it cannot be true.

No, I cannot want it *not* to be true.

No, I do not want Enyo dead. I never did, I could never—and why? When he did what he did to me?

Because I killed his family.

Godolia killed mine and I did worse to it. I did the same to him.

And it did not fix anything. The violence. The death. I did not recognize that until it was already done. Enyo saw that earlier than me. Maybe it happened while his pen was under my skin. Maybe it happened the first time—all those times ago—that the corruption held within me and I surprised him with the way I treated him. Like we could be friends. Like he did not need to kill me.

I know what I would have done if I were him. And so it makes even less sense now—why he treated me as he did, when I was not a loyal soldier but a threat all this time, when I made him laugh and he pressed his shoulder to mine and he was so, so careful—and I do not think how I feel about him is something he had stitched to my thoughts.

That *terrifies* me.

That I grew to love him all on my own.

That he loved me, too, I think, despite . . . despite.

So I say it again. "No."

I am shaking. Dissolving. My head in my hands, now, trying to force stillness because I really am going to break apart; I am going to split into a thousand pieces, and it's happened too many times. I have already had to put myself back together too many times.

A hand alights gently on my shoulder. Just for a moment, I think it's Fray, and I think I might kill her for it.

"Bellsona?"

I start at his voice. Push him back with a gasp, and then a snarl, and then my hands are in his shirtfront, shoving him back into the wall. His head tilts down to me, unbrushed hair slipping against his temples, and he *smiles*.

"Missed you, too," Enyo says. "The good doctor said she has cleared you to see me. I came right away."

I let him go and lunge across the table at Fray, who lets out a startled gasp, tablet and pen clattering to the floor. A test. Of course it was a test, and now I am going to kill her right here in the dining room.

But Enyo grabs my ankle and yanks me backward. I twist, the small of my back against the table's edge as I plant a foot on his sternum to shove him away. I could be executed for it. I hardly care.

"Wait your turn," I spit, but he only grabs me again when I turn for Fray, this time lifting me clean off the table with an arm around my waist.

"That will be all, Doctor," he says with a strain in his voice, and Fray scrambles for the exit.

The doors shut behind her, and I wrench myself out of his grasp. Heaving. Breathing—I only realize this after he notices it, and then see, with perfect shock, that he does not care.

"Are you all right?" His hand is gentle on my arm. "Did they hurt you?"

"I failed," I say viciously. *Thank the Gods, I failed.* "They got away."

I wait for him to press me on it. But he just brushes his thumb lightly against the gash marring my cheek.

"Let's get you a Spider."

"Get off me." He steps away immediately, which just makes me ache more. "Have you killed her yet?"

"Who?" he asks, even though there is only one girl I could be talking about.

"Starbreach." I watch his reaction, and I have the sense he is doing the same to me, though his expression remains neutral.

"No."

Relief pops in my chest. I need to see Jenny. I need to get her away from here. But how do I get to her? I turn it over in my head, but after a moment, Enyo speaks again.

"Do you want to see her?"

My heart pounds in my chest. *Careful, now.* "I am not sure what good it would do."

"Another chance, perhaps."

He holds out his hand. "And," he adds, "I have something incredible to show you."

There is something dark settled in his voice. But I take his hand anyway.

CHAPTER TWENTY-SIX

ERIS

We fall asleep at some point, and the kitchen lights are still on when I wake up. This time the glow crawls in accompanied by the hum of lowered voices. I ease off the bed and drift to the stairwell, footsteps silent under my bandages.

I crouch on the stairs just before the bend, where the voices are audible if I strain.

"—not a discussion, Haan."

Sheils, calling Zamaya by her last name, which she and I both know Z doesn't like. I haven't seen the captain since we got here.

"I wasn't asking permission," Zamaya says, a dangerous, wire-trap edge to her even tone. "The Zenith is still in the city. We still have a shot at this."

"You are using that boy as an excuse for getting Miss Starbreach back. We both know how that ended up for Eris."

I flinch, and there's a pause where I think they must've seen me. But I'm out of sight.

Then Sheils goes, "Mwo?" Another pause, and then sharper, "No, tell me what that look was, Eunji."

Someone clears their throat. "Well, Soo Yun, as you may recall, Jenny has been working on those, uh . . . refinements to the Pilot Mods . . ."

It's Dr. Park. Mods? Refinements? What the—

"I know that," Sheils snaps. "Jenny is smart enough to get herself destroyed before they can think to look any closer at her."

Wrong move. I can feel the shift in the air from here.

"Fuck you." The pure poison in Zamaya's voice makes me shiver. Then she's moving toward the stairwell; I stand and step into the reach of the light. "Eris—"

"What's going on with Jenny?" At some point I changed out of the dress and into Nolan's sweatshirt; its large fit and the words coming out of my mouth make me feel exactly like a small child. "What refinements?"

Zamaya's gaze slips off mine. "I've asked Sheils to siege Ira Sol with the Hydras."

I know she's trying to throw me off, but it works anyway. "Taking them out of the Mutts?"

"It's not happening," Sheils says icily, arms crossed. She looks like she hasn't slept since I last saw her, silver hair coming out of a braid made days ago, everything about her posture tight.

"You have to." The words are nothing at all. Maybe ridiculous. Because Sheils doesn't have to do anything.

None of us ever have to do anything.

We could've all run by now, me and my kids, blissfully unconscious the next level up. The Gearbreakers would've damned us deserters, cowards, but they wouldn't have come after us, not like Godolia does to the ones trying to flee the villages. We've never had to fight, never had a gun to our heads telling us to hurry up and save the world, and yet, it's the funniest thing—we're here, again. In *pieces*, again, again, again.

Sheils fixes me with her black stare, lips curling. "You can ask any other Pilot to take their mecha out. You know how I run this place. The Hydras are underground, and they are sure as hells going to stay that way."

It happened after her first run, after Sheils came back and told her Pilots what their Windups had been built to do. They'd already known, of course, but seeing it in action is different. There'd been a resource village I'd never heard of that had blown their train tracks, that had waited for the Windups to come, and were ready for them when they did. They'd been planning for months, their forest set with trip wires and charges and pits filled with twenty-foot sharpened spikes. They took out a Berserker, a Phantom, and then a Valkyrie that came to put down the rebellion—an instance completely unheard of, save for a small brigade of people called the Gearbreakers that was gaining a reputation on the opposite end of the Badlands.

But they hadn't known about the Hydras. No one had known about the Hydras.

It was too wet in the rainy summer season for the Phoenixes to be effective, but Sheils didn't even have to enter the forest. Just stood at its entrance and uncurled those long fingers from those skeletal palms and let the poisonous gases pool into the undergrowth. She used a single tank, a single digit of her hand.

Jenny told me this. I don't know how she got the story out of Sheils. But doing the math, Sheils would've been about the same age as Jen. Not that Jen hasn't killed a lot of people, too. But that isn't really the point.

I look past Zamaya to drop my gaze directly on Dr. Park; her lips immediately press into a tight line.

"What refinements?" I say.

The doctor doesn't say anything, but whatever the truth is, I can tell she wishes it weren't.

"Okay, then!" I turn and stalk up the stairs, flinging on the lights to the infirmary as I barrel in. "Up! Time to get up!" I yank blankets to the ground, hands drumming on the metal bed frames. "I'm calling the Gearbreaker Council. Get the hells up!"

They've followed me up like I thought they would, Dr. Park looking bewildered and Sheils looking a little pissed.

"There is no Gearbreaker Council anymore, darling," Zamaya says, leaning her weight against the doorway.

"I'm a captain, and I'm the only one here. I'm eighteen. That means there's a Council. Look alive, soldier," I say, leaning over to pat Nolan's cheek.

"You're dead," he grumbles.

"You'll have to wake up and kill me first. Okay!" I realize, faintly, that I'm acting a little like Jenny. I stop in the aisle between the rows of beds and turn to face everyone. "Listen up! We're sieging Ira Sol."

Theo picks his head up from his pillow. "When?"

"As soon as possible."

"Ugh."

"Shut it. You're not coming."

"Wait, I was kidding—"

"You're shot." I point to Nyla. "Broken leg." I point to Nova. "Broken head." I point at Seung. "Also broken head."

"It was already like that," says Gwen, lying on her back with her strawberry-blond hair spilling over the footboard, brown eyes flicking up to me from between the bars. "Yours, too, apparently."

"We're getting Jenny."

That gets their attention. Sheils scoffs, brushing a strand of hair out of her eyes as she looks out to the hangar.

"We're going to multitask, Sheils," I snap, and something simmers in her expression.

"Yeah? You already tried killing the Zenith. Seems like your sister did, too. What makes you think you could do better?" she shoots back, but I'm ready for it.

"A larger scale. Jen was going for the kid—we're going for the city. We have the numbers and the Windups to hold it."

"But that's not your priority."

"Yes, it is." I laugh, and I'm surprised by the way it sounds. My voice is thin and bright from the exhaustion and maybe a slight hysteria, but my laugh comes out ragged. "Those Mech-vesper kids are going to become killing machines and Godolia is going to make them *grateful* for it. I didn't know there could be Badlands kids so faithful, but I saw it." It's the same thing Nyla was talking about with the Academy students. "Don't tell me what my priorities are. Godolia is giving kids an out from the shitty situation *they* created. Mods and mechas and killing, and it's going to be a form of worship to them. Tell me, I mean, I am *begging* you to tell me—how the hells is that supposed to be right?"

Sheils is laughing, too, and it matches mine in the complete cheerlessness. "You Gearbreakers are such *hypocrites*. Saving kids from killing, is that what you are doing here? Take a Godsdamn look at yourselves." She turns to snatch Zamaya's wrist, pulling her hand high and into the light, each brown knuckle marked with a gear. "When did you get your first tattoo? Your first kill? Ten years old, right? That is when they start throwing you headfirst into the mechas' path. You want to talk about what is *right*? None of you have retrospect of the chaos here. You are *children*, and you are so saturated with violence you cannot even see how wrong it is that you were forced into it in the first place. You are no different from the Academy students, you—"

She stops short. She realizes that even Zamaya isn't looking at her, that we're all looking around at one another. Waiting for her to get it.

"What?" Sheils demands, voice still hot. "What is it?"

"Sheils . . ." I cross my arms around myself, straighten as much as I can. My palms are flat, so I can feel my fingers against my ribs. "We know."

For a moment, she's just still. Hand still wrapping Zamaya's wrist, and then she drops it, pushing her fingers through her hair, tearing through the pleat of the braid. She laughs again, once and short, not furious anymore, just startled.

"I—Deities." I've never heard her use the word before, or stutter for that matter. Her black eyes drift across the room, the room full of battered kids, waiting to heal so they can do it all over again.

"We didn't ask for it, but this is what we are." We were told there were bad things going on in the world, and that we could stop it, and so we tried. We're still trying. "We shouldn't have to be like this. We don't want other kids to have to be like this."

I look at my crew's faces. Nova's head resting on June's arm. Theo and Arsen shoulder to shoulder, arms linked, now. Eons ago I looked at all of them from the limb of that Phoenix and told them to run. I'd take care of the Valkyrie, no problem, no fear—why would I have fear? Why would I waste myself like that?

But we are so far past that. We're in so fucking far over our heads we can't remember where the surface is. The world's too dark now to pretend the things that come out of the shadows don't scare us shitless.

I can't hide it. I'm terrified. We're all terrified, but it's not about us. So we're going to keep going anyway.

"Soo Yun . . . ," Dr. Park says gently, a hand resting on Sheils's sleeve.

The captain's surprise has slid away, replaced by an impassable expression. But it's the look in her eyes that makes this real.

I take a breath. It's not relief. It's not even to steady myself. It's just to move. *Okay. Okay.*

"Fine," Sheils says, teeth showing in her grimace, belladonna-twined fingers clenched at her sides. Suddenly I can picture her young, Jen's age with the fire to match, with Godolia promising her sanctity. But the deity they made her into wasn't divine, and it wasn't good. Sitting down here won't change that, and I think she knows it. "Well, Miss Frostbringer. You have your army."

CHAPTER TWENTY-SEVEN

SONA

"Holy hells," I whisper.

Jenny's black eyes trace a slow line across the lavish room from Enyo to me, standing still in my shock.

Should I be shocked? It's Jenny. She is capable of anything, and because she knows it—perhaps *just* because she knows it—she will do anything. But I never expected this.

A panel set into her arm. Opened, so the light can graze the silver sockets. Enyo's fingers pinched lightly to her nose, one hand around her mouth, to show me. I would be surprised that she was not trying to bite his hand off—maybe it is more Eris's style—if not for the glint in her eyes. She is liking the performance.

Enyo pulls his hold away. Jenny's chest still does not rise with breath, and she shoots me another grin, like there is absolutely nowhere else she would prefer to be. Even bound to a chair, Jenny suits the room—the library of what will be the Valkyrie floor—backlit by the midmorning cityscape in her red dress, the bruise eating the left side of her jaw tugged by the corner of her smile.

Enyo places her silk gloves on the reading desk at her right, straightens, and looks at me over his shoulder. My mouth drops open. He has the giddiest expression on his face.

"Good Gods," I say, "you are impressed?"

"What? It's pretty incredible."

"Ah, kamsahamnida, bitch boy," says Jenny, beaming.

"Aniyoh, aniyoh. I must give credit where credit is due," Enyo says. "Do you have a colored contact in?"

"Oh, I haven't really gotten around to the eye yet. But I'm going to design it so it can see color. That is actually an added feature, I found, the colorblindness—remind me to take yours out, Glitch. Just one of those subtle, suppressive shitty things they like to do. And I'm going to leave the artificial-nervous-system thing out of my vessel entirely. It's an incredibly sadistic and unneeded thing, you know—it was just implemented to give your Gods a weak point. Can't have all-powerful deities, right, E? It would defeat their whole purpose."

"Certainly," Enyo replies cheerfully. "And your purpose?"

"Huh?"

"What is your purpose, Noona?" His words hover pleasantly, the air of the room doubling in weight despite it. "When I heard of your split from the Gearbreakers, from Voxter—well, from you *splitting* Voxter—I found myself wondering."

Jenny puffs out a breath to send a strand of hair away from her eyes. "'Gearbreaker' is a mindset, darling. I didn't lose a part of myself by leaving. I left pieces of Voxter, here, there, yes, but I have all my own intact."

"And how did you know?"

"Know what?"

Enyo's smile is soft. "To leave him in pieces."

We would not have assumed that Jenny killed Voxter on our own. She had been kind enough to let us know.

Now I remember how, a few minutes after I had first met her, Jenny threatened to do to me what she did to him—relieve me of my limbs and deposit me at the bottom of a lake. And then I got to know her, and I thought her capable of it, capable of everything, but I still could not imagine it. I have seen her break noses and spit poison and build vicious, wicked things, but what she did to Voxter . . . I have the stomach for a lot, but it still chilled me to my core.

I think it scared us both, me and Enyo. Starbreach was enough of a legend to begin with. Then she leaves pieces of the Gearbreakers' founder—two limbs, two arms, a torso, and a head—in the corpses of six mechas, half-melted so everyone would know it was her, and she becomes something more. Not just a legend, but a horror story.

Jenny does not care who thinks her mad, or a sadist. She only cares what kind of world she will leave behind.

"I'm a people person," is all she says.

Enyo takes his time searching her expression. I cannot pull anything from it, but Enyo has those eyes, those ancient, diving eyes, and his voice is gentle when he says, "Does all the intelligence in your head burden you?"

"No." Now Jenny does look at him, dead-on. "But I'll let you rephrase, Zenith."

He smiles. "Do you wish you could see less of the world than what you do?"

She does not answer the question. She only leans forward and flashes a vicious, megawatt grin that draws frost through my veins. "Now you're getting it."

"Thank you," Enyo says, like he is truly grateful. And right there, something in the tone of his voice eases past before I can catch it. "And are you only being so pleasant because you believe you are getting out of here?"

Jenny frowns, but only slightly. Her eyes trace the room again, to the guards standing at the exit behind me, to the books on the shelves, to the clean fireplace, to Enyo. Then to me, and I can see, just like that, that she knows *I* am here, too.

"I'm unsure," she says thoughtfully, frown slipping. I can see her turning over the look on my face, the curl of my hands at my sides, the way Enyo is still breathing before her when I could have snapped his neck by now. She looks back up at the Zenith, chin tilting high so her bruise basks fully in the sunlight. "You're unsure, too."

His smile, like an expanding fracture in a looking glass, splitting the room with the weight of it. The sadness of it, the slow broil of something like anger, but not quite. Frustration, weighed by a tiredness so immense I feel it in my own chest.

He turns to me. I do not know when the knife appeared in his hand, so thin that it seems like a fragile thing even when he holds it out to me and I take it from him. Like I could just drop it soundlessly on the carpet and we could all pretend it was never here.

"Bellsona," Enyo says, head bent over mine, name carved into my temple. His voice is smooth, like it always is—his tell is in his fingers, how they lie just a little bit too tight around my wrist. Wanting to run, just a little bit. Eris once told me my tell was in my hands, too. One and the same, Enyo and I. Almost. The kind of likeness that could have made us despise each other, if we were not so desperate for each other.

It's why he waits until I look at him to say it.

"Kill her."

CHAPTER TWENTY-EIGHT

ERIS

When the sun comes up, the mechas crawl out of the mountain one by one.

The scene feels hauntingly familiar. Me, in the head of Sheils's Hydra Windup, watching as the glass mat rolls under her steps, cords spilling out of her opened forearms. June and Arsen stand on either side of me, looking out the eyes and into the dawn-streaked mountainscape. It's their first mecha ride.

Well, the first they've been invited to, anyway.

Thirteen Hydras. A Berserker, two Phoenixes, a Paladin, a Phantom. There wasn't a single defected Pilot who wanted out of the fight. It has to be enough.

The goal is to take control of the Badlands Academy sky-scraper, where the Zenith is. Sheils barked out the logistics as I trailed her through the Mutts hangar, surrounded by the screech of metal as Windup after Windup was eased open, God after God wound to bathe the cavern walls in searing red light. Some of the mechas hadn't been touched for forty years, since the Hydras defected en masse, but they move just fine.

But no gas. Sheils was clear about that. Her Hydras would use blunt force only.

The Paladin, the Berserker, and a Phoenix take the lower guard, a couple of miles away as we move east, to look out for the Windups that attacked us at the cabin. The Paladin can take a heavier hit than the Berserker, but hopefully neither of them will need to fight—they look just like every other one of their kind out there, save for the faded paint jobs. That's what we're hinging on, until we get close enough to the city that it's too late to call for backup from Peaks-patrolling Windups—Godolia thinks every God out there is on their side.

The Phantom and one of the Phoenixes go ahead of us to take point on the Leviathan guarding the river, which Sheils estimated had moved northward, in case we were planning to cross the water after fleeing the cabin. We didn't then, but that's the plan now, across the Gillian and then southward, where we'll hit the Academy campus first rather than the rest of the city. While our mechas surround the skyscraper, the Gearbreakers will go inside and find Enyo. And Jenny, if we can manage it. If she's still alive.

Nolan, Gwen, and Zamaya are in Astrid's Hydra. Best to spread out, you know, in case one of us doesn't make the trip.

The rising sun glances harshly off the river when we make the valley that borders the Gillian, everything brushed red through the Hydra's eyes. Down the slope of the land, about a half mile out, the Phantom and the Phoenix hesitate on the shoreline. The other Windups flank us left and right, holding steady. Sheils's head is tilted to the side, listening to the comms.

"Go," she says, and I know she's watching the lazy surface of the river.

The Phantom and the Phoenix wade up to their waists, slowly, and pause about a quarter of the way across the water.

Then they ease onto their stomachs, water smoothing over the massive limbs and the metal plates shifting musclelike on their backs as they begin to swim.

"The ground drops off," Sheils tells us, and I glance at her. When I look back at the water, both Windups have disappeared.

"Oh—" Juniper starts, and the river lights up.

"Move, move, move!" Sheils shouts, and I knock against my crew members as the Hydra begins to sprint. I push myself off the glass of the eyes, teeth gritted, and between the palms of my hands the Gillian is rushing up to meet us.

Water breaks from the surface in towering plumes, shot through with light and flame, and Sheils's Windup pitches left with a tremor that I can feel in my ribs. It throws me to my knees, and the river hisses against the glass as we go down.

That's when I see it—through the red glow cast by the Hydra, drawn down into the depths of the water, I see the Phantom writhing on its knees on the rocky bed of the river. Some large, dark thing is wrapped around it, a clawed, webbed hand peeling back the metal of the Phantom's cheek. The mecha flinches before going limp.

The Leviathan lifts its fishlike head, burning with a crimson gaze, and I realize why Sheils wanted to move—it needed to reload. She sent the first two Windups as torpedo fodder.

We step over the dead, blasted remains of the Phoenix and kick for the surface. I watch the Leviathan untangle from the Phantom and make for a nearby Hydra, plucking it down by its ankle as it tries to make for the opposite shore. The Godolia mecha's motions are effortless and fluid in the water, the fins on its back contorting in response to its movements to allow it to easily overtake the Hydra, sluggish in the resistant environment.

I've never been in a Leviathan's head—the only Leviathan takedown I've even heard of was by the infamous Gearbreaker Hookplunge, dead about twenty years now (hunted and caught by a Phantom), who caught one like a fish with a massive network of underwater wires lined with explosives. Their winding setup is different from the other models—the head of the Windup is already flooded, so the Pilot can swim rather than be tied to a glass mat, and it can take water into the rest of the mecha or dispel it, depending on its desired depth. Jenny thinks the entire design is brilliant. I think it's completely horrific.

I can tell Sheils wants to turn back for the snatched Hydra, but she doesn't. She just brings her head above the water when she can manage, and we're greeted by the lush greenery of the opposite shore and the valley bordering it, the dawn sky above peppered with flocks of retreating birds.

And then it's gone. Water froths against the glass, and we're back under the surface with a force that jars my teeth against my bottom lip. Sheils hits the glass mat with a choked gasp. I wipe the blood away from my mouth with the back of my hand and look to see her on her stomach, one leg lifted behind her. We've been grabbed.

"Shit—" Arsen breathes, on his knees with an arm clutching Juniper to his chest. "What—"

She bats him away and heaves herself to the Hydra's eyes, her hazel complexion paled and dyed red. The riverbed is angled beneath us as we're dragged deeper and deeper below the water. It levels out after what seems like forever—we must be four hundred feet below the surface now, dark except for lines of crimson light thrown by the mechas and the thin threads of sunlight cut short above our heads. It seems like there shouldn't be a river this deep, but Jenny did say this all used to be an ocean.

Sheils is flailing, fighting. She twists onto her back, chin thrown to her chest, and the violent pitch of the floor sends the rest of us toppling to the back of the Hydra's head. I brace myself on the skull to see Sheils's knee rising to her chest, extending slower than her real form could normally manage. There's a Leviathan braced over the Hydra, fins arched and cutting above us. Sheils delivers a push kick into its gut just as its three claws sink into her left side, right below where the ribs would be.

Sheils shrieks as the Leviathan is forced off her. For an aching beat, I remember Sona's scream on the frozen lake, Victoria digging into her Valkyrie's eye, looking for the physical Pilot.

"Three of them!" Juniper shouts, gaping up at the scene before us, a battle between Gods. She's right—there are two more Leviathans than we originally thought, not just the one guarding Ira Sol. They must have been called in from their guard at Ira Terra and Ira Luna. The riverbed is littered with fighting Hydras and pieces of the broken Phoenix and Phantom. The Phoenix's arm cannon extends toward us maybe seventy feet away, branching off a shoulder ruptured with cragged metal. One of the Leviathans ripped it apart by the neck.

"We need to help!" I yell, upright but unsteady on the angled floor. Sheils is halfway off her glass mat, but she's still connected to the cords. She's still fighting. "Sheils!"

"I'm fucking busy!" The Leviathan has circled back now, recovered from the kick and pushed off the riverbed. Sheils gets her hands raised just in time, her leg already up so her Hydra's knee catches the Leviathan in the ribs, and just like that, she's twisted and we're on top of it.

"Which one of your tanks is empty?" I flinch as the Leviathan's hand reaches to tear at our mecha's cheek, but Sheils knocks it away. "Sheils—!"

"Right hand, forefinger," she grits out, straining as she attempts to put her Windup's weight on the Leviathan's neck. "Why the hells—"

"We're going to blow the Phoenix's cannon. Get your right hand to it." I grapple for Arsen's sleeve, meet his wild eyes with my own, spitting my words rapid-fire. "What do you have?"

"Enough," he shoots back, and he, Juniper, and I are dropping down the ladder into the neck.

It's freaking dark, the artificial nerves always making for shit light, but it's even shittier now—from the chest down, their luminescence is submerged, only glowing in faint, useless bunches, and the water is rising fast.

"Go," I snarl, and we leap off the ladder to a beam, toward the churning, shifting part of the wall. Gearbreakers don't usually mess with a Windup's arms—they get narrower, and the gears and mechanisms there move a lot faster than the rest. Getting clipped means getting pulled in, which means most of the bones in that particular limb getting ground into meat paste.

The entrance to a mecha arm looks like a mouth about twelve feet across, with a ladder that extends from the entrance down into the bicep. Easy, except ringing this mouth are gears clicking all the way around, and the fact that this entire machine is twisting as Sheils defends herself. If she moves the wrong way, if she's knocked to her back or if she's knocked at all, we'll be shredded.

"I'm going," I say as the Hydra shudders around us. The

waterline has risen to about ten feet below us, sloshing down into the arm. "You're going to toss me what you have, Arsen, give me your bag—"

"I'll go, Eris—"

"Then you're going to get back into the head. I freaking mean it."

His mouth sets in a tight line. "In the front pocket. You'll want to pull the one in there last—it has a longer delay on it."

I wait for the barest lull in Sheils's movements and push off the beam. My feet pass over churning gears, and then the arch of my foot hits a ladder rung. I fall forward, pitching down into darkness, and catch myself inside the limb. I turn, and Arsen's haversack is already flying toward me.

When it hits my chest, as I catch it, a violent quake from the outside pandemonium shudders the whole mecha, and Sheils moves her arm. I'm torn out of view from them both, gripping onto the ladder, then coast back to see that Arsen is gone. He's in the water.

June doesn't even look at me before launching herself off the beam, just a streak of brown-green hair and then she's gone, too.

I'm frozen with panic. One arm clutches the haversack to my chest, the other seals me against the ladder, heartbeat a little cannon in each fingertip. Then water licks up and over the entrance of the limb, and I'm drenched and back in my body, and I'm crawling down. They're fine. Fuck, fuck, I need to—just don't *think* about—

The walls of the bicep are lined with artificial nerves, lighting the way to five massive metal tanks that ring the ladder just above the elbow. The water is really pouring in now, in my eyes and pasting my clothes to my skin, slick against the rungs as I turn my back to them.

Decay. Which one leads to the forefinger? Each tube spirals down into the hollow of the hand, already submerged. Holding my breath, I knock a fist against one of the tanks, then the next, and the next. *Thunk. Thunk. Clang*—again—*clang.* Hollow. Please be hollow.

I feel around the edge of the tank for the cap. It's about as big as my hand, set near the ladder. *Think, think*, I beg myself as I twist it open, holding my breath—according to Jen's story about Sheils, it should be empty, and if not—don't think about it.

The cap's off and in my hand, no poison fumes sloughing the skin from my fingers. I let the cap drop into the abyss, sucking in air as another stream of frigid water douses me from above. The river's filled the Hydra's arm up to my ankles now, sloshing into the open tank—good, good, we'll use that to carry the bombs.

There's something in the Hydra's fingers, or maybe the wrist, that changes liquid poison to poison gas. It won't filter something as solid as a grenade, which is what we seem to be working with—and a *lot* of them.

"Good Gods, Arsen," I breathe, peering into his bag.

So. First grenade will get lodged in and blow apart the hand. The second batch will have free leave of the mecha. Any one of them get into that Phoenix cannon, filled with gasoline—that's our out.

I run my hand along the side of the arm, across a length of artificial nerves. The water in the tank immediately starts sucking down—Sheils got the message. The mecha feels like it's braced, defending from a hunched position—over the Phoenix, hopefully. I just have to trust Sheils. And she's absolutely going to murder me for this.

I pull a grenade from the haversack. The pin goes between my teeth, and I drop the explosive into the tank. In the back of my head, I know Arsen artistically put labels denoting fuse times on the handles, but I don't think I remember how to read right now. Let's go with seven. *Seven. Six. Five*—pull another pin, drop, another pin, drop, another—*boom*.

The water almost immediately jumps up to my midthigh.

Rot. The rest feels autonomous, the movements ticking off my body: I overturn the bag, grenades spilling into the tank and dropping down below, rip the delay bomb from the front pocket, pull it, drop it, ditch the bag, climb climb climb for my life.

This water, cold and quick and up to my waist—it's probably filled with poison, too. It's the inhalation of it that'll kill me, but still, it can't be good for me.

I make it to the top of the ladder. The water in the arm is up to my neck now, and still more of it is pouring down onto me from the torso; I'm choking on it, trying to see past it and the path *out*, and realize I have to wait for it to overtake me. I can't swim up a waterfall and past those limb gears. I'll have a better shot once it's flooded.

If you discount the whole drowning thing, but you know, semantics.

What the hells am I doing? I think as the water crawls up my cheek, past my nose once I take a full breath. *I am so gearfood, I am so freaking d—*

Boom.

Is there another word for it? Because this is different from the first blast. I feel the tremor ring through me, like my body is completely hollow, and I'm thrown clean off the ladder.

Black, then bright stars. The small of my back smashes against something wide and hard, and then I'm pinned against it, blind, below water, with the oxygen knocked out of me.

This is it. This is it, and it hurts—

A hand clamps around my wrist, then three, and my head's above the surface, gagging on air. Arsen and June hold on to me, and as one we kick for the ladder running into the neck. Spots bleed against my vision as I cling and force myself up the rungs, spilling out in a limp heap in the head. June and Arsen, both with a matching, rapid string of profanity, turn and seal the skull hatch.

I tilt onto my forearms, vomiting up water, and choke out, "Sheils—"

We're moving. Sheils is on her knees and on a single hand, the other lifeless at her side, the riverbed beneath us. The left eye is cracked, water leaking in a glossy sheen onto the floor. But it holds. It holds, and then the sun is shining in, and the mecha shudders as it collapses onto the shoreline, which means Sheils collapses. The floor goes completely upright beneath us as she slides headfirst toward the side of the head, but Arsen plants his feet against it and catches her by the waist. I crumple against the metal skull alongside Juniper, everything aching.

"Deities," June rasps, my soaked ribs pressed against her soaked ribs. "Let's never do that again."

"Did it work?" I breathe, staring out the eyes. A handful of Hydras stand against the backdrop of the mountains, others unmoving against the grass, dropped there like unwanted dolls. "Did—"

Down the river, I see a single Leviathan arm, half-submerged and gleaming with the risen sun as it floats along.

"It worked. Phoenix bomb. Gotta jot that one down for later," Arsen says thinly, ripping out Sheils's cords.

Sheils snaps back into her body and shoves away from him, then wraps a hand around my arm and lifts me to my feet. Her gray hair is loose from its tail, curls pasted with sweat against her temples.

"Sorry—" I start.

"We need to move to another mecha," she snarls, both eyes burning. "They know we're coming now."

CHAPTER TWENTY-NINE

SONA

Enyo knows.

Could he tell right away, even after seeing that the thought of him dead *destroyed* me, that I was not the same person I was when I left?

That I was not the same person he made me into?

Not entirely. The part of me he made, but did not intend to—that is what hovered. The part of me that loves him viciously.

The part of me I could not carve out if I wanted to, and I *don't*, because it only hurts when I weigh it against the part that needs to end this, that needs to avenge myself.

So I hold the knife. I walk over to Jenny with his eyes on the back of my head, and then on my cheek as I turn, backlit by the cityscape.

I cut her left binds first, then her right.

Jenny laughs, rolling her head to look at me, and I can see all the way down her throat as the sound crawls up and out, sharp and harsh against the softness of the library.

"Okay," Enyo says quietly, and his voice *breaks* on the single word.

Then Jenny snatches the dagger from my hand and lunges for him.

"No!" I move, faster than I ever have in my life, between

them now and knocking her arm off course, but she seems to expect it and Enyo barks at the guards to stand down as she grabs me and we crash into the nearby reading desk.

I try to move my fist, but there's resistance, glance to find my sleeve pinned to the surface by the tip of the knife. A round paperweight has materialized in Jenny's palm, leveled above my head, and I remember the first time she tried to kill me, on the Winterward ice a million years ago. She hesitated then, like she hesitates now.

I drive my knee into her stomach and snap my shin to her ribs, twist as she spirals back to wrench the knife from my sleeve. And then we are both frozen, sudden quiet dropping over the room.

Enyo's eyes are already on mine when I look at him, our mouths twisted, both our chests heaving with the same hurt.

"Gada," he rasps to Jenny.

She laughs again, but the sound is frayed this time. She runs a hand through her hair, a nervous gesture I recognize from Eris, but I have never seen Jenny do it herself. "What do you mean, 'go'?"

"I said *go!*" He takes ahold of a lamp and sends it crashing into the bookshelf just behind my head, splinters spraying my curls. It startles me so much I drop the knife, the blade soundless against the plush rug. "Go! Just fucking leave!"

The guards at the door step forward, unsure, and he turns on them with the same rage. His features are naturally sharp, all fine lines, but the pretty delicateness in every edge has dissolved under the dark roll of his voice.

"Let her pass or I will have you strung up in the courtyard alongside the renegades."

Jenny comes closer to me. At first I think she is going to

attack again; my shock is so complete I do not think I could stop her. Enyo has never lost it like this, not in front of me. After Heavensday, his collectedness wavered, but it has never shattered like it does now.

But Jenny only leans over a little to pluck her silk gloves from the reading desk, taking her time pulling them on and up to her elbows. She gives me a glance out of the corner of her eye, then glides past Enyo. She winks at him, but he is not as amused as he was a couple of minutes ago. Neither is she, not one twitch of a smile across her smeared lipstick.

Jenny pauses between the guards. Turns, and—because of course she does—savors the moment she walks out alive.

And I think, for a second, that she cannot possibly understand *why*. Then she looks at me.

"You two are good for each other," she says, but what she is really saying is, *You two are really fucking each other up.*

And then she is gone. Enyo sends the guards to the hallway, closing the doors himself. They shut with a thud I can feel in my throat.

I feel numb. "You let her go."

He laughs, cheerless. "Yeah," he says, sounding like he hardly believes it himself. "I think I should care more."

Then Enyo turns back toward me and just . . . sinks.

He lets me pick up the knife from the rug.

Lets me stand before him, blade trembling in my hand.

My palm on his shoulder, now. Push him to the floor, and I am on my knees. The tip of the knife stills over his heart.

His hands splay limp, unmoving, unprotecting, one wrist grazing my shin.

I remember that day we moved his desk, letting the iced tea glasses sweat puddles onto the floor while he worked on the ground with his feet up against the window, and I counted the times he glanced up at me just to give me a smile.

His lips part, but he says nothing. Waiting for me.

What am I waiting for?

I bare my teeth, the sob coming soundlessly. "Where do I put all this *hate* you gave me?"

This entire time, I have hated myself. For what I did to this city, to him. His kindness saving me and sickening me all at once.

And now, I realize that hate was familiar. Not a manufactured feeling from the corruption—no, it'd been in me for a long time now. But in a different position.

Clever, really, how they did it.

But I can recognize it, now. Where it used to be, because before, I only had hate for one thing.

Corruption took the hatred I had for Godolia and shifted it onto myself.

"I wanted to die," I say quietly, and Enyo makes this small, choked sound. I never said it out loud before, could barely bring the thought to the surface. But I know it was always there. I think he knew that, too. My voice cracks. "You did that to me."

One of his arms rises, presses over his eyes, sleeve blotting the tears on his cheeks. Just for a moment before he seems to force it away. The anger is completely gone from his features, evaporated like it knew its host was not built to sustain it.

He meets my eyes with that look that gets me every single time, the one that peels me back and leaves me feeling bare and wholly, entirely unjudged for it. It's his apology, this stillness. Because he can never, ever afford to be that kind of person out loud.

"Say something." The heat breaks in my eyes. I double over, knife blade beside his ear. *Let it sink.* I *can't.* "Say something!"

His hand lifts, and gently settles on the back of my head. I break. Brow to his collarbone, knife still balanced in one hand.

"I'm sorry," he says. "I was so scared. They needed a miracle."

Me. A soul saved. A vessel returned home.

Gearbreakers dead in the grove.

A nation held up by its belief in a child Zenith, small in the face of the power he has, crushed under the weight of a billion souls that are his responsibility in this frantic, feral world.

"It was never your loyalties, Sona." Voice hoarse and heavy, fingers in my hair. "They were never real. They are not why I grew to love you. I—I didn't mean to. You were not meant to see."

"See what?" I whisper.

He turns his head, and I lift mine. Kisses my wrist, and says, "That I do not want to be this."

Can you see? In my Valkyrie, wires feeding divinity into my veins. *Can you see I am not* this?

Can we not want to be alone, here?

"I'm scared, too," I say. "I am sorry, too."

CHAPTER THIRTY

ERIS

"This isn't right," Sheils mutters.

We're with Jen's crew, all gathered in Astrid's Hydra—which cleared the river battered but still functional—making our way south to the city. The walls should have been teeming with Windups by now, anything and everything the Zenith had to throw at us. But besides an Argus on patrol farther north and a Berserker that coasted closer to the city—maybe coming off its own shift—both of which other members of Sheils's unit took out, there's no one.

Then we're over the valley sloping down the back side of the Academy and into the city, one rogue mecha after the next. It's not even noon.

"Look," Gwen breathes beside me as we reach the gardens. I follow her gaze, prepped for the worst—like I have been this entire time. But it's just a helicopter, black with double sets of rotors, clearing the river and making its way east.

Dread, heavy and cold, drops into the base of my stomach.

There's about two thirds of our Windups left after the fight with the Leviathans. Half of those drift off to the wall bordering the river, the others gathering in a loose ring around the Academy. Astrid's is the closest, and it's down the ladder and out the heel and then we're on the Academy steps, Zamaya leading with an arrow already nocked.

But we pause outside the two-story entry doors. Because they're open, welcoming us into the hall where I danced with Sona barely more than a day ago.

Zamaya, more furious than I have ever heard her before, growls, "What the *hells*."

Jenny is sitting on the floor, facing the windows looking into the courtyard. My first bewildered thought is that they never cleaned up the hall—Jen's made a plate of food for herself from the uncleared banquet table, untouched on the ground next to her skirt. Which means they definitely haven't removed the Gearbreaker bodies. My second thought is also, *What the hells*, but it comes with no anger, just blank shock.

Zamaya runs toward Jenny, dropping to her knees and crawling the last few feet, and then Jen's head is pressed between her tattooed hands. I don't hear what they're saying to each other; I make it to them as Jenny is shaking her head, and I spit viciously, "Where is he?"

Jen's lips part, no sound coming out from the dark, smeared lipstick—I realize she's at a loss for words. She has never, *ever* been at a loss for words before, and it scares me. And then I remember seeing the penthouse lights from across the river, the only lit level once the alarms stopped blaring.

Then I'm running for the elevators. He'd be up there, with the best view, the golden fucking spot. June and Arsen shout and take off after me down the adjoining hallway. There's an unconscious guard slumped by a set of double doors beside the elevators—Jenny's work, surely—and I lean over to snatch the key card clipped to the inside of her jacket. Out of the corner of my eye, open doors; I see the room she was watching is full of Badlands recruits and their families, still dressed up and looking out of place for it, shrinking in on themselves when Juniper and Arsen catch up to me and see them, too. They exchange a look with one another, and that's when I go through the elevator doors and slide the key card home, finger jabbing the button for the penthouse suite.

The doors close ridiculously fast, June and Arsen looking thrown through its split before it seals, and then it's quiet, and I'm alone, and I sink against the glass overlooking the cityscape.

That helicopter. The coward *fled*, I *know* it. I'm shooting up toward an empty room, toward the next bad feeling. I could pull the emergency stop, but what good would it do. I have to keep moving. I have to keep moving or everything is going to catch up to me and I'm just going to—

Would killing the Zenith really make it better? Better for everyone else, maybe, but for *me*? I'm being selfish—*no*, maybe I'm just fucking wondering, because all I'm trying to do is keep more people from dying in droves, but I'm *rotting* for it all the time now—do I not get to at least *wonder*?

The elevator doors open. There is a knife strapped to my hip, and I free it as I step up the still corridor, boots silent against the dark hardwood floor. Mirrors hang against wallpaper detailed with small flowers; I pass a room with the entrance ajar, and look into an empty kitchen with gleaming countertops. A split in the hall is set with a teeny sitting area, delicate-looking chairs with pillows and a low table holding a rock garden.

More doors to the left; to the right, two slack bodies, throats slit, blood drying against their guard uniforms.

I step over them into what looks like a library. There's a chair set oddly in the center of the space, a bundle of cut ropes settled below the armrests. Pieces of a shattered lamp.

Papers thrown all over the carpet, blank spots blotted all over the room.

I drop the knife. I wrap my arms around myself.

The midday light has turned hazy, long clouds dragging across the sky. By the window, she stands in the soft glow. Still in her tattered suit, collar messy with the buttons undone.

Sona turns toward me. "Eris?"

And I know.

I know it in the way she says my name, and when she says it again her voice breaks, and I do, too. I step forward, and there's no clashing, desperate kiss, just us around each other, like all the wayward threads I had been carrying inside me find their ends in all the ones she possesses, untangled lines.

"Oh Gods," I whisper, lips to her shoulder, her arms around mine, so tight I can't breathe, so close I don't want to. "OhGodsohGodsohGods—"

"I'm sorry," she whispers. She buries her face in my hair. "I could not do it."

"Couldn't do what, love?"

"Do not hate me."

"Never, never."

I feel her breath stutter up her chest. Then, "I let him go."

CHAPTER THIRTY-ONE

SONA

Four Months Later

I have an odd dream. I think, I think . . . but I flinch awake, chest heaving, and it's—gone.

I am here.

She's here.

Here, under dry, cool air sliding out from the vents, muted under the weight of the blankets, light dulled in that soft, early-morning way. The feel of Eris with one set of toes under my knee. I breathe. My heartbeat levels.

Staring at the light striated on the ceiling, I pick away the curls sticking to the sweat on my temples and ease upright. Eris is on her stomach with a hand stretched out across my ribs in her sleep; now it falls to my lap, and I drop my head to brush my lips against her bare shoulder.

"Good morning," I murmur, admiring the way the black, feathery lashes lie against her cheekbones. "Do you want coffee?"

"Rot," Eris slurs, chin sinking farther into the pillow. Then, after I put my mouth to her neck and she pushes me back, lightly, "Tea."

I pull on her T-shirt—hem only reaching my waist, which I kind of love—and a pair of boxers and wander down the hall to the kitchen. Juniper is leaning over a steaming tea kettle when I come in, and plants a kiss on my cheek as her greeting, sliding a mug to me. She is an early riser, too—unlike Arsen, who's sitting upright and asleep on the tiled floor beside her legs.

I wrap my hands around the warm porcelain, stamped with the Valkyrie insignia. This would have been their floor, if the Badlands Academy had ever opened—the penthouse usually would be reserved for the Zeniths, if this were Godolia and not the Badlands. But it is, and so there are Valkyrie jackets in every closet, and Enyo is back safe in his city. Perhaps wondering how best to blow this entire place off the map.

"I like the new hair," I say, pushing the thought away. The silk of steam rises from my cup and warms my cheeks.

"Thank you." Juniper grins and pinches a strand of pale blue between her fingers. It was pink yesterday, violet the month before that. Eris and I cannot figure out where the hells she's getting the dye. "It's for my confidence."

"Checking the mine charges today?"

She nods. "Every week for forever."

"At least it's working."

Not the explosives, exactly—we are all hoping we never have to see if those work. But the idea of them is what we rely on, how we are holding the city and why an army of Godolia Windups is absent from the city's outskirts. Jenny and Captain Sheils came up with it. Ira Sol, Ira Luna, and Ira Terra sit atop the most significant ore vein in the entirety of the Badlands—but Ira Sol holds the richest part of it. It could supply Godolia for the next three hundred years. That means leverage.

That means Jenny planted magma charges to destroy the

entire underground mining system if we ever saw a single enemy Windup within ten miles of the Ira Sol border.

Godolia is operating on the same assumption that it always has—all rebellions, eventually, will be killed. So it becomes a delicate balance, then. The stronger the Badlands-controlled Ira Sol gets, the more likely it becomes that Godolia will think to cut its losses. The more likely it becomes that Enyo will give an order to turn it all to ash.

The kitchen doors swing open. It's Nyla, grinding her Mod eye under the heel of her hand, yawn splitting the air.

"Nice shirt," she mumbles, hand skimming across my upper arm in a sleepy greeting. "And nice hair, June."

"I'm pretty," Juniper notes brightly, and nudges a foot against Arsen. "Get up, please. I'm ready to go."

Arsen gives a half wave as he is dragged away. Nyla traces a thoughtful finger around the rim of her mug as I fill up one for Eris.

"Big plans today?" she asks.

"Refugee placement," I say. "You?"

"Patrol." She smiles. It's a shy one, and nice. "Along the tracks."

"Riveting."

"It is."

We mean it, the feeling in my chest something whole and warm. I almost did not believe Eris when she told me about the Mutts Pilots—the defectors, the ones like me. It's nice, being here with Nyla, on this side of things. She looks like me.

Back in our bedroom, I set Eris's tea on the side table and make the bed while listening to her rummage through the closet. After a minute she stomps out in her bra, the strap of her overalls unclipped and folded over her legs.

"Hey, I was looking for that shirt," she snaps, always so cheery first thing in the morning.

I look at the plane of her pale stomach before taking a slow sip of her tea, then set it on my knee and say, "Come get it."

A stonelike look crosses her face as she steps over to stand between my thighs. I put my palm to her cheek, thumb following the fine line of her jaw, and just before our lips can touch, Eris moves her face away and takes the cup from me. She leans away to take a sip while her hand wanders up my bare side, and my breath is coming quicker now, the innocent clink of the mug against the table, and her mouth smells like tea as it draws from my collarbone to my neck. I drop my chin to catch her sooner, a shortcut.

The same jolt every time. When I expect the good part to be over, it hovers instead.

"I *just* made the bed," I say once she pulls back to take off my—her—shirt, on my back now and her with her ribs against mine.

"You did a good job."

My fingers skipping down the ridges of her spine, I tilt my head toward the door as Eris drags her lips just under my jaw. "Th-that's your sister's knock."

"Go away!" Eris calls harshly, voice barbed, pressed closed to my skin, but the door opens anyway. She kisses me again, unperturbed, words coming out in the spaces she comes up for air. "I said—rot—what do you want?"

"To avoid a mass famine today, and maybe tomorrow, too,"

Jenny says, gliding in and stopping short before the mirror hung on the wall.

It's only when Eris notices Jenny left the door ajar that she scrambles off me; Jenny is not one to poke fun, or care enough to do so, but the crew certainly will—not in ill spirit but because Eris *hates* it. I sit upright, the back of my hand against my mouth to clear the wetness. Then I pull on her shirt again. She shoots me a quick, vicious look before grabbing mine from the desk chair, clips her overalls into place, and asks hurriedly, "Did Ira Terra send the food shipments?"

"No. Wirefuckers." Jenny puffs out a breath, then whirls from the mirror with her hands on her hips. She is wearing her dark gray canvas jacket—even though it's the middle of summer—to hide her arm panels. My throat goes a bit dry.

This was the trade-off: Jenny tweaks my Mod eye so I can see color, and I do not mention to Eris that her sister is turning herself into a Pilot piece by piece. *Unless she asks, of course*, Jenny had added with a wink, because Eris won't ask. Because it's such a ballistic thing to do that Eris won't even think to consider it.

It is ballistic, and dangerous, and she did it because she wants to protect everyone as much as possible.

And I know this is a secret and it's bad I am keeping it from Eris, but I also know she would understand why I am, because I am doing it for Jenny. Jenny is what is holding this all together, this fragile safe haven, a heavy and volatile thing. People are scared. They might be scared of starving or Mechvespers or the Gearbreakers or Godolia, but fear is the core of it, and that breeds panic. That is what can destroy everything.

"Did they not send it, or has the train not arrived?" I ask.

"The former would mean the latter, Glitch," Jenny sighs. She kicks her way over to the window, pulling up the blinds, morning cityscape gleaming in silver angles. One long fingertip drums on her bottom lip. "But yes, yes, what we do know for sure *is* the latter." She twists a strand of hair around her fingertip thoughtfully. "Why am I in here, you ask? Looking for that June girl. We might have to blow up some mine tunnels if we figure the delay is intentional. If they're finally trying something."

Ira Sol is the southmost of the Ore Cities; Ira Terra the northmost, with Ira Luna set between them where the Gillian curves. Terra has the fields that feed all three of them. No one wanted to have ties to Godolia, but when that first food train came to a stop outside the north border, and we checked it head to toe and found nothing but viciously needed supplies, we took it.

We keep taking them, scanning every single one. No one has died from poisoning, and the train doesn't explode on the tracks feeding into the inner city.

Ira Sol is the infrastructure we needed, to house Badlands people needing somewhere to run to, but there were fifty thousand people already here. None of the Iras are like any of the other resource villages that Godolia will simply raze when they step out of line. The Cities do not step out of line. The people here are another piece of capital Godolia thinks will be eventually returned. But not if they starve.

That is what most of us figure, that it's why the trains keep coming in.

I do not think I would be the only one if I dared to think differently.

These past few months, Jenny keeps stealing looks at me,

and me at her. Waiting for one of us to voice it. And Eris is quiet, but I can tell when she is thinking about it. How it might be true.

That Godolia is not merciful, but Enyo might be.

Eris rubs her eyes. "June and Arsen probably caught the shuttle to the mines already."

"Yeah, fine, I'll meet them there." Jenny turns to leave, then pauses abruptly at the door. "They're being safe, right?"

Eris draws her hands away from her face. "Huh?"

"I don't need another mouth to feed."

"Oh my *Gods*—" Eris shrieks.

"Well, with you two I don't need to—".

"*Ace*, Jen! They're ace! Out!" Eris barks.

"Yeah, that doesn't necessarily mean—"

"Deities, obviously, Jen, but I know they—oh my Gods? But it's none of your business? Can you just *leave*—"

I throw Eris a glance that she immediately catches—I *love* that, that she is already looking straight at me. "Wait," she says to Jenny.

But her sister is already walking away, ignoring us, and I follow Eris out into the hallway as she heads for the elevator.

"Jenny," I call, "if we are having problems with the supply line, then ... the refugees ..."

Jenny jabs at the elevator button. "We're not turning anyone away."

"Are we telling anyone?" asks Eris, slowing beside me, about ten feet away when Jenny steps into the elevator. The weight of the air has shifted so quickly—it seems better to keep our distance.

I hear the chime of the key card reader, and then Jenny faces us, hand dragging through her hair. Through the closing elevator doors, she says quietly, and without a smile, "You two. Always with the destructive tendencies."

CHAPTER THIRTY-TWO

ERIS

In the sudden silence of the hall, Sona threads her fingers through mine, squeezing. "Hey."

"Hey."

"Are we good?"

Milo used to ask me that, or I would ask him that, after our stupid fights, after he'd make me feel bad or I'd make him feel bad; that's how we thought we'd end it, fix it, with a question shot like a challenge. *Are we good?* was always just *Are we done with the current bullshit?*

This is so far from that. It's *I'm asking because I'm good if you're good.* It's better.

I squeeze back. "We're good."

"Whoa—" I grab a little kid's arm as he tries to wriggle by, shoved out of the line of people making their way toward the shuttles waiting by the water gate docks. His bare feet shuffle on the wood platform. "Who'd you come with?"

He pokes one of those jabby little-kid fingers into one of my exposed tattoos. "Cool."

"Stop that," I snap, eyeing Sona through the crowd. She's at one of the wooden stalls handing out backpacks—filled with rice, water, bandages, thread, tea bags, a few other sundries—to the refugees as they drift off the boat. She's laughing at me now, and hides it behind her hand when I shoot her a glare. I straighten, the boy's wrist still in my grip. "Hey! Anyone's—uh—child?"

A black-haired lady in her thirties, fuming and distressed, bats her way out of line. "Rohan, I am going to—oh! Oh. You're the Frostbringer."

I flash a thrilled grin—I legitimately can't help it—and smother it. "Here's your kid."

"Appreciate it." She smooths an absent palm down his unruly curls. He lets it happen.

"Yeah. Where are you coming from?"

"Sahil."

My breath stutters for a moment, but I manage to say, "Sahil, huh? That's a rough go, getting to the port from that ravine pass."

"Took about three days, yes. I thought it was wasted effort when I saw the mechas on the shore, but the boat just passed them by." She throws a tired, thin hand over her shoulder, at the ferry moored at the docks, the one that putters up and down the Gillian collecting any refugees it happens across. It took a while, but the Hydras got the message spread decently far across the Peaks and the Badlands deserts—Ira Sol is taking everybody. Resource village residents, runaways, deserters. You want out from under Godolia's thumb, you make your way here. "Turns out they were there to escort, not to slaughter."

Now my throat is dry, too. "Strange, huh?"

She smiles dazedly, turning her dark eyes toward the city. "Yes. I don't think that's changing anytime soon."

Another ferry unloaded, another shuttle full of Badlands

refugees peeling off for the empty residences, for a whole other life. Families go into apartments in the city, individuals to the vast number of empty rooms at the Badlands Academy, which is now the Gearbreaker headquarters.

The boat heaves away from the docks for the open water gate, back on another round. We've had a small fleet going non-stop for the past few months. During the first few weeks they were full of people when they left Ira Sol, too—Mechvespers, fleeing for the other Godolia-controlled Cities. We're not turning anyone away, and we're not forcing anyone to stay who wants to go. Jenny says deproselytizing the general population is a waste of time; I can't help but agree with her.

But most Mechvespers have stayed. I know it's probably that they believe Godolia's reclamation of Ira Sol is inevitable. It even might be that they're scared to leave—from what they've been taught about the Gearbreakers, it's a reasonable theory for them that we're just shooting whoever is gullible enough to get on the ferries. But there have been some outliers. Showing up at the Academy, literally just walking straight out of their apartments and up to the front doors, saying, *If this is real, I want to help.*

I cross the docks and lean my weight across the countertop of Sona's stall. She's dropping small pouches of sunflower seeds into half-filled backpacks. I shift one closer to her, and she thanks me with a kiss on my cheek.

"What is it?" she asks when she pulls back. Her curls are gathered in a short tail away from her face, but a few of them have escaped the elastic to touch against the fine corners of her eyes, softened in their concern. Of course she can tell something's off.

"That lady and the kid were from Sahil."

"Oh." She sets the next sunflower pouch down. "Did they—"

"Know it's nothing but craters now? Didn't seem like it."

We got the report about a day ago. It goes like this: The Badlands-controlled city of Ira Sol is inviting everyone, but if Godolia catches wind that their resource village is emptying due to people accepting that invitation, there are going to be Windups coming to take it off the map. We're getting steady numbers now, but it should be more. Much more. Jenny's and my crews will do a run when we can, but it's hells leaving the city now. It seems like the Zenith has thrown most of his army into the Peaks—they touch any of our boats, the mines are done for—but besides that, it's all still Godolia territory.

I roll my cheek on the heel of my hand. "We should be—"

Sona's long fingers rest on top of mine. "This is important, Eris. What we are doing."

"I know. It's just—"

"Quiet?"

"Yeah."

She leans closer. Her hand presses on mine with a sudden fierceness, and her voice has gone dark when she says, "Be grateful for it."

"You are completely creepy sometimes."

"I am serious, Eris," she snaps, drawing her touch away, picking up the next seed pouch with slightly more aggression.

"Hey, whoa. I know." I fold my arms around myself to keep from reaching for her. "I like the quiet. You know I do." We're on the empty sprawl of the docks, completely alone. A few months ago it would have been dotted with workers prepping mecha piece shipments, but now it's just the low, muffled buzz of the city a mile off and the soft sound of the water chewing at the concrete posts. It's muted enough that I can hear when she breathes if I pay attention—which I do, always, without even thinking about it.

"It's just . . . this isn't quiet. Not really."

Because we're not just here to guide the refugees from the ferry to the shuttles. Anyone could've been assigned to do that. We're meant to pick people out of the crowd, if we think they need to be picked. It would only take one decent spy to bring this whole place down.

So there's no one on the docks but us. It's getting to be high summer, and the day is a rare one—clear skies, morning mist burned off by the sun hours ago. And yet. I'll wake up in our bedroom or be in the Valkyrie library with the crew, a night storm beating at the windows, and it'll be better for a few hours, but I know it's waiting for me: the feel of the air, taut like a hair-wire trap, like it feels now.

I'm nervous all the time, and it's fraying me, and I'm . . . embarrassed by it. I don't tell her. And I don't tell her I'm not sleeping as well as she thinks I am.

"Next boat's coming in," I murmur, turning for the water as the ferry rounds the corner. Then Sona catches my wrist.

"Eris," she says, leaning halfway over the counter to reach me; it kind of looks ridiculous, but her eyes are steady on mine. "Give it time."

I open my mouth just as a thin, cheery shriek splits the air. "Heeeeeeyyyyyy!"

I thought it was a ferry, but it's a smaller vessel, one that turns on a dime right before it hits the docks to send water sloshing all over the concrete. Nova's at the wheel, of course, Theo looking a little pale at her side. They spend the day taking trips around the Gillian while the ferries do their routes—which sounds fun, but what they're looking for is water mines and Leviathans, especially since we haven't had *any* sightings of the latter in a few months. Because that would be the best move, wouldn't it, gathering the mechas to block the waters, stopping the supply trains, leaving the city to just choke on itself.

I can't help but think it's because of Sona.

The Zenith let Jenny go for her, just for the chance to talk to her, because he saw that he had lost her. Would he let this city go, too, for her?

I check the time with the sun, and call, "You're not supposed to be back yet."

"Yeah," Nova shouts back, "Zamaya radioed us—we're supposed to collect you. We're checking on that food train that's missin', where the tracks run beside the river. Some Hydras are coming to take you guys's next shift."

Then it's better again. Nova's grinning like she can't help it, wind sweeping her hair back—she's started bleaching it religiously again, and the sunlight blanches it almost colorless. Theo shrieks, huddled below her, clinging to her pant leg as she jerks the wheel just to mess with him. Sona and I sit at the pointed bow of the speeder, one of her ankles twined with mine and a leg stretched across the gap to brace next to my hip. We're heading north, fast, Novs hugging the shore as close as she dares.

I talked with Zamaya on the radio when we boarded—apparently our Windups tagged the train just outside Ira Sol territory, almost midway between our border and the walls of Ira Luna, dead on the tracks.

Sona and I have talked about it before, often, that the only reason we've held Sol is because we control Gods. The awe factor of the Hydras means we've created a viable heaven, even without a Zenith. Droves of the Mechvespers still gather at the city's edges when our Windups come back from their daily patrols, lips pressed to fingers and then to their eyes as they bow their heads. It's one of the most ridiculous and frightening things I've ever seen.

It's terrifying, the power of the Mechvespers' beliefs, and it's terrifying how it's probably what's keeping them from taking up arms themselves. We couldn't do much to stop them besides having our mechas flatten them in the streets—which, *dark*—but besides that, we are vastly, laughably outnumbered.

But it's been a few months. Jenny's finding her stride; Sheils is raising up an army of more Pilot defectors, the mountain hangar filling up slowly but surely with Windups that we control.

Now I can see the gray-black body of the train, alien and harsh against the line of the water and the lush valley sweeping up at its west side, dotted with wildflowers bending lazily under the breeze. There's no smoke or damage I can see, no visible reason it's come to a standstill, the note churning static in my chest. *Something's off.*

"Stay in the boat," I say when Nova pulls closer to shore, and step from its edge onto the gravel outlining the tracks. It crunches under my boots.

"Hey!" Theo protests. "But Glitch—"

"I wasn't talking to Glitch. Back!" I snap my fingers when Nova loosens hers from the wheel.

Sona lands on the ground beside me, throws them a winning smile over the line of her shoulder. "It's all right. We will just be a moment."

"When did I lose all authority?" I mutter as we pick our way toward the train, leaving the boat and the two fuming kids behind. "Oh, and hey—when the hells did you take it?"

She chuckles. The sound carries mutedly against the empty stretch of land. "You are paranoid, Captain."

"Oh no, love, what I mean is please, *please* do a coup. You're already so close, and I am so very tired."

"You are not excellent at taking orders."

"I'm excellent at everything." A beat. "Confirm, soldier."

Her mouth twists as she tries to hide her laugh, cheek turning away so her freckles catch the sun. "Ah. Love you."

I feign pain, clutching my side, and stumble on the rocks. She catches me immediately. I look up at her with a dazed, shit-eating grin across my lips.

"Dramatic," Glitch tells me.

"Heal me of it," I say, and she kisses me on my temple.

A shriek erupts behind us. We both spin only to see Nova trying to clutch a writhing Theo.

"Oh! Tell the kids to stay in the speeder so we can have this moment *alooooooone* together!" Nova's skinny arms are wrapped around Theo's middle, trying to plant a kiss under his chin. He's bent halfway over the side, trying to get away from her, mousy hair shaken from its tuck around his ears.

"Cease!" he protests, boat shuddering under his resistance. "Wither!"

"*Dead*," I hiss, heat bursting in my cheeks, and Sona doesn't hide her laugh this time as she tugs me away.

But it's good to see them doing better, really. It had seeped in only hours after we took Ira Sol—how many we'd lost, who we lost. It was us who had to cut the bodies down from the grove, us who built and lit the pyres and watched the smoke smudge the sky. It didn't matter how we had parted from the rest of the Gearbreakers, that they threw my kids out, that they considered me a traitor. We knew them.

Sona and I walk around the train, feet on the rails when we can to avoid the crunch of gravel. Not all the trains in the Peaks are automated, but this one is, per the agreement—no outside souls in the Gearbreakers-controlled city. We stop on the right of the frontmost car. A panel is set into its side; I press it to pop it up and reveal the control module, a large tablet and a bunch of buttons lining it. I look at Sona. "Do you know anything about trains?"

She smiles drily. I would say, *What are we even doing here? We are so not equipped for this* if I weren't already thinking it all the time.

Zamaya said to check the cargo—as in, check to make sure it's not filled with soldiers or bombs, et cetera—and we'd figure out our next steps from there.

We drift over to the other side of the car. I nod at Sona when she looks at me, hand around the door lever, and she tugs it open.

Sunlight streams into the dark, silent box. We check the crates one by one, making our way across the dozen cars. Apples, heads of napa cabbage, bags of dried berries. All intact.

We're finding nothing—I wish I could say it made me less nervous, but it doesn't, because a train doesn't just stop for no reason. But I can't really see some kind of sabotage like this being Godolia's style; if they wanted to mess with the train, they could've done it when it started in Terra or passed through Luna. They could have done it months ago.

Then there's the other problem, the fun, new one: the radicalized Mechvespers, or RMs. We don't think Godolia is ordering them around, but they still serve it, so it's almost the same level of *bad*. Where the mechas are sent to destroy an emptying resource village, the RMs will descend to try to pick off the fleeing refugees. Godolia doesn't kill people like that; it flattens, or burns, but it doesn't gather people up all neat and cut their throats.

That's what we saw about a month ago, a group of Badlands people that had been heading westward from a town called Bano for the Ira Sol ferry. Their bodies in a line, their blood on the sand. Jenny had said, "Oh, joy, another *thing*."

It gets a little confusing, the semantics of the Mechvesper religion; it's only recently that I've found out that the dogma differs slightly from region to region. The RMs entangle their deities with Godolia directly—they worship the heavens and the Zenith alike. But for others following the religion, the Zenith means something to them, too, but not as much as he means to his Godolia people. Not as much as the Windups, since not all the Badlands recruits and Mechvespers have fled Gearbreakers-controlled Ira Sol. Or maybe it's a matter of proximity. Closer Gods.

Or, you know, maybe they're just pretending to be cool with the Gearbreakers until their Zenith comes and saves them all, or gives them the go-ahead to murder us all in our beds.

We're at the last car now. This one's a lot cooler than the others, full of cold boxes instead of crates. I ease open a freezer to find stacks upon stacks of frozen fish cakes.

"Do you know how to make eomukguk?" I ask Sona, who's on the far end of the car looking into another freezer.

"Soup in the middle of summer?" she says, weighing a bag of frozen vegetables in her hand.

"Yes, please."

"Then yes, I do."

"*Yes*," I hiss as I open up the next cold box—it's a refrigerator this time, filled with glass jars of fermented cabbage, green onions, and radishes. "I haven't had this in forever."

"Take one with us," Sona says. "I think we have covered everything, yes?"

I look around. We'll have someone out to fix the train now that it's swept, but that feeling in my chest hasn't wavered. It's too quiet. "I guess."

She loops an arm through mine, soft where I'm rigid. "Frostbringer. Take a breath with me."

I do. Sona smooths a hand down my spine, pausing in the middle of my back. "And again." Her ribs swell against mine. "Lovely."

We seal up the train car and make our way back toward the speeder. Both Nova and Theo are down to their bras, sunbathing on the small stretch of deck; Novs springs up when she hears our footsteps. "You took *forever*."

"You two seem completely unhappy," I say, hopping into the boat and helping Sona over the ledge. Not that she needs it.

Nova shrugs, then crawls, first into her T-shirt and then upright to the wheel. As she turns over the engine, she remarks, "We've talked it over, and we've decided to start a band. Nova and the Haywire Kids! With an exclamation point, of course."

"I never agreed to that," Theo says, pulling on his shirt and sitting up so his shoulder is against my knee.

"Nyla has the voice of an angel," Nova coos, easing the speeder away from the shore and spinning us back south. "Wouldn't you say so, Theo boy?"

"I'm playing the drums," Theo tells me.

"Wouldn't expect anything else," I say, and wave the jar to him. "I got kimchi."

"Cabbage pickled in fish sauce. Yum," Novs hums over the rush of the wind. "That's not sarcasm. I could never disrespect my roots like that, no sir. What was wrong with the train?"

"Just stopped," says Sona, and briefly chews the inside of her mouth before she sees I notice. So she's anxious about it, too.

"Okay . . . ," says Theo, straightening. His pale eyes drift toward me out of habit only—I've never been one to sugarcoat anything for my crew, but that's never what they're looking for anyway. They've seen me arrogant and they've seen me broken; I'm not steely like I used to be, like I was supposed to be for them. Truth be told, I don't know what any of them have come to expect from me. Maybe it's just what I expect from them—to be here. That's enough for me. That'll always be enough.

"Don't look at me," I snap regardless. "I don't know what the hells is going on ever."

He just stares at me, head lolled back onto the seat, and then subtly tries to swipe the kimchi from my hand. I drop it before he can, the glass rolling on the warm, plasticky seat toward the nose of the speeder.

"Gimme," Theo protests, flipping over onto his knees. I grab the jar as he lunges for it.

"You've been doing nothing all day," I say, the corner of my mouth lifting when I see Sona smiling at me, both arms extended at either side on the railing, collarbone lifted and gleaming in the light. Deities.

"You told me to stay in the boat!"

"Exactly," I say, holding the jar up high as I hook my knee over his shoulder, pinning him against the seat. "Like I said—"

Black.

What—

Wait, but—

Quiet and dark and no wind, no nothing . . . Then a splitting note, like it's wound around a string, shot out into the void.

Flattened. Flattened on my side. Thin threads of an image crawl through the black, and then it comes back—the white skin of the speeder and the twist of the mountains above it. Blue sky. I'm still down, I'm lying on the seat, head hit the railing and it slid down at a bad angle—that's why everything's smearing. I'm not breathing. Someone's screaming. Everyone's screaming.

Everyone's covered in blood.

Sona puts her hand on my shoulder, and the air hits me again, shoots down my throat and I spit it back out. "What—"

"Don't move." She's screaming it, red on her teeth. *"Don't move, Eris, don'tmovedon'tmovedon'tmove—"*

"We're almost back!" Nova's half sobbing, half shouting. I bring my eyes past the shell of Sona's ear, see Theo still on his knees, mouth dropped open and frozen.

"Theo!" Sona begs, and he's out of it, on his feet ripping off his shirt and bringing it down, down, down, onto—me.

My hand.

No.

My wrist.

My wrist.

My wrist.

"Sona," I say, tilting my head back, grinning. Tears pinch my eyes. I'm laughing. I'm screaming.

"Just stay still, love, just stay still," Sona rambles over and over again, like she's praying. Her head bends over mine, my hand crushed in hers, the one I have left. She twists over her shoulder, my blood webbed across her cheek, a spire of it connecting her lips when she moves her mouth, when she shrieks, "Call Jenny!"

There's a piece of cabbage on her neck. It's all over Theo's hair, dying the strands red twice over. Red pepper flakes speckle the deck. Everything smells like vinegar.

I lose it. I laugh so hard I can feel my stomach quaking and my heartbeat sledgehammering in the raw flesh ending my arm—like I'm lying in a field with a mecha walking around in a careful, close circle, every step lifting me clean off the thistles.

Then it all goes black again. Like I'm pressed down into it.

CHAPTER THIRTY-THREE

SONA

Curled up next to her in the hospital bed, I bring a fingertip to her temple. *Gentle, now*—Gods, *please* be gentle—I smooth a strand of night-black hair behind her ear. She usually stirs when I touch her in the middle of the night, moves closer to me. This time she remains still.

I close my eyes, the pillow already wet with my tears, and nudge my brow against hers. Above us, the fluorescent light panel stutters. I feel like we are the only two people in the world, taking up the least amount of space we can manage, leaving the rest a vast, frightening thing.

This world is frightening enough as it stands.

The kimchi jar exploding midsentence, glass and then cabbage and then flesh and then bone, red against the backdrop of naked sky—

That was it, I think. The worst thing I have ever witnessed.

Jenny thinks the bombs were activated by heat. That they would have detonated on the way to the refugee apartments, or even within them, leaking their cold as soon as they left the train.

She had met us at the docks. I can still conjure her expression, vividly, the fear behind the careful, simmering calm, Eris between us as we rode back to the Badlands Academy hospital. Her sister stroked the curve of her shoulder; I remember watching it and her seeing I was and tensing, but she did not stop. Then, when Eris was under Dr. Park's careful attention, immediately forced herself onto the next step—figuring out what had happened.

I could not comprehend it. Eris lost her hand—how could Jenny be worrying about all the others, about the staggering number of *others*?

Because she is cold, and better than me for it. That is what will save us all.

"We're blowing the mines," she had said in an even tone, pacing the length of the hospital hall.

I waited until she reached one end and turned back toward me to answer. "You assume that this is Godolia, and you make yourself a blind spot."

Jenny reached the other end of the hallway, turned back to pass me again. But then she changed her mind.

She shoved her arm under my throat, my spine clattering against the wall. I let her, watched her expression through the hair in my eyes. She had fixed my Mod, so everything was no longer doused in red, but her cheeks were.

"You should have killed him," Jenny snarled.

"I know," I said, throat working against her hold. "I know."

She stepped away from me. Zamaya, leaning against the opposite wall, said, "The RMs, Jen. Could've been them, too."

"Wirefuckers." Jenny turned again.

"Yes," Zamaya agreed.

There would be no one to punish unless we caught them, and we won't, or I might, and I am sick of killing and it does not matter, not now.

I could peel them apart, piece by piece, now.

Eris looked so small when they brought her back from

surgery, barely an outline under the blanket. Like I could fit her in my palm.

I could not help it. When it was quiet, when we were alone, I peeled back the sheet, took in the unweighted wrist wrapped in its clean bandage. The fingers that lined my ribs just this morning, gone. The hand that gave me my first tattoos, gone.

Obliterated.

I kiss her between her eyes.

This time she moves.

Just a little. Just a little closer to me, and I think to myself, *If it was him—*

And the thought stops.

What, Sona?

If this was Enyo . . . what then?

Could you kill him?

Could you kill him, like you thought you could, before he went still to let you do it?

He had killed those guards, the ones who had witnessed him letting Starbreach free, that would have witnessed him letting me live. That last image of him, standing in the frame of the two doors, blood on his sleeves. He had looked back at me, and what did he say?

Don't think about it.

Please do not dare think about it.

And then Eris moves closer, and the thought moves past its locked place, because love like *this* and love like *that* are of the same caliber—I cannot help but see that they are echoes of each other.

Sona, Enyo had said, blood splashed across the softened corners of his eyes. *Could you do me a favor?*

Yes, I breathed, still on the floor where he had left me, raw and lightheaded with what I was allowing him to do. *Yes*.

And he had laughed when he said it. Like I would see him again; he would just be right back. *Try not to think the worst of me*.

"Tell me you did not do this."

"Sona?" Eris murmurs, eyes closed. "You say something?"

Did I?

"No," I whisper. "Keep sleeping."

"Don't leave."

"I am staying right here," I whisper, pushing around the tightness in my throat. "Right here."

The crew comes through later on, flits about Eris, propped upright in her bed with her arms folded around herself. The kids look like they have not slept, but it's not a dreary morning, all of them with their usual sharp banter and teasing. Eris says over and over again, "Get out, oh my Gods, all of you are so irritating, leave me alone." Not meaning it, never meaning it, smiling everywhere except on her lips.

Eventually Dr. Park comes and shoos them away, leveling me with a long look that I return while Eris chuckles, "Just try to get her to go."

The doctor has no prognosis for the hand, since there is not a hand to look at. Splintered ulna and radius bones, smoothed and fused with metal bits in surgery and layered with artificial flesh that will be partially absorbed by Eris's own as she heals. She needs a few heavy Spider sessions along the top of the wrist and the side of her forearm to even it out. Torn arteries, but we got pressure on her arm before she lost too much blood, and the transfusion did what it was supposed to.

It could have been worse. Eris could have been holding the bomb to her chest. But what she says is, "It could have been Theo."

I squeeze her shoulders, my arm draped across them as I sit at her side.

Jenny comes once the doctor leaves. She brushes her dark eyes over the both of us and snaps at me, "You missed your shift."

"I could not care less."

"Jenny," Eris says thinly, pushing herself up more. "Did you—"

"The mines are intact." Jenny crosses her arms, leaning on one leg, head tilted toward the window overlooking the Gillian. "Someone overtook the train controls remotely; that's how they got it to stop dead. I hate that computer-code tech stuff, honestly—you know I like the physical shit. I thought maybe Godolia had staged this to make it look like the RMs, right? *Oh, why would we do that when we could have simply stocked the explosives in Terra or Luna?*"—I blink; Jenny's Godolia accent is impeccable—"but I looked at the bombs. They're crude. Ugly little things. Doesn't seem like the smooth, pretty treats those Godolia sadists make in their labs."

Eris laughs roughly. "You're salivating."

"I'm going to make you something really cool. Would you like that?" Jenny breaks from her stance to round the bed, dragging Eris's hurt arm above the covers. "It's going to be metal. You'll have your full motor functions with practice."

I see Eris stare at it numbly for a few moments before closing her eyes, dropping her head against my shoulder with the barest tremble to her mouth. My heartbeat throbs in the base of my throat.

"You're making me a hand, Jen?"

"Yes," Jenny breathes. "Do you want a cryo function?"

"Huh?"

"Do you want me to put the cryo serum tech in the thing?"

Silence.

I cannot see Eris's expression, but I watch Jenny watching it carefully, watch as she leans back the slightest amount. "Oh . . ."

"I don't," Eris says icily, but her voice is shaking. "I don't. I want my gloves back. I want my *gloves*."

I've fought Jenny before. I was not planning on doing it again, ever, but if she is mean to Eris right now—

Jenny pulls her fingers from Eris's bandage, drags them softly across Eris's leg as she steps back, a light, natural motion that could be cast off as unintentional. It's not.

"You're so demanding," Jenny says, her tone bored, and leaves.

Eris turns her head from my shoulder. "I feel like a needy child," she hisses, so the quake in her voice only makes her sound harsh.

"You are the furthest thing. Why do you not want—"

"I'm not trying to touch you and kill you, or the kids," she snaps. "I'm so sick of hurting people." I watch as it bubbles up and out of her. "Killing the Nivim invitees. Killing *all those people* on Heavensday—it's not making it better. I just want to make it better."

Here it is. A piece of me that is a piece of her, too. The desperate, violent acts feeding guilt feeding *sadness*. We have saved people. We have destroyed people. It does not balance out, even if it was what was needed, even though I would not take it back if I could.

"We have to be better than the bad we have done," I say. "You said that to me once. It's true. It's so true, Eris, but being good does not erase the bad parts. Those we have to live with. It's going to be the hardest thing we ever have to do, and we do not have another choice, but you are not doing it alone. You will not be alone with this."

I shift on the bed so I can face her, so I can softly press my palms to the curves of her cheekbones and hold her there. Waiting until those black, black eyes roll up to me, glossy and simmering. The curve of her nose with its soft, wide tip, blushed with her efforts to keep from crying.

"I know you are ashamed. I am *never* going to be ashamed of you."

Eris swallows hard. "I don't know if I can be."

"Can be what?"

She puts her hand on my wrist, leans in and kisses me. Then she pulls back to press the next word right against my lips, like a shock down my throat. "Better."

CHAPTER THIRTY-FOUR

ERIS

One Month Later

"Oh," I say, squinting down into the jar. "Ha, oops."

Juniper whirls on me. "Oh Gods, what?" Her deep brown eyes drift from the container of salt I'm holding to the bowl of cake batter sitting innocently on the countertop. She brushes a fingertip against the rim and sticks it in her mouth, and her jaw unhinges. "Eris, you—*how*—"

I raise my hands as she takes a step toward me. "I am so sorry."

"Sona!" June shouts, taking the cake batter bowl and shoving it behind her, into Arsen's chest. He takes it easily and moves for the sink, the knot of his apron half-loose at the small of his back. "Sona—!"

"You're summoning her to *collect* me?"

"Absolutely!" she hisses.

"Fine! I'm going! I'm not appreciated around here anyway."

"I adore you, never come back ever," she calls after me as I drift into the hallway. "Check on Nova, 'kay?"

Novs is in the dining room, setting up the streamers. There was a lot of decorative shit lying around in the floor's storage—I guess even Pilots throw parties—which is good, because it's Theo's birthday today, but we're kind of combining all of ours into it, too, since we haven't really had room to celebrate anything since . . . the last Inklings party in the Hollows? Is that right? But with the Ira Sol numbers coming in steadily, there are enough free hands that the crew's off from shifts once a week.

The wonderful little freak is balanced with one foot on the table's edge and one on the armrest of a dining chair, hands above her head, trying to wrap a purple streamer around the branchlike arms of the chandelier.

"Assist me," Nova says weakly when I laugh at her from the door.

When we're done, we stand at the entrance, our hands—the metal of my right one cold, even over the fabric of my shorts—on our hips, assessing.

"Looks good," I say. "Where's Theo and Nyla?"

Nova trots over to the dish cabinet—that's right, this place is so freaking lavish the plates get their very own living quarters—at the back of the room. She presses an ear to the door, gives a sharp nod that shakes her blond hair loose from its bun, and swings it open.

Nyla is indeed inside, as is Theo, both in various stages of undress, both springing apart as the light reaches into the closet. Nova lets out a little string of giggles and books it, and Nyla bounds past me screeching, "I am going to *murder*—"

They ricochet out into the hall, leaving Theo and me alone. The pure smugness on his face tells me immediately what he's about to say. "Do *not* even think—"

"You were really onto something with Pilots, Eris." Theo pulls his shirt on, shit-eating grin still intact when his head pokes out of the collar. "Excellent kissers."

I'm about to start yelling, but instead jump as Sona's hand

snakes around my waist, and then her lips are on the shell of my ear, sending static down to the small of my back. "Is that true?"

I writhe and throw her a venomous look that says, *You little shit*. I know she doesn't adore public affection—she's doing it just to make my face flush, which it is. "Decay."

"Heard you were looking for me."

"You heard wrong."

Sona draws her eyes over my shoulder to Theo. "Hi. Happy birthday."

"Thanks, Glitch. I'm having a good one."

"I noticed."

Juniper fixes the cake somehow, and after candles we decide to pack it up and take it down to the water gate, lie out on that summer-warmed dock. None of us really likes hanging around the grove, or the gardens next to it. Besides, that's where the Mechvesper invitees—the ones who stayed—frequent during the days, hoping to catch a glimpse of one of our Windups out on patrol.

As we move across the green toward the gate, we pass by people lying out in the grass themselves, some wide eyes drawing to Sona and Nyla—the latter of whom blushes viciously—but mostly keeping to themselves.

"It's a beautiful day in Gearbreakers-controlled Ira Sol," Nova shouts, and flips into a cartwheel across the grass.

Mechvespers are different from what I expected. Awestruck, and docile for it. Not all of them—the RM displays we've seen outside the walls are proof enough of that—but some.

Were the mother and daughter from Nivim like that? Would they have stayed here, and been lying out in the grass today, waiting to feel the chord of amazement strike in their chests as a Hydra made its way to the hangar? *Clinkclinkclinkclink*—

"You are fidgeting," Sona says beside me, the basket with the cake, which she insisted on carrying, pressed protectively to her chest.

"I'm fidgety." I stop moving my hands. "I didn't realize it before, that I move my fingers so much. When I'm anxious." *Now I can* hear *it*. "Or is it new?"

"No. You always did that. Why are you anxious?"

So I don't have to respond, I reach up to twist one of her curls around my forefinger—my left one, so I can feel its silkiness. Nova's right. It's a beautiful day. I don't have to act like the sky is falling down, because it hasn't yet.

Well. Besides someone blowing my fucking hand off.

But we had a good four months, and another month of quiet now. More safeguards and sweeps were set up for the trains, but we've found nothing, and we think the bomb was the RMs'. Not Godolia's, not the Zenith's. And if I had to choose one . . .

But I feel safe inside the city. I've had to remind myself of that a lot, that even though I'll roll on the new hand in my sleep sometimes and flinch awake from the cold of it, there's Sona beside me, and the kids up the hall, and a city spread around us, still on the map.

So why am I anxious? Just the guilt. Just the nightmares. But I'm not the only one.

We reach the docks of the water gate, the sun dragging slowly out of the sky, the last ferry out and back an hour ago.

Sona sets the cake on one of the stalls as the rest of the

kids lay out towels and kick off their shoes. I trail her, like I tend to do.

"I'm good, really," I say. "The moment's passed. I'm a brand-new girl."

Sona's elegant fingers trace against the side of the cake. She tastes it, savors it, and says with her eyes closed, "You can tell me when you get all dark and deep and scary."

"Why?" I say, grinning. "You already know instantly when I get all dark and deep. And scary."

Face impassive, she takes another fingerful of frosting and deposits it on the tip of my nose. "You are not funny."

"That's okay. What do I need humor for when I'm so edgy and cerebral?"

Sona leans her weight on the countertop, chin on her interlaced fingers as she looks at me. The light daze of the sunset weaves gold into her curls as she studies me. *Studies me.* Good Gods.

"Kiss me," I say, heat in my cheeks and sugar on my nose, and lean in for it.

But at the last moment she strikes her hand out, flattens the frosting halfway up my nostrils with her palm, and straightens to call, loud and scandalized, "Oh, but in *public*, Eris?"

It earns immediate cooing from the crew.

"In public?" Nova shrieks, and lunges for Juniper. Nyla and Theo jump around them, a tired-looking Arsen with Nova's feet in his face, chanting, "Affection! Affection!"

Sona laughs, throwing her head back into it, and the sound is the best thing ever, as always. But she still looks to find me unimpressed under all the frosting in my pores, and coughs. "Ahem. I was kidding. Kiss?"

"No, no," I say, wiping the frosting away. "You're right. Too public."

I don't let her look fully disappointed before I snatch her hand.

"I guess we are just going to have to run away."

"But our parents, Eris!" she gasps instantly, grinning. "Whatever will they think?"

"We will be far enough by sundown that it won't even matter."

"I guess we'd better start going, then."

"I think you're right!"

I take off down the docks, pulling her behind me, past the kids to its end, weight tipping against the railing as I pull at my laces.

"Do you even know how to swim?" I jeer as she kicks off her boots, too.

"Do you think they would have let me graduate if I did not?"

I pull off my shorts and fling them at her. "Do you know how to chill?"

"Do you—"

I leap from the railing, fingers split and stretched in the air, and hit the water in a cold rush. I come up just to glimpse her shoes neat on the docks, socks and pants left to warm on the railing. Her shadow moves over me, and I go under again.

The water is dark and quiet, cold humming against my bare legs and up against my stomach as I sink, and I find her when she breaks the surface. We come up, both sucking in breaths, grinning like idiots.

The crew crows at us from up the path, and we slip under the cooler shade cast by the docks, pulled by the slight current.

There's a frail-looking ladder dropped down into the water, looking abandoned and out of place against the stoic concrete; we catch onto it, on opposite sides, her knee hooked around the side rail under my arm. When I try to kiss her between the rungs I smack my head.

"Wiref—"

She picks up my right wrist from the water. "Did Jenny say this was waterproof?"

"No," I say, watching the metal glint with droplets. "But if it electrocutes us I can call it poor engineering."

Jen used lightweight metal so the weight difference is slight, but it's there, when I reach, when I move. I'm still relearning how to shoot a gun. It responds to my thoughts, so Jenny says whatever functions I'm lacking is my own fault; I'm the one hesitating, not it.

I see the look on her face and add quickly, "It's not a crisis for me, Glitch. I know I'm human and stuff."

The side of her mouth quirks. "Good Gods. Is that how I sounded?"

"No! I, like, I just meant—" Then I see she thinks it's funny. "Well, yes, actually. I'm pretty close."

"You are *not*."

"Well, maybe not now." I laugh lightly, eyes drawn low, tracing the metal of my fingertip against the line of her fore-arm panel. "Right?"

My leg knocks lazily against hers, sky going hazy above our heads, primed for a storm, but it's not in any hurry. Sona watches me trace.

"Right," she says softly, and draws her fingertip up to the corner of her left eye, the one that throws itself in shuddering circles of light against the water. "This was not why I felt unnatural. I thought it was, and all of it is so present, you know, so easy to blame. I know now." The palm of her hand slides against the metal of mine. This calm, this quiet, like a mirror tilting to sharpen light into a point. "I wasn't human because I was hateful."

And she's wonderful.

And the thought, black to its core, comes up anyway. *Is that why you didn't kill him?*

It's horrible. It doesn't really go away. And it's just noise, water pressing my T-shirt to my stomach, hers reaching for my ribs between the rungs. I kiss her, or she kisses me, but I'm finding more and more often it's us catching each other halfway. Noise, like static, like nightmares. It's not as real as this is.

When Sona pulls away, she smiles, even though she must have seen the question written on my face. She knows like I know—nothing holds a candle to this.

And then her smile snags. Freezes.

She's no longer meeting my eyes. She's looking at something behind me.

Look.

The thought crawls up as my knuckles go white around the ladder, all the warmth of the past moments gone as fear bleeds through me. Up the deck, the kids have gone completely still, save for June taking a step back, stumbling and catching herself on the heels of her hands without a cry. I can see the whites of her eyes.

You have to look. That will be the worst part.

I turn my head toward the water gate.

Wrong, wrong, wrong. Dead wrong.

This part is the worst part.

Past the mouth of the gate, maybe fifty yards out. Two of

them, water up to their slitted nostrils, flat red eyes peering into the city. Straight at us. I realize, with complete, dreamlike horror, that the Leviathans broke the surface soundlessly.

The words come hollow in my head. *We are so small.*

We don't speak. Sona eases herself onto the ladder. I round its side railing, limbs sounding harsh as they drag through the water. I lift myself up one rung, the next, the rest, crawling silently onto the dock. The concrete is warm under my knees, my heart humming and *what is happening what is happening ohgodsohgodswhatishappening*—

We're running. The sound of our bare feet resonates mutedly across the empty waterfront.

Just us and the deities at our backs.

I get it, like I do every now and then. Why people bow.

CHAPTER THIRTY-FIVE

SONA

Jenny detonates half of the mines.

We wait for the next part. All of us in the dining room—Gearbreakers and Hydras. Wait for the bombs. For the mechas to come rolling in, like a wave of liquid metal over the borders. But there is nothing, not even the Leviathans anymore, gone about ten minutes after they surfaced.

Jenny is pacing. Trying to figure out why he did it.

She speculates that the Leviathans must have arrived in the morning, when it was still dark out. Then the sun rose and the first ferry passed right over their heads, unloaded a meager number of refugees, and drifted out undisturbed. So did all the others.

The Windups stood there all day long, planted on the riverbed, hidden beneath the froth.

Then they rose, just to stare, to make themselves known.

"Nothing up to this point, nothing—" Jenny's words are quick and below her breath, hands twitching from her pockets to her temples to her hair. She is only talking to herself.

"I think we need to evacuate," Captain Sheils murmurs from her seat at the table.

"Stabilizing population, finally, rainy season . . ." Jenny is at the window now, rapidly tapping her fingers against her lip. Shrugs quickly, and we all watch her. "Wouldn't be the ticket in the rain, is he just regretting it now? Or maybe it's just boredom, left us on the map for the rainy season—I mean a rainy day—ha! Or the devout. Inspiration? Months ago . . . wouldn't do just to make us flinch now, wouldn't—"

"Yes," I say quietly. "He would."

Just to make us flinch. Just to induce panic.

I do not want to be this.

This is still my world.

Eris stiffens next to me. Jenny turns, and I meet her eyes. "And to see," I say, "if you would stick to your word."

After a moment of silence, after a moment of the gears clicking in her brilliant, cruel head, Jenny rolls her neck and straightens with a cold laugh.

"Fine," she says, and the frenetic energy is gone from her voice. Now there is deadly calm. "Just fine. And now he knows."

"Knows what?" Eris asks, voice low.

Jenny flexes her fingers at her sides. The same ones that set off the mines, let the tremors shudder through the entire city. "That we're playing my game, too."

"Everyone who saw them is in this room," Sheils notes, nodding to my crew. The others watched it off the wall's surveillance footage. They could not see Eris and me pulling ourselves out of the water, the blood draining from our faces. "This cannot get out. It'll panic more people than it will help to know."

Or inspire them, like Jenny said.

A laugh, high and shrill, splinters through the heavy air. I look to see Nyla, at the back of the room where the rest of the crew has chosen to cluster, hands over her mouth to cut the sound short.

"Ny?" Theo starts, touching her shoulder. She flinches away before pulling closer, hands clawing his shirtfront. The proximity washes his freckles over in red light.

"It's been months," she chatters, like there is no one else in the room. "I was wrong. I was wrong . . ."

I see Eris glance at Jenny, who gives a sharp jut of her chin, and then we are both pushing back from the table, moving the crew into the hall and then the closest bedroom, which is ours. Theo guides Nyla onto the bed and has her sit. Her arms loop around herself as she begins to rock.

"I thought he left us alone." She is smiling, but it's a shaking thing, sucking down air, tears in her dark eyes.

I kneel down in front of her. "Nyla, love. It's going to be okay."

"You are *lying*." Another peal of nervous laughter. And then she begins to sob. Folds into herself on the bed, black curls shuddering on the comforter. "You are not safe here. No one is safe here . . ."

Eris closes the door. One by one, we join Nyla on the mattress, curling around her, around one another. I think to myself, *We are all seeing it in our heads, over and over again.* The Leviathans breaking the water. The other bad memories that spill from the one, liquid terror.

I reach for Eris's hand. She lets me take it, the look in her eyes distant. I close mine, and remember—and it's strange to, now—that I left the cake on the stand. And then, that it was me. I left Enyo alive.

Who he is does not matter in the face of *what* he is. I should have known that. Should have swallowed it, and put him down. I feared this, I remember now with Eris's hand in mine. That he might become something worse.

CHAPTER THIRTY-SIX

SONA

I start awake in the early gray morning without knowing why, temple on Arsen's shoulder, one arm draped over Eris's middle. I detangle myself, hand rising to my eye to keep its glow from waking them. Standing at the foot of bed, I count them out. Nyla is pressed between Theo and Nova, sound asleep. I understand her panic. It's worse, when you thought you were done running.

The bedroom door is open. I shut it and then move into the bathroom and turn on the cold water, one hand pulling my hair back as I cool my face. I think I was having a bad dream, and sweat slicks the nape of my neck. I lean my weight against the sink, and take a moment to breathe in the quiet before raising my eyes to the mirror.

Across my features, there are words, shining under the red of the Mod.

Bellsona.

I stumble back, hands scrambling to the door to make sure its lock is in place. My touch knocks the switch on the wall, and my eyes sting at the sudden light. I turn, slowly, back to the mirror, and—the glass. The glass is covered in red marker.

Bellsona.

Stop.

I can't look away.

Bellsona.

Do you remember the night you pierced my ears and thought about killing me? You scared me more than I let you know.

I forgot, when you were with me. That I was always meant to be something terrible. But I was not meant to love you so much, Sona, so I'm running, I'm running, I'm running…

Can you meet me?

The woods before the tracks meet the city. Tonight.

I read it over and over, until the floor suddenly tilts and I kneel against it, brow to the tiles. The tap is still going, the sound static under the heartbeat in my ears.

Someone in the tower, communicating with him. Who walked right past all of us sleeping to scrawl these words on the mirror. One of the invitees? Someone who came in on the ferries, walked right past us? Were they carrying this note to begin with or did they receive it, somehow, when they were already past the walls?

Nausea pinching in my gut, I lift my head, finding it all still there, done up in red. This is unprecedented. A heresy no one would ever dream would come from a Zenith.

Is that what this is? Heresy?

I'm running.

Could it be true?

You scared me more than I let you know.

I press myself up from the floor. With shaking hands, I take the towel from its hook and run it beneath the tap, and shut it off. I stand in the silence, water dripping from my hand. I think I am about to do something wrong.

He scared me, too.

I raise the towel to the mirror, and let the words bleed away, as my family lies asleep in the next room.

I have to tell them.

Red ink bleeds down my arm.

I will tell them.

After tonight.

It is raining, mist churning in the undergrowth, clouds overhead all day long. We spent the day prepping Jenny's new strategy. Citywide curfew starting at eight o'clock, taking the mechas out of the hangar and stationing them around the Academy, just in case. She says we can fight grounded deities better than a fleet of helicopters overhead. Says she will hold off blowing up the rest of the mines since we all made it through the night, and because the foodstuff delivery came through this morning— extra sweeping found it fine, bomb- and poison-free. Says the Zenith could rain hellsfire, but now he knows Jenny's finger is on the detonator button—he will lose what is left of the mines.

"Thank Gods," she said dramatically, but I could tell by the rings around her eyes that she had not slept, "that you two embarrassed the Archangel design enough, because that—*ha*—that would have been bad. Guess things do happen for a reason."

The Leviathans at our water gate seemed like his idea. Just something flashy before he ran—was that it? He would have critical eyes on him all these months for not doing much about the Ira Sol takeover, and maybe this move relaxed them. When they found relief in the act, he ran. It would explain why the Windups did not blow us out of the water.

Turn around.

I do not turn around.

Past the grove, past the gardens, and up the wooded hill that rises north of Ira Sol. The tracks that feed into the city are on my right, though I cannot see them through the mist and rainfall. My heart pounds fresh heat through my chest, breath coming out in light clouds. He is close. I know he is close.

He wants to be better—I wanted to be better, too.

I can convince the rest of them. Eris saw good in me when she helped me leave the Academy, when she brought me home. We have all done unspeakable things, from a place of hate sown inside us so early that we should have grown around it. It should have been so a part of us that we could not recognize it was there at all. But I've seen it in him—the recognition of that achingly *human* beat when we had the same thought, when we leaned into each other without even touching. It is bigger than the city, bigger than the way we grew up.

And through the mist—movement. A hood, a gloved hand pressing against the trunk of a tree. Staring out into the woods.

"Enyo?" I whisper.

The name is swallowed up by the rush of the rain. Same with my footfalls against the dead leaves, as I move forward.

I reach out.

He is here. It is all over. Maybe I was lying to Nyla, that it was going to be okay, but I can say it now. There is nothing chasing us anymore.

My hand rests on his shoulder.

My other hand grapples for the sword at my side. The one I brought just in case.

It's not him. It does not feel like him.

But they are quick. It happens in less than a half second.

The figure turns, something hard brought down with a force that cracks my temple, splinters white across my vision I am on the ground *look look look* I open my eyes to look and only see fingers feel them dip into my left socket and then there is another hit that jolts my limbs at my sides, *stay awake* there is rain filling up my head—

Black.

Black.

Black.

CHAPTER THIRTY-SEVEN

ERIS

The crew come in soaking wet from running around in the rain outside. They find me on the library's couch, with a book I haven't even looked at, eyes trained to the window.

"Where's Sona?" Nyla asks, flicking her hair, which splatters Theo. Nova mimics her, also splattering Theo, and the two throw a perfectly synchronized thumbs-up while he stands there dripping, in shock at the alliance.

"Don't know," I murmur, turning the page I didn't read. Yeah, okay, I'm a little sore with her. Yesterday meant that Enyo might not be done with us, and I don't like being reminded that we should all still be scared. But I'm not going to scream at Sona for not killing him. That's not going to be something I hold against her.

But I needed a little distance today, to tell myself this. I think she did, too. Different reasons, of course, but so what? It's not like anything can shake the soul mate out of either one of us.

"Godsdamn it," I mutter, and turn the page, another that I haven't absorbed a word of. I pinch too hard, and the paper rips between the metal of my fingers.

I hear the elevator chime up the hall, then footfalls. I straighten, then slump back a little, ready to see her, but real casual—but it's Jenny who comes through the door. Her black eyes flick around the room.

"What?"

"Where's Glitch?" Jenny demands.

"I don't know!" I snap. "I'm not her keeper!"

"Eris," she breathes; now I do straighten. Her tone is wire tight. The crew goes completely still, too. "Come with me. Now."

Silently, I get up from the couch and trail her into the hallway.

She's holding a tablet in her hands and scrolls through it until there's an image of a map—the Ira Sol cityscape, the Academy campus, and the surrounding terrain and river done up in blue lines.

"She's gone," Jenny says, and points to the woods north of the city that the train tracks wind against. "She was here, and then she was gone."

"Holy fuck, Jenny, *what*?" I'm aware of the dead silence inside the library, the kids listening in. "Are you *tracking her*?"

"Yes," she says. "Well. Her eye."

My thoughts skip blankly for a moment before snagging. Jen fixed color back into Sona's Mod a few months ago. Took it out of her head and said to come back for it in an hour; I was there.

"First my gloves," I breathe. "You—what, is this like an addiction or something?"

Jenny just laughs. It rattles out of her. "Don't be an idiot."

The sound chills me. I shake my head, feet shifting a step back.

"No," I say. "She's here. She's back with us."

Not an addiction. Jenny placed the tracker in case she ever went back to Enyo.

Is that all she put into the eye? I know now how skilled Jenny is as an explosives expert, too.

Deities. Later. I'll deal with it later. Now—

I turn to the library and kick open the doors. "Come on. Sona's missing." Every eye goes wide. "Don't just stand there. It's okay." *Calm, calm, I'm calm.* "We're going to go look for her."

I literally trip over her.

"Shit, shit, shit!" And then I'm on the ground and her curls are in the undergrowth and there's blood on her face. That image. It's just this image, the rest of the world fringed by mist—not even noise, not even my own words, just the silent twist of my throat as they spill from me. "Sona! *Sona!*"

I move the hair out of her eyes, and she blinks awake. She's alive, and she's shuddering, and I realize I'm staring into an empty socket. She twists to empty her stomach onto the forest floor.

She reaches up to touch her temple, toward a lump the size of an egg, and I catch her wrist. Her eyes—eye—drifts to me, distant and glossy.

I don't know what to say. I don't know what I do say, just let the whispers crack from me, breathless, so I'm gasping on them, forcing them out.

You're okay. You're okay, I think. Something like that.

I don't realize it until later, after we get her back into the tower and into a hospital bed—I wasn't trying to reassure her. I was praying.

CHAPTER THIRTY-EIGHT

ERIS

We stand in quiet, after she tells us the whole thing. Me, Jenny, Zamaya, and Sheils, crowded around her bed. I feel different, still numb with the shock of finding her like that. She won't even meet my eyes, the left one new in her head.

"I'm sorry," she whispers as the others leave, but my own gaze is off her, keeping a careful watch on Jenny. My sister looks back, her hand on the door, looking right past me and at Sona.

It's like we're on the Winterward ice all over again, one Valkyrie drowned and another smoldering behind us, and Jenny picking apart the threat in her head.

I take a slow breath as the door clicks shut. Sona puts her hand on my wrist, and I shake my head. *Give me a minute.*

It's not hard to picture what Enyo might mean to her—even though I hate him, even though I stay up late at night sometimes imagining what I might do if I had the chance. As if it could untuck every horrible thing he did out of her head.

But I don't know him.

Just like I didn't know Sona. Just like I hated her, too. War is only able to eat its way forward across generations because the *others* have a singular face, and it's blank. It's easier to fight, easier to kill when it's just a tally knocked off Godolia's numbers, when it isn't real, breathing people, not really. Just the heavy, sick *hate* sitting in your gut.

Enyo let Sona live. Moreover, he let *Jenny* go, which says just how much Sona means to him, how he pushed it all back just so they could have words, and killed his guards afterward because they might have seen how he let Sona hover with that knife over his heart.

Jenny's been taking her as a convenient protection charm. But that might not stand anymore. And I know it hurts Sona more than this hurts me, that she kept this from me and wandered out into the woods alone, so I find her hand.

"Do you love him?"

"I do not like boys," Sona returns, but her words come hoarsely, because she knows I know this, and she's deflecting.

"You know that's not what I meant."

I can't take it, and my anger is bullshit, and I put my weight on the mattress to curl up beside her on the bed, cheek against her collarbone. But before I can do it, she says, "Stop."

"Why?" I ask.

"Be a little mad. Eris. Yell at me. Get off me." Poisonous smile, and her words tumbling out in sharp, broken fragments. "Did you not hear me? Stop *touching* me!"

I immediately flare, voice just as vicious as hers, spitting, "I'm not going to punish you just because you think I should. You can't do that. You don't get to ask that of me."

"Why the hells do you think you could be safe from me? What I did—"

"Oh, love, I'm safe from you." I lean in, so her gaze singes against mine. "I'm arrogant and you're—you're fucking *obsessed* with me. You keep things from me and then you come to bed and you lie to me and you love me, and you're good, and the rest of it is just—deities—it's just—everything else. It's *nothing* else, Sona. I am so far past picking you apart. I *know* you, you dumbass. 'Get off me'—you know what happens when I do that?"

I pull my touch away, and she catches it. I don't smile at it; there's no triumph here. For a half second, her bottom lip trembles; she suffocates it by pulling her hand from mine and brushing her knuckles against her mouth, laughing a little, disbelieving and helpless and so, so sad all at once.

"He was just . . . lost." The fight crumbles out of her. "I just—I just used to be so *sure* of it, Eris." Her fingers lift to drag through her hair, and her chin turns toward the windows where the lights of the city push back the black night. "What was good. What was bad, *who* was bad, and who had to die and who *had* to live and—"

I can see her teetering, toward fury or toward grief, before tucking her shoulders against a sob that splinters her whole body. Guilt.

"I *hated* you, Eris." She says it quietly. "He made me hate you, and he made me t-*terrified* of you, and I . . . I really was going to kill you." She laughs a little, the sound hollow between us. "Enyo let me live. That is bare-minimum treatment, I want you to know that I know that. But he was angry and grieving and then he was himself, like *us*, just—just a fucking *kid*, wanting to do what he could. Protecting who he could. And I'm sorry. I thought—I am so sorry, Eris."

I go to her. I fold myself against her outline and push the rest of it, all of it, away. We stay like that for a while, me breathing in the scent of her shirt, her tears dripping into my hair.

It didn't seem like protection, not at first. Not the easy way the world looked like to me, with its clean lines and clear cruelties pasted on the opposite side. The killing of entire towns. An Academy full of children, so they could grow around the things put inside them, so they could set properly, irreversibly. Windup upon Windup, excess upon bloody excess. I'm here *now*, and so it shouldn't matter that before all of this, Godolia was the one being suffocated by the nations that once made up the Badlands; it shouldn't matter that their first mechas and their first Pilots were fighting *back* instead of just fighting.

But I'm looking at things differently than I used to. The systems in place are violent and horrific and that makes hating them simple. But then there's the people, messy and complicated and *human*, and unexpected for it.

I'm screwing up all the time, but at least now I recognize the mistakes I made *are* mistakes. Not like how I used to think trusting Sona was a flaw, or how I thought attachment was a liability, because that was what was taught to me, that the kind of world I had ended up existing in was one that would eat me alive.

What Sona feels for Enyo . . . that's not a mistake. It's clarity.

"I don't want you to think you can't feel like this," I whisper into her shirt, hands between my stomach and her ribs, the right one pulled into me so she can't feel its cold. "Okay? We don't ask each other to feel like anything, or to feel less—I'm not letting any of us go on like that."

Not her. Not the kids. Not me. My parents wanted me to be cold because they thought it would save me. But it's making me sick and it's making us rot. And maybe what everyone needs is the hardhearted Gearbreakers, not people but shields and sharp edges. Maybe I can understand it, but I'm not going to waste myself like that. I want us to be selfish, and together, and better for it.

"Don't hide it from me." I curl in around the dark thought, what she must have felt when she saw it wasn't him and she was all alone. "I don't care if you think you're bad. Don't hide from me."

After a moment, she murmurs tiredly, "There is nothing else for me to hide from you." Her arm drapes across my shoulders; she curls into me, too. "He's done with me."

Which could mean hells for Ira Sol. For all of us.

But we'll get to it in a second. Our lives under threat, again, again, again, the worst of it all the time now.

It's fine. It's just us, right now. Her breath and mine and the quiet.

When I wake up, still tucked into her side, there's a dark, tall figure watching us from the corner of the room. I quickly press myself upright, metal hand falling on Sona's shoulder.

"Get up," I hiss blearily. "Jenny's going to kill you."

Sona's eyes blink open, red glow coming in starts across Jenny's calm expression. Then she rolls over. "She would have done it already."

"So she's obviously still thinking about it!"

"Yes, I am," Jenny agrees, in her faraway, thinking-about-it voice.

"*Sona.*" More frantic now, jostling her.

She bats my arm away and pulls up the blankets.

"Okay," I breathe, in utter disbelief. "We're going to have to talk about this lack of self-preservation later."

"If there is a later," she murmurs, expression hidden by her hair.

I glance back to see that Jenny's moved closer. I scramble off the bed and take her by the wrist, yanking her into the hall.

"You thought she was going to run," I say, quick and low and pleading. "*Listen to me.* She didn't—"

"Wasn't much better," Jenny says, her tone even, "than what she was actually doing."

"She told us."

"Afterward."

"Isn't it more important to figure out who left her that message?"

"If there was someone," Jenny says. "There's no one on the elevator surveillance cams coming up to the floor during the night. Besides my crew." Jenny flashes a sharp grin. "Insinuate it."

No freaking way. "They could've taken the stairs. No cams."

"Or there was no one at all, and Glitch's mind is still fucked up."

"She has a lump growing out of the side of her head. They took out her *eye*." My voice is cold. "You could stand to trust my judgment, too, you know."

"She's fooled you before. A pretty suit and a smile and some flirting was all it took."

"Deities," I gasp, heart twisting, "you fooled me, too, Jen! You said we were going to go to the opening to get her, bring her *back*. You didn't tell me you were going to try to kill Enyo. And Sona is the *only* reason he let you walk out alive after you failed."

Jenny takes a measured pause, her fingertips grazing her

temple to push back a loose strand of hair, the motion methodical, steady. Her eyes flick down to mine, and all of a sudden, she's our mom. I mean, Jen's even wearing her coat, like she always does, so I'm back in the Hollows and Jenny's next to me at the dorms' entrance. She's fourteen years old, smacking me away when I lean too close, both our spines against the bumpy concrete wall as we wait for our parents to come back from their run. Appa comes up and he's exhausted, weary smile pressed in light kisses against both our crowns; Mom trails behind and she's simmering, like she always did after an unsuccessful take-down, pinning Jenny and me with the same exact look Jenny's pinning me with now. Tired, wired, and a dare all in one.

For a while, I always thought that look meant, *Tread carefully. You're on thin ice.*

It wasn't until Mom was gone that I realized it wasn't that at all.

Tread carefully. I'm *on thin ice.*

"I don't know if this was him," Jenny says.

"What?"

"The Zenith kid. I don't know if this was him."

"Sona said . . . that there was a memory, written out. Her piercing his ears."

"But I don't see why he would need an eye," Jenny says, and adds, half to herself, gaze drifting up the empty hospital hallway, "There's only one reason for that Mod."

To see out of a Windup.

"You think someone's making a Pilot," I say low. "Inside the city. An RM? Or—"

"I don't know," Jen murmurs. "I've put watches on our mechas. I'm going to have them brought closer to us, keep an eye—Gods. It would only take one Hydra . . ."

She goes still. I see it playing out in the look in her eyes, the gas coming in. She always sees every bad thing playing out. It's how we've stayed alive so far.

"You're watching her," she says gruffly, shrugging out of it. "You don't leave her side."

"She's loyal to the Gearbreakers," I snap.

"Don't act like it's going to be such a pain, doing what I say." She brushes her hands against her jacket and begins to walk away. "And have your crew on standby."

"For?"

"For if I'm right. And we all know the chances of that." Jenny sighs. Sharp, like it could be a laugh if it wasn't so flat, if she wasn't grinning so widely now that I can see the corner of it even with her head turned away. "If they're putting her eye in another Pilot, that tracker's going to come back online."

CHAPTER THIRTY-NINE

SONA

It rains for three weeks. The halls of the Academy tower seem muted under it—footfalls are lighter, voices of the Gearbreakers and Hydras drawn low, without our intending to. Except Nova, who has a quiet spell that Eris says has happened before. All of us waiting, all of us tense. If I was right and Enyo sent us the Leviathans just to make us nervous, he has achieved it. But Jenny kept her word, too; I know he does not want to lose the remainder of the mines. The trains with the foodstuffs still roll in, and we pause before every first bite.

I apologized to the rest of them, for keeping the note to myself. It startled me, like Eris did, when they were angrier at my going about it alone than my believing Enyo was waiting for me at the end of it. But still angry, fractured trust, and I pressed my hands to my eyes when the heat broke in them from the shame of it. Did I really do something so stupid, for an image in my head of all of us together—Enyo and Eris and me and the crew—and all of this so far in the past that we forgot we used to be so afraid of one another?

"Well," Nyla said, voice high and unnerved by my crying, hovering with the rest of them at the foot of my hospital bed. "You know! She would have already killed us in our sleep if she was still on Godolia's side! So, it's good! Right? Right?"

"Maybe," Theo said drily, breaking the beat of awkward silence that followed. "Whoever wrote the note didn't kill us, either."

Juniper hurriedly clapped her hands together before the thought could settle. "Well, that's absolutely terrifying. I love you, Sona, and all of you, very, very much." Palms clasped, she looked to Eris. "Let's stay close together forever."

Her tone was bright, a smile on her lips while she said it. But she did not mean it lightly, and we did not take it as such. We have stayed close. We sleep in the same bedroom or in the library, and when either Nyla or I am slated to go out on mecha patrol, the rest of the crew is there when we leave and when we come back, waiting in the rain.

Slowly, I can feel all of us easing the tension in one another, even the silences growing hazy and calm after a couple of weeks. Eris finally learns how to make a proper cake from Juniper. Arsen teaches me chess. The Valkyrie level has a sparring room, which I did not know about until Nova silently pulled me into it one day and picked up a sword. Even though I am out of practice, I touched her wrist and moved her stance into proper grounding, and since then we have been having lessons in the early evenings. I forgot how much I missed the feel of a sword in my hand.

One night, I ask Eris to give me back my gears. In the library, she kneels in front of the arm of the couch and takes my hand with hers, sheathed in plastic gloves. It feels familiar. I can tell she is nervous, with her new hand, but I want it to be her, and she is doing well and she notices it, too, like I'd hoped. Between each gear I press a kiss to her temple. Seven in total, one for each of the crew, including Xander.

This is what I have. Not a burning world or a chest full of guilt or someone who could have been good, if it was at all fair. They are what is real.

When she is done, Eris sits back on her heels and blinks back tears—once and they are gone—and she turns toward the rest of them.

"Anyone else?" she asks. "I know all our counts are kind of off, but . . . you know." She shrugs. The motion seems easy, and it makes me smile and ache all at once. "It's whatever. It's good. Nyla?"

"Oh no," Nyla says, palms up, taking a step back into Theo. "I have never destroyed a Windup."

"You took one away from their army," Theo points out, and tucks his head over hers with a smile. She flushes red. "Counts."

"Counts," echo the rest of us.

"Doesn't have to be a gear," Eris adds quickly. "You can get whatever. Arsen's better at the art stuff, though, so I'd hand it over."

Our explosives tech bobs his head and flashes a calm, double thumbs-up. Juniper, beside him on the loveseat with one knee over his, gives a helpless, pleased laugh, and touches her fingertips to her mouth with a bashful smile when Arsen glances at her. "Nothing," she says. "You're just funny, that's all."

I see Theo and Nova exchange looks.

"Wow," Theo says, "you guys haven't been gross in a while." Nova nods.

"Can't!" Nyla squeaks, when gazes drift back to her. "I—needles. Do not make me. Please . . ."

"Oh, Ny, we won't," Juniper says quickly.

"Even though we tattooed Glitch while she was sleeping,

because she couldn't feel it. Back of her neck, so she couldn't see it, either." Theo shoots me a grin, chin on top of Nyla's head. "Surprise!"

Nyla shrieks and jolts out of his hold. Nova immediately tackles her. I touch the nape of my neck as they go rolling across the rug under my feet. "Is this true, Eris?"

"Not sure," Eris says. "Lemme see."

I turn and hold up my hair. Eris brushes her thumb against the spot—gently, gently—then pulls back and says, "Yep. But it's very tasteful."

"So you do not have anything to worry about, Nyla," I say.

Nova untangles from her, green eyes looking back, hair a blond tangle on the rug fibers, and says, the first thing she has spoken in weeks: "I want one."

June turns to bury her smile in Arsen's shoulder. Theo buries his in Arsen's other one.

Eris smiles, too, a tender thing. "A gear, love?"

"No," Nova says seriously. "I want a smiley face. On my face."

Silence. Nova blinks up at us, waiting.

"Metal," Nyla breathes from the floor.

That is how Jenny finds us, Nova laid out on the library's couch, head in Arsen's lap, where he's just finishing poking a little smile at the corner of her right eye. I look up as she leans against the door frame, and know that it is serious by the way she does not comment.

Eris stands. "It's up, isn't it?"

"Just a few minutes ago," Jenny says, fingers curling around the tablet in her hand. I have not yelled at her for putting a tracker in my head without my knowledge, but only because she decided not to kill me. A daily practice. "You ready?"

Eris looks back at the rest of us. Nova ghosts a fingertip across the bandage Arsen placed over her fresh ink and nods. "We're ready."

It is odd, here at night, and I thought things could not get stranger. Jenny has the mechas cast around the gardens like abandoned playthings, and when we head toward the emptied city streets, the lighted gaze of Nyla's Berserker—Jen did not let her skip out on her assigned guard to come with us—traces our path, scares our shadows long and thin from our forms.

1718 Ursula. That is where the tracker last pinged; Jenny's waiting on the radio in case it moves.

None of us speak as the buildings grow tall, silently noting the faces pressed close to windows upon windows stacked up into a cloud-smothered sky, ignoring us completely, completely fixated on the deities standing quietly just up the hill. The curfew is unpopular, but the fortification is doing good for us—the Mechvespers' Gods came bright and shiny into this world from Godolia's whims, but they are currently strewn about our lawn, and awe is so much more intoxicating when it can be fed so easily.

Jenny would be with us, but all of us feel better with her watching after the new outdoor hangar—the first and last line of defense. It is me, Eris, Nova, Juniper, Theo, and Arsen, and in the black gaps slicked beneath the darkened streetlights— only a fourth of them lit under the curfew—we run.

Theo started it first, taking off up the gutters and then stopping, teetering before the edge of the light, like the asphalt dropped off instead of being stripped bare by the overhead bulbs. He waited for us, all of us walking together in the beam, and then the night slipped over our toes again and Eris took my hand.

It is a senseless, bright thing. Chasing one another in the dark. Tripping over the light, reddened cheeks, flyaway hair, pretending we have been moving so slowly the entire time.

We get close to our destination, eventually, and Eris says harshly, but quiet, in the empty cavity of the street, "I fucking hate the city."

I think we all get it. She is not talking about this quiet, uninhabited night with the summer just starting to leach from the air—we would be just like this, just be here forever, carving circles between the skyscrapers until the streetlights burned out, if we could. But we are not the only things here. There are worse things here.

In the dark gap we are subconsciously loitering in, I cup my hands around my mouth and shout, "Fuck this city!"

Eris looks so *dumbstruck* while the kids ricochet in the shadows, flapping their hands and repeating me, distracted. My arm loops around Eris's waist so I can kiss her, daze her, and do it again because it's funny. Because she can hate the city all she likes; I am trying to keep her from hating the rest of the world, too.

"Careful not to forget it, love," I say into her ear. "You're obsessed with me, too."

"Oh," she snips back, "you didn't want to keep your limbs?"

"You and your sister are so alike. I am positive Jenny has asked me something like that before."

"*Wither.* Let go of me."

"Ha. You—"

"Sona," Eris snaps, and now she is not looking at me. I let her go. "Hey! There's a curfew!"

She is shouting, head turned up the street, and all of us follow her line of sight, to someone turning on their heel and taking off at a sprint down the mouth of an alleyway.

"Gods damn it—" Eris is running, and so we are, too, passing right under the street marker that reads URSULA.

There are doors scattered down the length of the alleyway, one on the left swinging shut as we make the corner. Eris has already freed the mallet from her belt, but in her hurry her stance is all wrong—a strange, biting hum throbs against my eardrums, and the force of Jenny's frequency modifications shatters the handle and part of the doorjamb and sends Eris off her feet. But she is up before I can even get to her, grime on her hands and halfway up her leg from the dirty coating on the pavement, boot meeting the remnants of the door. The entrance leads down into an unlit stairwell.

We pause, an animalistic, fight-or-flight hesitation, going still like we can sense some unseen creature crouching over us.

June traces the side of the building and murmurs the numbers under her scarred fingertips. "Seventeen eighteen."

1718 Ursula.

Eris breathes. It draws a solid line across her shoulders, and she says, low and steady and rough, "Arsen. You're up."

A flash-bang is produced from his haversack, alongside a handful of thin glow sticks that crack into lines of green in our hands like ignited circuit wiring. He offers the ring to June, who grins and pulls it free, and he lets it clatter down into the stairwell.

A flash of white, and Eris tosses her glow stick and slides down after it.

But she stops short, after our feet move off concrete stairs, her light reaching into the darkness. Green luminescence traces open air, a thin railing. Semirusted bars and a set of grated stairs drip from the platform.

"Eris?" Nova whispers.

This isn't just a basement, the air cool and open and massive to carry the smallness of her voice wide before smothering it.

We are not alone in the room.

Footsteps, unseen and far, far below, patter like raindrops on stone, and then a hiss. Metal against metal, and I know that sound; we all know that sound. A door.

Eris frees the radio from her belt, the sound of momentary static grating my teeth, and she says quietly, "Jenny?"

"I'm here." Instantly. Like she can hear it in Eris's voice.

"You need to get here. Right now."

"I'm on my way. What? What is it?"

Eris looks at me, a mirror, just as scared shitless as I am. I do not think we are meant to change this quickly, to go from kids playing in the empty dark to this, a minute later—kids drowned in red. "It's a hangar."

I cannot see her when I reach for her, but I hear her perfectly. We are all completely silent under the groan of metal, the tick of gears beneath iron flesh, as the mecha a dozen feet away winds into consciousness. There is only one in this odd, deep space. I could be laughing, laughing about how the number hardly matters. One or one thousand, we have already started out in a grave.

"Come on!" Eris shrieks, shaking me from the thought. "Come on—*shit*—we are so not fighting it here—"

Tripping up the stairs and cutting up my palms for it, I am last to surface. The mecha reaches for me, fingers crawling up concrete and across the blood smears I leave behind. We spill into the alleyway, and it's odd; it's a whole different world with an open sky above us, and then I realize all of it is leaning.

No, the building is leaning, narrowing the cloudscape.

The mecha is coming aboveground.

"My Gods," June whispers, stunned, and I grab her wrist and Arsen's as the ground begins to lift beneath us. Concrete tears below our feet, and maybe I expected it to be like a breaking of a bone, but it's not—it booms more than it snaps, and then we are running again.

Hells, the thought ricocheting in my head as I try to keep upright, *I am not dying underground I'd rather be crushed flat—*

We make the intersection with the rest of them. Theo turns, scrubbing his hands through his hair as he goes completely pale. "Oh fuck, Eris, what do we—"

"I—" She is breathing hard, arms around her ribs, eyes wide and terrified. "Gods. Fuck. *Fuck* this. We're going to do what we usually do."

The skyscraper is coming down, glass body tilting oddly at an angle up the alleyway, as the Windup's wrist and hand creep onto the asphalt from within a cloud of debris. A whole building full of people.

I am holding their wrists too tightly—June snaps hers away, Arsen testing a tug and then wrenching free when I do not notice, cannot notice anything but the indistinguishable blots of faces pressed to the tilting windows. I take a step back, mouth unhinging, everything from the supports to the pavement to the people to the mecha screeching in their own ways.

Not again—

No—

Get it together. This isn't Heavensday.

I suck in a breath, then another. *Get it together and* move.

But something else moves first.

In the distance, a few blocks up, another skyscraper leans on its foundation like a thistle wilting in the sun.

"Eris!" I shout, and she whirls on me, tattoos heaving against her collarbone. She sees it, too. "This isn't—is there—"

This isn't the only one.

Her shock snaps from her, and then her teeth are bared. "*Go.*"

Running back toward the Academy tower, alone, boots hitting trembling asphalt. I can feel them in my molars, climbing, sprouting from their hidden caves.

I almost miss it, standing on the shadowed grass, hilariously, awfully. I choke on a laugh as I put my eye to its black boot, and climb. It does not matter that I have never Piloted a Phantom before. It does not matter which deity I wind—I have never felt much like a vessel anyway. I just feel like me most of the time now, and that does not flee from me when I put in the cords, click by cold click.

One hundred and seventy feet tall, and I still feel quite like myself. Still scared. Still watching a city crack apart at its roots.

CHAPTER FORTY

ERIS

Another reason why I hate the city? It's no place to fight a mecha.

Gearbreakers like open spaces. We don't need buildings to burst apart or narrow paths to get trapped in or fifty thousand people waiting to be collateral.

We need—*oh Gods*—fingertips cold at my side, heart thudding as the mecha's arms come aboveground, reaching for us—we need to *not be here*—

"Now!" I yell, and we break left. The hand reaches just past us, and there's a flash of June's biting smile, half grimace, as Theo and Arsen boost her onto the wrist. We follow her, down on the street as she takes off up the forearm. A tube has dropped from each of her sleeves, connected to sacks of fluid bound to her sides—we haven't done a run in a while, and that means lots of time to come up with new shit.

That means the mecha's other hand reaches for June and *winces* back when she slashes her wrist out, a blade of black liquid meeting its fingertips with an instant hiss of steam.

The thing is so incredibly ugly. It doesn't even have a proper face, just two uneven red eyes like they were shoved hastily into place. Jenny's Archangel was a patchwork piece, but this—undetailed limbs, panel edges gaping, the entire structure groaning with its movement—it doesn't have the sense of a sloppy effort, but rather a desperate one.

Tip: You never want to be between a Windup's arms. The rest of us are between the mecha's shoulder and the edge of the building, coming up on the alleyway. The skyscraper is already down, people already dead, *more of them* crawling onto the streets. The *how* of it doesn't matter, doesn't matter, *doesn't matter*—one Godsdamn thing at a time, and I swear the thought is a nail driving down into my head. I can sob all I want about it *later*.

"June!" I shout, boots already on Arsen's hands, ready to jump, and she turns to grab me but sees it in my eyes—the dripping fingers of the mecha's other hand rounding back to reach for her, and she lets herself fall forward onto all of us. Scattered between the edge of the alleyway and the building's corner, among rubble and broken glass, and the metal bastard has the audacity to start to tuck its arm, elbow into ribs and us between the two. Halfway on my knees, I bring the hammer to the mecha's side and Nova leaps over me to slash at the opening with metal-shearing knives—new, of her design and Jenny's engineering—two of them in her hands and the back of her arms bleeding down into her shirt from when she helped to break June's fall.

We don't talk, just *go*, one by one, sliding down the side toward the front of the chest as the cragged gap above us goes dark, blocked out by a metal limb.

Hells. We're scattered, and I'm upside down, caught and flipped with my ankle in a bundle of artificial nerve-cords, and the mecha is still moving.

The inside of the mecha is moving.

We're not alone.

And someone is screaming. The thought slams into me—
It's one of my kids—and I've ripped myself free, sliding toward

the sternum. But the angle changes, tilting cold metal on the back of my legs and then on my knees as the Windup begins to stand up.

I don't look—just shove my weight off the surface before it becomes a free fall, body clattering against a beam. When the air is forced out of me, feet dangling into empty space, a hand wraps itself in my hair and forces my head upward.

And I think, *Trojan horse wire*fuckers.

As another person appears to lift me onto the beam—just kicking me off might not kill me, though neither would kicking me in the stomach, but they do that anyway—I gag on air. Mechas below the city, mechas coming aboveground. They got Sona's eye—are the other ones going blindly?

I sweep my leg across the ankle of one of them when he goes to kick me again. He screams as the small of his back hits the beam, and then he's gone, and I'm up, knocking the other off the edge. But I grab the back of her shirt before she can fall, the fabric slick in the metal of my hand. I slide my knife to her side, blade cutting cotton but not much else, but we both know that will change if the mecha moves more hastily—or if she doesn't answer my next question.

"How many Windups?" I haven't sounded like this in a while. I haven't felt like this in a while. Angry and nothing else.

She looks at me over the curve of her shoulder; I should let go then, if only because the dread hits me so fast it startles me, but I don't, because I freeze with the feeling of it. It takes me a moment to understand what she's done, because she's done it so silently and so simply—tucked herself right into the knife, sending it right between her ribs, turning so her hand is on my wrist when she looks me dead in the eyes. It takes me a moment to notice the warmth running over my fingers, and the look on her face.

She's not triumphant, or coy, or sanctimonious. She's happy. Fulfilled.

"Can you count the Gods?" she asks me quietly, and then she just . . . lets go of me.

"Eris?" It's Arsen, from the far end of the beam, but I hear my name distantly, like it's fed down a tunnel. And then it all stutters, time and vision and the mecha wrapped around me. When I blink again I'm on my knees, Arsen's hand between my shoulder blades, and my lips and throat stinging with the bile I just emptied over the side.

"Okay." The word shakes out of me. "Where are the others?"

"It was June's scream," Arsen says, voice small. That wrenches me back into place, pins the nausea in my stomach as an insignificant thing, and then I see her, or just the electric blue of her hair, a smear in the dark down below.

Arsen sees it, too, but stays beside me when it's clear she's moving, climbing, and she heaves herself onto the beam. At first I think there's cuts on her face, but then Arsen touches his fingers to her cheek and it's blood splashed there, on the surface.

"I got one," June breathes. She shakes one sleeve, faintly, the hidden tube stitched inside. "Maybe another."

A cheerless grin spasms across my lips. I thought I smelled singed skin.

"All right," I say, tilting my chin toward the ladder. "Let's go."

But we've been beaten to the skull. Nova and Theo stand outside the Pilot's glass circle, both heads snapping toward us as we enter, but my eyes go to the cityscape daubed outside the tinted windows. They haven't taken out the Pilot yet because of it—because if you cut down the vessel while it's moving, the whole God will collapse. It wouldn't be a problem in the Badlands desert, but here . . .

"Rot," I spit. I *hate* the city.

The Pilot can hear us just fine, but doesn't speak, just keeps splintering the asphalt as he carries us rapidly toward the Academy. But we reach the end of a block and he turns his head slightly, still on his path but so we can glimpse it, his mouth forming into a tight line and some stinging kind of elation curdling in my chest.

Another ugly mecha appears up the intersecting street, but this one is already grounded, one leg *liquid* up to its knee, running into the gutters. Its head has put fissures through the east city plaza—Jenny timed it exactly right so it wouldn't take out a skyscraper or two on the way down.

"Wither," Theo says viciously to our Pilot. "Now you're *screwed*."

"*Nope*—oh." Arsen takes a step back from the ladder hatch, knocking into me. "Hi. I thought you were a Pilot. Uh. The bad kind."

I glance down to see my sister dragging herself up from the hatch. She has her goggles on, magma gloves deactivated, one brushing her hair off her shoulder and the other snapping out to grab the front of Arsen's shirt. She looks down at him, splits her expression with a grin, and says, "You'll find out why I think that's hilarious later."

"How the hells did you get in here?" I rasp as she releases our explosives tech.

Jen lifts a shoulder and shifts her backpack around to

her chest. She reaches into it and retrieves something—some*things*, and my heartbeat goes heavy in my ears—and juts her chin at the Pilot. "End this day for me."

I pull on the gloves she hands me. Left first, then right, black fabric over the biting glint of metal—I didn't realize how cold it was, all this time.

"Hold still," I say to the Pilot. The blue light curls over the nape of his neck, and I set my touch right there, the other drawing up the length of his leg the moment he puts his weight on it.

The mecha doesn't make it out of the step. When I pull away there's already vapor curling off the Pilot's frozen skin in delicate clouds.

"Jenny?" I say. The rush of the new cryo gloves, what I've just done, what I've just stopped—the thought of all of it is gone, just like that, when I hear how my voice sounds. Like a little kid.

I look over my shoulder. Jenny's standing there with the rest of them and they all look so, so young. "Come on," Jen says. "We have to clean out the rest of them."

Sona's up on the road that rings the Academy campus, in a Phantom Windup, ripping open the cheek of the last patchwork mecha when we make it out of the cityscape. Its stomach is split, Nyla in her Berserker picking through. Jenny must've warned them over the comms, that the bodies aren't empty.

Jen doesn't even glance in their direction, just stalks toward the Academy, occasionally scrubbing the heels of her hands against her crow's feet. The gardens are in chaos, another junker mecha splayed across the green, holes blown in its ankles. Zamaya's work. Hydras and allies scatter between the deactivated Windups, grass stomped flat, flashlight beams pulsing against night and metal, and Jenny mutters to herself.

"What?" I say, straining to match her stride. "What did you say?"

"Damn it. *Damn it*. Did we get them all? We've missed some. Sheils!"

The captain's head snaps in our direction, mouth set in a tight line as she stalks over. She has her Hydra jacket on over a pair of sweats and a tank top, graying, bedhead hair drawn back in a tangle behind one ear.

"Hello," Sheils greets viciously. "Did you earn some more tattoos tonight?"

"Did you search them?" Jenny shoots back just as harshly. "Did you find everyone inside?"

"We're combing." The fight flickers in and out of Sheils's eyes and the line of her shoulders, belladonna fingers picking at her pockets. "Ha, you know . . . This never happened when we were underground."

We don't even know what *is* happening.

"Z!" Jenny shouts, and I turn to see her crew coming out of the collapsed junker. There's a body in Nolan's hands, and my heart seizes before I realize I don't recognize them, and that there are panels in their arms. Nolan drops the dead weight, and Jenny immediately kicks the body onto its back, leaning over to look at its eyes. Natural and natural. I was right. The rest of them were moving blindly.

What the hells is this?

My hands are sweating in my gloves. That damn question—*Can you count the Gods?* I'm sure she hadn't shrieked it, but that's how it's carved into my head, like her lips could be right next to my ear, jaw unhinging—

No.

You can't count the Gods.

Because humans panicked. Because we needed saving and then we just *kept making more of them*, until we needed them closer, needed them to have physical forms and then closer still—we needed to be able to be their vessels. The Gearbreakers always made it sound so easy—Godolia was playing Gods, which was fucked, and it still is, but it's nothing so lucid. This isn't some power trip fueled by unlimited resources. It's a systemic desperation for protection.

Protection from what?

From nothing. From a world we scraped into blankness. It's so easy to be haunted, to be tense and scared and primed for the worst after the worst comes again and again, and faster when you're looking for it.

My fingers are on Jenny's sleeve. She looks down at them, eyebrow quirking, and then at me.

"Jenny," I say steadily, "we need to move our Windups out of the city."

"What?" she says, the word a dry laugh.

"I'm not kidding." I'm trying to grapple her here, trying to see my own dread snag in the black eyes we share because it needs to, because it's back, that same bad feeling. It's all about to get worse. We have mechas dead all over the city and we're going to follow them if she *doesn't listen to me*. "They were trying to get to our Windups, or knock the tower over, or just kill us, because they're always trying to do that—but what the hells kind of plan was this?"

Mechas thrown together, patchwork pieces, just like the

bomb in the kimchi jar. Chaotic, indulgent, and reckless—that scares me. We didn't see it coming, and now we don't know where to put it. Even Jenny didn't see this playing out in her head.

"We need to get the mechas *out*, Jen. Something isn't right. Something else is about to happen. I don't—it's just this knowing in my chest, and, Jenny, I *can't*—"

There's a moment, I think, when she's going to turn away and I realize that I don't know what I'll do if she does. I might just dissolve onto the grass.

"Come on," she hisses, hand around my arm suddenly, and she's dragging me back toward the Academy and away from Sheils. Jen barks over her shoulder to the general pandemonium, "I want guards in those heads around the clock!"

We reach the base of one of the Hydras and Jenny pulls me to the side—next to those freaking toes—and grips my shoulders, pinning me under her stare. Every word precisely carved, she tells me, "We can't move our Windups. You know that."

I do know that. I know that as soon as we move the mechas out, we might have more coming in, and they won't be ours.

"When it happens . . . ," I say. "When whatever happens happens, you have to *end this*. It has to be *done*, Jenny, because we're almost done, okay? We're—we need to be done living like this."

She grabs my chin. I didn't expect her to. My lips part as she tilts my face left to right.

"What—"

"You look so much like Mom."

I flinch away from her, hand up to my mouth. "Please," I snarl, like that's going to scrape the softness off my past words, off my thoughts. "She'd be disgusted with me."

"No. You sound like Appa, and she loved him, and—it's just, you look like her. Sometimes. I hadn't noticed."

My cheeks are burning. "Did you hear me at all?"

"I heard you."

That's all I'm going to get from her. I'll just have to trust it. "Thank you. For the gloves."

I leave her to go over to the base of the unwound Phantom, getting there as the door in its boot opens and Sona comes out. She wraps almost her entire weight around me, my face against her jacket, arms tucked around her ribs. Not a perfect fit exactly, but it feels like it.

"What's happening?" I whisper into her shoulder.

"An act of worship . . ."

Her voice is distant. Cold spills into me. "What?"

I try to pull away, but her hold tightens. I feel her heartbeat jumping in her chest.

"Eris." The name's feverish from her lips; I barely recognize it as mine. "I think they are shrines."

CHAPTER FORTY-ONE

SONA

Four Windups. Nine Pilots.

They were scattered among the rest—stationed alongside them in the junker mechas, we think, in case the Gearbreakers came—all without artificial eyes, but with panels sunken in their arms, wrought with wicked infection. *Hasty jobs*, Dr. Park tutted. Some just slowly cooked in their own skin, under-insulated pieces shoved into their veins—we do not know where they were getting them from.

The RMs we found in the four junkers—alive—are not so much talking as they are babbling.

About the Zenith.

About being presented with a holy gift, a vessel's eye, to mark his favor.

A call to bring the shrines above the earth.

It's a rare Mechvesper practice, I explained to Jenny, *building a full mecha, no weapons and no Pilot. Solely for prayer.*

The shrines could have been under the city for decades, until someone brought them my eye Mod.

Four Windups, trying to make it onto the Academy campus. There are a few ways they might have intended for it to play out. Maybe just a rampage, to knock the tower out of the sky with as many Gearbreakers as possible trapped within. Destructive. Simple.

Or, they were trying to get to the Hydras.

Older models, with doors that open without a retinal key.

You scared me more than I let you know.

Not scrawled in red across a mirror, across my own features, but his words, his voice in my head against black. I startle awake, glow of my Mod spilling from me and against the nape of Eris's neck.

I check the clock on her nightstand. Three A.M. *Go to sleep*, I tell myself, a joke, my weight already on my feet and my feet already on the carpet. *Just sleep.*

I pick over the kids—Nova with us on the mattress and the rest of them buried under blankets on the floor. The halls are dimly lit, lazy, yellow light soaking warmly into the dark floorboards. I drift by the other crew's rooms, listening for a laugh, the turn of a book page, but all is silent. I stand where the path splits, still for a moment, making sure. Then I turn for the elevators.

"This lighting is obscene," I say to Jenny as I push open the doors to her lab, or at least to the back of her head, the hunch of her shoulders. The fluorescents burn white above us, the night pressed against the sheet of windows to our right, seeming to recoil from the glass.

"If I knew you were going to be up this late just to bother me, I would've put you on skull guard," Jenny mutters. I sit on the edge of one of the lab tables, metal cool against the back of my legs, and glance out the windows toward our garden hangar far, far below.

We have a guard in each Windup head, and a guard at

each base. It's not enough, not enough to give them a gun and a radio and a time frame—we need more people. We checked every mecha top to bottom but they are, of course, massive.

Massive, and strange inside. Gearbreakers know it the most—there are plenty of places to hide in a God.

Jenny had the winding cords ripped out of most of them, save for the one constantly on guard—but nothing that cannot be easily fixed. No, we need them to be easily fixable in case *we need them.*

I think Eris was right. We need to move them out of Ira Sol.

But I understand Jenny's frustration. Her fear.

Jenny finally looks up, snapping her fingers at me when I try to get a glimpse of what she is working on. "Do *not.* It's ugly right now. Why are you here?"

I lift a shoulder. "Cannot sleep."

"You're checking up on me." I do not answer, and she extends a hand. "Now, bukkeuleowo hajima. I hate timidity."

I edge closer.

She snatches my wrist and brings my fingers to the base of her head. Through the silk of her hair, my touch scrapes against something cold.

I jolt back. Jenny is grinning when she says, "Boo."

"*Why* is it outside your head?" I spit, touching the base of my own neck, where if I press—I never have, and I won't—I will feel the syncing chip, too. The Mod that likes to fry the Pilots who flinch against it.

"What, and I would rather have it against my brain stem? Yeah, no. Fuck that." Jenny laughs, leaning back in her chair, fingers intertwining behind her head.

"There is no way it works," I hiss. "How the hells do you have it connected to anything—"

She snaps her black eyes to me, and I fall silent. That's on me—doubting Jenny Shindanai is a waste of energy.

"You know why they have it inside you, right?" Jenny asks me. "It's a sloppy design. If they set it wrong or it heals wrong, that's a Pilot with a liquefied head. But if they need to kill a vessel, that gets it done, hm?"

I am quiet.

"What?" she jabs, as my fingers drift to my right forearm panel. "What happened to you?"

"Enyo—when we first met—" I add, because that piece feels important. "When we first met, he . . . he turned on my nerves again. To take my tattoos out."

Silence. I can hear the hum of the lights above, Jenny tilting forward now, elbows balanced on her knees as she stares me down.

"Well," she says. "That's fucked."

"Is it? I had not noticed."

Her smirk cracks apart into something darker. "Yeah. It kind of is, Glitch." She taps the back of her neck again before standing. "Anyway, yeah. That's why it's there, and that's why I thought we couldn't siege Godolia."

"What?" She is moving toward the elevators, flicking off the lights as I trail behind her. "What do you mean?"

"I mean that little Zenith switchboard, or whatever the hells it is, the one that allows control over Pilot bodies—it has a range. Ends at Godolia's borders, or so I figured—oh, right. You've been wondering why you've been alive and stuff if this is true?" I open my mouth, but Jenny just shoves ahead, thumb jabbing at the elevator button. "The microchip takes in the physical information, so to speak—touch and sight and pain—as it is applied in real time to the mecha, and is able to . . . oh, how do I explain this . . . actualize the sensations through the Mods in your body. It's not like the switchboard sends something to the chip that says *time to fry*. I don't think there would be a program like that in place: Flip a switch, kill a Pilot. That would be too big a vulnerability with the right renegade group."

We go into the elevator, and she hits the button for the ground floor. I am too engrossed to ask what it is we are doing. Jenny turns her back to the doors, leans against them so she can watch the city grow taller and taller outside the windows.

"So," she continues, "if I've got it right—and you know the spectacular chances of that—the killing part of the teeny kill chip in your brain only works if you're plugged into one of their Windups. The mecha is what kills you—Godolia can remotely overextend the amount of aforementioned physical informa-tion that is pushed through the chip, making the God sensitive, making the chip heat and the vessel go *pop*." She smacks her lips together. "See, you're alive because they didn't know you were the darling little traitor you are until you left the limits. You're alive again because when you came back, it wasn't their mecha you were piloting."

I follow her as the elevator doors part and she stalks through the Academy entrance hall, where months ago Jenny danced with me, cut and crushed me under black gloves and a silk dress and a megawatt grin. Now, we are both in our socks, going along soundlessly.

Jenny pushes into the cool autumn night and stops, drop-ping herself on the entrance steps beneath the unlit strings of bulbs reaching from above the doors. She puts her hands on her knees, stretching her spine tall, eyes closed and head knocked back.

"What are we doing out here?" I ask, quietly for some reason, taking a seat beside her.

"Shush," Jenny says, each fine-edged feature lifted toward the blackened cloudscape. "Here. Plant your palms against the stone of the steps. Do it. There you go. Sit up. It feels like a crisis every single second, doesn't it? We're fine one moment and getting battered the next, so the former doesn't feel like it counts for much. What a shitty way to see it. Look. Stretched thin all day long and landed here all the same. This can feel just as enormous as the worse parts."

"It's cold," I say, feeling a bit dazed, feeling the gaps between my clothes and my skin. And it startles me when she speaks again, because she does so very softly.

"It's quiet."

And then the words are gone completely, swallowed down like a pill into the stomach of the dark.

Quiet, and still, and I just—breathe.

Mechas strewn before us, shadowed edges of limbs, fingers dropped in half curls toward the earth. Eris sleeping just fine above my head. The slow stretch of the lungs in my chest, and hold still. Just for a minute, just for now.

Deities.

People generally think Jenny has a screw loose. Brilliant, but batshit crazy, like her humming while she pulled my eye from my head to slit open its ring like an egg in her palm, easing out the color-blocking Mod. Like her spitting on it, and crushing the lens under her coffee mug to send it splintering.

But considering the circumstances, Starbreach might be

the sanest of all of us. She should not have had to learn how to cope so quickly, so early in her life, but it seems like she did, if only because she had to.

Footsteps sound in the building behind us. The doors swing open as Jenny drops her head all the way back to peer at her four crew members, flails and twists onto her feet after Gwen leans over and flicks her captain between the brows.

"Banned!" Jenny shouts, gathering Gwen's shirt in her fist.

"Mm, joh-a," the sharpshooter yawns. "I'm going back to bed."

"Nah. You're in the Phantom skull over there; Seung's got your base." Jenny shakes Gwen slightly, and then slightly harder. "Joh-a? Is that joh-a enough for you, you little brat—?"

"J-joh-a—*good*, fine, whatever," Gwen yells, skittering out of her grip to clutch onto Seung.

Zamaya, a riot of violet hair and dangerously tired energy, snaps her hand out onto Jenny's shirt. I freeze, expecting an immediate fist struck against the archer's tattooed cheek, but Jenny, a step below her, leans *back* with a sheepish grin.

"Did you have a bad dream, gorgeous?" Jenny asks, palms up.

The stony look across Zamaya's features does not twitch. "You're going to regret putting me on this shift, darling."

"Ha, uh, Nolan—?"

"Don't look at me," he says.

"Insubordination!" Jenny growls, straightening and tearing Zamaya's hand away, but she keeps it in her grip as she turns toward the mecha garden. "You two are on the Hydra," she spits. "That one, so get—that's—"

She drops Zamaya's hand, fully facing the Hydra she was gesturing to. Its back is to us, the stack of its sculpted vertebrae mangled and elegantly detailed at once, like the teeth of a serrated knife. Jenny's silent as she takes a step forward, closer, thinking and seeing something we do not, and just like that, I know.

This past beat of quiet—it is the last one we will have for a while.

The line of Jenny's shoulders shifts. Tilts to the left, just a little. Then she takes off running.

We follow after her, shouting, but no one can catch Jenny, and when we get close she turns, making for another Hydra, and another. At some points I can see just a sliver of her expression and it—it—*deteriorates.*

There is fear there, across Jenny Shindanai's features.

And then she just stops, like a black pin dropped in the middle of the green. Her head turns slowly, slowly, at the Hydras reaching up around us.

"*Jenny*," Zamaya hisses, grabbing her arm. "What is it?"

"They're standing wrong," Jenny breathes, her next words ricocheting in a high, thin laugh. It's the most terrifying thing I have ever heard. "They're off balance."

Zamaya releases her. Jenny gives another laugh, short and vicious and then done, and she pulls the radio from her belt and pushes past us for the Academy.

"We're evacuating," she snarls into the receiver as she shoves into the entrance hall. "I want every single floor cleared, *now.*"

"Starbreach." It's Captain Sheils's voice, cottony, a moment out of sleep. "What the hells—"

"We missed some. We didn't find them all. They might have been in the fucking deities the entire Godsdamn time."

"Jenny—"

"The Hydras are missing tanks. Or they've been drained."

"No . . . ," Seung breathes, hands on top of his shaved head, and I just—look at the gears tattooed down his wrist, ink following the veins, my heartbeat thudding, I do not understand, it's slipped past me, what is wrong here—is anything wrong here?—and then *thud* the tilt of Jenny's shoulders *thud* poison as arteries in the mechas' limbs *thud* off balance *thud* missing *thud* tanks.

Jenny pulls the fire alarm. It's like she split the world.

Sound draws in a white bead across the air, emergency lights popping and dying and popping again, and the radio cracks to life in Jenny's hand one more time. Sheils's voice.

"Don't come—"

Jenny snaps her head up, and then she *pushes* Zamaya, her mouth unhinging in her shock.

"Get out!" Jenny *screams*. "Go! *Go!*"

I look up.

To the row of vents lining the ceiling.

To the clouds trickling silently from the grates.

"Shit . . . ," Zamaya whispers, face completely drained of color.

I have never seen any of them stunned like this, but Jenny is moving, Jenny is shrieking, and then they are all outside, scattered on the steps.

"Stay the fuck outside. You come inside and I will kill you." Jenny's voice breaks. It breaks, and I feel the line of its fragment in my chest, the strangest thing. She flinches against it when she hears it. "You'll like it better than the gas in your lungs."

Then she is on me. Hands on my cheeks and it startles me, forcing my eyes up to hers, *thud, thud, thud,* and I realize—Jenny wants me outside, too. Wants me outside and away from all of it, but she needs me here.

"Listen to me. It's going to be okay. Don't breathe," Jenny snarls. "What did I say?"

"Don't breathe," I whisper, and above the night of her hair, the gas has become heavy enough to have color, green-gray silk stripping down the walls.

Oh no.

The words small, so completely small in the back of my head.

Oh no.

"Exactly." Jenny swallows hard. Scowls. Releases me. "Now go get Eris."

CHAPTER FORTY-TWO

SONA

The elevators split open to the Valkyrie floor. Lucky to have gotten here so quickly, and so selfish for thinking it—most people, believing this is a fire, will take the stairs.

But I am going to be selfish.

I tear a mirror from the wall and smash it to bits on the elevator threshold; when the doors begin to close, perhaps to go collect and save someone else, they spring back open. I do not care. I just don't *care*.

"Everyone get up!" Screaming it into the hallway, and I realize the blare of the alarm is nonexistent. *No.* Did it malfunction? "We need to—"

It's already here. Curls of poison nestle in the corners and tangle in the rug fibers, mist rising around my boots.

Why the hells are they not—

I shove open our bedroom door. It's the same moment Nova manages to pull herself out of our bed, and lands on the rest of them where they writhe.

Sweatshirt pulled up to her chin, the fabric soaked with bile where it meets her mouth. Her hands spasm and reach for Theo's bloodless face.

I am there, dragging her away and dropping her into the hallway. It's worse inside the room, the gas stinging tears into my eyes when I go to grab Theo. Or maybe it's just because

Juniper's halfway on her knees, her scream choked silent, arms under Arsen's ribs, heaving him upright.

I do not see Eris. I don't know where she is.

"Gods—" I let Theo go next to Nova and scream, "The elevator! *Go!*"

"S-Sona," Arsen croaks, teeth chattering as I pull him and Juniper into the hall. "Ny—"

"*Go*—Nova—" But I turn to see her form spasm with a violent cough, and red splatters the wallpaper. "*No.*"

The panic disorients me, vision warbling with the sting of the gas in my eyes, and I do not understand it.

Why Theo, heaving himself onto his forearms, has a gun in his hand.

For a glittering, surreal beat, I think he is aiming for me.

But he is shaking all over. The shot buries itself in the bedroom ceiling.

And then something heavy and hard slams into the base of my neck.

The floor tilts, and I slide down the door frame, the nausea immediate. A hand wraps itself in the front of my shirt, drags me upright, and there is a light being shone into my eye.

No. Not a light.

A Mod.

"I never understood it," Nyla says, rolling a paperweight in her other hand, "why the Zenith liked you so much."

She slams it against my temple. My vision stutters white, and I know: It was her in the woods.

Is it true? Are you taking Pilots? Them finding her, in the mountains. Guards slain, their blood dried on her face. *If I'm wrong, can you make it quick?*

"He sent you," I slur. "From the beginning."

"I thought I was chosen," Nyla spits, and slams a kick into my stomach when I try to move. Her next words are a shriek. "But *you were—*"

Another kick.

"*—in—*"

The next one makes me choke.

"*—his—*"

Something cracks and—

"*—head—*"

One more to the head, my chin meeting the door frame and then the floor.

Somewhere past the ringing in my ears, another gunshot. This one goes wide, too, and in my clipped vision, I see Nyla turn and pluck the pistol from Theo's sweat-slick hands, the gesture easy. She stands there for a moment, simply watching him shudder and choke, before turning back to me.

"I could have blown all of you off the map months ago. But he wanted to keep you. Wanted to test you, is what he said."

She makes the mistake of leaning too close, and my hand snaps out. But she does not even flinch when I drag my nails across the length of her cheek, split her skin open in four lines, pinking, and then reddening. She wraps my wrist in her grip and pins my other hand beneath her foot, blood rushing to my fingertips.

"But then we were here. He let *Jenny Shindanai* go. I guided the Mechvespers to put those bombs on the train and still *nothing* from him. Nothing but a message to be delivered to *you,* in this desecrated place, in the first few weeks. I kept it to myself. I thought he had lost his mind."

I remember her senseless laughter. We mistook it as terror. But it was relief.

I thought he left us alone.

Until the Leviathans. My thoughts reel, absent of pain, but the panic distorts them just the same. Nyla thought them a sign for her to begin her work.

Were they a sign?

Enyo sent me a message.

Enyo left us on the map, all these months.

"Sloppy work, the Mechvespers. But hey. Got me on patrol in the Hydras. Got me the gas, little by little," Nyla says, and presses the muzzle of the gun into my cheek. "Oh, but not just yet, Bellsona. I watched you burn down people I loved, so safe from your place in the sky." I think her voice shakes, just a bit. I cannot be sure. "You are going to watch your family die, too."

The gun pulls back only to snap forward, and then it's black.

I blink awake what must be seconds later, blood over my chin and down my throat. Broken nose. Nyla is standing over Theo, who's attempting to crawl up the hallway with Nova under one arm. His gun in her hand, Nyla kicks him viciously in the side before she raises the barrel between his brows.

"He did not think I could do this," Nyla says, poison curling at her feet. The gun gives a single, bare quiver in her hand. Her voice frays, high and shrill. "But I did. *I did this.* I would've gone down in the hellsfire from the beginning!"

"You—" Theo croaks. "You were one of us."

Nyla frowns.

And then Juniper is on her, body knocking into Nyla's arm, and the gun goes off. Plaster pops from the wall directly next to Theo's head. My hold slips, bile sloshing up my throat as I buckle again. *Get the fuck up.*

"You are right," Nyla purrs at her. "The gas will get the rest of them in a few minutes. But I am not sure about your tolerance to toxins at this point, Badlands *freak.*"

I lunge forward, but Nyla's already thrown Juniper off and plucked her back up. Entangled a hand in her riot of blue, blue hair, the gun set beneath her chin.

"Don't—" Juniper snarls, eyes bright, and this isn't—

Bang.

Blood

up the wall and it's

done—there's no time

Nyla is already moving on to Nova, the green in her eyes small in her whites, *shrieking,* blood on her teeth, on her hands, her hands on Juniper's head—

And then I have Nyla against the floor, hands around her throat, use the grip to bring her up and then down, once, twice, her feet kicking underneath me, a third time, and now it's a crack instead of a thud. Her eyes spin back in her head. Flickering light.

"Where's Eris?" I scream, and scream, but it is all happening too quickly, the body is already slack in my hands. I lurch to my feet, just *moving,* tearing Nova away, and it's, "*No, no, no,*" the words a moan, rolling out of her in a low swell, "we can't leave her—"

I drop her in the elevator, go back to drag Theo, trip over June when I try to lift him, fractured sob pulling from my throat, and then we are past her. It is just two more times over, to get Arsen. He is gray, but his skin still blisters under my touch.

He tries to push away from me when we get to her.

"Please, please, Arsen," I beg, and he chokes, a wet, horrible hitch, and shudders so violently he jerks out of my arms onto the ground, and reaches for Juniper. Hand in her matted hair, and his spine arches through the T-shirt as he shudders again and empties his stomach, sobbing as he inhales, taking more of this poison inside him. "*Please—*"

Dragging him now. Away.

Oh my Gods. Oh my Gods.

On the floor of the elevator, Nova is colorless and curled in on herself, Theo twitching around her, one hand on the back of her head. I put Arsen down, his mouth drawn in cold, silent horror, and punt the mirror shards away.

"I blocked the elevator vents. Jenny's waiting for you downstairs, okay?" I choke out as I press the lobby button and step out. "Just one more minute. Hold on."

The doors close. My hands clamp over my mouth, catching a whimper I did not know was coming.

I do not want to turn around. To see her again.

I want to sink to my knees and scream until I'm raw.

But I have to find Eris.

I cannot look at her. It's just the lithe line of brown ankle at the end of her pajama bottoms, the gas swallowing one set of scarred fingertips against the carpet. It's still too much. I look to the ceiling, and it's a mistake, find her blood, and the bullet hole, and the matter—

I stumble against the wall, push off it.

"I'm sorry," I murmur, delirious, leaving her behind. "I'm so sorry."

CHAPTER FORTY-THREE

ERIS

My fingers rise to the wood of the bathroom door, cheek slick against the floor tiles. It's Sona. She's here. She's screaming. *Everyone get up! We need to—*

Stand up.

The thought comes in a fog. I woke up and she was gone. I couldn't fall back asleep. Came in to draw a bath, in the dark, and someone closed the door behind me.

I didn't realize it until I went to turn on the lights.

Didn't see the gas until they came on, until it was already in me.

This isn't good. The nausea lurches in my stomach, spills at the base of my throat. The ground angles underneath me, vision slipping up the crack of the door. I don't remember collapsing. The faucet is still on. Water on the tiles.

A gunshot.

The sound breaks through my delirium. They need me. I can't get up.

Someone's talking. I can't pull meaning from it.

Another gunshot.

I'm on my forearms now, tears streaming down my face—I take it back. I'm sorry for all of it. I'll leave your Gods alone. I'm sorry. I'm sorry. Don't take them away—

Bang.

A muffled thud, a weight slumping against the floor. A half second of silence while my mind goes blank, before the air splits with an arching, cold-blooded shriek.

Nova. It's Nova's.

"*Nonono*," I sob wetly, clawing at the door. "Don't hurt them, please don't h-*hurt* them—"

The taste of blood in my mouth, and black dots fleck the light.

Something inside me shudders, and I realize it's all getting darker and darker—

CHAPTER FORTY-FOUR

SONA

My touch traces her spine, head turned and tucked to hers. *Deities,* I start, trying to remember, *please remember,* Umma at the head of the table, her clasped hands raised to her brow—*Deities traced around this mortal outline I ask for your glorious protection*—

Nyla blocked the bathroom door with a chair. Eris was already unconscious, soaked with the water from the over-flowing tub.

The poison is everywhere, and she is already gray. *She needs air.*

I slam the bathroom door shut behind me. Rip the towel bar from the wall and send it crashing through the window above the tub, and drag her, biting down on my cries. My socks sink into the water, stark and odd against the porcelain, and leave her there, slick and draped over the rim, clattering out again to seal the vent under the sink. Hands shaking, I soak a towel and drop it over the grills, and stumble over to do the same to the slit below the door.

"Come on," I sob, sloshing back into the tub, her back against my stomach as I smooth her hair from her eyes. They are half-open now, gasping at the fresh air trickling too slowly through the smashed window. "It's okay. It's okay."

"Where are they?" Eris moans, half gasp and half cry,

rocking in my arms, sending water onto the floor. She shudders, then vomits over the side. Shaking her head, begging me. "No, no, *no*, S-Sona—"

Her weight suddenly slackens, and I ease us back into the water, one hand jerking to shut off the faucet. In the silence, her dark, dark eyes roll up to me, no—*stay calm*—the whites—*stay calm for her*—of her gaze glossed over in red. Blood webs her lower lashes, little crimson canopies strung between the black threads.

Her head is against my collarbone, tilted back. She takes in a breath, lifting my arm where it's strung around her waist. The air snagging somewhere under her skin, like a needle catching on a record—*tick tick tick*—and then out again—*tickticktick*.

My mouth in a tight line, I turn my face into her hair. *Just be right here. There is no next part. She's here. She's here.* Tears spilling down my cheeks, I close my eyes, fumble for the prayer and come up blank. Eris shudders, a quiet, pained cry splitting from her.

It's too late.

I was too late.

"I don't want to die," Eris says, her voice small. "I'm scared."

"Don't worry," I murmur into her, holding her tight. Fighting to keep a tremor out of my words. "Hey. Remember when you told me about how we were all going to live next door to one another? Somewhere quiet. With a porch."

Her fingers tighten around my arms, breath coming quick and shallow.

"Can you picture it for me, Eris?" I whisper, heart breaking in my chest. "It's summer, and it's warm. I make a stupid joke and you threaten me for it. The sun goes down. We sleep in the next day. I'll make the bed. I'll make you breakfast. If you ever get dark and sad I will open the windows and you can sit in the middle of the kitchen floor until it goes away, love.

"It will always go away . . ."

CHAPTER FORTY-FIVE

SONA

We lay out the bodies in the rose garden, blossoms dead from the nightly cold snaps, one white sheet after another until the lawn is pockmarked with fabric. I straighten when it's done, wipe the sweat from my brow and lean, lean, lean back, so much that I fall. I have not slept in so long. I let my curls tangle in the grass and watch the clouds, high and thin and pale, scar the sky. Hand on the edge of the sheet beside me, like I am waiting for her stomach beneath it to lift, to realize I have dreamed up all of it.

From above, the bodies must look like seeds waiting to be pressed into the soil, even if they are to be burned instead of buried. Even if I won't go upstairs like no one will go up the stairs, because as many people as we have on the grass around me, there are more slicking the steps.

Eventually Jenny comes to loom over me. "Sleeping on the job?"

"Go away," I say, wishing Nyla were still alive. I want to make her beg for her Gods.

Her God.

It did not matter, finding the stolen tablet Nyla had used to communicate with Enyo, hidden so simply in her bedside table. Finding his letter, sent to her to be distributed to me, mere weeks after we took Ira Sol. Months ago. I can see why she chose not to show it to anyone. *I thought he had lost his mind.*

Dear Sona,

Do you remember the night you pierced my ears and thought about killing me? You scared me more than I let you know.

I forgot it, when you were with me. That I was always meant to be something terrible. But I was not meant to love you so much, Sona.

You were supposed to be heartless. I laugh at that now.

I needed a miracle to ease the masses. I hurt you. I made you into something else. You just kept coming back, until I thought it finally stuck. But. Ira Sol, and Eris, and I came back here.

And good Gods, forgive me. It all seems so much less.

We pluck our inheritors from the streets. There are so many orphans here, but the babies are the ones chosen for it. We are built up like code. This whole place is shot through me, grown around me, but I grew around it, too, ingrained like a tumor—which one of us is the tumor? Zenith, or Godolia, or it does not matter. Removing one kills the other kills both.

They know it, too. My guards, my Pilots. They panicked when I tried to run. I just tried to walk out onto the street, through the front doors—you would have laughed at me—thinking I could just disappear. They shot me when I stepped off the campus. Then they didn't let me die.

I think, maybe, I could not be the first one who has tried. I think now I know where my power ends. The one thing a Zenith can never do is leave.

I do not want to hurt anyone else. But I think, for this to end, I have to have a part in it. I have to have my end in it. You only win when there is no one to fight back with. Know that it's Eris.

It's Eris.

It's Eris.

I remember my heart hitching in my chest, reading those words on the screen. All of them need him, to suffer for them, to pin this entire consuming system in place; he is not at the top of a tower but at the center of a body grown around him. Stuck, ligament to bone, vein to heartbeat.

You are not telling me something.

It was Nyla, telling him that Eris and Jenny had gotten the invitations, where we were at the cabin. Nyla thought he was holding her back for a chance to test me. I think it might have been true.

And then I failed.

And this letter . . . he did not care that I did.

Zamaya noted that the letter lacked an apology, but I think moreover it lacked purpose. I mean something to him, and so he left us alone, and in the end it did not even matter.

But perhaps today I am just bitter. I am mourning. I did not care to pick over it like Jenny did, thumb skimming over her sister's name.

"The doctor wants to see us," Jenny says now, and I jolt up immediately, follow her across the graveyard and into the Academy's elevator. She hits the button for the hospital floor.

There is a chance the entire building reeks, but I would wager that neither of us have breathed since last night—was it only last night?—but I do notice the chill. In the bath with

Eris on the top floor, we could not see how our mechas had gathered around the skyscraper, shattering window after window to force the gas to leak out.

"They're in room nineteen," Jenny says when we exit. She makes her way for Dr. Park, coming up the left hallway to meet us.

I am immediately numb. "Wh— Are they awake?"

"Enough," Dr. Park says, and I'm gone, skimming through the numbers and pushing through a door, hand choking the handle as I freeze on the threshold, chest heaving now—it smells clean, actually, and sickly so. Two pairs of eyes latch onto me.

"Sona—" Nova murmurs, and I am out of it, next to her with my cheek pressed to her temple. She looks so small in the bed, limbs thin beneath the blanket, plastic mask looped over her mouth and nose like the rest of them.

I press a reverent kiss to the side of her head. Lean back to see her bottom lip warbling, to see Theo looking at the ceiling, fighting to keep the tears in his eyes. Arsen has his gaze up, too, but I do not think he sees anything at all. Face blank, limbs slack. Motionless, except for the rise of his chest, his breath brushing the curls on his left cheek.

But he must feel me staring at him, because his black eyes drift over to me. There is the bright shock of grief beneath the unfocused glaze.

"Sona," he says, voice ragged, the voice of someone five times his age. "Where's Eris?"

Eris.

She was cold when Jenny found us, when Jenny lifted her from the bath. That was it. I thought, *This is it*, she is gone and it's just me and that low, cracked sound that came spilling out from Unnie's mouth, the one that is going to be chasing me for the rest of my life, and I—I am just going to be this hollow, haunted person.

We bled for one another and then bled into each other, did not realize it was happening at first and watched it happen when we did, smearing edges, softening lines. How young we were, thinking we belonged to each other; we could never be anything so simple. We fell into each other so completely that I cannot mourn her without mourning myself.

And then Eris had moved, shook, and I realized it was the bath that had gone cold and not her blood, and Jenny snapped her teeth closed and the world clicked back in line.

I put my hand over Nova's when it tightens around my wrist, and breathe, "She's alive. Dr. Park has her in the intensive care wing. She cannot breathe on her own." Tubes down her throat, plastic curled against raw flesh. "Has not woken up yet."

"Why are you here?" Theo croaks, and he means, *And not at her side.*

I lift a shoulder, tired for a while now, and suddenly, too much so to talk. I have not been away from her for long—Hyun-Woo and Dr. Park sent me out when it was time for her chest X-rays. But it's not just to see her lungs—it is also to make sure the fine line of her bones is still intact. Captain Sheils says that everyone reacts to the poison differently. Nyla was right—June took it the best of all of them, most likely because she has been around the fumes of her own corrosives for a time now.

"So," Arsen says, the word chipped out of a dry, scraped

throat. His eyes still drifting toward me, the rest of him unmoving. "What do we do now?"

They are all looking at me. Looking to me, and I—

I have nothing to say to them. Nova's expression distant, odd without the firecracker grin, Theo's freckles rubbed dull under the hospital fluorescents, and Eris . . .

Eris on the edge of that black, black ledge, and I have nothing.

Nothing but the thought that this isn't over.

The fact that he could have had those Leviathans come in past the gate, could have blown us all off the map months ago, that he tried to *run*, that he is just a kid—

It does not matter. He knows it does not matter.

Because they think him a God, and they won't let him leave.

So. I guess I lied. I do know what we do now.

Shouting erupts from down the hall.

I turn a couple of corners before I find the source: Nurse Hyun-Woo, protests near incoherent with shock, reaching for Jenny's arm as it pins Dr. Park by her collarbone against the crisp white wall. Jenny does not even glance at him as her free hand sends him to the floor, leaning over the doctor easily with her height. Both women are perfectly calm.

"I'm getting Soo Yun," Hyun-Woo spits, rising to hurry past me.

Jenny ignores him, ignores me, saying silkily, "Now, as I was saying—" but I am paying attention only in beats, stockstill up the hall because what if—what if this is happening because Eris—my hands around my mouth and I cannot feel my feet underneath me, realizing with total indifference that I am about to sink to the floor when Jenny snaps, *"Stop that."*

It is directed at me, and my sight tightens back into focus on her. But she is already done with me, and then I remember that sound she made when she pulled Eris from the tub. Jenny would not be calm like this, just at the point of danger, if Eris was gone—

"—I'm not asking," Jenny breathes, each word as steady as her hold against the doctor.

"You cannot—"

"The hells I can't. I run this place."

Dr. Park laughs, a particularly reckless choice, with her spine to the wall and Jenny so close. "And you hate it."

"But that doesn't change it," Jenny snarls easily. "So—"

"*What* the hells are you doing?"

Someone else moves past me, and Captain Sheils is tearing Jenny away by her forearm, lifting it up high like someone would wrench back a child. Jenny lets her but does not break eye contact with the doctor, and I see it perfectly clearly across her features, the moment when her calm flips over into something jagged.

And then she is screaming.

"I am *done*." She pulls against Sheils's hold and it startles both of them, Jenny clawing for the doctor's coat as she shrieks, "It goes to Eris, or I am *out*, and you can let this city starve and burn and dissolve for all I care! Throw the entire thing into the twin hells and fucking *let go of me*!"

Sheils does not, but Jenny manages to break from her anyway, and when I think she is going to go for the doctor again she is right in front of me, hand around my wrist and her words pushed and sharpened through clenched teeth. "We don't have as much medicine as we thought we did."

And I understand, right away. Jenny is not throttling me,

too, because she knows I am not going to fight her on this. Ha—no, I am going to be selfish right alongside her, going to let every other person in this building fighting for their next breath take their last one. All of them can think terribly of me, terribly of us, but we—we're just human.

We are just kids.

We tried our best. We tried to save as many as we could, and we have given up so much of ourselves for it, and we will carry so much worse because of it.

But not this. Not Eris. She is not going to weigh on us like this.

"You need her," I hear myself say. *We need her.*

"We do not get to pick and choose," Captain Sheils says, voice steel. "There are people who are worse off than her, who are going to *die.*"

"She is not going to be one of them," I shoot back, aware of Jenny's fingers tensing around my wrist. "Do you really think your Hydras can keep this place together? You did not even want to take Ira Sol in the first place."

"Which is why you *cannot*—"

"Leave?" I laugh, and it is a cold thing, splintering my throat. "Watch us."

But I do not move. It turns over in me, what we are lacking, where we could get it, clicks into place with what I want—need—to do.

Get Enyo.

"Heal her," I say. "You do that, and we will get you more supplies."

Dr. Park laughs, the sound rough. "And from where would that be?"

Jenny gets it. She scoffs, and lets go of me. But just like that, we are tied. This isn't something I can do without her. It isn't something I want to do alone.

I am scared to do it alone.

"Godolia," Jenny says. "We're going to get it from Godolia."

On one shoulder, making myself small on the edge of Eris's hospital bed, my fingers slip between hers to watch the feathered line of her closed eyes, the brief slope of her nose, the hard mouth softened in her sleep. Parted around the tube that rises from her lips, feeding in air, and I cannot help but think of the plastic line it draws down her throat as her chest rises under the blanket.

"This feels familiar," I whisper to Eris, and I wish it were not true, wish it truer, because at least she was awake the last time we were here.

The X-rays came back promising, and now the medicine is reaching her system, dripping from an IV that hangs above us. I do not know what is in it—some impossible miracle compound that Jenny tried explaining to me. Like the Spiders, I do not understand any of it, how it works, how Godolia could possess such an essential in bulk and only keep it for themselves, besides a handful scattered like chicken feed across the Cities. What is happening to Eris, what is happening to dozens of people across this floor—it is all curable.

"Love . . . I have to go." Brow bent against the side of her head, the silk of her hair. "I know I promised I would stay.

I'm sorry. I have to go do something really stupid, and it has to work out. I cannot have the world like this. I do not want us to live in a world like this, and deities—I promise I would just run from all of it if you asked me to. We could just leave and let it all burn down behind us, and I would be so happy, love."

The hum of the fluorescents softens everything, IV dripping in an even, quiet metronome, so when I shudder I feel out of place.

"I'm sorry. I am getting your hair all wet. I told Jenny about the empty Phantoms that stand as Devoid guards in the desert. They rotate at the end of the week, brought back to Godolia if a part of them is broken, so we are going to break one. Stay here and sleep. We'll bring back the medicine." Gently, I bring her hand up to my lips, brush a kiss against the back of her knuckles, and whisper against them. "I am going to take away their last God, and it will make them stop."

I was so cold for so long that I thought I had simply frozen over. Woke up from the Mods surgery and thought myself a completely horrible thing, and I—thought that would be it. I would be sick with the thought of myself, and I would get used to it. Hateful, but alive. Sad, but still standing.

And then came Eris.

When it was all supposed to be so vicious, and she ended up in my life all the same, like a missed stitch.

"It was worth it," I whisper, words murmured into her skin. "Everything that happened to me. Everything I am going to carry with me, and hurt for—it was all worth it, because it dropped me right next to you. I love you. I love you while the world is ending, and I love you when it goes still."

I press my lips against her temple. I know. I know I am

being cruel again. Doing this while she is asleep. Because she would say it if she were awake. *It's all shot. Run away with me, Sona. We could be* so *happy. We could let it all burn down behind us, and we could be so happy.* I could not say no to her. It's everything I want.

CHAPTER FORTY-SIX

ERIS

Wait—

Blurred edges, lights flashing, no—I'm blinking, trying to anyway, one set of fingertips feeling threads of the blanket pressing me into the mattress, the other I can't feel—oh, ha. Bomb. Metal. Right.

Oh, right.

I'm dead.

I don't know what I was thinking.

I thought it would feel better. *Seriously?* Do I not get to feel better, even now? I hurt all over, dry from the inside— good Gods, are you *serious?* You do not get to do this to me. After everything—I can't—you *won't do this to me*—

I'm awake.

Alive, and upright, spine curved and rising through the split of the hospital gown, staring at the fibers of the bedspread, breathing to find it less painful than last time, and I hold the inhale, hold it, hold it, and let it go in a jagged, horrible laugh.

"Sona Steelcrest," I rasp. "You're so fucking *dead.*"

It's the middle of the night. I stand in the doorway of room nineteen. Count. Count wrong. Count again. And again.

"No," I say.

Three kids. They blink at me in the dark.

I shake my head and say it again. "No. Where's—"

"It was Nyla," Theo croaks, mouth moving behind the plastic mask. "The bomb in the train. Sona's eye. The gas. J-Ju—"

His words clip. Arsen puts his arm over his eyes and breathes in, the act ragged.

The feeling goes out of my legs. I slide down the door frame as the grief eases open in my chest, twists inward into a black hole. I'm hearing the gunshots. I'm hearing Nova's scream.

A sob pops out of me, hand going over my mouth to catch the next one. *Where are they?* Sona hadn't answered. I shudder, my head going light. No. *No.* I was so close, feet away.

I left them all alone. I failed them. I failed June.

"Eris," Arsen whispers, so softly, and I realize how loud I am, crying so hard I've barely taken a breath, barely can see him extending his hand. I crawl onto his bed, and he curls around me, holds me while I shake. He's shaking, too.

This isn't how I was supposed to be with them. I was supposed to lead. I was supposed to protect, and comfort, and get them up to do the next fight, to do it all over again.

Instead I clutch onto Arsen and choke out between my sobs, "I'm sorry. I'm sorry. I should have—"

"It wasn't your fault," Arsen growls, and I've never heard his voice as harsh as this, but his hold tightens around me. "Don't, Eris. She'd hate you for it."

But we both know that wouldn't be true. June doesn't really hate anyone.

And Nyla. I can't believe it.

I am going to take away their last God, and it will make them stop.

"Sona left," I murmur. "To try to save him."

Maybe he did leave us alone, for the most part, because he's better than the rest of them. It just doesn't matter, and Sona knows that. It's bigger than him. It's fanaticism, and fear, and religion. Ancient things, bigger things.

She knows it.

And she still thinks this can end with him alive.

Arsen laughs, the sound dark. "Don't even get me started on her."

"She's doing it for us. She's—she's trying for *us*—"

"You're leaving, too." I almost don't catch it; Nova's voice is small, maybe the smallest I've ever heard from her. I turn my head to find her green eyes half-open, words worked out from beneath her oxygen mask.

I feel the smile flicker onto my face, already there before I realize how cruel it is to them, even if it's unintentional, even if it's only there as a reflexive thing to keep me from crying more.

"You're sick." This comes from Theo. He tries to lift his head, but it doesn't work, so his words float up to the ceiling, where his blue eyes are drawn, glassy with his own tears. "You're fucking sick in the head, Eris."

Arsen's hold slackens from me. I press myself upright, and the nausea comes instantly—the poison is still in me, cleaved through me. I'm sweating through my shirt and still cold, so, so cold.

I'm quiet when she's quiet, still when she goes still. Sona's moving now, and so I'm up. So I'm going. It's as senseless and as simple as that.

"I'm sorry," I say again. "I'm awake, so I can't just stand here."

I stand. Nova scrambles upright—it must hurt—and tumbles to the foot of the bed, catching my wrist. I look down her arm, feeding from her hospital gown, and into teary eyes. She tugs the oxygen mask away, and I see chapped lips, and at the corner of her right eye, the little smiley face that Arsen pressed into place. It wasn't that long ago. It seems like so long ago.

"Don't go," Nova whispers, and then her voice breaks. "We lost."

That.

That kind of breaks my fucking heart.

And I think of Juniper. Her head tucked over my collarbone, green hair soft against my sleeve as she painted another tattoo into my skin with the tip of the needle, grinning at something sour I had said, grinning, all of them grinning—it hasn't all been bad. *Of course.* The two words in my head, against the barbed curl of my hurt. *Of course*—of course there have been good parts.

Breath swelled so perfectly in my lungs with a mecha blocking out the sky above us. Bare feet on the fire-warmed rug. New drawings pinned to the walls. Running in the shadow-wrought, empty streets. Them leaning against me, me leaning against them. Sona wearing my shirts. Holding in my laugh, laughing until my stomach aches. Hurting less. Realizing it suddenly and all at once. Pause, let it steep. Let it stick.

"She's going to try to save him," I say. "And I can't let it happen."

Nova's hold drops from me. I follow it, hand on the back of her head to kiss her brow, quick and breathless, and I've stepped away.

"I want us to be done. I can't do this again," Theo croaks, but his words are burning. "If—can we leave when you come back? Can we just *go*, Eris?"

And that tells me a lot. Tells me I'm loved, so, so recklessly, with so much sadness and fear and care and hope all at once—acting like it's a given, me coming back.

"Yeah," I say, because we should have done it years ago, when I realized how much I loved them all. Should've packed up everything we could carry and walked right out of the dorms, into the forest, and let it all crumble behind us.

Alive. Together.

"We'll go," I promise. "We'll run."

CHAPTER FORTY-SEVEN

ERIS

On my way to the elevators, I brush past a white coat in the hallway. My leaving is not exactly subtle, with my bare feet smacking the tiles and my sweat-soaked hospital gown, and Dr. Park turns as I push the elevator button. *"Eris Shindanai!"*

"Is the gas cleared upstairs?" I ask as she stomps up to me. "I need pants."

"You—we have been looking for *you*—"

I draw a slightly aching but full breath. "What the hells did you give me that I can stand up straight? Or did you just give me a new set of lungs?" The last part is a joke, but her expression stays strained. "Wait—ha—"

"I did not. I did, however, give you a large dosage of nano-synthetic stem cells and bio—"

"Actually, I don't want to know," I interject. Any needle that isn't held by my crew sends me right back into my first Academy stay. "It should've gone to my kids."

Dr. Park's face goes red—I mean, really *red*—and I open my mouth, but she's already yelling at me, "That was one of the *last*—"

"I know." I raise my hands, the metal of my right fingers flecking the fluorescent lights into smaller dots against the elevator doors. "Gods—yeah, I know, Sona told me, and now she's gone, and I'm—I'm going after her. Oh. Can you give me a ride?"

Dr. Park blinks her dark brown eyes. I've thrown her off; I didn't know I could do that. "A ride." She says it slowly, like she's sure she's misheard. "To Godolia."

"You escaped on a med helicopter, right?"

"I . . . did." Then she laughs. She's far from amused when she says, "You are just like your sister."

It takes too much energy right now to be either offended or thrilled by that. "She's gone, too, right? With her crew? Where's Sheils?"

"Yes. Yes." Dr. Park somehow flaps a perfectly steady hand. "Soo Yun is somewhere on the floor."

"Don't tell her we're leaving. Let's—"

"Eris," Dr. Park says harshly. "I cannot stop you from going. But I can*not* come with you."

"Oh. Okay," I respond as the elevator doors finally peel open. "Fine."

I try not to think about it too much, the quietness of our floor, the blood splattered against the walls. Don't think about June. June. June—Nyla. Yeah, let's think about Nyla.

Here's that scary and dark place, Glitch. Here's Nyla here, and there, and there.

Jenny had the right idea, with Voxter.

My blankets are tangled on the bed, like it's one of those lazy mornings when Sona didn't make the bed right away, like I could lift the corner of the comforter and see the long stretch of her calf with her toes curling at the sudden cold, could hear her bark me away and then catch my wrist when I pretended I'd go.

"You're dead," I mutter under my breath as I tug on my overalls, grab the cryo gloves from the bedside table, and the new leather-rimmed goggles Jen gave me after the patchwork mechas, like she knew I was going to need them. "You better be alive when I get there because you're *dead*."

Then I kick into Theo's room and get a pistol from one of the many he has hidden around, the same kinds of hiding places he had in the Hollows—on the windowsill, in his laundry pile, taped under the bed frame. I grab the last one and head for the elevators, back to the hospital floor, where I pick through the rooms for Dr. Park again. I find her at the foot of an unconscious patient's bed, push through the door, and raise the gun to her head. "Hi. Let's go."

She glances up at the gun for a moment and then right back down to her tablet. "I told you I cannot."

I grin. I am so, so tired, and my body's wrecked; I'm not even sure if I can fight right now, hence the gun—convenient and lazy and I deserve both. "I'm not asking."

Now she's the one who brushes past me, out into the hall, and moves for the next room. I shoot the wall next to the door handle as she reaches for it, plaster spewing, and she glares at me. It's immediately obvious she's more irritated than shaken, meaning she's not shaken at all and very, very irritated.

"You do understand what has happened here, do you not?" Dr. Park growls. "You missed my meaning—you can shoot me, but I cannot leave. I am the only doctor here."

"Oh," I say. "Oh. Sorry. Right. I'm on a lot of drugs, right?"

She sighs, and pulls up a new screen on her tablet and types something into it. "Nurse Hyun-Woo will meet you on the helicopter pad. He is the one who flew the both of us out. But he will not fly anywhere near the walls, even if you are planning to put that gun to his head—the cannons will kill both of you just the same."

"I—right." I lower the gun, feeling childish. "Can you tell Sheils I left?" A beat. "And to check on my kids, if I don't—"

"I am not your messenger," Dr. Park snaps, and then she's gone through the door in a rush of white fabric. Okay. I did deserve that.

I ride the elevator back to the Valkyrie floor and then duck into the stairwell, drag myself up the last flight of stairs, and shove against the wind to get the roof door open. It's sick, that we had an exit so close, but it was the stairwells that got the worst of it—they'd filled up with poison so thick you couldn't see through it. That's what Sona told me, anyway, voice floating down into that dark place I was in. I think that's why I thought I had died—it was suddenly quiet, without her, and I didn't know how long it had been like that.

A massive, sleek four-rotor helicopter sits on the painted circle, like the one Sona took out during the Archangel test run. It's something I think she'd dwell on more if the Hollows hadn't burned down that night.

It's probably only a few minutes until Hyun-Woo makes it up here, but I'm anxious and the wind cuts right through me so it feels like I'm standing there forever, thinking about Sona and Jenny and her crew and where they are. Have they made it to the city? It's sunset, gold and pink skies heavy with clouds. If I heard right, they're trying to go in through a Phantom. Hope they don't get caught, that they'll be brought right into the belly of the hangar and just—wreak havoc.

It's shitty. A chaotic barb of a plan, forged in their desperation, and barely a plan to begin with—all of them had to have known that going in.

But Hyun-Woo finds me at the railing, looking down into

the gardens streaked with rosy light and the bodies, lined up like some nervous, twitchy kid is counting out rice kernels. Out past the grove, they're stacking a pyre high with furniture stolen from the rooms that won't have a use anymore. And that's it. This is us—sick, mourning, dead, burning our dead, frayed, coming completely undone. This is it.

We've ended up like this, and it's all we have left. Desperate attempts and a tiredness like a sickness sunk down to our bones, and just enough anger to keep us awake. And it has to be enough.

Hyun-Woo drops his sullen eyes to the pistol at my hip. "You just pissed off the only doctor who's going to treat you when you're pummeled by dawn."

Pummeled. I can take *pummeled*. I'm already pummeled.

"Thanks," I say. "Can we go see my girlfriend now?"

"Is that all this is? You're not trying to take down Godolia today?"

"I'm . . . helping."

But he's right, to some degree.

It was always Sona who was going to be the end of all of this. I think I've always known that—it's a thought that dropped into my head when she put Victoria's Valkyrie through the ice, three days after we met. It was this moment of, *Oh. You might be it.*

And then I lost her. Even then it was like I was waiting around for the day I was going to hear she'd slit Enyo's throat in his sleep, and it would've been cataclysmic and *horrific* and completely unsurprising, because she's so kind but so precisely brutal when she needs to be, and now—it's the same.

And Enyo knows it, too. He knows her, too.

He knows her, so he loves her. That's it.

She's going to wander right up to him, and he's going to let her.

And that moment.

She knows this ends with him, even if she did come all that way to take him back with her, to save him from his deification. But she will think about it in that moment, that she could end it, that she should. But she won't. She won't. Because his hands will be down. Because he'll be standing still.

But I can.

With a grunt, Hyun-Woo pulls down the helicopter stairs, then glances up and past me. I turn around, hairs prickled at the base of my neck. In the mouth of the stairwell entryway blinks a collection of red lights, and then Sheils steps out onto the rooftop, Hydra jacket brushed black in the dusk. Her half-ignited glare is pinned to me, more searing than the city lights rising at her spine.

"Just where," the captain breathes, "do you think you are going?"

CHAPTER FORTY-EIGHT

SONA

We stop. Without the pulse of our steps through the sand, the silence is startlingly immediate. Wrapped around us like a jaw waiting to snap down.

"Well," Seung says mildly as he raises his arms in a leisurely stretch toward the black sky. "This blows."

Gwen spits out a colorful stream of curse words that ends in a hateful "—cking clouds! *Fuck!*"

"Holy hells," Nolan barks at her. "Can you keep your head?"

We were on a ferry for most of the night, over a black river under a black sky, watching the water for Leviathan fins. Then we abandoned the boat near the closest path to the foothills and walked over the ridges and into the desert, railways cutting like ink paths through the blankness. Then we could see by the dull, sparse lights of the pair of resource villages hugged against the hills. I do not think any of us appreciated it enough, but that was hours ago, miles of Badlands ago, and we were different, less bitter people.

I keep my mouth shut, but it's only to quietly work my teeth down to a fine, flat line, to keep from screaming, too.

I look up at Jenny as she brushes past my shoulder, now circling the group with her eyes turned to the Badlands desert. This is why Devoid guard works. Enyo knew that the rainy season would block out the sky at night. A Badlands in the colder months versus a Badlands in the summer is a very different desert. You can see the entire stretch of celestial bodies in the winter.

Now, the Badlands are black. Flat, wet sand stretching on in an indistinguishable plane of nothingness. No flashlights—it would draw a deity right to us. So it is just the sound of one another's steps and the compass in Jenny's palm.

Zamaya's next to me, close enough that I can see the expression on her face as she looks at Jenny circling—they can all see me; the only light is the one that bleeds past my shut lid—and under her breath, in a voice half-irritated and half–completely fascinated, Zamaya says, "What the hells are you seeing?"

Jenny straightens and says, quietly and clearly, "Shut up."

It is silent immediately, and Jenny frames her gloved hands against the sky, unignited; fingers relaxed as she turns, graceful in the surgical motion. Then she stops. Her chin lifts to the sky. "We're here."

And then I see it. Twenty feet away, twenty stories of pitch-black mecha. Metal blocks out most of the horizon, and we still almost missed it. My mouth goes dry first, a beat before the pin of fear draws a cold, thin line through my head—not because of the Windup, but because of Jenny. She had felt the tilt of the sand under the Phantom's weight.

"Close your mouth, Glitch," Jenny says. "You'll catch sparks when the drilling starts."

I should be relieved. Instead I could easily double over and empty my stomach into the desert.

If we had gotten this close to the last one without seeing it . . . well. We were about five hundred feet to its left, about four miles back east. A flash of lightning, and Zamaya's head snapped to the side, and then, just the barest amount, the mecha's did the same.

Because for every garrison of Devoid guard Phantoms, there is one that is wound. The rings of its eyes can only be seen when one looks at them head-on, but it can sure as hells see just fine.

We are lucky. That's it, that is what we are working with. Luck—well, and Jenny.

So we actually do have a shot at this.

First: the entrance to the mecha. The door would let me through with my eye, but it might be registered and flagged back in Godolia. We need another way in.

In total silence, using a knife with a hair-thin blade of ignited wire, Nolan draws an inch-long slit on the first layer of skin on the Phantom's ankle, opposite side of the door. Jenny, standing at his right, hands him what I think is a pen before he hovers it above the incision, and a thin light burns out of the tip. Jenny waves him aside after a few seconds to check his work, squinting down into the half-inch laceration.

"Do you want to—"

"You have steadier hands than me," she murmurs, cutting him off. "You can't do the repair, but you'll make it as neat as possible for me. Good. Lightly, now."

She hands him another laser saw, this one thinner, beam width nearing the edge of a sheet of paper. Then there is light reaching up from the cut, faint and blue, and Jenny goes, "That's the ticket."

That is how they do it, inch by pained inch, to outline a

hole that will fit Nolan, the biggest one of us. The horizon is dark purple by the time they have finished, the night's work a disk of metal ringed in its strange blue glow, and Jenny pulls two magnets with handles from her bag and attaches them to the disk. She and Seung, straining with the effort, haul the disk up and out and let it drop onto the sand.

Before us now is a sheet of artificial nerves, but they are nothing like the ones twisting around in the mecha's guts—no, the skin is what marks Godolia as the technological elite. The Windups themselves may not move with an exactness to the Pilot's real form—Valkyries come the closest, which, admittedly, is *close*—but the nerves of the skin are perfect sensory imitations of the ones both already in the human bodies and the second set threaded through mine. It's an intricacy that is awe inducing.

Nolan cuts and removes the nerves in a sheet, which Jenny carefully rolls up and places in her bag. Next is the two-inch metal layer, which goes quicker without the concern for damaging the nerves, and Nolan shoves it brutally, lets it tip forward to send a solid, single-note *clang* ringing up into the calf and the stomach of the Phantom. I can see the entrance door in the Phantom's inner ankle and the ladder, spiraling up into blackness.

We climb in. It takes some maneuvering to get the disk on the sand back into its place, but Jenny was right: Even with the sweat breaking out on his forehead, Nolan's incisions were perfect, the disk sliding in smoothly when it is lifted back into place. He secures it with a ring of sealant, ear to ear with Gwen and Zamaya in the entrance so that they can hold back the outline of cut nerves as it dries. I am up on the ladder, watching the scene from the calf because there is not any room to stand, watching as Jenny sits back on her heels and scrubs at her tired eyes with her knuckles, watching as she breathes out slow, slow.

"Nolan, take a rest," she says after a moment, shrugging off her gray jacket, folding it at the base of the entrance. Her tattoos completely envelop the rise of her collarbone, drip off her shoulders in straight lines, ending in uneven lengths past the straps of her black tank top. She runs her palms up her arm panels and then stretches them out wide, breath coming in sharp, dialing in.

"The rest of you are on," Jenny continues, her voice calm. "Remember to make sure the wirefucker can still move; an incredibly inconvenient ache is what we're going for."

We spend the hours working at the two rotator cuffs, loosing every other tiny, razor-teethed gear just so. This needs to feel like malfunction, not sabotage, which is why Jenny is kneeling on her jacket to stitch our entrance—nerve by delicate, unforgiving nerve—back together. We are done long before she is, around what must be midafternoon outside the Phantom's body, waiting up in the torso save for Zamaya, who braves several trips downward to the hollow of the leg to check on Jenny.

I watch her crawl up from the dark, limbs fed through the ladder rungs beside the nuclear heart. Zamaya pulls herself onto a small platform below my feet, hand lifting to bat away a sheet of wires and nearly knocking Gwen right into the mecha's stomach. But the gunner only rights herself and says gently, hand patting Zamaya's knee, "She needs a break."

"Yes," Zamaya says, venomous but quiet. "She does."

But it does not matter. Who knows how many more have already died since we have set out from Ira Sol? My stomach gnaws on the fear lining it, and the thought of Eris and what I am going to say to her if—*when* she wakes up, what I am going to say to Enyo to get him to take my hand and follow me out of the city.

And just behind us, the systemic structure of a billion people collapsing in on itself, onto a blank gap in the shape of his outline. Total chaos.

I have not gotten away from it. I do not think I have ever been away from it—this same kind of violence, on the same massive scale.

It goes like this: I leave Godolia behind blood soaked, every single time.

Once I would have reveled in that, before I knew I was not built for it, like a sickness down to my bones and when I *just kept going*, when I could not seem to stop. I cannot bury the girl I once was because I need her, angry and hateful and withering for it, and I need her to bear this so that the people I love now can survive it.

So that I can walk away and let it all crumble to dust behind me, because I cannot do it any longer. I am just so tired and so heartbroken and so fucking selfish, and I do not care. I don't *care*.

I want to save everyone, but I think it might kill me.

I won't outlive the ache of it. Bodies thrown apart in my wake, again, and I won't forget the weight of it.

But it's for them, dropping a billion people into pandemonium. It's for Eris and the crew, in the city I have left behind, and Enyo, in the city I am turning toward. That is it. That is the planet I am standing on, the deities I am hinging on, and I am sorry—but not enough.

I know that everything else just blinks out, that nothing

else matters to me past the people I love, and it's not something I can stop. I'm sorry. I do not want it to stop.

"Holy shit," Gwen breathes as metal tendons begin to sigh and shift around us. "It worked."

We waited, just under the hip opposite the ladder, after Jenny called up that she was finished. We found her, sheet-white and slick with sweat, the dark circles ringing her eyes washed in the blue glow of the repaired nerves, then blackened entirely as the rest of us worked to heave the two inches of metal flesh back into the entrance.

Then, sometime later, the roar of a massive helicopter, the *thuck thuck thuck* of its rotors beating against the mecha. And then the sound of the door disengaging, and us watching silently as a Pilot climbed into the leg and up, up, up, Mod eye outlining her form in red.

Jenny, on the pelvis platform with her feet dangling into the void of the thigh, produces her compass from her haversack, lips twisting harshly as she cranes her head over its glass face.

"Northwest," she reports, bobbing her head. "Good. Good. Looks like those aches are working."

"And the entry wound's good?" asks Zamaya, and I catch the gloss of her eye roll when Jenny snaps her chin up at her, incredulous. "Good Gods, Jen, I'm just *asking*—"

"You're just *wounding* me—"

The archer's smile is poisonous. "You're such a dramatic bitch."

Jenny laughs, short and pleased. "Oh, darling, please say that *again*—"

337

"Can we—" Seung tries to cut in, and then visibly strains as Zamaya repeats herself, as requested. He reaches up from the support he is balanced on to bat at her knee where it dangles next to Jenny's, hissing, "Can we go over the plan for when we get to the *hangar*?"

Jenny looks at me, which means of course they all look at me. "Well," she says. "You're up."

I am the last Valkyrie—Enyo said he needed me in the city at all times in case of another attack. It made sense. The only time I left Godolia under the corruption was when Enyo was standing next to me, in my Windup's skull as we headed for Ira Sol.

And I am the only one out of the lot of them who has been inside the hangar. It is an exact duplicate of the former Academy hangar, I explain, a cavernous expanse beneath the city street filled with barely a sixth of the Windup army Godolia once garrisoned. Their aim is the twenty-first floor, the hospital, separated from the hangar by monitored elevators and a monitored stairwell.

"Not to mention the entire floor of Windups and Pilots," mutters Gwen.

"I'd rather chance that," Seung hisses. "Honestly, what we're doing—"

"You want to argue we won't be more protected inside a mecha?" Zamaya shoots at him.

"Oh, sure," Seung says, "except our plan is to climb."

"Oh Gods," Gwen groans. "That really is the plan, isn't it? When the Pilot can be fried off the side of the skyscraper at any moment. Oh Gods—"

"Only the Zenith has that power," I say. "And he won't use it."

"You are hinging on that guess extraordinarily," Nolan mutters.

But he is looking at Jenny, not me, and she is meeting his eyes with the void in hers and says, with perfect calm, or perhaps it is weariness, "Yes. We are."

"Oh good," Nolan responds, in the driest voice I have ever heard. "As long as we know."

I say, "They might put a gun to the Zenith's head and tell him to implement the mecha's kill switch, the one that will be scaling the skyscraper below his feet. Spark the chip in their brain and fry them to every end of their natural nervous system. But either he knows it will be me, and he won't kill me, or he won't know, assume someone is coming to kill him anyway, in which case he—he won't stop them, either. And we need to switch mechas," I add quickly, making myself go very still to brace for the flare of indignance, which spikes the air immediately. "After what we have done to this one. I had not realized what—"

"It's fine to climb," Jenny snaps, and slashes an accusatory stare across the rest of them. "Didn't I *say* to keep it—"

"It *is* fine to climb," I repeat quickly. "But the journey to the streets will batter the Windup enough, and we will be fucked if I need to fight."

We cannot take the elevators, or the staircase. But we can take a mecha and work through the underground tunnel that feeds from the hangar into the Badlands, the one that runs just beneath the city streets. We will come up out of an exit we make, and then we will climb. Up the side of the Academy, completely visible, laughably bold with it, and Enyo will just watch it happen, because of everything I just said. But minus the latter portion because . . . because he *will* know it is me.

I know it senselessly, just as senseless as the sudden, cold line that draws itself down my spine, and I completely miss whatever Zamaya sneers back at me.

"Hello? *Glitch*," Zamaya snaps at me, "so we'd have to move out onto the hangar floor?"

"Um, *hello*, and *why* would we need to fight?" Gwen queries just as harshly.

I open my mouth, ready to laugh at her, but Jenny says, "Don't be disgustingly naive."

"Naive," Gwen scoffs, crossing her arms and knocking her head back into a pipe puckered with valves. "Maybe I'm just being optimistic."

"You've said you actively hate optimists," Seung returns.

"That was unfair of me," Gwen shoots back. "I haven't met anyone stupid enough to be one."

"You're all stupid," Jenny says offhandedly. "And I think this is good. I like this—I want you in a Valkyrie, Sona."

"The Valkyrie"—there were only two left after Heavensday, and one I took and left in Ira Sol—"is garrisoned halfway across the hangar. We can move to the Windup nearest to where this one gets stationed."

"You're better than anyone in that hangar. If we're fighting, let's fight," Jenny presses, and Zamaya seems to get something I do not, a tattooed hand flattening to Jen's shoulder. Jenny shrugs her off. "One will be better than two, anyway."

"Two," I say.

The thud, thud, thud of my heart, and it's like it is just then that I realize where we are, in the stomach of a mecha—no, I had realized that, actually. It is only now I feel I have been swallowed up.

As Jenny tilts her chin back, hands drifting up beside the

pale pillar of her neck, elegant, long fingers dipping for her left eye.

A black contact balances on her finger pad, and Jenny picks up her head and grins at me.

"Deities, Unnie," I hear myself say, words dissolved into a thin laugh. "You are a dramatic bitch."

It's not to jab at her; it has the effect I intended, her smile white hot and splitting wider, slow within the crimson cast spilling from her left socket. And the Pilot says, voice poisonous silk, "Yes. I'm aware."

CHAPTER FORTY-NINE

ERIS

My boots hit dirt, and I realize, with a bit of a start, that it's cold now.

I breathe it in, feel the path it carves down to my lungs, cooling the soreness scraped there—then it catches, chest wrenching in a coughing fit that almost sends me to the ground. When the tremors die down, I find there's a hand rested between my shoulder blades, and Sheils says, in what is probably the gentlest voice I've ever heard from her, "You good, Shindanai?"

"Shi-bal," I spit, throat stinging. *Fuck.* It's one of the few words I know from my dad's side of the family, though Jenny's the one I picked it up from.

Sheils laughs a little, and goes, "Eodi apa?" which I find, after a beat, I know, too—*Where does it hurt?*

Deities. I've really just been handed the language siphoned down to the bits that fit into that golden Gearbreaker lifestyle. That's depressing.

"Pibu apayoh," I return, which means *my skin hurts.* It shouldn't be true but is actually really freaking true. And I'm still sweating all over.

Sheils, in fact, did not try to throttle me for leaving like I thought she would. The general state of things wasn't the only reason she was looking frayed—Jenny had left, and took only her crew, plus Sona. I doubt she even considered asking the captain to go with them, back to the place they've been running from for forty years.

But Sheils was more worried about Jenny than I thought she'd be. So worried that behind us, in the now-stilled helicopter, the rest of her Hydras are unloading from the hold, bags clinking with tiny metallic notes.

Or maybe it's not just worry.

They kept their mechas underground for decades, trying to keep exactly what happened from happening. And this, being here again—they're facing it, in a way.

"Haven't seen this place in a while," Astrid says, kicking a boot against the flat of the Badlands desert. Wet sand furrows under her assault, lit only by the cast of the Pilots' eyes. "Looks exactly the same, doesn't it?"

"You can't expect forty years to heal a nuclear-fried spot," mutters Sa-ha, another Hydra.

I straighten fully once the nausea settles into a manageable amount, and look past them and the black body of the helicopter to the horizon, where lights rise like sharp, needled teeth. The Godolia cityscape.

Sheils turns slightly at my side, searching for something in the dark, and points when she finds it. "That's our target."

Up ahead, maybe four miles south of the city, there's a mouth in the ground, ringed by faint lights. But that's not what marks it. What marks it is the crimson-slick profile of the Paladin guarding its perimeter—the underground tunnel that feeds the Academy hangar.

"Shit," one of the Hydras breathes. "How the hells are we supposed to take that?"

I almost roll my eyes. Then I snap my welding goggles

over them, my hands at my sides flexing, relaxing within the cryo gloves. And then I feel it over the hurt, over the nerves threatening to shake me so hard they'd just fall out of me, like a glass wall coming down: Perfect clarity. Perfect excitement.

"Oh," I say, zipping up my jacket so I don't get too cold. "Pretty quickly."

I don't stop moving as I barrel out of the mecha's ankle and collapse, heaving, onto the sand, just breathe in the shock of the cold air and push myself upright. The Windup is down on one side, and around its heel I catch a glimpse of Captain Sheils's clenched teeth as the Hydras bolt for me. I'm already turning away, facing the tunnel entrance as they begin to help one another up onto the top of the Paladin's palm, fingers the length of train cars limp against the earth.

The cryo gloves and the sonic hammer have proved a brutal pairing, and Paladins are the slowest ones to begin with. But that fucking *climb*—my ribs feel like they've tensed inward, prodding the desperate shake of my lungs, and all of a sudden black dots are crowding the view of the fluorescent-seared tunnel entrance, my mouth bone dry, and I thought I was going to be fine but I think actually I—

"*Eris*," Sheils calls harshly, above and behind me, and my focus snaps back together. She stares me down from atop the hand, the Hydras around her rustling in their bags to drag out cannisters of spray paint. Caps are thrown aside, and the *hiss* of the aerosol streaks the air already humming with what I realize is, in fact, not only the ringing in my ears, but the scream of alarms.

I watch, dazed, as Astrid lets a line of paint loose as she books it up the Paladin's arm, streaking the Paladin's dull green-gray coat with blue, bright and bold and *glowing*.

Damn, I think faintly, *the kids are going to be sorry they missed this.*

They've already seen us—we're not hiding. We also have to know which mechas are ours when we get into the hangar; the paint is a functional thing, but that doesn't stop Sa-ha from standing on the Paladin's neck and drawing a curve from the side of the Paladin's thin, serious mouth, the smirk bleeding an eyesore pink.

"Eris!" Sheils shouts again.

"I'm good," I call up, though I don't know if it's true.

"I know that," Sheils snaps, and flicks her tattooed fingers irritably to the mecha behind her. "You know this is going to hurt like a bitch, right?"

I shoot her as much of a shit-eating grin as I can manage. "I cracked apart the left eye for you."

Her upper lip quirks in a snarl, and she turns from me, flashing the snake emblem of the back of her jacket as she makes for the head. Maybe I should've mentioned that she also needs to unplug the dead Pilot from his cords, and that there's blood on the glass mat. But maybe she's already assuming it. It's slicked all over my wrists anyway.

I face the tunnel again. From the concrete maw, there are footsteps attached to a weight so massive the force of them is crawling up my legs. I straighten, plant my feet in sand washed in the cold blue of my gloves, lifted slightly at my sides as if I'm placating. I'm not.

Behind me, the Paladin pushes itself off the earth, and rises.

"All right," I say, and I bite down on it, force the next breath out in a growl, slow and steady. "All right. I've got this. I've got this."

And it clicks.

This moment, the thing I'm addicted to, where everything lines up all neat and narrow and it's just me and the thing I have to beat—there is a kind of stillness here.

"Okay." Steady, now. Yeah, I'm steady; I'm at the last part of the end of the world, and I'm freaking solid. "Come and get me."

I admit I left a mess of the Paladin, but Sheils is a fantastic Pilot.

I mean, she is *damn* good. When the two Arguses come charging up the mouth of the tunnel, and I let the cryo serum loose in two screaming, brilliant bolts that tear back the dark of the sky, it's the only advantage I have to give her—she steps right over me and runs them down.

When they're twin messes of crushed and ice-shattered metal, the Paladin turns and lays out a palm for me. I don't think it's ever something I'll get used to, those massive fingers curled above my head; it would be such a simple thing to forget the weight I press to her palm, to close her fist slightly and blink me out of existence. But she doesn't, and I watch the long bulbs of the fluorescents run above the domed curve of the Windup's battery-guard helmet, speckled with neon paint that swells artificially even under the harsh lights.

It's a pretty straight shot, but not one we travel alone—I feel the next sets of footfalls long before the Phoenixes' forms appear in the distance. I'm also not oblivious to the cameras that dot crevices in the concrete walls. We must be under the city by now; I wonder, but only briefly, if the streets above will feel the flush of the heat that's about to choke up the passage. Briefly, because this makes twice in the last forty-eight hours that someone's not only trying to kill me, but beat my physical form into an entirely different shape.

Sheils seems to know this, too, because she lets me down. My boots hit concrete so smooth it seems clinical, and I realize two things:

One, there's a split in the tunnel. I'd been focused on the lights and the footfalls and on not letting the quake of the Paladin empty out all the water I'd chugged down in the helicopter. The path that the Phoenixes are growing bigger and bigger on seems a newer addition, curving away from the old one, unlit so I can't see so far down it, but I can see enough. Concrete walls fissured, split with a quick and brutal influx of heat, a firepower that the thermal cannons of the approaching Phoenixes couldn't match—couldn't even come close to. This tunnel connects to the old Academy's hangar, the one Sona collapsed with the last missile in her chamber, thick with Jenny's magma serum.

Well, *shit*. We can't be that far into the city, can't be that close to the Academy's ruins, and yet the pure molten heat of the blast made it all the way up the concrete streaked below my feet. *Shit, Jenny*. We would've been screwed if she'd been born on any other side but ours.

Oh, right, and two—there's a Berserker coming up on our flank. Maybe one that just got off its rounds.

A Berserker is about the worst thing a Gearbreaker can face without cover. Phoenixes are a close second with the long range, but they need to charge up—Berserkers have ribbons of ammunition that run up the lengths of both their arms. You ever have the pleasure of watching a Berserker with a frozen hand try to catch itself on the Badlands desert, because your driver got its feet twisted around and your corrosives expert is a sick freak that likes to go for the ankles? Its wrist splits open, and it's just bullets, belts and belts of bullets glinting under the bright bite of the sky like golden pomegranate seeds.

I gesture to the Berserker. Sheils notes it from far, far above, and her mecha takes off running for the Phoenixes. This Windup could fill me with lead, but there's some air left-over with artillery, while you can fill a room wall to wall with fire, so, yeah. I have a slightly better chance, especially if the wirefucker doesn't see me right away.

I hurry into the heat-fissured tunnel, back pressing to the wall just before the turn, just out of sight from the main path. It's curved slightly instead of being a neat corner, because a century or so ago, or whenever this damned place was carved out, the architects thought to themselves, *I think I'll make this be where Eris Shindanai dies.*

I swallow, the movement harsh against the raw dryness coating my throat, eyes flicking up to the grubby ceiling before closing, before begging for my heartbeat to slow. It's going to look for me. Whoever's manning those cameras will be in that Pilot's ear, telling them exactly where I am. And if I didn't know that a few seconds ago, when I felt the force of the Berserker's every footfall thud against my sternum, I know it now, now that it's closer and the thudding slows, because here's what it's going to do—because it's the most terrifying thing it *could* do: slow to a stop, and then curl its massive, grisly face, eighteen stories above my head, around the curve.

It will almost be more terrifying than the next part, where its haze of bullets evaporates me.

But—and it's ridiculous that this is what might save my life—but its foot will not be against the wall.

Its arm is going to be in the way, and all the Windup classes below Valkyrie can't move their legs past the width of their hips. Because here's the one thing that mechas will never be able to imitate about the human form: the softer bits, the parts that stretch and pull. Windups are all sharp edges, and that makes their movements linear, clipped—even the intricacies of Valkyries give their actions a jaggedness, albeit slight. Usually none of that even matters in the moment. Usually.

This time, it matters. This time, it makes it so when the Berserker's footfalls are so close that they make me light on the ground, when its head leans and red light glides around the curve and cleaves across me, I *move*, between the wall and the metal of the Berserker's base, and I'm gone.

Concrete explodes in my wake with the force of its artillery, but I'm already behind the mecha when a chunk of it hits my ribs, knocking me to the ground. I've had a cryo glove pressed to the flesh of its foot and then to its heel the entire way around.

"Got you," I rasp, the taste of blood flecking my tongue, clenched fists bursting with light and frost as I force myself onto my back and crush them together. As the Berserker turns, both palms blurred with an unending stream of rounds, I unfurl them as one.

And it's not going to work. I realize this, with all the attached *I'm dead* implications, in a split moment the light shrieks from my hands—it's going to be a direct hit to the mecha's stomach and it's not going to work, because this glorious, glorious shot is not going to stop it dead in its tracks and that's the only thing that's going to save me now.

Shit, Sona, I think, faintly, and then, a skipped heartbeat later, *Shit, Jenny.*

It *shouldn't* work—but I forgot.

These aren't my old gloves.

My old gloves wouldn't be

sending

the

mecha

down.

Fluorescents burst halfway up the length of the tunnel as the Berserker's palms jerk involuntarily upward, my arms thrown over my head instinctively as bullets shatter glass and concrete alike, raining down in the sudden dark. My slack jaw is what saves my teeth from cracking apart from the force of the Windup's entire weight crashing against the ground, frostbitten gut fragmenting with a sound like the splitting of a frozen lake.

The bottoms of its feet rise far above me, but it's down and I'm *alive* and the metal blocks out the rest of its ugly, mangled corpse. The breath ticking in my lungs like it's trying to count my ribs, make sure they're all intact, and they are— bruised, but whole.

"Sheils!" I call, even though there's no way she can hear me, picking myself up off the ground as quickly as I dare to. "I'm freaking *invincible,* holy *hells,* did you see what Jenny—"

The triumph dies, dries up into sand in my chest cavity.

Up past the mist rising out of the Berserker's cold spots, there's smoke filling the tunnel. A Paladin's paint-marked hand still and awkward against the wall, and the Phoenixes are down, and it doesn't matter, because again—fucking *again*—the ground is shaking.

And the force is coming from both sides.

At my twelve, their approach is already moving the smoke, sending it billowing to fill my lungs. I'm so, so tired of breathing in poison—I think that's why I turn to my six, where the exit into the Badlands is a sweet, night-black spot in the distance, blocked out by the body of another Phoenix, and right behind it, a pale mark that might be an Argus.

Where the hells did I hear that Godolia was running out of mechas?

"Shit, Sona," I say, out loud this time, the words a laugh as the delirium and exhaustion hit me at once.

Mechas at my back and mechas at my front. So. This is it.

I should have listened to her and stayed put. I wouldn't feel it hitting me, that animalistic panic of an alive thing about to be a dead thing.

But *honestly* . . .

"Honestly, love," I say through gritted teeth. I square my shoulders, flicking my fingers to send cryo serum and ice splintering on either side of me. And next to the panic, there's anger. That's the stuff that numbs me down. That's the shit I can work with. "What did you expect?"

CHAPTER FIFTY

SONA

I extend a hand to my left. *Wait.* Eyes leveled on the Phantom Pilot, still in her ending stance save for her hands, reaching for the cords spilling from her forearms. She plucks them out neatly, one by one, nearly methodical, and it is an odd, unexpected thought, but that is how I know that she is a good one. A good fighter—that she does so with precision, without excess, without adornment. And this—Zamaya burying an arrow in her temple as soon as the last cord drops from her fingertips—is not indicative of a lack of skill. It is simply not a fair thing, but then, neither side has ever been quite fair.

We drag the Pilot's dead weight from the mat, warmth soaking my sleeves by the time we have cleared her. Jenny has taken center stage, hands ghosting silently over the cords suspended in the air. I open my mouth, and her black eyes snap to me.

"Don't," she says. "I don't want to know what it's like until I *know*."

"Hurry *up*, then," Gwen barks in a feverish voice, unflinching under Jenny's cold stare. "You know they're expecting that Pilot to be spilling out of here any second."

"Gwen," Zamaya says softly, but it's a warning. "Give her a moment."

Jenny turns. Squares her shoulders, face lifted toward the

Phantom's eyes, the hangar that stretches beyond them, pock-marked with deities. Takes in a deep, deep breath that lifts the line of her collarbone and the tattoos pressed there. Lets it go, lets it all go, and reaches for the first cord.

"Has Sheils ever told you what separates the good Pilots from the greats, Glitch?" Jenny asks, shivering as the first socket fills with a *click*.

"No," I whisper. I have a strange, enormous feeling in my chest that I cannot name—some sense that what I am witnessing before me is *immense*.

"Well. She did mention you. After she saw you tear apart that patchwork mecha in the gardens. *Look*, she said, *she fills up her body*, or something like that. Some Pilots don't, I guess. Some hesitate, because they know in the deep-dark of their heads that this is a form that is false. A second skin, and not just skin, not just them."

It surprises me. I have been conscious of my real body when I am wound, but it's just so . . . distant. An afterthought. I thought that was how all Pilots felt.

"And that's because, halmeoninim says," Jenny continues, with one arm fully attached now, black lashes drawn low as she begins on the other, "of the massiveness. That's it. So used to picking up our chins to look at the sky—maybe, even, so used to bowing low to the things greater than us. Used to thinking there are things greater than us."

Her fingers pause, the last cord balanced between them. Jenny Shindanai tilts her left cheek over her shoulder, red spilling over all of us, dark hair slipping down her back.

"I don't understand it," she tells us. "I don't understand how people can't see it. We are so much more tremendous than we give ourselves credit for."

And then, Jenny smiles. It is electric and cold and shock-dead serious all at once.

"Except for me, of course," she says. "I know I am immeasurable."

She clicks the last cord home.

For a moment, she is absolutely still. Then she rolls her shoulders back, right, and then left, and then together as one.

Nolan says, "Does it hurt?" which for a beat I think he is referring to winding, but then I remember that we had spent the entire day making sure this Phantom's Pilot did, in fact, hurt.

But all Jenny says is, "I've fought in worse states."

That entices a dark chuckle from Zamaya, which stops abruptly when Jenny flinches—barely a tilt of her chin, but it's there. "Jen?"

"Whoa," Jenny breathes, dark eyes wide. They flick to the left before narrowing; at the same time her smile twists into something more vicious. "That's a little cool."

Cold sweat breaks at the nape of my neck. "What?"

"Oh. You'll see," Jenny says. "I'm going to move. I think I see the Valkyrie—ah, would kind of love to try *that* out sometime—hurry along to the boot."

"I—"

"You'll have cover. I'll meet you outside, yeah?"

Sliding down the ladder in the neck, the last sound I hear from Jenny is a laugh, little and pleased, as the mecha takes its first step forward. Good Gods. This is bad—laughably *terrible*—a mecha moving when it is not supposed to be moving is going to be marked.

Really, I am expecting the door to open up and a bullet to immediately enter my head.

But I open it anyway. Because if Jenny says I will have cover, I'll have cover.

And I find that I do, when the door slides out with a whisper of metal on metal, when the light slides in with harsh insistence—just not in the way I was expecting.

Jenny has set the Phantom right next to the Valkyrie's base. It is still clear, immediately, that in the time it took for me to drop from the mecha's head to its feet, the Academy hangar has dissolved into chaos.

No one even glances in my direction as I move onto the open floor. There are hurrying bodies, the gray uniforms of guards and jacket-clad figures sprinting for mechas, shouting, the scrape of metal boots moving against concrete. Alarm lights flick in white flashes, glinting against the Valkyrie's sharp lines. I steal through her boot and climb, and my arm panels pop back by muscle memory only—*what the hells is happening?*

I wind, with the barbed, bright feeling that the answers lie there.

And I am right.

Suddenly, I know what Jenny thought was a little *cool*: the small space now carved out in the corner of my vision: a video feed, pasted on the image of the hangar in pandemonium like it is physically tangible, instead of a broadcast dropped directly into my Mod.

Eris.

It's Eris, just for a moment, in the hangar tunnel stepping off a paint-splattered Paladin's palm, until she is gone out of frame, up around into the blind spot of the old Academy's abandoned path. There are voices resonating in my head, Godolia Pilots sounding off as they wind, the barked orders of captains, but I barely pay attention to them. I just stare, dumbfounded, at the spot on the video feed Eris just vanished from.

She is awake. She's *here*—how the hells is she *here*?

"Eris," I rasp. "Oh, love, you are so *dead*."

CHAPTER FIFTY-ONE

ERIS

I— Did I really miscalculate this?

I'm facing the wrong way. The mecha at my back—hangar-ward—is getting to me first. I'm only turning when it's made it out of the smoke, when it's half-shrouded in gray and massive and I'm dead-smack in its path. Like, *deities*—rescind my tattoos now—how the hells did it get here so *fast*—

And nothing. There's nothing in my head now, just a blank spot that the bone-dry terror has clicked into place, because . . . that's . . . that's a Valkyrie.

I'm *frozen.*

Move, move, please please move, begs my voice in my head in a body completely stock-still, and then it's on me, a hundred and seventy-five feet of vertical metal and I stand at five fucking three and then it's just . . . just— Oh.

Oh.

The hair next to my ear lifts up and back. The Valkyrie's next footfall is a line of static up my spine.

I turn, unbreathing, as the fear in my throat crumbles into disbelief.

It stepped over me.

And with a single, fluid movement, so elegant it is almost

delicate, the Valkyrie frees the sword from its back and cleaves the Argus shoulder to hip.

It goes down. It goes down, metal scraping concrete scraping my eardrums, and all I can think, with perfect clarity, is, *I know that hand.*

Heat rushes against my skin as the Phoenix nears to an assault distance, tunnel charging with warm light, but I don't even have to think about running—Sona snaps a roundhouse to its thermal cannon, splintering the wall with the force of it, and when she doubles back, her heel meets the Phoenix's iron jaw. The metal furrows as easily as the rug does when the crew was chasing one another up and down the hall.

Her stance resets perfectly as the Godolia Windup stutters. It raises its digited hand, locking the wrist supporting her blade before Sona can cut it down, but it doesn't matter, barely hitches the fight, because she's already slamming the brow of her helmet to the Phoenix's wrecked face. Then there's distance, just for an *instant* before Sona closes it, her stomach almost pressed to the Phoenix's if not for the sword hilt between them, the one she flipped in her hand so seamlessly I hadn't even realized it, until the black tip of the blade is fissuring out of the side of the mecha's neck.

The Valkyrie steps back, pulls the sword long and slow from the Phoenix's gut with a teeth-rattling screech of metal, lets the Windup fall slack off its end.

And then she waits for me.

The door in the mecha's boot is open, and I am already through it and climbing, heart thundering in each rib and fingertip, body gasping for air and rest and about a thousand other things it needs less than who's at the top, who turns when I get there and looks me dead in the eyes even with those cords spilling from her forearms, even though she can't see me. Her hands are lifting anyway.

I almost knock her over. I almost topple the entire deity. But she's solid. My arms thrown around her neck and hers around my waist and a fierce, sharp breath I can feel fill her lungs ricocheting against the air spilling from mine as I say, the words quiet and hurried and nearly incoherent, "You're so dead. I'm so fucking pissed at you."

Sona laughs. She kisses me hard against the temple, keeps her mouth there as one hand travels up my spine and to the back of my head, like if she lets me any farther from her I'll just drift away. I won't. "You were supposed to be unconscious until I got back."

"Well," I say, helpless like this. I think I really was angry at her before. Now she's close to me and I don't know how the hells I ever thought that would be sustainable.

"I missed you," she says.

"That's so unfair." But it's maybe also exactly what I deserve. For all the shit we've been through, we deserve each other like this. "I missed you, too."

"I figured. Seeing as you are here."

I smile against her cheek in a way she can feel as *you're on thin ice.* "Don't push it, Glitch. And you can't even see me."

"Yes," she agrees, and kisses me anyway.

It's short. It's just a second before we break and I say, "So. War."

"Ruins everything."

"Uh-huh."

Sona tilts her head, those large, fine-edged eyes open and

blank and staring right past me. I untangle myself from her and step off the mat as they flick to something I can't see.

"There are Pilots with paint canisters in the hangar," she murmurs. "Know anything about that?"

"No," I say as she begins to move the Valkyrie over my Berserker takedown, the corner of her mouth quirking. Up ahead, Sheils's Paladin is up—thank Gods—and then *off the ground*, fists colliding with the ceiling of the tunnel with a force that makes me flinch. Concrete rains down in car-sized chunks. "What the hells is she *doing*?"

Sheils is next to a Phantom. There's something wrong with it—you're not fantastic at Gearbreaking like I'm fantastic at Gearbreaking without noticing when something's wrong with a mecha. The shoulders are set just a bit looser than they usually are—but I'm not as concerned with the set of them as I am about the line of them, the posture so perfect and held so effortlessly that it just screams vanity.

That, paired with the fact that it's just standing next to Sheils and not trying to kill her, screams *Jenny*.

"That's Jenny," I say numbly, and Sona's eyes flick to me.

"It is," Sona says evenly, and after a moment, when I'm still quiet, "Eris?"

"I'm fine. I'm good," I say.

"You are smiling." Shock is drawn in her voice.

"Yeah, I'm smiling." I press my palms to the cool red glass of the Valkyrie's eyes, grinning at the Phantom as we near it, close enough that I can see Zamaya and Nolan and Seung and Gwen gaping back at me from its head, and Jenny, wound, and the glint of a Mod eye in her skull and the glint of her teeth. "I just won a bet against the crew." I wave at the Gearbreakers. Gwen blows me a kiss, Nolan grabbing Seung to shake him as he points at me; Zamaya's features flicker in what I know to be a harsh, disbelieving laugh.

"Well," I add, glancing back to see Sona's mouth dropping open, "against Nova and Arsen—June and Theo thought Jen was ballistic enough, too."

The night comes through in veins, and then in wounds, as the ceiling tunnel cracks and crumbles and comes down.

Then it's horrific. I mean, it must look *horrific*, the mechas clawing themselves up and out onto the open street, next to a moving patchwork of fleeing, shrieking bodies. And the Valkyrie rises.

"Twin hells." The words are so soft that at first, I think Sona's the one who said it. And then a beat later it hits me that it was me, that she's silent and staring with her spine straight and each finger curled, watching the chaos we've just thrown like a sheet over the cityscape.

She's thinking what I'm thinking, like we tend to do.

Oh.

We've ended up here again.

"Okay." This time Sona is the one who says it, her voice just as soft. "We are going up. I want to hit the fog and go in from there."

I say, "Okay." Because I might as well.

Her feet turn on the glass mat. Outside the crimson of the Valkyrie's eyes, the city seems to turn with her, skyscrapers shot through the pavement like teeth, every edge electric with light, every part of the night shocked away with neon or wire or bulb. It makes it so the straight path of the street bordering the

Academy tower seems anything but—the strange, mismatched glow blurring the cityscape, blotting out any evidence of elegant, sharp lines.

It makes it so I can see the panic perfectly, as the three mechas—us in the Valkyrie, Jenny and her crew in the Phantom, and Sheils piloting the Paladin—move into the grove of golden trees that cluster at the Academy's base.

And crush them like their branches are matchsticks instead of solid metal.

Sona reaches up, and the Valkyrie's black fingertips shatter the glass of the eighteenth story like it's nothing at all.

And then, just like she said—we're going up.

This is insane. I can meet the eyes of the people within, rubbernecking to the windows until they stumble back with mouths dropped open, emitting shrieks I don't have to hear to feel them in my head, and Sona has her head tilted back now and so goes the floor angling under my feet. Then it's just glass above, the smooth plane of the skyscraper, shooting for the smog swallowing up the city lights.

We don't speak, like if we speak it'll all snap—a hand around the mecha's ankle, the skyscraper giving in to the weight of the deities latched onto its face, the chip in Sona's brain turning her nerve endings to ash—

I feel light, so dizzy with exhaustion and the decay that has half-cooked my body and us thinking we could do this, us *doing this*. Like we weren't here before. Like the worst part of us hadn't come after we were here before.

I look at her. The cosmic dusting of freckles drowned out in red, those massive, half-moon eyes, the carved jaw and the weight of it against my temple in my muscle memory, the mouth that can shift so arrogantly and smile so fully. I like it best like that—I like it in every form, but I like it grinning even more than when it's against mine, because it's bold, every single Godsdamn time, because Sona takes her happiness boldly.

So when the Valkyrie moves into the smog, when there's another brittle cough of glass as the length of its arm reaches in, hooking around something I can't see, when the lights from the city drop away and it's almost completely dark, save for the mat glowing beneath her feet and her eye glowing in her head, I move for her.

Both of her arms are outstretched, an elegance to them even now, like she's reaching for something. I step between them and pluck the cords from her sockets and look as she lands on her own two feet again, right next to me.

For a moment I don't speak; neither of us does, just watching each other as we wait for the mecha to unhook, to send both of us down to the earth again.

It doesn't. I glance over my shoulder, just for a second, just to see the Valkyrie's reflection pressed to the window of the abandoned Academy level before the smog sighs back into place, and the world becomes blank.

Here we are again. Alone in the head of a deity. A breath apart.

"Can we wait a minute?" I ask, and I know I'm asking a lot.

"Yes, Eris." My name is careful on her tongue, like it always is, handled like a sharp thing.

"I'm okay," I say.

She waits. Waits for it to build in me.

"I'm okay," I repeat. "That's it. I'm okay. I've been thinking all wrong. I've been thinking like I've been so broken apart by everything that I'm unfixable, that when it's good it's just going to be bad again, because, ha, look at the track record, right?" I lift my hand, metal sharpening the light that spills from her and redirecting it to the wall. I watch the glint scrape the skull until I realize that Sona is watching me with her shoulders braced, and then I turn closer into her and put my hands to her ribs and ask her, *really* ask her, "But how the fuck am I supposed to live like that? Things get better. *People* can get better." I'm holding the proof right here, in the warmth of her skin, the quick thrum of her heartbeat nudging against my own. "You're just . . . You feel so much realer to me than all the bad thoughts."

Heat flushes behind both of my eyes, and when it breaks, Sona catches the tears, both palms against my cheeks to lift me upward. She studies me for a second. Studies me, and then kisses me, slow, slow, slow, and the noise like static in my head smooths over, eases away like it's the simplest thing. There's stillness. Like there isn't a heart thudding in my chest or mechas crawling out of the street or a boy a few stories up with minutes to live.

And that thought, of course, scatters it. I pull away from her, and Sona leans to brush her lips between my brows before straightening.

She's silent as she lets me work. I touch an ignited glove to the side of the Valkyrie's skull, letting the frost root good and deep before shattering it with a kick. Air spiked with smog and the chill of autumn rushes over both of us, and I reach up to snap my goggles into place. I survey the slope of the Valkyrie's cheek and the spiked shoulder armor cascading below. It's massive, like every part of the mecha is; it still looks like a narrow landing pad.

But we make it, snagged in uneven stances between the trunklike spikes, instead of disappearing soundlessly into the clouds below, and then less soundlessly against the asphalt below that. Sona goes first, me trailing her down the arm, a metal bridge over the drop that stops at the elbow—past that, we both have to duck our heads to get inside, the Valkyrie's bicep almost as tall as the story itself.

Alarms blare in white flashes, but if I had to wager a guess, I'd say that this floor is already deserted. We've landed in a dining room, rich green carpets and a sleek table half in splinters; this is probably a mecha unit floor, but it's not like there are a ton of Pilots left to begin with, and whoever is alive is probably already wound or on their way to the hangar. We pad out of the dining room and into the hall, where the Valkyrie's wrist lies, fingers powdered in plaster where they're buried under the wreckage of a decimated wall.

"Paladin floor," Sona says in a low voice. "Five floors down from the Zenith wing. Stairwell's this way."

We have to pull ourselves over the Valkyrie's wrist, landing on another stretch of lush, rubble-strewn carpet. There are ajar doors, unmade beds, one nightstand occupied by a mug stamped with the Paladin shield insignia. Sona turns and stops after the hallway splits left and right, and we take a left, and she unhinges a cylinder from her belt loop.

"Did I show you what Jenny made me?" she asks, and before I can say anything, she tightens her grip and flicks her wrist. A curve of black metal springs out from the cylinder's side to sheath her expert grip in a knuckle guard; at the same time a blade unfolds from nowhere, tip arching toward the floor molding. She moves her thumb affectionately, gently, and the bare edge of the sword *ignites*, a line of lit wire crawling from grip to tip. She stands there looking all too pleased with herself.

"Damn," I breathe. When the hells does Jenny *sleep*?

Sona flicks her wrist again, and then the blade and the knuckle guard retract, just a cylinder again that she tosses into my startled catch. Just as startling, she then closes the distance between us, palms on my hips as she watches me turn over the compact sword in my hands. I look up at her, and she steps away, shoving open a door into an unlit space.

"Stairwell," she says, feet unmoving just before the threshold, smiling and waiting for me to go first.

So I do. Why wouldn't I? Then I realize that I'm still holding the sword, and it's only when I turn back to her that I register that this doesn't look like a stairwell, it looks like a storage closet—and Sona, with a motion so fluid I barely feel it, takes the sword from my lifted palms by pulling the cryo gloves clean off the tips of my fingers.

And then she shoves me back.

I hit a cold floor and some sort of bucket, plastic clattering as I kick upright, but she's already shut the door by the time I'm against it, and I feel the snap of a heavy lock fall into place.

"Glitch—"

"Love," she breathes, inches away, "I know why you are here. I . . . I just need a minute with him."

I fumble for my belt with hands that feel raw—but there's no hammer. Her hands on my hips—she'd taken it right off me.

"You can't—" I growl, stepping back, but the door doesn't even budge when I throw my weight against it. My words are chipped as I push them through teeth clenched against the flash of pain. "Don't go *alone*."

I hear it when she takes a step back. Or maybe I just know

when she does. *No.* She could be heading for a room filled with guards. She could be killing herself doing this.

"Don't." I'm begging her. I'm choking on air trying to separate it from the bile of panic in my throat. "Sona, *don't*—"

"I just—" Sona starts. "I just need to talk to him."

And then she's gone.

Just. Like. That.

CHAPTER FIFTY-TWO

SONA

I place the gloves and the hammer on the ground, right outside the door as it shakes again with the weight of her body. Then I run.

Up the stairwell. I cannot stop moving. If I stop moving now I am either going to turn around for Eris or I am just going to stop. And I cannot do either.

And then—a door. Metal and dull and unassuming, like the hall past it won't be clotted with guards, the air thick with bullets the moment I push through, like he is not just up the hall and the sight of him is going to hit me like a kick in the chest.

I press my ear to the cold surface, the rapier unfurling sleek and quiet at my side, my other hand pawing the lump weighing the inner pocket of my jacket.

Arsen won't mind, I think, that I went through his things before I left.

I pull the flash-bang's first pin with my teeth, ease down the door's handle around it, and pull the second. Let it tumble inside and shove the door back closed, just for a moment, and it goes off with a ring threaded through both ears even through the barrier, and then I am pushing through. Sprinting low, ignited blade angled in a steady hand at my side, thinking *necks*, thinking *ribs*, thinking—there's—there is no one here.

I am alone.

I straighten, eyes flicking up the hallway. The Zenith floor is less decadent than those of the mecha units'—black doors, all closed, perfectly white walls set with dark frames, wood floors glossy under my feet. Enyo usually joined me for meals on the Valkyrie level, slept in its rooms a few times until I caught him doing it and shooed him back upstairs. Every time I went to see him in his office, I would pace these halls with my sight set forward. It's not what I do now, so I do see it. Them, exactly where I thought they would be, which is why I avoided them, in the picture frames. The Zeniths.

Some of the photographs are arranged by age—shoulder to shoulder, each unsmiling face looks straight into the shot, even the little ones and their tiny heads and tiny necks rising from black collars, breasts stamped cleanly with the Aether Tree insignia—and some seem candid. A girl around five years old holding the finger of a teenage Zenith reading off a tablet. Three around Jenny's age with their heads tilted back, the feet of a mecha in the near background. A group of them around a dining table, the wood strewn with flour and pale flat circles of mandu dough and metal bowls lumped with kimchi stuffing, the completed dumplings and their soft, pinched arms set on a tray at the center. It's a New Year's tradition—Heavensday—and my gaze catches on a boy with his black head of hair turned away from the camera who could be Enyo. But I could not say for sure. Could not say if this was his last celebration before I dropped into his life, from the sky.

Then he is screaming.

And he has been in my head for so long, and just in my head, that, for a moment, I think he is still only there.

But then I turn the corner, and his office doors are ajar, and it is the back of one guard disappearing through them and the faces of the two others snapping toward me, and I realize it's real. Enyo is real in my ears because he is suddenly so close, and I have moved, and there is a jolt of my shoulder back and then the jolt of it forward as my blade moves from the guard's right temple to his left jaw, and the next soldier is at point blank range and he shoots me again, I think, tears the skin stretched over the slope over my collarbone. But then his hand is gone, the gun with it. We are ribs to ribs, my sword between his.

I step back. He goes down. All of three seconds and I am soaked through, their blood and mine down my throat, and I am still moving. Pushing through the half-ajar doors to find my eyes latch onto his fingers first, pale and long and blood streaked, too, find them tensing around the trigger.

The bullet cuts into the hallway, close enough to my head that I reach up, dazed, after it buries itself in the red-speckled plaster behind me, to catch my hair as it settles back down.

Enyo, slack jawed, puts the gun down, and I find the rest of him.

His black hair is messy, long again, half of it tied up and the rest wild around his fine jaw. It's that and the fact that the buttons of his shirt are all off by one loop, and the look in his dark eyes, that make him seem frayed, like this whole time he has just been sticking his fingers in electrical sockets. So long that he has grown bored of it. It's been *so long*.

"I—" Enyo starts, voice rough and low, like he has not used it in ages, or his scream has scoured it down.

The gun twitches at his side, barrel draped in his unrolled sleeve. The barest amount of wind lifts the fabric lightly from his wrist—there is no window anymore, I realize. Glass peppers the carpet like bits of blasted aether. Glass we pressed our feet up against when we were finished moving the desk and the afternoon seemed to hesitate.

Socks on shoeless feet, pale cheeks ruddy and so, so much tiredness in the brushstrokes of his eyes, Enyo looks lost. I cannot imagine what I look like, dripping red puddles onto the floor. I cannot imagine what he is going to say.

He swallows hard, throat moving, and then his tongue flicks over his lips before they split in the smallest, smallest smile. "Hi."

I could slug him across the face.

"I could slug you across the face," I say hoarsely.

"Yeah. I believe you."

At his feet is the crumpled body of a guard. The one I saw going in when I made the corner. Judging by the rug, he was bleeding out from his chest. He is still, now.

Enyo tried to run, so they locked him up in a tower. They could not let their God wander off. He tried to do it again, in the chaos we brought with us.

"Did you mean to shoot me?" I ask.

Enyo laughs. It's a helpless, quiet sound. "I missed, did I not?"

"Barely," I spit.

"I thought you were the next guard."

The next. He was planning on killing all of them.

"Nyla," I say. That's all I can say, my eyes burning into his.

The gun drops to the blood-damp carpet without a sound. He swallows. "What did she do?"

I shake my head. "No, Enyo, what did *you* do?" I take a step forward, another, and he takes one toward me, stepping beside the body of the guard, and then I am close enough to shove him back as my next words break out of me. "The shrines. The gas. The Leviathans—was it to push her? Inspire her?"

"No," he breathes, hands landing on my wrists, tangled in his shirt. "The Leviathans—I hadn't done anything for months. I—I wanted to leave all of you *alone*—"

"Why—"

"For *you*, Sona!"

"And the Windups still razing villages in the Badlands?" My throat is tightening, even as I scream at him. "Is that for me, too?"

"It was for *them*!" Enyo shouts, letting me go to throw his hand out toward the broken window, into a broken city. His voice rings, and then bleeds out into silence. His fingers drift back to the side, the boiling point of the moment suddenly drained. His words come quietly. "It—I was supposed to be for them."

"What are you doing?" I am tinged by something, rage or sadness. I can barely feel it. The details are blown out by a sudden numbness. The wind picks up and plays in his hair, his gaze still set outside. "Enyo. Do you want to leave?"

It could all be different, if he left with me and then just vanished into the Badlands, anonymous and insignificant. Would that sate the RMs, the ones in the Windup army and this entire damned city that reveres him? If he simply disappeared?

I cannot say, *Leave with me.* I cannot say, *I am taking you from here, and it is going to be okay,* we *are going to be okay,* because he has to be the one to say it.

I can't reach out to him. He has to be the one to take my hand.

I stand completely still. Watch the rise and fall of his chest, the stretch of his ribs brushing the wrinkled shirt. Somewhere beneath it there is a scar—no—somewhere beneath it there was once a bullet hole that they healed perfectly.

"Do you believe they are Gods?" Enyo asks. "The Wind-ups . . . Do you think we have brought the Gods here?"

The answer is yes. I would be a fool not to think so, not to see it. They are Gods. Manufactured incessantly, but Gods nonetheless. Just because they are not mine, just because they are my nightmares, does not change what they are to other people. "I think we made a mistake."

Enyo turns. My chin tilts down so I cannot see his face when he stills in front of me, inches away. I think of nothing, studying the black fibers around the misdone buttons, studying how they move, just slightly, as he puts his arms around me. Then they are gone. I am against them, pulled into them, feeling the thud of my heart incomprehensibly vivid against one cheek until I realize it's his. That he is holding me.

And this, finally, is when it hits me. The kick in the chest, but not so much a kick as a lightning strike. It takes *everything* not to beg him, everything not to take his wrist and *just start running*.

He is here, right where I left him. And how I left him, down to the blood on his hands and the blood on mine, and the same terrible world crowded around us.

We have done the worst to each other. We have been the worst of ourselves with each other.

But then he breathes, and I know. I know that he did not put himself in my head in the place that he is, full of sadness but devoid of hatred, because he breathes like I breathe with

Eris, and how she breathes against me. Like he is taking his time, finally, finally. Like he's home.

Enyo murmurs, chin balanced on the top of my head, "I have killed so many people."

The words sound half to himself. Cold bleeds in from the broken window. Outside, the city is nothing, a blank sheet speckled with skyscraper heads, looking as though they are temporary, passing thoughts, only briefly coming up for air above the smog.

Tears break at the corners of my eyes. "Me too."

"It was for them." His voice shakes. "I swear it. I swear it."

A billion people, in his city.

My crew, ink-blotted kids, with a nasty habit of picking fights with deities. It was all for them—every killed guard, every Archangel missile. Leaving him alone here, to be their God above Gods.

We can be better than the bad we have done. We have to believe that.

He brings my fingers to his lips, and then he lets me go. Steps away.

"This is for you, Sona," Enyo whispers, breeze in his black hair, cooling the tears on his cheeks. "But I'm sorry. I'm sorry. It's for them, too. To inspire them."

His eyes are on mine, and I can almost see it. *Miss Steelcrest, I am not going to kill you.* That pen in his hand, the grief tucked under his calm. *We are going to accomplish such great things together. There is no need to worry. Take comfort.* His hand on my temple. *Godolia is a merciful place.*

Can we not want to be alone, here?

"You did not believe it was true, that I was this," he says. "I love you for it, and for so much else." He takes another step back, feet moving over ruptured glass. "I . . . I wish I were not this."

"Wait." The word comes out a whisper. My body feels numb, distant.

He is already gone, over the edge.

CHAPTER FIFTY-THREE

SONA

Eris is holding me back, glass in my knees and in the palms of my hands as I lean and there is nothingnothingnothing over the edge, not even a scream except the one in my throat.

"I'm so sorry, Sona, oh my Gods, I'm so sorry, love—"

It might have been the same exact thing she would have said if she had frozen him, shattered him across the rug, but how could it matter now. Tell me how the hells that could matter now.

I am panicking, like it is not already done, like he has not hit the ground by now. Like he is not *gone* by now.

"He thought he did not have a way out." I am nothing but the sobs fissuring my body, crying into Eris's shoulder, and it is just small and so, so dark here. "He thought he could not just *run.*"

"I know," Eris whispers, each feverish word broken. "I know."

I—I was not enough.

In the face of all of this, in the face of everything built up within him—did I know that nothing could have been enough? Not me. Not his desire to run, or the good in him— not against the bad that is here. It is colossal, and it feeds itself, and it fed itself on him, like it feeds itself on all of us. The difference is that where it is in my veins, it is in his head. And now I know which is worse.

I feel Eris shift. Her head moves, seeing something I cannot look at, and she murmurs to me, "We're moving back a little bit."

We do, crawling from the edge of the broken window to the hollow under the desk, and Eris touches a kiss to my temple before untucking herself from me. Dazed, I pluck the glass out of my hands as she leaves, and there are screams in the hall. I'm not understanding much, suddenly, in a numb kind of way, and liking it. He was just here. I do not understand how he was just here and then he was weightless and then he was gone. He is gone.

Eris comes back. Holds out her hands, the gloves unprimed when I take them but freshly cold. Her metal one feels thinner than her left.

"How did you get out?" I ask her as she leads me into the hall. Ice splinters the clean walls, my breath coming in clouds as we move past upright, frozen forms.

"Forcefully." Eris eases open the stairwell door, and the panic spurs again—this cannot be it; I have spent minutes up here, I've only just gotten back to him, and her grip pulls taut on mine, tracing it to find me still, so, so still. She looks up at me and steps closer to me and says gently, "Sona. We have to go."

"I—I do not know where to put this." Like *this* is something I could roll up and drop somewhere in my pockets, but I am indecisive. When I laugh, the sound is helpless. "Eris—I cannot— How do I *do* this?"

How do I live with this?

And Eris says quietly, temple pressed to my jaw, "Slowly, love."

More guards in the stairwells, a Pilot or three, and they are gone in a blur of blood and frost and screams, and then we are back in the Valkyrie. We work our way down to its feet, and Eris breaks our way out of its ankle and onto another level of the Academy—training rooms, empty mats with a few practice Autos milling around, abandoned midtraining. Drop down another floor and we have made it to the hospital, where the face of a Phantom presses to the east-facing hallway windows, its eyes flowing from the sockets in trickles of melted glass.

A girl in a gray canvas jacket, the gash on her cheekbone and the bruises smudged in the rips of her trousers regarded unceremoniously—meaning not at all—comes rushing past us, pauses, and doubles back only to tear Eris's hand from mine, hold it high and tight.

"What," Jenny snarls through her teeth, "the *hells* are you doing here?"

"She came here to kill Enyo," I say. Both their gazes snap to me—Jenny's narrowed, Eris's blown wide. Like she is scared I am going to recognize what I just said, like I am going to bolt. And it would have been terrible, if she had done it, it would have been *horrific*—but I cannot imagine what she would have to do to get me to cast her from my life completely.

"And did she?" Jenny asks, Eris's hand still held fast.

And Eris realizes I am looking at her. Unflinching. She blinks back the tears in her eyes and says, "He's dead."

Jenny releases her and takes a step back, the backpack and haversack jostling against her tall frame. She gives a single, short laugh, and then says, "Well. Shit. Okay. Where's the comms room, Glitch?"

"Above the hangar."

"Wondrous." Jenny promptly drops everything she is holding and flaps a gloved hand at the window, past the Phantom staring in. "Take the medicine for me. We're going downstairs, so—oh—have you seen the current happenings?"

We turn, and we look, down to the streets below. Windups heave themselves out of the cragged asphalt around the exposed tunnel, like an opened vein, some splattered with paint that sears viciously bright in the dark. An Argus with ankles dripping green, torn apart by the bite of bullets from a nearby Berserker. A city block and a half completely ignited with two Phoenixes still brawling up its length—paint marking one of them a Hydra Pilot—flames clawing up its tallest skyscraper. Bodies pressed into the asphalt as wet, glinting spots.

Faintly, I notice the ground is shaking beneath my feet. I thought it was just me trembling.

And then, all at once, I feel very distant from all of it.

I feel exactly the size I am. And it is so small beside everything else.

Silently, I reach for Eris's hand, only to find that she is reaching for mine, too.

"I don't know why I thought this would end any differently," Eris says, taking the words right out of my head. She tends to do that a lot. So I know she means it in the sense of the Gods in the streets and the cityscape burning down and us, here for it and just—us.

We have been so cruel to each other, and then the world

was so cruel to us, too, that we forgot to keep up with it, and in the beat of that hesitation we fell in love. I turned around and realized I was looking for her all the time. That did not change when I lost my mind, and that does not change now, with a boy dead on the pavement and an era easing to ash below our feet, and still so many deities everywhere.

I know I would love Enyo less if I had not loved her first.

Is that not how it goes?

Is it not so much easier to love once we know how it feels?

"Come on," Jenny says, and it takes me a beat to realize that her voice is . . . softened. She has already turned away from the view. "Let's get the fuck out of here."

So we go numbly, weighed down by the medicine bags. I focus on the feel of Eris's hand in mine to remind myself that this is real and I am still here; I think she is doing the same. I do not ask her, and we do not speak. We work our way down. There are bodies—those unfortunate enough to meet Jenny's crew—but it is just us otherwise, us and the push and pull of our shadows under the flicker of the emergency lights.

We pause on the ground floor, Jenny pushing out of the stairwell to glance across the Academy lobby. Black marble runs sleek and empty under high ceilings dripping with thin lights, and, outside the line of windows, another Berserker pulls itself out onto the street. A Phoenix's boot, streaked with blue paint, crashes down inches outside the doors, rattles their hinges and the thoughts in my head.

Faintly, I wonder if they have found Enyo's body by now. And, as if Jenny has the exact same thought, she says, "So who's in charge now?"

"Power would revert to the mecha captains," I hear myself say. "If there are any left."

"There aren't going to be," Jenny says, and lets the stairwell door slam shut. We keep moving.

The Windup communications floor is a low-ceilinged space filled with screens. Floor-to-ceiling windows that rim the entire perimeter look out onto the hangar floor. I have never seen it bare before, the neatly painted boxes of the mecha units blank as gums absent of teeth. This level is a flurry of movement—Jenny immediately takes the shirt collar of the one guard stationed at the stairwell door, and, after using it to slam him against the wall, puffs out an indignant breath when she realizes no one has batted an eye at us. Technicians in black uniforms just continue shouting at one another over the glow of the tablet tables.

"Hey!" Jenny shouts, scoffing when still no one looks at her.

Then the air of the stairwell behind us is electrified with a series of gunshots in quick succession, and everyone, including Jenny and me, glances back to see Eris with a gun smoking in her hand, eyes black fire. So that is how she got out of the storage closet.

A technician slams her hand on her tablet, screaming, "We need backu—"

Eris flicks the barrel of the gun past my temple and shoots her in the side of the throat, and Jenny, before the body hits the floor, says brightly to the stunned room, "The Zenith is dead. This is Valkyrie Captain Bellsona Steelcrest; she is now your commanding officer. She'd like you to pull up the haptic monitors of the entire army."

Not a single person moves.

Jenny's grin sparks viciously. "It was worth a shot."

She reaches down and plucks up the limp guard by the

front of his uniform and flicks on her glove. The fabric immediately smokes and deteriorates in her grip, and the guard hits the ground with his chest cavity sloughing over his exposed sides. He flecks the wall in pale droplets.

"Out," Starbreach says, wiping her palm absentmindedly on the door.

Eris and I move to the side, away from the rush of bodies. When they clear, I realize Jenny had snatched one out of line—a small man completely drained of color. She throws him onto the nearest tablet table.

"Active haptics," she barks, and the sweat on the man's palms leaves streaks as he navigates the screen with shaking fingers. The surface splits into a grid, each stamped with a Pilot ID and a unit insignia. Jenny's narrowed eyes sweeps over it, taking in the information and spitting out the next question before I can even think to consider it. "What are these red markers for?"

"F-Flagged Pilots," sputters the technician. *Our* Pilots.

"Clear them," Jenny says, and he does, and she shoves him aside. She gives an experimental tap on one of the remaining Pilots, blows the box outward. An Academy-standard picture flickers into place, a bored-looking boy in his twenties next to a quivering set of vitals and a diagram of his Phoenix Windup, the left leg flashing a cautionary red.

Jenny wraps an iron grip around the technician's wrist. "Okay," she says. "Show me how to kill him."

He was already colorless; now he is a corpse gray that matches his hair. "You cannot. The Zenith—"

"—is dead," Jenny hisses, but suddenly the technician is shouting over her. "—is the only one who can give this order!"

Jenny backhands him. It snaps his chin a full ninety

degrees to the side; he hits the floor only for a moment before she has picked him up and thrown him back against the tablet table. She is so utterly calm that it makes the shake of my hands infinitely more apparent. Eris's mouth is pressed into a tight line, focus dropped to the technician with the gunshot through her neck.

"The only God in this room," Jenny breathes into her captive's ear, "is me."

But he just shakes his head, shoulders quaking with sobs. Jenny takes the back of his head and slams it into the tablet so hard I am shocked it does not crack apart, lets him slide limply to the floor. Jenny flicks the Pilot's haptic screen with a disgusted breath.

"Here," I whisper, ghosting my fingers over the corner of the tablet, where there glows the Aether Tree insignia. The mark of the Zeniths.

Jenny presses it. A box pops up, outlined in blue, above a digital keypad. She does not even pause, her fingers quick—*21019*. My Pilot number. The screen flashes red; Jenny does not blink.

2512121915141.

My mind hitches on what Jenny is going for. *2* for the second letter of the alphabet? *Bellsona*. Another flash of red.

1915141.

Sona.

Red.

Jenny's grin turns rictus. I realize she is putting her entire weight against the table. I realize I am still bleeding, and that I am going a little cold.

"Not you," she murmurs—to me, I think. "I'm out. Any ideas?"

I press a hand to the blood, at once distantly surprised and completely nonplussed that I had forgotten about the open wound in my shoulder. "Eris."

"Shit, Glitch," she breathes, staring at my hand for a heartbeat before she drops to her knees and begins to tear her way through the medicine bag. "Why the hells didn't you say—"

"No," I murmur, looking to Jenny. "It's Eris."

Jenny's fingers move. *518919.*

You only win when there is no one to fight back with. Know that it's Eris. It's Eris. It's Eris.

No flash. The keypad and the box just disappear.

Eris stands. A plastic vial of Spider capsules hangs from her fingertips.

"Why?" Eris whispers, meeting my eyes as Jenny goes to work. Now, when Jenny brings up the expanded haptics, there are more live vital diagrams, both of the natural and artificial nervous systems, as well as medical listings of bodily functions. She finds something, touches something, pulls back as the entire box goes dark. Just for a moment. Then she is on to the next one, killing the next one, flooding those divine Mods, felling deities on the streets above our heads.

It's for them, too. Her tattoos rise in her slow inhale. *To inspire them.*

Liar, I think.

I think.

Eris peels my jacket back from my shoulder, hisses at the mess of blood chewing at the tattered shirt beneath. Gently, she squeezes a Spider capsule and lets it crawl into place, its metal legs so fine I barely feel it. I barely feel anything.

"Why?" she asks again, quieter this time.

Is it not obvious? I want to say. *I love you a lot.*

It is obvious. It would still not make sense, not right away. She is the root of it. Why I was able to love Enyo and why the corruption would not stick, could not stick, why he is gone now. Because he would not have gone if he was leaving me alone. I am anything but alone, and it is not a question of blame—it is a question of people mattering to one another despite the Gods cluttered here, the hate still poisoning us here. The scale of it should have rendered it impossible; the violence should have shaken anything human out of this era, but here it is. It came down to love, and it wrecked us, and yet still it hovers.

I do not know how to say any of this to her without completely falling apart.

But maybe someday.

So I take Eris's hand, and all I say is, "It is chaos out there."

Then Jenny goes very, very still, and says, "Oh. *Shit.*"

She works fast. All the Pilot boxes are darkened, lives blotted out, which means the lives of our allies saved.

Except for one.

I glimpse steady vitals, dark, unkempt hair chopped around a teenage girl's face, and then—as Jenny grabs both of our arms and shoves us toward the stairs, spitting something about *locked haptics* and *go go go*—beside her, a unit insignia.

A moon, one half outlined, one half dark.

But the Pilot is not in a Phantom Windup. The insignia does not match the diagram of the mecha beside her picture.

"That's not—" Eris breathes. "I thought—"

"Me too," I say as we make it up the stairs, push into the abandoned lobby with a head-on view of the hole in the street. "I thought he had it destroyed."

From the broken asphalt, the opened vein, the mecha pulls itself into view.

Halo first, glinting under the press of the flaming cityscape.

Then the wings. Tucked into its pitch-black spine until it makes the edge, and then within, the Pilot rolls her shoulders back, and lets them unfurl.

The light of the fires is gone, suffocated under the cast of its massive, cleaving shadow, and, all at once, the street and the calamitous filth scraped across its surface are glazed in a pure red glow as the Archangel lifts her head.

"They locked the haptic controls on it. I don't know who had the gall to do it," Jenny whispers, each gloved finger flexed at her side. She laughs, the sound brittle with the same disbelief swelling in my chest.

"Their fail-safe," Jenny says, "the one deity they wouldn't let him kill."

"Damn it," Eris says. The marble below our feet flushes as she sends her cryo gloves roaring to life. We burst out of the doors and into the smoke-flooded night. "We need to get it before it gets off the ground—"

The Valkyrie is still stories above us, but the head of a felled Berserker lies at the corner of the courtyard. I meet Eris's eyes for a moment, and then we both go bolting for it. She cracks open its eye, iron temple crushing the sidewalk, and I grab her arm.

"Stay here."

"Like hells," she spits. "Get me close."

The Archangel, about a block up, is rising from its knees. The last thing I see is the flames of the burning cityscape glinting off its night-pitch metal, and then we are through the eye, ripping the dead Pilot from their winding cords. I snap them into my own arms as Eris drags their body away. The hair on the back of their head is singed and black. Jenny's work.

The last cord I click into place on my knees. I wake up looking across the pavement and the courtyard, the darkened sky blocked out by the rise of the Academy.

I push myself upright. Somewhere, I feel Eris's hands, helping me as the floor angles. Glass beneath my feet, street beneath my stance, and on either side, levels upon levels of skyscrapers sloughing away, dropping down, down, down beneath me.

The Archangel's wings breathe heat, shudder the air. In my vision, an artillery count flashes red.

I breathe, filling up my body. "Here we go . . ."

Eris's voice is electric. "Let's get the wiref—"

The Archangel's head turns, red gaze cutting across me, and I grasp its wing in my hand, bringing a fist to its jaw. The scream of metal on metal sounds like the world coming down.

It does not even get a chance to flinch back. My vision flashes blue, and then white, and cold scrapes across my skin, the distant, distant form, as Eris lets her power loose.

Frost branches jaggedly across the junction of its neck and shoulder. Now it does flinch, and iron splits, and screeches, and something else is shrieking from the wing in my hand—

Pain. Bright against my ribs, blistering heat and I feel none of the chill that Eris has put around us—around me there is fire. It flickers in the windows as I lose my footing from the impact of the missiles.

We were too close. I should not have—

Against the street now, my ears ringing.

Gods know where my real body is, but the cords are still against my skin and I am still staring up at the darkened sky, and then to the Archangel blocking it out. It's looking at me, fear clotting in my chest. I hold out my hand and there's gunfire rippling from me, and then the oddest thing . . . it's snowing. Snowing glass. The Archangel has its arms thrown over its eyes, ricochets bursting windows apart. It's not moving toward us. It's strange. It's strange. I'm still burning down, flames dancing in the fragments.

"Eris," I murmur. "It's snowing."

"You hit your head." She whispers it. Or she's screaming it, I'm unsure. "You—"

Did I? The air is alight, sparks like gold. We are still alive. We shouldn't be. "She's not attacking . . ."

I am not sure if I say it aloud. Sound snaps back into place. She was screaming it.

"—hit your head! Sona, *get up!*"

I'm pushing myself up, and the Archangel is moving. Away, into the city, wings lifting, shadows arcing over the street. Then they burn away completely; with a rush of heat and a plume of blue flame, the mecha's jets shriek to life.

It's fast. I fire again, the pulse of it beating in my chest, and Eris moves again, but the Archangel is too far away, the blast from her gloves dying in the air we clash into a moment later.

The Archangel leaves the ground, wings decimating the cityscape. It does not look back.

Something's off. I reach out, fingers curling around the

Archangel's ankle, but there is heat coming off the wings and Eris is screaming and begging, "Don't let go. You can't let go—"

I'm not sure if I do.

The Archangel kicks, my grasp leaving it, and, tether gone, clatters against the side of a building. But only for a heartbeat before it is moving again, pulling itself up a dozen levels at a time, drawing its limbs in fire against the shroud of the night and then—it hits open air.

No missiles. Not even a glance down—enormous, delicate features out of view, lifted toward the heavens as it pushes from the cityscape and into open sky.

The smog swallows it whole.

My hand is still extended. I reach up my other one and rip out my cords.

I wake to find myself tangled up in them, halfway across the Berserker's skull. Skin pink and tender, same as Eris's, from the flush of the heat, the floor beneath my ribs still warm to the touch. Disoriented, I reach for her as she sinks to her knees beside me.

"It's gone," Eris says, her voice small. She hiccups a laugh. "Well. We're fucked. I love you."

Hellsfire will rain at any moment from the blankness above. Because that's what they do. That is what we have done. Over and over and over again. I reach for her hand.

"Wait," I say. My voice comes hushed. "Wait . . ."

The streets are littered with dead Gods, life electrocuted out of their Pilots where they stood, splintered, supports moaning under their massive, dead weights. Collapsed in the forests of the Peaks, dropped onto the sand of the Badlands deserts. The last Leviathans sunk down onto the riverbeds.

I think the Archangel realizes it, too—no, the Phantom Pilot tangled up inside it.

I see her face in my head. Feel her age in full.

The image of it comes in a flash. Her in the hangar, feeling the tremors above, like the city was about to come crashing down. Her climbing the Archangel's ladder, in panic, in heresy, needing its wings.

I know. I do not know how I know. Maybe because I have just come from a city of runaways. Maybe because I have been a scared thing for so long that I can recognize another right away.

Or maybe it is just because I am a damn good Pilot, and a Gearbreaker, or just the girl holding Eris's hand, hopeful and hopeless for it, listening to the quiet. It hovers.

This could be our last moment on earth. It is not a terrible one.

But I think Eris feels it, too. She looks at me, dark eyes bright.

"It's gone," she whispers. I do not think she means to.

Her hands land on my cheeks, head bent over mine and the wild black of her hair crowding the daze of her expression, and for a moment, I cannot speak.

It threads through me like an electric shock, like I am nothing but the ends of my nerves and where my skin meets hers.

"It's over," I whisper, fingers wandering up to her wrists. "It's done, Eris. We survived it."

She does not move. The moment hitches around us, like it would be the simplest thing to take her hand and tuck ourselves inside it, just let the timeline ease past us.

Then she blinks. Tears fleck the pale curve of her cheekbones.

Then her temple is to mine and there is no air between us, nothing between us except the thud of our hearts pushing us back, but that does not matter—in the gaps that stagger them, in those inevitable, still moments, we drift back together.

ERIS

I keep my promise. We run away.

For a little while, at least.

It's clear that Silvertwin has been empty this entire time. Even standing in the house, it's so quiet that we can hear the crew pattering up the dirt footpaths as they explore the forest. Afternoon light glows through the sycamore leaves, stained cherry red, brushing the dust of the floorboards in lazy shivers. From the mouth of the hall, I watch Sona put her bag down and lean her weight against the small breakfast table, eyes drawn low and steady. She exhales, and her head tilts, loosing a deep brown curl from behind her ear.

It graces her cheekbone when she glances up at me. "You look unsure of yourself."

"I'm very sure of myself," I say, but my voice is a whisper. I clear my throat, feet shifting below me. I asked her if she wanted to come here, to her old home, alone, and I was surprised when she said no. Even more surprised when I asked her again, just to be sure, and her answer lifted in a laugh.

Sona smiles. Her hand extends toward mine, and, because it's muscle memory, I take it without thinking. My metal glints sharply between her soft fingers; they tighten around mine without hesitation, like there's skin to feel it. There's not, but it's the weight of it that I focus on.

She leads me through the house, picking through the kitchen cabinets, where everything that was rotting is done rotting, telling me in a light voice that her umma was a great cook, and how her father would carry her upstairs when she fell asleep on the loveseat. There's a photograph stuck on the small refrigerator, and Sona plucks it off the magnet by its curling edge.

"Oh my Gods," she says, soft and delighted. She turns toward me, hovering by the countertop, and holds it out, the movement graceful, like the rest of them.

I put one hand on her waist as I duck my head over it, vicious joy popping in my throat at the baby photo. "You were so stupid cute."

"I *am* so stupid cute," she says with a wink, and then, when she notices the expression on my face, "What?"

"Nothing," I say, heat burning in my cheeks. She just looks happy, is all.

It takes a wrenching moment to work the back door open, cool autumn air sliding in over the stone steps, and then it's us moving around the furniture to liberate the dust bunnies and set them free over the back steps. It gets dark, and in the neighboring house we can see out of the kitchen window, a flame lights a candle, revealing Arsen. He lowers the match, dribbling with smoke. For a moment, his head knocks against the cupboards and stays there.

I can almost see her—June, sitting on the countertop, smiling, dropping her chin to the top of his curls.

A little while later, Nova glides in through the open back door, followed more tentatively by Theo. She immediately flops down on the loveseat, tangles her hand with Theo's when he passes by. He pauses in his steps and stays there, fingers intertwined, turning his head to observe the room. Arsen comes in a moment later and drifts over to put his chin on Theo's shoulder. The boys look at one another, nose to nose, and one of them murmurs something that makes them both grin, their next words punctuated by a laugh.

The power hasn't worked for a while now, but Sona makes doenjang-jjigae on the portable stove we brought along. There aren't enough chairs for all of us, so we eat the stew sprawled out on the kitchen floor, while I fiddle with the radio that Jenny made us bring along. For a moment, the feed sparks from static to a now-familiar looped message—*welcoming all to the Ira Sol sanctuary. Ferries and shuttles available from the Gillian Conflux port, the Hana River port, the west and south Godolia wall terminals*—until I hit the right channel, and say around a mouthful of tofu, "Jen?"

"Yo," she says, and I think I hear Zamaya's snort in the background. "You guys find the place empty?"

She means did we find Silvertwin lacking of mechas. Lacking of an Archangel, which we still haven't found. Jen's all keyed in to the haptic systems of that single Pilot—if she winds again, we'll know it, and we'll prime for it, but she hasn't. But I feel it in my gut—Sona's right about this. The Pilot just might be a kid who got scared, who ran. There's no shame in saving yourself.

"Yep," I say, my shoulder against Sona's, backs against the cupboards and my knees over her jeans. "We're good."

For now. I'm trying to focus on it.

"Well," Jenny says, voice distracted, like she's fumbling with something else, "good."

I haven't asked her how she's taken it. I don't know why the hells I've even been thinking I should, but I have—I don't think she liked killing like that. Frying Pilot after Pilot with only her fingertips, drawing those flatlines across their hearts while she stood still. If I know anything about my sister, it's that she wears her violence blatantly—it's the only part of her that's hideous, and she doesn't hide it. I'm sure some other part of her, blinking out vital after vital, thought it felt like cheating.

I'm not going to ask. That wouldn't be fair. It's over, and Jenny's going to bear what weighted her the same way she always does—the best she can, which is saying a lot. I don't know if I'm ever going to cope with it as well as she does. I don't know if I'll ever see the world as anything but something that's waiting to tear me to pieces—but.

But I'm still growing up.

And, lately, I touch the people next to me and my hand scrapes against the sky, and the thought comes with perfect, unrushed clarity—the Gods aren't anywhere but here.

"We'll be back soon," I say to Jenny.

A pause. There's some sort of scuffle, and that's definitely Zamaya's hard laugh, pried out of her in the way only Jenny can manage. Jen says, "Yeah. Take your time, Eris."

"Okay," I say, even though she's already gone, and it's fine; my temple is on Sona's collarbone. She tucks her chin to brush a kiss to my cheek, the movement offhanded and light, just a given. "I will."

SONA

Heaven is still a mess. Godolia lies in partial ruins, new, hungry powers already rising amid the chaos to pick out what they want to save. Who they want to save. But Jenny is a hells of a diplomat. Every week, the Badlands-controlled Ore Cities ship out supplies, enough for comfort but not glutton—if we ever hear of new Pilots, new mechas, Godolia will never see another train car. They need us—they have always needed us. It is only now that it is clear—they cannot eat their Gods, whose bodies still litter the streets.

At night, I dream of the train tracks being snipped away, black threads of iron curling in on themselves like shy things. From above, Godolia looks like a speck in the white. Detached, adrift. Enyo lies on his back in the sand, a thousand times bigger than all of it, listens to the cityscape with his dark eyes focused on the clouds.

Often, I wake up crying. Then, always, Eris is awake, too, and it is a little better, and a little more so when the sun comes up.

The sun is gone now; I am hip to hip with Eris in front of the sink as we wash the stew bowls, Arsen breathing life into my parents' fireplace, find the good parts hovering, find them everywhere.

The flames catch. Our shadows ease away from us, press against each other on the countertop.

Nova suddenly scrambles upright from her place on the floor and books it for the back door. "I forgot to get something!"

Eris and I watch her disappear out of the reach of the light, into the forest and then back again a minute later, blond hair a flare against the shadows. She barrels in and lets something roll from her arms and thud on top of the fireplace. One of those old music systems.

Theo lets out a low chuckle. "That thing is ugly as hells."

"Beauty is subjective," Nova says without missing a beat. Her fingertips twitch over the nubby buttons. "Found it in the closet of our house. Didn't check if there was anything in it. Let's find out."

She pops in the red button. Something whirs inside, speakers crinkling numbly, and then—the first note.

"Well," Arsen says, head lolling back on the couch, smiling softly. One tattooed hand tucks under the other on his stomach. "That's lucky."

It's something that builds, and Eris says quietly, eyes dropped to the suds on her fingers, "It's nice."

I love you, is my next thought. I do not say it, but I tell her anyway, quietly drying her hands with a cloth and then taking them, our bare feet shifting against the tiles. My arms drop down her back and hers around my waist, my chin to her temple as we move.

I thought I would hear ghosts, when I returned here.

But I did not come home alone.

This would not feel like home, alone.

"What is it?" Eris murmurs. "Are you thinking something profound again?"

"Again?"

"It's one of your habits, Glitch."

I laugh a little at that. "You must think a lot of me, Frostbringer."

"I'm sure you're fucking shocked."

"Fucking astonished."

Now she laughs, the hum of it against my collarbone.

I draw my breath in slow. Take my time with it. Feel the lines of the tiles under my toes. Feel the warmth of Eris's skin and the love in my chest and the age in my veins.

And happy.

"Tomorrow," I say, "let's sleep in."

Her smile spills into the dark of her eyes first. "Let's stay up late."

We do. Dancing in the kitchen, and later stepping silently over the sleeping kids to close the back door. It might look like we are staring out into the black, and not at our hands as they reach for one another, as we lean into each other.

And I think, distantly, it will go like this:

Eventually, she hands me all the bad things she has done. I do the same. It is not so easy to be good, to make ourselves good, but sometimes, it feels like it is. We open the windows when we remember the Gods, when we can't sleep, to see only sky again. It's okay if we need the reminder, even when it starts to get cold. We can wear our jackets in the kitchen. We can keep each other close.

So. I'm okay.

I really think I am going to be okay.

My name is Sona Steelcrest. I am human. I am a Pilot, a Gearbreaker. Metal and flesh and fire and bad dreams, and more than any of it, I am the girl holding Eris's hand. I am never too far from home.

ACKNOWLEDGMENTS

Okay. So. I have been incredibly mean to my characters. But I still stand by the claim that the Gearbreakers duology is a love story, both in the sense of what Eris and Sona find in each other and the family the crew finds themselves a part of. The message here is hope, despite. Crumbling world, malicious gods and systems, and it all doesn't hold a freaking candle to what people mean to one another.

People are reading this sentence and maybe the story before it? I don't think I'll ever really wrap my head around it—all I can try to do is express how much it means to me, though truly, truly, it goes beyond words. Ha ha.

To the girl I'll never be able to stop thinking about. Do whatever you want.

To Ty. Hope the art checks, dude.

To Mom, my wonderful solid ground. Thank you for always letting me take things at my own pace.

To Dad, who I can rely on being in my corner, always.

To Kiva, you vivid soul, and Mira, who I am so happy to have met when I was pretty sure there wasn't anyone cool left to meet. You both leave me in such awe, such happiness. I'm just going to follow you both around forever because I can work from anywhere. So. Love you.

To Alex, Tyler, Kayvon, and Jerimiah, for feeding me consistently.

To the D.A.C.U. (I don't think I can write out what that acronym is for, but if you're in the know, you're in the know). Tashie, Chloe, Christina, Rocky, I love you all, you're my idols, and we're the new age. I can't wait to read absolutely everything that comes from your glorious minds.

To the roundtable group. You're all so strange and I'm constantly scared of every one of you—thanks!

Emily, thank you so much for your insight, for pushing the duology to be the best that it could be. I always love the emoticons in your comments, too.

Morgan, thank you for being the absolute best publicist a girl could ask for.

Taj Francis, Mike Burroughs, and Mallory Grigg, thank you for making the covers of my little mecha duology prettier and more intense than I could've possibly come up with in my head.

To everyone at Feiwel & Friends, who gave such a good home to the Gearbreakers duology.

To the little things growing on my shelf. Grow, please.

To the Castle, where we have always lived.

So. I think it's a happy ending, and maybe that it's okay not to know it right away. It's better to wait and see. Builds the suspense, right?

Thank you for reading this Feiwel & Friends book.
The friends who made

possible are:

Jean Feiwel, *Publisher*

Liz Szabla, *Associate Publisher*

Rich Deas, *Senior Creative Director*

Holly West, *Senior Editor*

Anna Roberto, *Senior Editor*

Kat Brzozowski, *Senior Editor*

Dawn Ryan, *Executive Managing Editor*

Celeste Cass, *Production Manager*

Emily Settle, *Associate Editor*

Erin Siu, *Associate Editor*

Foyinsi Adegbonmire, *Associate Editor*

Rachel Diebel, *Assistant Editor*

Michael Burroughs, *Senior Designer*

Ilana Worrell, *Senior Production Editor*

Follow us on Facebook or visit us online at mackids.com.
Our books are friends for life.